ROBERT ROTH

Into the Lightning Gate

Book One of The Gates Saga

**JETSPACE
STUDIO**

Contents

A Note About Pronouns

I made an editorial decision early in my writing process to identify characters with gendered pronouns only when their gender was already known by the narrator. I referred to every other character exclusively with they/them pronouns when pronouns were necessary. Instead of resorting to gender markers, I included additional information to help readers decode any passages with multiple non-gendered characters, adding context clues such as hair color/length, skin tone, style of dress, profession, and actions. It will be challenging to some readers who are used to having the world defined explicitly in binary genders and assume someone's gender based solely on their appearance and presentation. However, it's essential to let go of such assumptions. If you're challenged by this, I urge you to lean into your discomfort and embrace the fact that, even if you could see a particular character, you still may not know their gender. For the sake of this story, how they identify doesn't matter much anyway.

THE AGENT

«STATIC»«FLASH»

She crouched silently in the shadows, carefully hidden in a small room off a mostly disused side corridor. Somewhere dark and silent. With a thought, a glowing, blue-lined map flickered to life in front of her, projected directly into her brain's optic processors. She surveyed the schematic, first locating her position and then her target. It was close.

The map flickered away with another thought, replaced by her command menu. She selected one of the items, watching it grow a brighter blue than the rest. Then she waited, timing it for the perfect moment to trigger the command–the moment when the nearby security guards were positioned so the program could achieve the most optimum impact. Their precise locations were fed to her through passive sensors, measuring everything from nearby temperature differentials and air movement to tiny vibrations in the floor and walls around her.

Ten seconds.

Three seconds.

Execute.

The local power grid abruptly suffered a severe malfunction, plunging the area into total darkness. She stood up from her crouched position and moved through the nearby door into the corridor. She was a shadow in the dark.

«STATIC»«FLASH»

She flicked a gloved finger, scrolling through the menus that swam across the holographic display like a school of neon fish, finally landing on the one she was looking for. She selected the command to load the data to local memory, pulled a slim data crystal from a small pouch on her belt, and stuck it into the waiting port. A tiny yellow light flashed above the port, indicating a connection to the console, and a new icon appeared on the display screen. She herded the mass of data on the screen toward that icon with a small gesture, starting the transfer to the data crystal.

An alert popped up in her vision. Her sensors had detected signs of movement outside in the corridor. She glanced down at the prone figure of the station guard that lay crumpled at her feet. She'd disabled them before they could raise any alarm, swiftly snapping their neck with a sickening crunch. She knew that her combat suit's stealth field shielded her from any station scans, so either she was about to be visited by a guard on their regular patrol route, or her subversion of the station systems had somehow triggered a silent alarm. It caused her no concern. Based on the floor vibrations picked up by her passive sensors, she estimated that she had another twenty seconds before being discovered. That was fine. She only needed ten.

A quiet tone sounded from the console. The data transfer was complete. She removed the data crystal and returned it to its pouch on her belt. Moving swiftly, she pulled a blade from a sheath at her waist and got into position. By the time the door slid open, she was in place beside it, her back to the wall. She observed a blaster barrel poke through, followed by the armored station guard who was holding it. She dropped her stealth field, shunting its power into the electro-muscular servos in her armored suit, then struck–a quick and powerful chop with the side of her hand at the guard's neck. Their head tilted back. Twisting around with a dancer's grace, she shoved her knife into their throat. Close enough for a kiss, her breath fogging up their closed faceplate, she watched their eyes roll back in deathly ecstasy as their lifeblood quickly drained away. She withdrew the blade and shoved the guard's dying body back in one fluid motion. The remaining guard had barely registered the disturbance ahead before suddenly dancing with the corpse of their former partner.

While the fumbling guard desperately tried to recover their balance, she lunged forward and slammed their helmet into the corridor wall. The guard's fog of dazed confusion left them defenseless against her blade as it stabbed into the soft, rubberized collar around their neck, slicing through the carotid artery, then severing the spinal column. Their limp body slid down to the floor, painting a sanguine map of their melee on the wall behind them as they bled out.

An alarm began to squeal, and the corridor's lighting shifted from bright white to blood red. But she was already gone—the two crumpled bodies in the passage, the only witnesses to her departure.

«STATIC»«FLASH»

A particle blast sizzled by, the radiant blue fire missing her head only by mere centimeters, as she ducked back into cover behind a corner. Three guards had taken up positions near one of the station's maintenance airlocks. They clearly knew where she was headed.

She was still on track for her exit, but she was cutting it close. Her timing had to be precise. She pulled a slim black disc from a pouch on her belt and set its timer for three seconds, then reached out and slid it down the short corridor toward her welcoming committee. The disc began to emit a hypersonic wail, and the guards started to scream, desperately covering their ears in a futile attempt to block out the piercing banshee cry.

Her mission timer counted down in the lower right corner of her vision. Thirty-five seconds remained. She launched herself down the corridor, rushing past the helpless guards, and reached out for the access button on the maintenance airlock. She punched it, and the door whooshed open. Thirty seconds. She jumped into the airlock, hitting the prominent Emergency Cycle button. The door immediately slid closed, locking and sealing the chamber off from the station with a series of loud clunks. One of the guards looked through the window in the airlock door and began to gesture wildly. The hypersonic wailing must've run its full course. It didn't matter. The door was sealed and couldn't be opened from the outside once the cycle had begun. Twenty seconds. The lights above the airlock door changed from blue to yellow, and a buzzer began to sound. Suddenly the door behind her blew open, and she was yanked out into space. The moisture from the scant remaining air crystalized around her like nighttime snow in the naked vacuum. Five seconds. Her suit was vacuum sealed and temperature-controlled, so she felt no discomfort as she sailed backward into the cold and black.

The three guards she left behind watched her in dumbfounded shock through the small airlock viewport. Then a new sun flared briefly to life as the station blossomed into an impossibly silent, expanding sphere of burning gas and twisted metal after the powerful explosive she'd placed inside finally finished its countdown.

But she was already gone.

«FLASH»«STATIC»

CAM

Cameron Maddock shouted himself awake. Momentarily confused, he looked around the darkened room, unsure of where he was. Memories of the strange, dark dreams that plagued his sleep were still fresh in his mind. Then the fog of sleep slowly lifted from his thoughts, and clarity began to return when he realized that he was safe and sound in his bed. Pulling a pillow over his head, he pressed it onto his face, muffling a long, low moan. It couldn't possibly be time to wake up already. He'd just gone to bed a little while ago. But the sudden chirping of his phone alarm quickly gave the lie to those thoughts, broadcasting its lively, eight-bit arpeggio with almost violent glee.

He reached over to his nightstand and silenced his phone. It didn't usually bother him, but sleeping had never been that kind of problem for him before. Cam never felt all that cheerful in the morning, although he'd been accused of it often enough by lovers and housemates. But when he woke up, he was usually awake and aware right away, with no additional start-up time necessary.

Staring up at the darkened ceiling, he tried to sort through the mess of strange images from his dream and maybe make them into something coherent, something he could

6

catalog and quantify. But the memories had already begun to fade like most dreams did, and he was left only with vague impressions that he couldn't make any sense of. Vivid dreams had always been a common occurrence for him, but his dreams had recently taken on a much darker tone than he liked. Not to mention how they'd started to interfere with his sleep.

The room slowly brightened as he laid there, thin shafts of gray morning light shouldering their way past the heavy curtains hanging over his windows. Dust motes danced brightly in fingers of light as they curled through the air. He watched them perform their tiny frolics before looking up from his pillow to spy the darkened monitor sitting on his desk across the room. It was no use putting the day off any longer. He shook his head softly, hoping the motion would throw off any stray remnants of his nighttime escapades. He had work to do.

"Good morning, Ego," he said into the slowly retreating darkness. The desktop monitor flared to life, cycling through a brief startup sequence before settling on a white text prompt flashing on a black background.

"Good morning, Cam," replied a voice emanating from the speakers on his desk–a dark and husky contralto that Cam spent weeks fine-tuning until he'd gotten it just right. "My data indicates that your sleep cycle was less than optimal."

"Thanks for the update, Captain Obvious," Cam muttered mirthlessly. Typically, the biometric data Ego captured from the sensors in his room would go without any mention. But, Cam usually slept like the dead and woke without complaint. It was good to hear that his bio signs matched up with how he felt, at least. He knew he'd slept like shit, and even the data supported that notion. "Be a pal and start the coffee, would you?"

"Right away, Cam." The grinder on the espresso machine in his kitchen immediately sounded off with a distant drone.

"What's on my schedule for today?"

"Your calendar is blocked off until five PM for the Bridgespan Biotech job. After that, you have a Farstorm raid planned with Tony Zhang."

It was the day of the Bridgespan job, of course. There was nothing like a shitty night's sleep before a day of fieldwork. But it didn't really matter. He knew he was otherwise well prepared. Once he'd had a shower and some caffeine, he'd be right back on track.

As if on cue, the rich smell of coffee started to waft into his room, delicious and earthy. He rolled himself out of bed and started stumbling toward the bathroom. "Ego, open the curtains. Then, pull up the code I was working on last night and load it onto my handheld."

"Right away, Cam."

Silvery morning light flooded the room as the motorized curtains began to slide apart. But Cam barely noticed as he closed the bathroom door behind him.

Stripping out of his shorts and t-shirt, he took a few moments to inspect his reflection in the mirror. Despite his sleep cycle being less than optimal, he didn't really look any worse for wear. He briefly rubbed the sparse black stubble on his chin and decided that he had at least a few more days before he'd need to shave again. His buzz cut would definitely need a touch-up soon, though. Then he reconsidered, wondering for a moment if maybe he should grow it longer again. But keeping his hair short was an easy fallback for him since his parents never taught him to properly care for his tight, wiry curls as a child. He'd learned how eventually, but it never seemed worth the effort to him by then. Leaning in closer, he made sure there was no hint of dark circles under the glossy, greenish-brown of his topaz eyes. It made him feel a little vain to look, but he'd never suffered from them before. That would no doubt change, he imagined, if his sleep patterns didn't get back to normal soon. But his eyes were bright and baggage free, as always, just like his deep, golden-brown skin had always been smooth and clear of blemishes. Well, except for the occasional bruise or scrape from his fanatical parents, that is. But he immediately shook that thought away. There was no use getting bogged down with shit like that, considering the shaky start to his day.

Still, the thoughts crept back into his head anyway, as he began to wonder what became of his adoptive parents. He hadn't spoken to them in years, not since they'd disowned him and thrown him out of their house back when he was eighteen. "After everything we've done for you," his hysterical mother shouted, her pale face mottled and red with rage, while his equally pale and blotchy father just stood behind her, silent and implacable. "After we took you in and raised you like you were our own, this is how you repay us?" But, then, he'd never really been grateful enough for their liking. He absent-mindedly rubbed his cheek, recalling the sharp crack and the sudden pain from her vicious slap. That definitely left a mark.

Nope. Not going there.

Sighing, he stepped away from the mirror and turned on the shower, waiting a few moments for the freezing water to start running hot and steamy. Once he stood under the water flow, his remaining tension melted away like snowfall in the warm sunlight. In the safety of his shower, he started fantasizing about going back to that cliché Craftsman bungalow in the woods of North Seattle. Then he could show them what their heathen-born, dark-skinned, adoptee child had made of himself without their overbearing, right-wing, religious nonsense holding him back. To let them know that the only reason he'd never fought back–even though he could have–was because he'd known that if he did, he would've probably won. And then, ultimately, lose, of course. His father may have been large and loud, but that was all bluster and no bite. And Cam had always known that, if it ever really came down to it, he could've easily bested the man. Of course, he'd also always known how things would turn out if he'd fought back. He harbored no illusions that his loving, white, overprotective, adoptive parents wouldn't turn on him in an instant if he'd ever fought back or shown any signs of serious resistance.

Once he was through washing, he rinsed himself off. Then, before he lost his nerve, he turned the water knob back toward the cold side. He jumped around lightly as the water turned frigid, and the shock of the sudden temperature drop charged him back up to full. After a few moments of icy suffering, he shut off the water and stepped out onto his bath mat, wrapping a soft, fluffy towel around his lithe, athletic frame to dry himself off. He was a little surprised at how often he kept going back to thinking about his parents. Had it been because the dream had shaken him so much? The shower helped turn his mood around, at least, since he was already starting to feel better. Some fresh, hot coffee was all he needed to seal the deal.

Soon enough, he was halfway dressed, sipping coffee from his favorite mug while he sat in front of the monitor in his bedroom, ready to get the day going.

"Ego, show me the Bridgespan schematics." The blinking cursor vanished from his screen, and a wireframe building map spun into its place. He looked it over once more. He'd spent many hours reviewing his plan, writing the code he'd need to pull the job off, and getting everything in order. He was ready. Still, there was a hint of lingering doubt. "What do you think, Ego? Have I missed anything?"

"Given the available data, your plan has a ninety-one percent chance of success, with a possible three percent margin for error in my calculations."

That sounded good, even if Ego's programmed confidence was less than totally reassuring. But Ego was probably right. Cam had always had a mind for problem-solving. Puzzles, games, strategy–those had always been easy for him to master. Programming, coding, and systems turned out to be just another type of puzzle for him, too. Once he'd learned the proper languages and taught himself the correct tools, working with those things was no different to him than playing any other game. He just needed to understand the rules.

None of the work he'd done for the Bridgespan project, though, could've come close to his most significant accomplishment: Ego.

It was true that there were a lot of personal assistant programs already on the market, especially from the big tech companies, and a lot of them were even free. But why would he ever want a bloated, overgrown search engine or online marketplace to mine and sell his data under the guise of assisting him? The idea was laughable, especially since he knew that he could write a better one for himself. It took more than two years of intense work before he'd started to see any significant results from his efforts, but by that point, Ego had been officially born, and the whole project had snowballed into an avalanche.

He still wasn't even sure what Ego's limits really were. He wasn't ready to call Ego a true AI yet. He'd hardly had access to the kinds of processing power something like that would've required. But the learning algorithms he'd written quickly overwhelmed the custom Nero Imperium server he ran at home. They still regularly taxed the rented cloud-server space he'd moved them to, requiring frequent storage and processing upgrades. And with its natural-sounding voice responses and almost scary heuristics, Ego was truly becoming a force to be reckoned with.

Cam always had Ego checking his code and reviewing his strategies, in part, to help him find any flaws or errors. Doing that also gave Ego a chance to learn. And, one day, Ego would be able to think and reason for itself, beyond the code that Cam had written for it. Until that day came, though, Ego was still a helpful virtual assistant, one that managed his calendar, tracked his finances, oversaw his system security, and monitored his biorhythms. And started his coffee maker.

"Ok, Ego, I guess that means we're set, then." He pulled his handheld off the dock on his desk and stood up to finish getting ready.

He put on the navy blue button-up with the Bridgespan Biotech logo embroidered in white on the chest pocket. He'd ordered it online from a custom embroidery site after he'd seen a lot of staffers wearing them during his site visits. His chunky, black, rubber-soled boots were shiny enough to look dressy to the casual observer. On top of the shirt went a simple, smart, gray jacket. A newish, charcoal gray messenger bag completed the look. His handheld went into a pants pocket. The rest of his toolkit went into the bag.

After a quick once over in his full-length mirror to make sure he looked the part, he nodded to himself. He was a little more stylish and put together than the average nerd, maybe, but he wasn't taking any chances. He knew from experience that the site security staff at Bridgespan could be a little jumpy. On his first site visit, he'd nearly been turned away by the staff at the visitor's desk for a scheduled meeting with their CTO. It hadn't even mattered that one of the uniformed front desk guards was Black. One look at the Brown guy trying to talk his way past the front desk was all it took to get a no. Even after they'd confirmed his appointment with the CTO's administrative assistant, the guard insisted on escorting him up to the c-suite offices. What was he going to do, graffiti the elevator wall? But, since it was a high-paying gig, Cam just rolled with it. It certainly wasn't the first time his appearance inspired special attention from wannabe law enforcement officers like that. In the end, it was all part of playing the game. When that game included appearing like he belonged in a place that he most definitely did not–like the secure areas of a biotech firm that he wasn't employed at–looking the part was just that much more critical.

Satisfied with his outfit, he grabbed his earbud case from his desk and popped one into each ear. The earbuds looked enough like their mundane counterparts to fool most onlookers. Like his handheld–which started its life as an ordinary, Gemtek Ruby smartphone–they were equipment that Cam had torn apart, redesigned, and rebuilt himself. Their full range of functions was more than those onlookers would've suspected had they been inclined to wonder about it.

"Testing," he said.

"Receiving," Ego replied into his earbuds.

"Open a secure channel to the handheld, Ego, and initiate Watchdog mode."

"Affirmative, Cam. Secure channel opened. Confirm Watchdog mode is active."

A collection of tiny sensors he'd hidden around the apartment turned on and would record anything that happened there while he was away. If there was ever an incident, and Ego couldn't reach Cam, it had a predefined set of actions it could take on its own, based on specific parameters. For instance, if someone were to break in, Ego could broadcast a warning message, disable the apartment's power, or even activate the fire alarm. He'd never had an incident like that happen, but, given his line of work and the potential for trouble that came with it, he thought it felt irresponsible not to have at least some basic security at home.

The Bridgespan Biotech building was just a quick Metro ride from his Van Ness apartment building down to the gleaming biotech centers of San Francisco's Mission Bay. Taking the city's light rail involved trekking down into the tunnels under Market Street and navigating the frantic crowd heading to and from the Metro and BART trains. He generally viewed the experience with an eye for swarm intelligence and fluid dynamics. Having that kind of distanced perspective helped him cope with the constant struggle of being in the outside world's generally hostile environment. All the systems in place to monitor people and control their access to spaces were not there to keep him safe, after all, but to keep people safe from him. Every trip outside the safety of his apartment or workshop involved infiltrating a society that viewed him as suspicious just because of the way he looked. Even in such a diverse, multicultural community as San Francisco, those systems all paid homage to their tech company masters and the flood of money they'd brought to the city. And those masters, invariably, were rich, white men.

The concourse was surprisingly free of police and security that morning, although he made a mental note when he saw a maintenance team who looked like they were installing a new camera. He would have Ego add it to his map of the area's surveillance system for a program he was working on to remotely sabotage facial recognition systems. Programs like that already existed on the dark web, of course. But again, to him, it was more about the challenge than the result.

He gave a white commuter in a knee-length skirt and six-inch heels a wide berth after he saw them quickly pull their expensive purse close before he nonchalantly tapped his handheld on the reader at the turnstile, mimicking the actions of the people in front of him. It beeped as the metal barrier unlocked and parted for him. He smiled as he passed through, long ago having subverted the farecard system so he could tap on and off without paying any fare or leaving any traces of his passing behind.

After wading through the crowd of anxious commuters on the platform, he stepped onboard the correct Muni train and settled back in one of the train car's remaining empty seats.

"Ego, let's have some music," Cam subvocalized. "Something cool."

The deep, jazzy beats of Revolution Jackpot's new trip-hop album began to thrum in his earbuds. Cam smiled. Of course, Ego didn't really know what Cam thought was cool. But, based on what he usually listened to at any given point in the day during his many various activities, its algorithm was able to determine what Cam would've probably chosen for himself. Ego definitely got it right that time.

By the time they arrived at the Embarcadero station, the train was mostly full, and some people chose to stand and hold the ceiling-mounted handrails. A stooped, elderly Asian passenger boarded at the station clutching large, reusable, pink grocery bags in each hand. But there weren't many choices for a seat, as the area reserved for seniors and people with disabilities was already filled with seated riders, including a middle-aged, white executive in a three-piece business suit who obviously didn't belong there. The exec looked up when one of the bags brushed a pin-striped leg but then looked right back down at a glowing smartphone screen, unconcerned. Cam frowned. He hated it when the apathetic privileged took advantage of things like that. So, he waved his hand when the senior was looking in his direction, then stood up and offered them his seat. They smiled when they sat down, murmuring something to him he didn't catch, and positioned the overstuffed bags in their lap. Cam noticed the suit in the senior seating area looking at him with obvious disdain, but he just met their gaze defiantly as he grabbed one of the straps hanging from the overhead handrail until they finally gave up and looked back down at their phone.

After the short ride across the Mission Creek Channel, Cam stepped off the train onto the outside station platform.

The others who deboarded with him all scattered to their individual destinations. As he crossed the street and started walking toward the Bridgespan building, he mentally reviewed his attack plan one more time. His primary advantage that day was the element of surprise. He was arriving two full days ahead of the date they'd verbally agreed upon for his inspection when he first took the contract. It was always possible that they could've been expecting something like that. Then they'd probably alerted their security staff to the possibility of his incursion. But, based on his experience, that was pretty unlikely. Tech executives always overestimated how prepared they were and how tight their security was. And when you evaluated a company's security system, it wasn't a fair test if they were expecting it. He usually found that surprise visits were much more revealing.

He readied himself as he approached the lobby, getting mentally into character. Then he pushed the revolving door and stepped into place behind a pair of genuine Bridgespan employees, blending in nicely with the flow of morning arrivals.

"Ego, initiate stage one," he subvocalized. The music immediately stopped.

"Stage one confirmed," came Ego's reply.

The building's large, glass-walled lobby was modern and stylish in that bland corporate style of so many startups with money to burn. A giant, silvery, abstract, metallic sculpture–undoubtedly costing them at least six figures to acquire–anchored the space. Only the oversized Bridgespan Biotech logo, an unimaginative echo of the famous, nearby bridge projected brightly onto the back wall, gave visitors any clue to who owned that particular space.

When Cam was halfway across the lobby, near the hand scanners everyone had to pass through to get to the elevators, his handheld started buzzing in his jacket pocket. He feigned a mild look of embarrassment as he pulled it out and looked at it and stepped off to the side to avoid impeding foot traffic. Then he tapped the green answer button flashing on the screen.

"Hello," he said aloud. The call was simple misdirection. He'd just needed an excuse to stand there in the middle of the lobby while he was close enough to the security network for Ego to break into it.

"Sigint initiating," said Ego in his earpiece.

"Oh, hi, it's great to hear from you." Cam kept up the ruse, his eyes pointed at his handheld's screen. "I'm just on my way into the office."

"Secure network found. Initiating access." A wireframe schematic of the wireless nodes in the area appeared on his handheld display, with the closest node highlighted.

"No, that's okay. I've got a minute." One of the security guards noticed him standing off to the side and gave him a questioning look. Cam shrugged apologetically and pointed to his earbud with his free hand. The guard nodded in understanding and went back to watching the employees scan themselves in.

"Network access acquired. Inserting biometrics now."

Cam smiled. "Oh, that's great news. Congratulations."

"Biometrics inserted. Withdrawing from the network."

"Ok, sounds good. Talk to you later." He tapped the red End Call button on his screen and put his handheld away. After making a brief show of dusting something off his pants, he looked back up and made his way to the hand scanners.

"Good news?" the security guard asked in cheerful baritone.

Cam placed his palm on the reader, and it immediately flashed green. Ego's network incursion had successfully added Cam's palm print to the employee database. He was in.

"Yeah," Cam replied, offering the guard a friendly smile. "My nephew's softball team made it into the finals. He's really excited."

The guard chuckled. "I bet he is." They paused briefly to check the display on their side of the scanner. "Have a good day, Mr. Martin."

Of course, Cam hadn't used his actual name in the fake biometrics file he'd created. "Thanks, you too," he replied before calmly walking on toward the elevators. Stage one was complete.

Cam rode one of the elevators to the building's third floor, an administrative level with minimal security and, more importantly, accessible, single-occupancy restrooms. He avoided the one closest to the elevator in favor of another farther down the hall. That particular restroom was located next to a locked closet that contained the floor's network hardware, which was a significant security flaw. The door was unlocked, so he quickly stepped inside and flipped the lock switch around, lighting the door's small Occupied sign. Then he pulled down the baby changing station table and set his bag down on top of it. Reaching into his bag, he pulled out his toolkit, then took out a probe attached to a short cable and connected it to his handheld. Holding that, he climbed onto the toilet seat, then reached up to the drop ceiling and slid the nearest tile up and out of the way. He reached into the dark space above him, next to the restroom wall, and felt around for his target. When he found the bundled cables he was searching for, he pulled them toward him so they'd be easier to reach, then used his probe to detect each cable's signal traffic, one by one, until he found the one that led to the primary security server. Bingo.

He carefully stepped down from the toilet seat and went back to his toolkit, putting the probe away and removing a small, matte black cube with its own short, looped cable attached. Returning to the toilet, he resumed his balanced stance on the seat and unlooped the cable, using a gripper on one end to clip it onto the cable he'd identified. He pressed a small button on the black box, and a green LED lit up in response.

"Ego, Initiate stage two."

"Stage two confirmed. Initiating network access. Access acquired. Routing to your handheld."

Holding the black box in one hand, he pulled out his handheld with the other and tapped the screen with his thumb. The display came awake to show a command prompt flashing next to the drive ID of the security server. Excellent.

"Show me the security feeds." Cam watched as Ego entered a series of commands faster than he could read them. But he knew what they were since he'd written them himself. The command prompt quickly disappeared and was replaced with a stack of thumbnail video images. He scrolled through a feed of every security camera in the building, stopping once he found the one he was looking for. Then he double-tapped to expand it and saw an empty hallway outside of a security door. The room behind that door was his next target. "Record ten seconds and loop the video on this feed."

"Affirmative. Recording. Replacing the feed with the video loop."

Cam stowed his handheld in his pocket, then stuffed the box and the cable back into the ceiling. Once those were secure, he slid the ceiling tile back into place.

"Insert the RFID for this device into the building security system and grant me full access."

"Affirmative. Initiating system access. Access acquired. Inserting RFID. Altering system privileges. Completed."

Satisfied, Cam grabbed a small black disc from his toolkit and slipped it into his pocket. He'd connected to the network with an ultra-wideband transmitter in the cube he'd left behind in the ceiling. It went through walls really well, but it was range limited, so he'd brought along a network repeater just in case. Stage two was complete.

He placed the toolkit back into his bag, slipped his bag over his shoulder, and flipped the changing table closed. After a quick check-up on his appearance in the mirror, he went back out into the hallway. His next stop was the sixth floor. Instead of returning to the elevator, he looked for the stairs at the end of the hallway. When he found the stair door, he opened it and started walking up the stairwell. Even muffled from his rubber soles, the sound of his footsteps still softly echoed through the concrete-walled chamber.

Then he heard a door slam closed above him, followed by the rhythmic pattern of footsteps descending the stairs. Someone else was in the stairwell. Cam pushed back on a sudden burst of anxiety. Only a handful of people in the building would recognize him, and the odds that any of them would take the stairs were comfortably slim. As the footsteps grew closer, he composed his features, reminding himself to remain calm and look like he belonged there. It was the easiest camouflage he could wear. He kept climbing, but the other person stopped on the landing above him. When he heard a beep and a click as they unlocked the door, he let out another deep breath, willing the tension from his body before he finished walking up the remaining flights to the sixth floor.

Once he was standing outside the door to floor six, he pulled the disc from his pocket and pressed the small button on top of it. A yellow LED flashed on and off for several seconds before changing to a solid green. Connection achieved. He set the disc on top of a firebox mounted to the wall in the stairwell, where it would be out of general view for the short time he'd need it. Then he pulled out his handheld and tapped it with his thumb, but there was no response.

"Ego," he subvocalized, "what's wrong with this device?"

"Running diagnostics, stand by. There is a fault at connector one forty-seven."

The power control for the screen. No shit.

He tapped the handheld against his hand–tap, tap, tap. He felt silly doing it, knowing that it was the go-to solution for non-techies everywhere, but then the screen flared to life, and he breathed a sigh of relief. If the screen's power control connection had somehow become loose, he must've knocked it back into place.

He switched to the camera feed, which showed that the hallway was clear. Satisfied, he placed the handheld against the wall-mounted security pad next to the door. The system beeped as it read and recognized the handheld's RFID as valid, and the door unlocked with a loud click. He pulled it open and stepped through into the empty hallway.

Being spotted in the stairwell would've been manageable. Getting caught on a secure floor without having gone through security was a complication Cam preferred to avoid. But it was a short distance from the stairwell to his next stop. He used his handheld to unlock the security door, then quickly stepped inside.

The space was hot, cramped, and, between the hum of the server racks and the industrial AC unit's jet-engine whine, really noisy. The server racks were his ultimate target, and they'd presented him with the most significant challenge in his operation. Typically, data theft was a simple matter of network access, and it could often happen without even needing to enter a facility at all. But Bridgespan took the extra precaution of storing their most valuable IP on an air-gapped server, with no connection outside this room and the terminals in the nearby research labs. Any data would have to be manually transferred from a terminal to a portable storage device and hand-carried out. Stealing data that way would've required either infiltrating the labs as an employee or using some tricky social engineering. Neither option would've been impossible, but they also would've taken the most time. Accessing the data directly from the server was so much quicker.

Cam lifted the bag off his shoulder and set it down on the floor. He knelt, reached inside, and pulled out a coiled-up cable. Then he stood back up and began to visually trace the pattern of wires connecting each server unit on the rack. Once he found the server he wanted to connect to, he plugged one end of the cable into it and the other into his handheld.

"Ego, Initiate stage three."

"Stage three confirmed. Initiating server access. Stand by." Cam saw the code he'd written for that stage rapidly scrolling across the handheld's screen. He'd finally reached the trickiest part of the whole operation. He hadn't known what kind of security he'd come across plugging into the server directly, so he'd made some educated guesses about what he thought he'd find. If he was lucky, they'd assume that only authorized users would ever have that kind of access. Then it would be a simple password request–if even that. If he was unlucky, there'd be a biometrics check involved. "Access acquired."

That was fast. "Show me the root directory." He watched the list expand on his handheld screen. Everything was there, every company secret and prototype, their entire set of IP. If he'd genuinely been there to steal from them, he could've robbed them blind.

Then his handheld buzzed. He was getting a call from Tony. Cam reluctantly pressed the answer button. "Hey Tony," he said. "Kinda busy right now."

"What? Shit, man, I'm sorry. Just calling to confirm the raid tonight. The Goobers are already pestering me about it, you know?"

The Goobers were their raid squadmates in Farstorm, the MMORPG they'd been playing together almost religiously. Cam and Tony had taken to calling their raid squadmates the Goobers, regardless of who they were at the time. They'd first given the nickname to a pair of German brothers whose last name sounded enough like Goober to make it funny, but they'd most recently bestowed it on a couple of teenagers that lived somewhere out by Sacramento.

"Tell them I wouldn't miss it for the world, I promise. Now

let Daddy get back to work, please."

Tony chuckled. "Yeah, yeah, sorry, man. Have fun writing your report or whatever computer shit you're doing."

"Fuck off, Tiger."

"Love you too, Mad Dog. Kisses."

Tony disconnected before he could reply. Cam smiled ruefully, shaking his head, then reached down to the bag at his feet, pulled out a slim, portable SSD, and plugged it into the server unit.

"Ok, Ego, let's have some fun."

Forty-five minutes later, he was seated at a window table in the coffee shop across the street from the Bridgespan building, listening to music with his earbuds while he enjoyed a nice, spicy chai. Some movement in his peripheral vision made him look around to see his client standing over him. He was flanked by the very same beefy, iron-faced security guard who'd insisted on escorting Cam into the building that one time. Hovering nervously behind them both was Matthew Ugumori, their head of Network Security. Cam smiled. "Hi, Ron. Matthew. Care to join me?"

Ron Freeman, the CTO of Bridgespan Biotech and Cam's client, nodded reluctantly before taking the seat across from him. He wore a perfectly tailored, charcoal gray suit that was probably Italian-made. It was only the second time he'd seen Ron in person. But his wardrobe remained just as impressive as Cam remembered it to be, from the spotless leather shoes to the impeccable knot in the crimson silk tie that almost matched the crimson hue of the noticeable reddening on his otherwise pale cheeks. Ron gave Cam a slight eyebrow lift when he spotted the Bridgespan logo on his shirt.

Cam just shrugged. "I take it you got my message?"

Ron cleared his throat. He was obviously having some feelings about this meeting. "I certainly did. Along with the entire research department." He looked back at Matthew, who promptly looked away. "You weren't supposed to come for two more days."

Cam shrugged again. "Come on, Ron. It would hardly be a fair test of your data security if you actually knew when I was going to show up, would it?"

The security guard, likely taking offense at Cam's tone, started to step forward, but Ron stopped them with a raised hand. "You were supposed to audit our security, Mr. Maddock. Not break into our facility and steal our IP."

"I did audit your security. As for your IP–" Cam started to reach down into his bag and noticed the guard immediately tensing up. "Come on, Ron. We're in a coffee shop. Everything's fine. Would you mind calling off the dogs, please?"

Ron's pale cheeks flushed even further before he sighed, nodded, and turned to his excitable escort. "Go wait outside. We'll be fine." The look on the guard's face said they clearly disagreed with Ron's assessment, but they nodded anyway and left.

"Thanks, Ron." Cam reached down into his bag and pulled out the SSD, setting it on the table and sliding it across to Ron. "As for your IP, I didn't steal it. I just encrypted it. Here's the encryption key, by the way." Ron looked down at it, then at Matthew, who reached down and grabbed the drive. "Now, as I'm sure your legal team just explained to you, the contract we signed didn't specify any specific method or timing for my audit. And it completely indemnifies me from any legal action you might be thinking of taking. It also binds you not to disclose any of my methods to anyone else. That's why the folks you asked about me didn't warn you."

Ron sat quietly for a moment, probably repeating in his head whatever mantra it was that got him into a C-suite office with a salary that could afford expensive Italian suits. "So?"

"You'll get a full report with my invoice, of course. But the short version is, you've got the basics down. The biometric scanners and the air-gapped servers are some of the smartest moves you could make."

"But?"

"Your signal security is pretty laughable, to be honest," admitted Cam. "And we have to talk about not locating important network cables where someone could easily reach them through the drop ceiling in the bathroom."

Matthew finally spoke up. "I don't think–"

"No," Cam interrupted, "you clearly don't." He looked back at Ron. "This is your network security chief?"

Ron nodded. "For now."

Cam shot a glance at Matthew, who'd suddenly gone pale. "I'll include my full recommendations in my report, Ron. I'm also happy to pitch you on some kickass firewall and encryption software that would take a supercomputer to break."

His client seemed to consider this for a few moments. "Fine. I look forward to reading your report." He stood up and offered his hand to Cam, who shook it. "Please see that you don't break into my building again."

Cam offered him his most gracious smile. "Next time, I'll make an appointment first."

CAM

Cam watched in amazement as Tony blew out a ridiculous amount of smoke from the joint he'd just hit. "Oh, man," Tony softly exclaimed, his voice tight, "I can't believe we actually pulled that shit off. We fucking rule, dude!"

Cam laughed. "Stop gloating and pass that joint over here, dickwad." Tony complied with a bow of his head and a little flourish.

The Farstorm raid had gone off without a hitch. Their squad infiltrated the targeted stronghold almost precisely according to their carefully devised plan. As Mad Dog, his Farstorm persona, Cam was in rare form. Using his recently acquired stealth cloak, he took out sentry after sentry while they were none the wiser. Eventually, their squad secured the artifact they'd been looking for without setting off the alarm. They'd also stumbled across the stronghold's security room, where Cam found a self-destruct button. So he pressed it. Who wouldn't have? That's when the alarm went off, but it was already too late for the enemy clan. When the five-minute timer started counting down, Mad Dog, Tiger, and their squad tore off on a mad dash for the exit, guns blazing. They'd lost one of the Goobers on the way out, but even he'd said it was worth it to watch the whole place go up in a massive fiery explosion in the end.

Cam took his own hit off the joint, savoring the sweet flavor as he inhaled the smoke into his lungs.

Tony poked a finger at Cam. "I told you getting that stealth cloak would be worth it, didn't I?"

Cam nodded while he exhaled, then passed the joint back to his friend and squadmate, "You sure did, Tiger. And now we have the Requiem Vortex Generator, too. At least until someone tries to take it from us."

Tony shook his head. "Nah, man. No one even knows we have that shit except for the assholes we just took it from. And they're not about to admit that our merry little band of minstrels just rolled into their secret lair and took it off their hands."

Cam laughed. "And by the time they can get their shit together again to come take it back–"

"We'll have already used it!"

Their daring raid was only one part of their master plan. With their stolen generator, Cam's stealth cloak, and a couple of really sweet Supernova Cannons that Tony lifted from the clan's armory, they were ready to take on their next big score, the infamous Syndicate Vault in the sky city of Volaris. But that would be another raid for another day. Their current celebration was all about enjoying their freshly won spoils.

Playing Farstorm was how Cam and Tony met. After they'd randomly teamed up in a raid to take out the same target a few years back, Mad Dog and Tiger clicked well as a team. With Cam's gift for planning and strategy and Tony's essential fearlessness, they'd been almost unstoppable. In the game chat, they'd discovered that they both lived in San Francisco, so the pair decided to try out a few couch co-op sessions, where it turned out that they clicked well as friends, too. They were both twenty-six, both avid gamers, and both shared a biting sense of humor and a general dislike for authority.

While Cam had made a handful of friends and acquaintances in the city after he moved there, Tony turned out to be one of the few people he'd actually grown close to. Cam had even met most of the Zhang family, including Tony's parents, sister, and several aunts, uncles, and cousins. Tony's mother basically treated him like another one of her own kids, which was sweet, and a welcome change from what Cam remembered of his own mother. Since Tony seemed to know everybody in town, he'd given Cam a social life that he probably wouldn't have had otherwise. Plus, Tony threw some killer parties. Cam enjoyed them, even when they got crowded. And, because Tony had a lot of family and friends in the city, his parties were always crowded. Cam even met a few of the guys he'd dated since moving to San Francisco at one or another of Tony's functions.

As his closest friend, Tony was one of the few people who Cam ever opened up to. He was also the only one of Cam's friends who knew what he actually did for a living, beyond the nebulous title of tech consultant.

Tony passed the joint back. "So, how much did you make again today?"

Cam smiled. "Fifteen grand, plus expenses. And probably a new contract for some firewall and encryption software." He held up the joint. "This would've helped at the meeting, though. For a minute, I was sure their security guard was gonna tackle me."

Tony laughed and took the joint from him. "Humboldt's

finest. Guaranteed to smooth over even the angriest client meetings."

Cam wasn't a heavy pot smoker, not like Tony was. But he did enjoy taking the edge off after a long day once in a while. "Seriously, though, you should've seen him. And their network security guy? I'm pretty sure he got tossed out onto the street right after they left. It was fucking intense."

Tony rolled his eyes dramatically before slapping Cam on the shoulder. "That was a fucking boss move, though, breaking into the place like that." He took another hit before passing it back to Cam. "Seriously, that was totally some real Phantom Division shit. No wonder our raid went so well. You've been practicing IRL."

Cam chuckled. "At least I didn't have to drop in from the ceiling hanging on a wire or some shit. Still, it kinda sucks getting someone fired like that. Before today, he probably thought he was good at his job."

Tony laughed, then screwed up his face and pointed a wagging finger at Cam. "You'll rue the day you crossed me," he croaked.

"Nah, I don't think he had the balls to speak up, not with how pissed his boss was. But, if he was any good at his job, then they wouldn't have needed to hire me. So thank you, Matthew Ugumori, for being shitty at Network Security."

Tony scoffed. "Ugumori? Is that Japanese? Hell, he's probably just mad you didn't back him up in front of his white boss. You know us Asians gotta stick together against white tyranny."

It was Cam's turn to roll his eyes. "Yeah, cuz I'm so totally Chinese." That had long ago become one of their inside jokes. Cam had the kind of racially ambiguous features that could've placed him in most any non-white racial group. But, since he was adopted, and there was no actual record of his birth, he had no idea what his ancestry really was. After much pestering from Tony, Cam had even given in and taken a DNA test a few weeks back, despite knowing that it wouldn't tell him much when he finally got the results. In the end, it didn't really matter. Cam still wouldn't learn anything about his birth parents or where he'd really come from. He was Brown. Whether that was because he was Black, Asian, Latino, Arab, or whatever didn't matter much in most white folks' eyes.

"Hey, my family thinks you're Chinese, so you may as well be," Tony shared. "Speaking of family, that reminds me. My cousin is DJing at Emphasis tonight, and I'm on the list. We should totally go later."

Cam glanced at his handheld to check the time. "That place in the Marina? Ok, yeah, that sounds like fun. But right now, I'm starving. We should eat first."

"Good call. Let's go get noodles and beer."

Cam's stomach gurgled loudly in response, and the pair dissolved into laughter. Still chuckling, Tony got up off the couch and walked across the large, open space toward his bedroom. The converted storefront he lived in was mostly just the one big room, with a galley kitchen set along one side and a bathroom and a bedroom in the back. Despite the size and the extra tall ceilings, it was surprisingly homey, with the furniture laid out in a clever way that divided the main room into smaller, more intimate spaces.

A few minutes later, Tony emerged from his bedroom, having changed out of his shorts and t-shirt into a more club-appropriate collared shirt and tight pants, with a light jacket slung over one shoulder. "How do I look?"

He looked great, of course, with his toned body, high cheekbones, full lips, and spiky, jet black hair. If he wasn't Cam's bestie, there would've been some definite sexual tension for Cam to deal with.

Cam stood up and brushed some ash from the joint off of his own shirt. "Like every bachelor straight guy I know."

Tony laughed. "Yeah, but you gotta admit I look way better than the rest of those clowns. And who knows? Maybe I'll meet somebody tonight?"

"Ah, so the real reason you invited me along finally comes out. You want me to be your wingman." Cam grabbed his jacket off a nearby chair and slipped it on.

Tony dramatically mocked a sudden chest wound. "Ooh, you got me good, Cam." Then he laughed. "Maybe you're right, but it's not like I wouldn't be your wingman if the situation ever called for it. You just never hit on anybody when I'm around."

Cam snorted. It had been a while since he'd gone on a date. Hell, it had been a while since he'd even hooked up with anyone. He always told himself that was because he was just too busy, which was true enough. Between contract clients and side projects, his schedule was pretty densely packed. But, when it came down to it, he knew it was really because he just hadn't been interested in anyone lately. A deep dive into the issue would probably result in admitting how he'd been using his own feelings of otherness to isolate himself from potential love interests, thus creating some sort of self-fulfilling prophecy. But Cam wasn't interested in that sort of introspection, at least not when he was about to go out for the night. And he was fine playing along with Tony's serial dating habits. Tony was his best friend, after all. But he also wasn't about to let his friend off the hook that easily. "That's because last time you went with me to the Bridge Club, the guys all kept hitting on you instead of me."

Tony held up his hands in appeasement. "Hey now, don't blame me if my beauty knows no bounds. I'm supreme arm candy." He turned and did a quick check of his hair using his reflection in the glass of a framed print hung on the wall next to him. "But we could go there tonight instead if you want. It's not like this will be the last time my cousin ever DJs."

Cam scoffed. "On a Thursday? No way. It's Country Night."

Tony scowled facetiously. "Ew, yeah. No way."

"Let's just stick with the original plan," Cam suggested, putting a brotherly arm around his friend. "We can deal with my love life some other time."

Tony ducked out from under his arm and gave him a friendly pat on the stomach. "Ok, lover boy. But next time, it'll be all about you."

A short time later, the pair were on their way to a new Chinese noodle joint up the street from where Tony lived in Dogpatch, laughing and joking, still pleasantly stoned. The once gritty, industrial neighborhood had gone through a gentrifying renaissance when the most recent tech boom brought in the new light rail line. Since then, it became the home to more than a few new bars and restaurants. It was a little too polished for Cam's tastes, with all the vast, empty sidewalks and bland, featureless new buildings. He preferred neighborhoods that felt more lived in and less like barren movie sets. But the pleasant, late summer evening was perfect for the walk, without even a hint of fog in sight.

The host at the restaurant knew Tony, of course, so they got seated ahead of everyone in line. They even got a free round of beers to boot. When Cam made a comment about it, Tony took mock offense. But he quietly added that his family gave the owners a loan to help open the place since they hadn't been able to get financing from the banks. Cam nodded knowingly. Tony's family was a benefactor for many such local operations, it seemed.

By eleven PM, the pair were on their way to the club, following a quick stopover at Cam's place so he could shower and change while Tony channel surfed on Cam's giant flatscreen. When the rideshare driver dropped them off at the curb in front of the club, there was already a line of people waiting. Since it was the Marina, it was mostly an upper-class crowd. Or, at least a group that was trying to look upper-class. But, since Tony's cousin was DJing, it was also a de facto Asian night, so the crowd at least wasn't all white. They got a few nasty looks from the onlookers in line, but Tony was undeterred and walked right up to the burly, black-shirted bouncer at the door. Cam wasn't surprised to see that they knew each other, too. They were both quickly ushered inside past the complaining crowd, with only a quiet admonishment for Tony to tell his sister that Leon said hello.

Inside, the club was body heat warm, saturated with the sickly floral scent of high-end perfume layered over musky pheromones so thick that you almost had to wade through them. The DJ, Tony's cousin, was laying down some tribal beats under a looping sample from Fortune Scarlet, one of last year's top R&B artists. Cam could feel the rhythm crawl under his skin and massage his heartbeat like a hand beating a conga drum. He smiled, knowing that he'd made the right call to come along. He'd spent way too much time in his own head already that day. A few drinks and a little dancing were going to do him some good.

Tony left Cam behind to go handle the drinks, navigating through the mass of people stacked up at the bar like a salmon swimming back to its spawning grounds. Tony had a way with people, a fearless charm that instantly placed them under his thrall. He never had to ask people to move out of his way. They just wanted to. Cam never mastered that trick, but he was ok with that. He had his own set of tricks up his sleeve.

As he stood there next to the dance floor, he watched the dancers' bodies writhing and undulating to the heavy bass beats like winds blowing through a field of tall grass. For a moment, he was reminded of a massive bird flock–thirty-thousand tiny creatures seemingly merged into a single organism that dipped and swerved through the sky, dancing to nature's own tribal beat. Then, suddenly, he saw every one of them, each dancer like a distinctly colored tile in a dance floor mosaic. That was his trick, to see not just the pattern, but all the pieces of it–how a dip and swerve on one side of the dance floor rippled across the mass of bodies, slinking along like an ocean wave, then crashing along the shore on the other side.

Tony soon returned with the drinks, which led to dancing. The dancing led to Tony veering off to make out with a hottie in a short, tight dress who'd been flirting with him. Cam, sweaty and hot, took that as an opportunity to plod through the tightly packed throngs of dancers to get to the bar and order another drink. He was lucky enough to arrive during one of the random lulls that happened sometimes, and found the bar mostly empty. Cam was even luckier to find that the bartender he'd been crushing on was standing right there, in a tight black t-shirt and dark jeans, running a dry rag across the metallic bartop. The bartender smiled, and Cam, feeling bold and riding the high from such a successful day, smiled right back at him.

"Hey there," Cam said, pitching his voice loud enough to be heard over the din of their surroundings. "You're Joe, right?"

The bartender nodded. "Joe Tanaka, yeah. And you're Tony's friend Cameron?"

Of course, he knew Tony. "It's just Cam, actually. How do you know Tony?"

Joe smiled again and ran a hand through his wavy black hair. "Everyone here probably knows Tony. He's sort of a fixture around here, I suppose." Then he stuffed the rag into a back pocket and offered his hand out. "Nice to meet you, Cam."

Cam grabbed his hand and squeezed. "Nice to meet you, too, Joe."

The bartender held onto Cam's hand for a moment, then let go, put his hands down on the bar, and leaned in close enough that Cam got a whiff of his cologne. "So, Cam," he said with a smirk, "what can I get you?"

Before he could answer, Cam was interrupted by the rowdy voices of a pair of blonde-haired, improbably tanned, poorly aging, former fraternity pledges. They high-fived each other over some secret, shared insight as they shoved their way in next to Cam at the bar. "Hey, dude, lemme get uh–," slurred the one closest to Cam with breath reeking badly of booze and cigarette smoke, before turning to their friend. "Hey

Spence, what the fuck are we drinking?"

"Shit, Trev," slurred the other one. "I don't fucking know."

Trev turned back to Joe. "Just make it a pair of double vodka Blitzes and, uh, two shots of Wolfhead."

Joe offered the faintest scowl, then shook his head. "Uh, no way, dude. You gotta wait your turn." Then he turned back to Cam. "Sorry about that. Anyway, what can I-"

But Trev wasn't having it, and slammed a fist down on the bar. "Fuck that! You can take care of his fairy ass after we order." Then they flashed Cam a horrid, drunken sneer. Cam knew that, if he wasn't careful, there was about to be trouble.

He put up a hand to keep Trev from closing the gap between them any further, then smiled. "You know what, Trev? You're obviously thirstier than I am. You go right ahead."

That only earned him a bloodshot glare. "Are you trying to fuck with me?"

"Yeah, you better not fuck with us," Spence added loudly, moving in closer and pointing a drunkenly menacing finger Cam's way, "or we'll fuck you up."

Cam glanced over at Joe, who made a slight nod and then lifted himself up on his tiptoes, looking out over the crowd, hopefully for the bouncer. Cam looked back at Trev and tried to keep his expression placid. "Look, there's no problem here. Just go ahead and order."

The glare transformed into a crooked smile. "Maybe I've got a problem with you now, ass muncher," they quietly growled. Then, before Cam could react, Trev shoved both hands into his chest and pushed hard, knocking him down onto the floor. Cam felt himself jolt at least one person's elbow on the way down and heard the bright crash of a glass smashing next to him on the floor.

Spence grabbed onto Trev as they lunged forward toward Cam, trying to hold them back, but Cam could see the drunken rage in his attacker's eyes and knew it would take more than that to stop them. He started to scramble backward, trying to find the space to get out of the way and back onto his feet, but the area was too crowded for him to move anywhere else. But he still managed to pull a hand out of the way just before it got stabbed by someone's high heel.

Then suddenly, the bouncers were there, two giants in tight black t-shirts materializing out of the crowd with a deftness that belied their size. Cam watched in relief as they enveloped Trev and Spence in their bulky embraces. Trev kept on struggling, trying in vain to throw a punch. But the bouncer shut it down, slamming them hard up against the bar and wrenching their arm back into a lock. Then, holding their arms firmly behind them, the bouncers pulled the pair away and started shoving them toward the exit.

Shaking his head in mild disbelief, Cam started to push himself back up when he saw a hand reach down in front of him. He looked up to see that it belonged to Joe, who must've come out from behind the bar. Cam grabbed the hand, letting the bartender help pull him back up. Once he was back on his feet, Joe let go, then brushed a bit of debris or something off of Cam's shoulder before handing him a dry rag. "Sorry about that, Cam. I'm not sure how those assholes even got in here that drunk."

Cam used the rag to wipe some of the spilled liquor and a few glass shards off of him, then handed it back with a sigh. "Thanks," he said, then shrugged. "It is what it is, you know. One too many vodka Blitzes, and suddenly your shit don't stink."

Joe ventured a smile. "Yeah, that's for sure. Still, it shouldn't have happened, and I'm sorry. Can I at least get you that drink? On me, of course."

It would've been a tempting offer under most circumstances, especially after the way Joe seemed to be flirting with him earlier. But Cam's mood was pretty much ruined at that point. While the club had been fun, raucous, and exciting before, it suddenly became hot, loud, and crowded. Cam just wanted to go home. He shook his head but tried to soften his refusal with a smile. "Nah, I don't think so. I appreciate the offer, but I think this is gonna be it for me tonight."

After a moment of careful contemplation, Joe nodded. "Yeah, I get it. I don't blame you for wanting to go." He reached into his back pocket, took out a small business card, and then wrote something down on it with a pen pulled from a nearby cup holder. He handed it over to Cam. "I'd still really like to get you that drink sometime, though. Here's my number. If you feel up for it, text me."

Cam smiled as he took the card and looked at it. "Ok, Joe. I will." Then he glanced around to see if he could spot his friend. "Look, I'm gonna go find Tony, then I'm gonna take off." He put the card into his back pocket. "But I'll text you, for sure."

Joe nodded, then put a hand on Cam's arm, biting his lower lip just a little bit in a way that almost made Cam reconsider his plan to leave. "Have a good night, ok?" Then he let go and started to push his way through the crowd to go back behind the bar and take care of the people who'd been waiting in his absence.

After spending a few minutes looking around for Tony,

Cam couldn't seem to find him. The noise and the crowd were really starting to get to him, too, so he decided that Tony would just have to deal with things on his own and walked back outside. The black-shirted bouncer at the door gave him a quick, apologetic head nod, which was a thoughtful gesture. Cam was mainly glad to be back out in the chilly night air, even in a yuppie enclave like the Marina. He pulled out his phone and summoned a rideshare car to get him back home. Then he tapped out a quick message to Tony, letting him know that he'd taken off before shoving his phone back into his pocket to wait. Glancing around, he realized that he was one of the few brown-skinned folks he could see around him, unlike inside the club. Still a little shaken from the incident at the bar, he inched closer to the bouncer, whose skin was so dark it almost matched their t-shirt.

"It's all good," the bouncer told him in a surprisingly deep and gravelly voice. "Ain't nobody gonna fuck with you while I'm here."

Cam looked over and nodded, grateful for the camaraderie and for not having to explain what was on his mind. But the moment was short-lived, as his rideshare car pulled up a short time later, and the driver leaned over toward the passenger side window and called out his name.

Once he finally made it home, after a whirlwind ride up Van Ness that he hardly even noticed, Cam stripped out of his dirty, alcohol-stained clothes and jumped into the shower to rinse off all the sweat from the club. After brushing his teeth and getting into a pair of comfy shorts, he crawled into bed, his head still swirling from everything that happened.

He lay there for a few moments, playing out a little mind fantasy of how the night could've gone. Should he have just stuck around afterward and taken the free drink? Maybe. No, that would've been stupid. He'd been in no mood for flirting and would've been shitty company. At least Joe had still given him his number. Was it too much to text him already? Should he at least wait until the next day, or even a couple of days, so he didn't seem needy or desperate?

Then he huffed and reached over the side of the bed to grab his pants and pull the card out of the back pocket. Once he had it, he picked his phone up off the charger on the side table next to him and tapped out a quick message with just his name, a smiley emoji, and a "nice to meet you." Then he hit send before he lost his nerve. Mission accomplished, he set the phone back down on the charging plate and lay back down on his pillow. As tired as he was after a long day, it still took him longer than he liked to finally fall asleep.

THE AGENT

«STATIC»«FLASH»

She moved through the crowded, covered market on autopilot, oblivious to the bustle of commerce happening around her. The mob of shoppers and tourists, perhaps unconsciously sensing the danger she somehow represented, instinctively parted before her, their raucous din falling around her in slow, rolling waves. The air was a wet blanket, laying on her cold and heavy, but the combat gear she wore kept her comfortably warm. She'd hidden it under a stylish coral raincoat and loose, flowing, white pants covered with a delicate blue floral pattern. Anyone on the lookout for her would've only seen another tourist trying her luck in the old marketplace.

But luck wasn't what brought her there. She'd arrived with a purpose.

She spotted her contact standing in front of an old flower merchant, ostensibly sampling some of the colorful, aromatic goods. He was a handsome man, with short, dark hair, terracotta skin, and a well-trimmed mustache with just a hint of gray. He'd dressed in a charcoal woolen suit and a sky blue dress shirt. He spotted her as she approached and smiled in welcome. She smiled in kind, staying perfectly in character, although the smile didn't reach her eyes.

"Ah, you made it." Her contact leaned in to embrace her, offering her a light kiss on each cheek. "What you seek is nearby," he whispered into her ear.

"Show me."

"Of course." He bowed to the flower vendor in thanks, then led her away down the row of market stalls. She followed him through the cramped space, ignoring the beseeching calls of vendors as she passed by them. She had no interest in their wares, only what she'd come for.

"There was some difficulty in obtaining it," her contact mentioned, his tone casual and light. "I will need to increase my fee for this acquisition."

She resisted the urge to lash out at him for his impertinence. He'd been useful to her, she had to admit. And it would be a hassle to replace him at that point. "That will not be possible. However, if you genuinely have what I seek, I will need you again for an additional task. We can renegotiate your fee, then, if necessary."

"I understand."

She didn't even have to look at him to know he was pleased. His greed, like that of most of his kind, was reliable enough to be predictable.

They exited the marketplace onto a crowded plaza anchored by a large circular pool with an extravagantly carved stone fountain in the center. Across the plaza stood an aging, brick building set with an ornate entrance arch flanked by rows of large, iron-framed, double windows.

Her contact gestured toward the old hotel. "I've taken a room there. We can–"

A flashing alert popped up in her vision, and she raised her hand to silence him. "We have picked up a tail."

Her contact remained unperturbed. "I see. Perhaps we should–"

She waved him off again. "I will take care of it. You continue on to the room. I will meet you there."

"As you wish," he agreed without complaint. "Room three seventeen." Then he turned and continued walking toward the hotel.

Turning with a flourish, her floral print pants swirling from the motion, she made her way back toward a nearby stall adorned with ornate, handcrafted jewelry. She'd been directed to avoid exposing her operation if possible, so she needed to discover if it would be required. She feigned interest in a jeweled pendant hanging from a hook on a thin silver chain but kept her attention focused on the large mirror standing in the back of the vendor's stall. She scanned the crowd for her tail. An icon overlaid her vision, designating her target as a tall, copper-skinned person with a shaved head, dressed in dark, utilitarian clothing.

The vendor noticed her interest in the pendant and said something to her, but she ignored them. Her mark seemed to be following her contact towards the building at the end of the plaza. They weren't there for her, then. Could they be there for the same objective that she was? Then the vendor said something else to her, more insistently, and she sharply told them to fuck off before she left the booth.

Her target had already passed by her position, so she started to follow them. It was clear that they intended to enter the hotel, and the risk of them discovering her objective forced her into immediate action. She quickly closed the distance between them, readying the emitters in the palm of her hand to deliver a stunning jolt, incapacitating her target enough to allow her to remove them from the field of play with little notice. She slipped between the final two bystanders in her path and reached out to make contact. But she must've given herself away somehow because, at that same moment, her target turned back and saw her. The two briefly made eye contact, and her mark knew they'd been made. She lunged anyway, hoping to stun them, but they quickly twisted out of her reach and started running.

She took off in pursuit, roughly forcing her way through the teeming throngs of people, shoving them aside when necessary, following the target icon when they disappeared into the crowd. Then they suddenly broke right and ran into a narrow alleyway on the side of the building.

She grunted and rushed in after them. A large, cement block wall at the end of the alley barred her exit. She glanced up and saw that her mark had already climbed halfway up the metal fire escape bolted onto the side of the old four-story structure. She rushed forward and jumped onto the metal railing above her, ignoring the ladder altogether. The sound drew her target's attention, and they looked down to see her still in pursuit. She pulled herself up and leaped onto the next railing, then the next, quickly closing the distance between them. By the time her target reached the roof, she was right on their heels.

They scrambled over the edge of the rooftop and scurried ahead to the far side of the building, perhaps intent on jumping away, but the twelve-meter drop to the top of the next building would've taxed even her enhanced structure. The only other building they could potentially reach was behind her. Her mark sighed in resignation, then turned and put their hands into their jacket pockets, calmly walking back to the middle of the roof as she pulled herself up onto it.

"Why are you following me?" they called out in a deep, booming voice. "Who are you?"

She replied by attacking, aggressively lunging forward to where they stood. They quickly dropped into a combat stance, then sidestepped her to avoid the collision. But she'd anticipated the move, planting a foot where they'd been and shifting her momentum toward their new location with an audible grunt. The change in direction was impossibly fast, requiring biomechanical servos to pull her reinforced tendons tight and prevent her from turning an ankle. She plowed through her opponent, knocking them down, then tucked and rolled, landing in a crouch to reverse her position and face them. She lunged again, but they were fast, too. As she neared them, they punched. She blocked, then counterpunched, but they dodged the hit and resumed their attack. As the pair came to blows, she realized that her opponent was a more capable brawler than she typically encountered, which meant that they'd likely been sent by her rivals. But she filed that information away for later analysis and focused on her immediate task.

The pair's arms almost seemed to blur as they each jabbed, chopped, and blocked. Her foe was nearly her equal, but she soon clocked the patterns in their movements, the subtle ways they telegraphed what they were about to do. She waited for it. There. An opening. She feinted a jab to their throat, which they moved to block, exposing their midsection. Then she slipped in a quick knife jab to their side, which threw them off balance, followed by a sweep kick, which knocked them off their feet. In a moment, she was kneeling on their back, grabbing for their arm to fold it into a lock. Somehow they managed to push up with their other arm and twist into a roll that knocked her loose. She let her momentum carry her into her own roll and popped back up into a combat stance to see them crouching a short distance away, gingerly cradling the arm she'd grabbed. She'd clearly hurt them, which meant their fight was almost over. That was good because she needed to end it soon, one way or another. She didn't know if they were working alone or not, and the fight could've been a diversion to stall for time.

"Why are you here?" she asked, her breath heavy from exertion. "Who sent you?"

Her rival's face was contorted with pain. "You know why I'm here–for the same reason you are, obviously."

She nodded her acknowledgment. If they knew about the data crystal, then others could've known as well. There was no more time to waste. She quickly raised an arm toward them, palm out, and triggered a disruptor pulse. The wave of excited energy particles struck her opponent as they tried to raise their shield, too late, and forced them backward, pushing them over the edge of the building. She heard a dull, wet thunk as their body slammed down onto the plaza below, followed by terrified screaming from the crowd.

By that point, she was already moving back to the fire escape. She jumped over the side of the building onto the black iron grating below her. Another disruptor pulse shredded the old fire door, sending shards of wood scattering into the darkened hallway behind it. She entered the building through the hole she'd just made, found the interior stairwell, and quickly went down to the floor below. The door to room three seventeen was locked, so she knocked loudly. Her contact opened it from inside, then swiftly backed away as she forcefully pushed herself inside the old hotel room.

"I heard the screams," he said mildly. "I take it there was some trouble?"

She silenced him with a look. All business now, she had no patience for his archaic sense of propriety. "It has been handled. Now, give me what I came here for."

He frowned but offered her no complaint. "Very well. It's here." He walked over to an older but well-preserved wooden bureau and reached for a small, matte black box that sat on top of it. When he casually held it out toward her, she could see that his hands were shaking ever so slightly. He was clearly afraid of her. Good.

She took it from him and briefly examined the box before flipping it open. Inside, nestled in folds of charcoal foam padding, lay a thin, rectangular data crystal. She was briefly struck by a flash of satisfaction. After all the time they'd spent looking for any evidence from the incident, any clue that could point them toward the one they'd been looking for, she'd been the one to find it. Surely that would mean she'd be allowed to continue following that trail. If not, it remained another success marking her exemplary track record. "This is it? You are sure?"

He nodded. "I haven't been able to break the encryption on it, of course. But the encryption itself was evidence enough that it could be what you're looking for."

Could be. No, that was not good enough. She looked back down at the crystal, then reached into the container and grabbed it. She let the container drop to the floor, where it landed with a soft thud on the thick, ornately patterned carpet under her feet. Wrapping her hand around the crystal, she closed her eyes and instructed her system to access it, providing it with decryption codes that were nearly 30 years old. There was a brief pulse as the codes took effect, then the decrypted data unfolded for her like an old map. And there it was, the information she'd been looking for. After all this time, she'd finally found it.

«FLASH»«STATIC»

CAM

Cam hadn't even opened his eyes yet, but he already regretted being awake. He had a throbbing headache. It couldn't be a hangover, could it? He rarely ever got those, and he'd hardly even gotten drunk at the club, anyway. Yet the ache was still there, settling in like a heavy stone sinking into the wet sand of his mind.

Laying still for a moment, he closed his eyes and took several deep breaths, one after the other, saturating his bloodstream with fresh oxygen, focusing on the steady, pounding thump of his heartbeat. The ache began to fade, almost as if he were willing it away, and, after a few more breaths, was gone. That was more like it. Then he remembered the dream.

His eyes shot open. What the hell was that all about? He remembered noise, light, and motion, but the frenzied details had already begun to fade, damn it. Another night of strange dreams, followed by another uncomfortable morning. Why was that happening to him? It couldn't be age. He was barely into his mid-twenties. Still, it had been many years since he'd struggled this much with sleeping like he had back when he'd first entered adolescence.

Like a lot of other burgeoning teens, his behavior had

become unruly with the onset of puberty. His parents, suddenly unable to control him, had eventually forced him to see a shrink. And he'd had strange dreams back then, too. Had that been why he always felt so out of sorts all the time? When he made the mistake of talking about those dreams with his parents, they'd just chalked it up to the hormonal changes of puberty. But Cam always knew that wasn't the problem since he had puberty-inspired dreams, too. Those presented an entirely different set of challenges, as he grew to understand that it wasn't just his skin color that made him different from the people around him.

When his behavior became more problematic than his parents were willing to deal with, they'd eventually convinced his doctor to put him on anti-psychotics. The strange dreams stopped then, but only because he stopped dreaming altogether. And when Cam finally stopped taking the drugs, the dreams hadn't returned.

He shook his head at the unwelcome memories. He wasn't interested in talking to another shrink and even less so in taking more anti-psychotics. They'd dulled his edge so much that he spent most of his early teenage years walking around like a zombie.

And there it was. Cam was thinking about his childhood again. That made it two days in a row. His unconscious mind must've been trying to tell him something, but the fuck if he knew what it was.

Cam rolled out of bed and launched himself into a quick round of bedroom calisthenics before rolling out a soft rubber mat and bending his body through a set of yoga asanas. After a shower and quick breakfast, he finally started to feel a little more centered, so he settled down in front of his computer to work on his report for Bridgespan. He pulled the data off his handheld, which had faithfully recorded his entire visit, then set about translating it all into a narrative that his clients would understand and appreciate. Following that, he appended a list of recommendations to improve the areas where he'd found their security lacking. Then he sent it off, along with his invoice and a follow-up message about his interest in bidding on their firewall and encryption upgrades. It would probably take them a few days to get back to him about that, once they'd gotten over their dismay at his unscheduled audit. And they would get over it. His clients always did.

He looked at his handheld, sitting in its dock. The damn thing had nearly betrayed him at the worst possible time. Cam knew he needed to crack it open and take a look at what had gone wrong. He'd already been thinking about giving it a few upgrades, so a visit to his workshop was in order. He could already feel a part of his mind planning out what he'd do there. He imagined the handheld's various internal pieces spread out onto his workbench, neatly categorized and labeled in some sort of cyberpunk dissection. Tinkering was an excellent way to distract him from the troubled thoughts he'd been having for the past couple of days. It never failed to put his mind at ease.

"Hello, Ego."

"Good morning, Cam." At least Ego sounded chipper enough.

"System status?"

"All systems are nominal. My latest debug protocol scrubbed thirty-seven thousand, nine-hundred sixty-four possible logic errors. I successfully ranked two million, one-hundred twenty-one thousand, seven-hundred forty-three new decision trees and incorporated them into my primary matrix. I also read a study on anti-gravity. It was so good, I couldn't put it down."

Cam chuckled softly. Not a day went by where he didn't regret introducing Ego to the concept of Dad jokes. "Ego, do a full cloud backup of the handheld, and reset the device firmware."

"Affirmative, Cam."

"And prep the workshop. I'm heading over."

"Backup and reset confirmed. The workshop will be ready when you arrive."

Satisfied, he got up and got dressed, deciding on a casual look more in keeping with his personal style than his workwear. He chose some slim-fitting but comfortable trousers, a long sleeve t-shirt with a Voidspace logo on it, and a pair of well-worn but well-loved canvas high-tops. His handheld and toolkit went into his messenger bag while his phone, keys, and wallet went into his pants pockets.

"Ego, activate Watchdog mode."

"Confirmed. Watchdog mode activated."

After a final glance in the mirror, he popped in his earbuds, grabbed his favorite dark gray hoodie, and headed for the door, shutting off the lights on his way out.

The sun shone brightly, but the air's crisp humidity cut some of the warmth out of its light. It was still reasonably pleasant weather for that time of year, though, and he almost didn't even need his hoodie. And it was a lovely day for a walk to his workshop.

After crossing over Market and making a quick stopover at a nearby coffee shop to pick up a little more caffeine, Cam started walking south toward Howard. It was late morning, and the downtown tech workers were already trickling out of their trendy, overpriced, open-plan workspaces in search of the day's lunch. Despite making his living off the city's tech sector, Cam didn't envy their slog or really even enjoy their company all that much. Spending his days hunched over in a cubicle, pumping out code for massive tech giants or, worse, risky startups, didn't appeal to him. He liked being his own boss. He always had. Some of that conviction came from a persistent feeling of not belonging. When he was a kid, when he was in school, even when he'd struck out on his own–he'd always felt that way. During his childhood, he'd chalked it up to being adopted. As he got older, he'd started to wonder if maybe he was just wired wrong somehow.

The San Francisco streetscape was easy enough to navigate after his years of living in the city. But he could still feel the underlying current in his thoughts telling him that things were somehow wrong. No amount of meds or therapy managed to banish that feeling. Sure, the meds had worked for a while, but only because they stopped him from feeling anything at all. His angst, whether consciously felt or not, had always been there. A lot of things were wrong, of course. Between racists, sexists, homophobes, transphobes, classists, and ableists alone, the world was full of haters. Not a day went by that he didn't hear or see another reason to feel like maybe humanity just wasn't cut out for its position on top of the food chain. But there was still something beneath that–or perhaps even more significant than that–that always made him feel like everything was a little off.

An incoming call dragged him out of his melancholy reverie. "Incoming call from Tony Zhang," the phone announced.

Cam tapped on an earbud to answer it. "Tony?"

"Hey, Mad Dog. How's it going? Are you as hungover as I am?"

Cam smiled. "You know, I did actually wake up with a headache this morning. But it's gone now."

"Jesus, Cam. I feel like someone wrapped my brain in a bunch of smelly old socks and played basketball with it." Tony paused and took a deep breath. "I probably shouldn't have done all those shots."

"Well, aren't you just the suffering poet?"

Tony gave him a low chuckle. "Tiger, tiger, burning bright, right? Hey, what are you up to? Wanna come by and smoke up? I'd love to hear the story of what happened to you last night."

He heard the flick of a lighter and the sound of bubbling water as Tony took a bong rip. "Sorry, Tiger. I can't. I'm headed to the workshop to do a little tinkering. I could head over later, though."

"Ah, shit." Tony's voice sounded strained as he held the smoke in his lungs before releasing a powerful exhale. "I told my sister I'd help out at the restaurant tonight." His family's business interests included, among other things, one of the more popular restaurants in Chinatown. His sister Summer managed it, and Tony helped out sometimes when she was short-staffed. "You could come by for a bite, though. She'd love to see you. But, first, you should tell me why you ended up ditching me at the club last night. I was a little worried."

Cam neared the building where he rented the space for his workshop. The area around it was being rapidly redeveloped by the flood of tech money gushing out of the Financial

District. He knew he'd probably end up getting pushed out before too long so that his building could be torn down and replaced by some tech company's ambitious new office. He noticed one of the street dwellers that hung out near his building sitting near his doorway again, so he fished a ten-dollar bill out of his pocket and handed it to them as he walked by. They smiled and thanked him, tucking the ten into an unseen pocket inside their torn and dirty overcoat. Cam smiled back, suppressing a sigh. How long would it be before the area ended up scrubbed clean of the more unfortunate souls like them?

"Hey, man. Are you still there?"

Cam's attention snapped back to the call. "Oh, yeah, sorry. And sorry about last night, too. Things ended up getting a little rough." He gave Tony a brief rundown of what happened before leaving the club the night before.

"Shit. Those fuckers. Hopefully, they got eighty-sixed from the place. But you're ok, yeah?"

"Yeah, just my wounded pride, mostly. But I did get that cute bartender's number, so it wasn't a total loss." Once he said that, Cam unwittingly checked his phone. Still no reply from Joe. But it was early, and he figured that a bartender would probably sleep late. "Anyways, I'm at my shop, and I gotta let you go. But I'll definitely swing by the restaurant later. See you then?"

"Sure thing! Later, Mad Dog." Tony hung up.

Cam shoved his phone back in his pocket, then pulled out his keys. First, he unlocked the outer gate and then the inner door before climbing the steps up to the next floor. The building had started out as an old auto shop but had enjoyed many adventures since, before being renovated and converted into light industrial and office spaces. It still had a lot of its original charm, though, with artfully preserved, peeling paint on the walls and refinished wooden floors full of gouges and oil-stain hieroglyphics telling stories from the golden days of auto repair. But it also had blazing fast fiber optic internet and an industrial-strength power supply.

He leased a partitioned space on the second floor that he'd set up for tinkering and other work. While programming and software were his primary income, he also did a decent side business building and repairing hardware. And the workshop was also where he built all of his specialty gear.

At the top of the stairs, outside his workshop door, he flipped up the cover of a small, wall-mounted touchpad and pressed his thumb to it. It beeped, then he heard the snick of the door lock and the thunk of his security system deactivating. Unlike his apartment, Cam had free reign to modify his workshop space. Most of the hardware he kept there was proprietary and one of a kind, so his security system was more robust than the one at home. Anyone who tried to enter the space using a standard key, or anyone who attempted to just break in, would get themselves a nasty shock–literally.

"Ego, I'm here."

The overhead LED panels came on as he walked in. His custom-built three-D printer already hummed quietly in the corner, warmed up and ready.

"Welcome back, Cam." Having a cloud-based assistant like Ego came in handy since Cam could access it anywhere he could access the internet.

Cam took off his bag and hoodie, hanging the latter by the door and setting the former on his workbench. He pulled his handheld and toolkit out of his bag and placed them on the bench, as well, then set the bag on the floor. Sitting down on his padded stool, he flipped on the task light hanging in front of him and tapped on the screen of the tablet that was sitting in a nearby dock, waking it. Like his handheld, his tablet started its life as something else—in this case, a top-selling, aluminum-bodied Gemtek Diamond. But, like most of the tech he'd purchased, Cam took it apart and gave it a thorough upgrade. Now its power rivaled that of most desktop computers.

"Ego, show me the schematics for the handheld device upgrades." The tablet screen filled with a rendered set of complex wireframe graphics. Since Cam had to crack the handheld open to fix the screen's power supply connection, he decided that he may as well add in a few of the upgrades he'd been thinking about, too. He smiled. It was going to be fun.

After spending a few hours printing and installing custom modules and fittings, along with a few specialty parts he'd ordered, everything tested out fine, or "nominally within acceptable parameters," as Ego would say. Cam applied a few touches of industrial adhesive, reconnected the front and back housings, and put the final screws back into place. The completed product still looked and felt just like the Gemtek Ruby he'd built it from, but it was so much more than that. He powered it on and watched it go through the startup sequence. So far, so good. He was about to set it back into the dock to test it when a Watchdog alert flashed on the tablet screen.

"Motion detected at primary residence," Ego announced through hidden speakers mounted on the workshop ceiling.

Primary residence meant his apartment. Cam wasn't aware of any maintenance visits scheduled for the day. Was there some sort of problem in his building?

"Show me."

The red alert box was replaced by a set of thumbnail images, one for each miniature camera hidden throughout his apartment. On one of the thumbnails, Cam watched two strangers walk through his living room. He grabbed the tablet and gestured to expand the video feed. The pair were each dressed in matching dark clothing, possibly coveralls or some kind of uniform. One of them held a gun.

Holy fuck. A gun? Who would break into his apartment with a fucking gun? Had that angry Bridgespan security guard sent a team to act out some weird revenge fantasy? That couldn't be possible. Could it?

Cam shook himself back into focus. Regardless of the intruders' motives, he needed to act.

"Ego, activate Torchlight. Authorization drama basin dialect tamarind."

"Torchlight confirmed." Back in the apartment, Ego remotely activated and wiped any pieces of computer equipment down to their system bios. Whatever the intruders took from him, if anything, wouldn't have any personal or incriminating information on it. His data was all stored on remote servers anyway, so he wasn't losing anything.

On the tablet, he saw the trespasser Ego labeled as Intruder One had already thoroughly tossed his living room. Cam expanded the thumbnail for a bedroom camera and saw Intruder Two, the one with the gun. Intruder Two stowed the weapon in a shoulder holster, probably realizing that Cam wasn't there, and took a small, black, rectangular device out of a pocket. Cam watched as the intruder waved the device around the room like an oversized fairy wand. Was it a signal detector? Soon enough, Intruder Two found the hidden camera that Cam was watching. He saw them reach for it with a gloved hand, and then the feed went blank. Shit. What could they be planning to do that they didn't want Cam to see? It didn't seem to be a burglary. And he already had both of their faces on video anyway. For that matter, why did they have a signal detector? They couldn't have known he'd have cameras or motion detectors. But they were clearly prepared for the possibility. It was really odd. What did they know about him?

Cam turned his attention back to the video feeds, watching as each one systematically went dark until only Living Room Four, the one hidden in his soundbar, remained. It didn't offer a great view but would be next to impossible to spot and very hard to detect since the wireless speaker signal provided cover for the video signal. Still, he watched intently as Intruder Two searched the room with the device while Intruder One stood in the center of the room and talked on a cell phone. It looked like they'd made a mess of things, but they otherwise hadn't done any real damage. Intruder One ended the call and said something to Intruder Two. Cam wished his cameras were good enough for him to read lips. He wished he even knew how to read lips. Then he remembered that he didn't need to.

"Ego, can you activate the input mic on the TV without turning on the screen?" Managing his home entertainment system was one of Ego's more mundane tasks.

"That mic is already live. Attempting to access audio feed." There was a brief moment of static, then the conversation the intruders were having started to broadcast through his speakers.

"–found them all?" Intruder One asked.

Intruder Two shrugged. "I don't know. I think so. I found at least one in every room. But this guy's got a lot of electronics, so I may have missed one."

"Okay. It doesn't matter. We were already on camera anyway. But The Boss is coming up, so if he asks, tell him you found them all."

"But the guy's not here. Why is he coming up?"

Intruder One shrugged irritably. "I don't fucking know. That's just what he told me."

"Fine, he's coming up. What do we do? Just wait here?"

"I guess so, yeah.

Shit. "Ego, are you recording this?"

"Affirmative. The video and audio feeds are being recorded. There is also an audio and video data cache starting from the most recent activation of Watchdog mode. Would you like to access it?"

"No, not now."

A third person walked into his apartment. Unlike the first two, they were well-groomed and nicely dressed, with a neatly trimmed mustache, dark business suit, and white shirt. Their collar was unbuttoned, and they had a more confident stance and swagger than their apparent subordinates. When they moved, it almost looked like they were gliding. Ego tagged them as Intruder Three, but Cam figured he must be the person Intruder One had called The Boss. Strangely, he almost looked familiar.

"He's definitely not here," Intruder One announced.

"That is quite clear," the Boss replied. His tone and speech were far more practiced than the two Intruders. Something about it, along with his confidence and poise, nagged at Cam. But he couldn't figure out what it was. "It's no longer a concern, though. We've located his phone. He is not far from here."

Cam looked down at the offending phone lying on his workbench. How the fuck did they get access to his phone GPS? Just who in the hell were these people? He grabbed it–a mid-range smartphone that he used for mundane things like calling and texting–snapped off the back cover and pulled out the battery and SIM card. He stuffed the SIM in his pocket, then laid the phone back down on the desk, grabbed a mallet, and smashed it until it was in pieces.

The Boss lifted a finger to silence something one of the Intruders was about to say. Then he tilted his head to the side as if he was listening to something. "It seems we've just lost the position of his phone. The timing of that is fascinating. Could it be that he's listening to us? Hello, Mr. Maddock? Are you listening to us?" The hair on the back of Cam's neck stood up. Before, he'd been more curious and bothered than scared. All of a sudden, he felt afraid. "No matter. We will find you soon enough, and then you and I will talk, yes? There's no need for you to worry. I just want to have a conversation with you." Shit, he shouldn't have smashed his phone. He could've put it into a drone or something and led them on a wild goose chase. Oh, well, he thought with a grimace—next time. "You two, move out. We'll be seeing you soon, Mr. Maddock."

Cam cut the feed, scrambled off the workbench stool, and started rifling through one of his cabinets. Not really sure about what he'd need, he hurriedly grabbed a few items and stuffed them into his messenger bag, along with his tablet and toolkit. He shoved his handheld into his pocket, wishing he'd had time to run it through some more QA tests. There wasn't anything else he could think of to grab, and there was nothing else in the lab to worry about except the server.

"Ego, wipe the local server."

"Please confirm."

What was that fucking confirmation code? "Authorization poet series honey village."

"Affirmative, Cam."

The fans on the server rack all spun up as Ego instituted a complete memory wipe. Cam stood, listening to their whiny drone, momentarily at a loss. He could feel the edges of panic starting to pick at the perimeter of his mind. But there was no time for that, so, with a deep breath, he locked it all down. Panic wouldn't help. Those people were just crooks, and, guns or no guns, he could deal with crooks. Just the day before, he'd infiltrated a multi-million dollar biotech facility and locked off their entire collection of private IP, undetected. Dodging a scrappy squad of mysterious villains in a city as crowded as San Francisco should be child's play for someone like him. There was no more time to waste, so, after one last glance around the workshop, he grabbed his bag and hoodie.

"Ego, initiate Thunderbolt," Cam said as he slipped his hoodie on. "Thirty-second countdown."

"Affirmative. Thunderbolt countdown commencing now. Thirty, twenty-nine, twenty-eight–"

Ego kept counting down as Cam opened the door and stepped out. After shutting the door behind him, he pressed his thumb on the pad until it beeped and kept it there until he heard the click from the door lock engaging. With Thunderbolt activated, it didn't matter how someone got into his workshop. Unless Cam gave Ego the appropriate shutdown command first, even he'd be in for that nasty shock.

He slid the cover back down over the thumb pad and went for the stairs down to the front door, but the sound of someone rattling the outside gate brought him to a quick halt. It could've been one of the local street kids testing their luck while hunting for an unlocked door, but odds were that it was one of his new enemies, making their first attempt to get into his building. Even if they didn't manage to get inside, which they almost certainly would, they'd still be waiting for him out front if he used that exit. That meant it was time for Plan B.

Cam turned around and rushed back up the stairs, then down the hall past his workshop door. At the end, a set of old metal ladder rungs were bolted to the wall—roof access. Cam had actually run a few scenarios where he had to escape from the workshop unseen. While he wasn't thrilled about having to put those drills to use, at least he wasn't totally flying in the dark. He pulled himself up onto the ladder, climbed toward the hatch in the ceiling, then pushed through out onto the roof. A screwdriver from his bag worked well enough to lock the hatch behind him. It was a substantial fire code violation, but he'd jump off that bridge once he'd managed to survive the jump he was already making.

The sun was still bright in the sky but lower than before, and the temperature had dropped. The vast, black, tar roof radiated the day's anemic heat upward, but the air still had a late afternoon bite. Cam zipped up his hoodie and crossed over to the side of the roof, where a neighboring building butted up against it. It was one story taller than his building, but there was a nearby utility box that Cam could climb on top of. He heard a loud thump as someone pushed against the locked rooftop hatch. That meant they were already inside his building. He needed to get a move on.

Cam jumped up from the top of the utility box and grabbed the edge of the other building's rooftop. He pulled himself up onto it, grinning at his sudden, impromptu parkour. Then he ran across the gravel-covered rooftop to the other side and jumped down to the rooftop of the building next to it. Since his building was in the middle of the block, he didn't have many options for a fast escape. The only building exits were in the front, to the street, and back to the alley. But if he put enough distance between himself and his workshop, he could probably risk a quick descent to the back alley and remain unseen. He climbed over a short wall onto the next rooftop, but that was as far as he could go. The next climb would've been up the side of a newly built, ten-story apartment building that he'd have to be a superhero to even attempt.

He jogged over to the back edge of the building and found the fire ladder he could climb down. Risking a quick glance over the side, he saw that the alley was clear, so he hauled himself over onto the ladder and climbed down to the pavement below. Without looking back, he hurried toward the street. He'd almost reached it when he saw Intruders One and Two turn the corner in front of him. He clocked them right away and quietly groaned in frustration. Seeing them in person, Cam realized that they weren't burglars at all. They were soldiers in black uniforms. Some kind of mercenaries, probably. And at least one of them had a gun, he remembered. But it was better to assume they both did.

Turning to run back the other way wasn't a possibility. Since he was a gamer, he'd already plotted out lots of potential cover. But he also knew it wasn't a situation where he could rely on the enemy AI to stay in a predictable loop. Besides, who even knew how many mercs would be waiting for him at the other end of the block? That left just two options. Get past the ones in front of him, or surrender to them.

The black-uniformed pair both skidded to a halt as soon as they saw Cam, clearly surprised that he was so far away from his workshop already. Intruder One held their hands up, palms out, in an almost placating manner. "Hey now, easy there, kid. There's no need for any more drama here. The Boss just wants to talk to you."

Kid? Fuck that.

"That's right," Intruder Two echoed, stopping mid-step and shifting to a more defensive stance. "Nobody wants any trouble here."

Those were nice words, but Cam could see the gun tucked into a ballistic nylon underarm holster, too. He felt his heart rate rising as he watched the one with the gun start to inch their way forward. Cam's palms began to sweat, his mind racing as he desperately tried to come up with a plan. If he could just think of something. If only–

Then a strange, steely calm descended on him, flowing out from the back of his mind and down through his body like glacial runoff in his veins. Feeling frosty and sharp as ice, time around him seemed to slow to a crawl as his neurons started firing on overdrive. His pulse pounded, deep and slow in his ears. And then he saw it. The soldier's rising chest as they inhaled. The subtle movement as they shifted their weight from the left side to the right. The slightest shoulder twitch as they readied their arm for motion. They were about to go for the gun.

A plan suddenly blossomed in his mind like a knife-edged flower, slicing its way through his trepidation and fear. It burst up from somewhere inside him, gift-wrapped for special delivery, perhaps from the same mysterious wellspring that flooded him with this hardened confidence. And yet, it was undeniably his plan, all the same.

Cam was moving before he even realized it, launching himself forward like a rocket, as if he'd done it a hundred times before. Each foot fell like a piston, pounding and pumping off the ground, propelling him forward at incredible speed. The geometry of his movements, and his foe's reactions, were so obvious they were practically painted right there on the ground before him. He moved impossibly fast, closing the distance between them before Intruder Two could even react. The merc reached up for their gun, not realizing that it was already too late., that their fight was already over. At the last moment, Cam twisted, changing his direction, and put all the force of his forward momentum into his right shoulder. He barrelled into the hapless goon like a sledgehammer. As Intruder Two flew back and fell down hard, Cam pushed off with his next footstep and started twisting himself around.

"Oh, shit, man," the downed mercenary groaned, rocking side to side like a tortoise trying to right itself. "You're gonna regret that."

But Cam had already moved on, his focus shifting to Intruder One. As his momentum swung him around, he lifted his arm up, made a tight fist, then thrust it out low and jabbed it hard into Intruder One's solar plexus. They let out a whooshing gasp as Cam planted a foot and completed the spin, swinging his other arm up and striking the side of Intruder One's head with the edge of his elbow. The enforcer crumpled, collapsing onto the pavement like a rag doll.

Cam loomed over them, breath heavy, his pulse pounding a slow, relentless drumbeat of grim determination in his head. Then he turned back to Intruder Two, who'd managed to turn over and push back up onto their hands and knees. "No, you don't," Cam spat before he planted a firm kick to their side, flipping them onto their back. Then he lifted his foot and slammed it down on the soldier's face, breaking their nose with a dull crunch and knocking them unconscious. As blood began to leak from the merc's ruined nose, Cam leaned down and grabbed the gun that fell from Intruder Two's holster. It was a matte black handgun that looked like the infamous Haas Dominator, forever memorialized in the first-person shooter game Final Attack. The Dominator was supposedly one of the most reliable handguns on the market. According to the game's hero, Carl "Carbine" Bishop, you could leave it submerged in water for a year, and it would still fire like the day it came off the assembly line. Some stamped characters on the barrel meant it was probably a Chinese copy. Hopefully, the Chinese had been faithful when they cribbed the design.

A distant shout made him turn back to spot another pair of identically dressed, black-uniformed mercenaries running at him full-tilt from the other end of the alleyway. How many more of these soldiers were out there? He looked down at the one sprawled at his feet, shocked, for a brief moment, at what he'd just done. But the cool detachment smoothed his inconvenient feelings away with another wave of savage calm.

Cam was gone the next instant, stuffing the Haas into his messenger bag as he broke into a swift jog he could maintain for a while if need be. That left him with figuring out his next move. Although he'd managed to escape from his workshop, he still needed a place to escape to. His apartment was no good. They'd probably left someone behind to watch the place. He definitely would've. It was time to seek a little help.

He slowed his pace, dug through his bag, and pulled out his earbuds, popping one into each ear. "Call Tony," he said, once they'd connected to his handheld, then stole a glance back over his shoulder as he listened to the other line ringing. There was no one behind him yet, but they would come.

"Hey dude," Tony said when he picked up. "Did you change your mind about–"

"Tony," Cam interrupted, "this is an emergency. I picked up some serious heat, and I need a place to lay low for a minute."

"What? What's going on?"

"I can't get into it right now. Can you help?"

"Shit. Of course, man, just lemme think." Tony paused, although Cam could still hear his excited breathing. "Uh, what about the restaurant?"

Cam placed Tony's restaurant on his mental map and then plotted a path to it as he turned right onto Mission. He could cut down through the underground stations on Market and then maybe head up through Union Square. If he passed a cab along the way–

"Yeah, ok," he said. "That could work."

"Cool, cool. My cousin has a place in the building upstairs. He owes me, so we could go chill there for as long as you need."

"We?"

"Come on, Mad Dog, you're my boy," Tony pleaded. "If you got heat, then I got heat."

"Oh, ok. Thanks." Cam glanced around as he approached the next intersection. "I'm not far from there. I can get there soon."

"Alright, I'm leaving right now. I'll just call over and let them know you're coming first."

"Thanks, Tony."

"No sweat. Gonna go jump on my bike just as soon as I get some pants on. You just make sure you get there."

Tony swore by motorcycle travel, especially on the crowded San Francisco streets. He almost had Cam convinced. It would've been nice to have a motorcycle of his own to jump on for a quick getaway at that point. "Alright, I'll see you soon."

Tony disconnected.

Cam continued onward, keeping his pace at a brisk walk to better blend in with the late afternoon crowd that was swarming around him on the sidewalk. As soon as he started to look for a cab, he got a sudden, intense feeling that he was being followed. He glanced back over his shoulder and quickly picked the two black-clad soldiers out from the crowd. But they'd made no attempt to hide and, once they realized they'd been spotted, both broke into a run. Cam started to pour on the speed since he no longer needed to blend in. The stoplight ahead turned yellow. If he sped up to a full run, he could make it across before it turned red and possibly gain a little distance on his opponents.

Then he saw who waited up ahead and skidded to a halt.

The Boss was standing across the street, flanked by a couple more of his mercenaries. Of course. The runners behind him weren't hiding because they wanted to be seen. They weren't chasing him. They were herding him right into the waiting arms of the Boss and his uniformed bandits. Cam needed to change direction. His instincts told him to go left, so he took off that way, crossing over Mission on his way to Market. He kept up a frantic pace, heedless of the looks he was getting from the curious passersby who weren't too jaded to look up from their phone screens. At least the late afternoon sun was low enough that he was soon engulfed in the shadows cast by the looming Financial District towers, which offered him a little additional cover.

When he broke right at Market Street, the sudden blare of car horns behind him made him risk a quick look over his shoulder. The Boss was climbing into the back of a shiny, black Bernier Faucon sedan that pulled up next to him, blocking all the traffic behind it. Shit. Still, he knew there was an entrance to an underground station just ahead, at the end of the block. If he could make it there before they caught up to him, that would negate any advantage the vehicle gave them.

His mind shifted into overdrive as he sought out a path among the bustling crowd, mapping the ripples of motion across the teeming sidewalk like he'd done the night before at the dance club. Reacting with lightning speed, he danced around a pair of shoppers as they wrestled with their unruly handfuls of shopping bags and quickly skipped around someone who'd bent down to pick up their dog's waste. Then he squeezed himself through a sudden break in a pack of tourists, their heads and cameras mindlessly pointed every which way, before ducking into the stairwell down into the underground station.

Cam slowed his pace as he descended, breath heavy, mindful of conserving his remaining energy. Possibilities blossomed in his mind as a whole new set of options opened up in front of him. The Boss would have to abandon his vehicle if he wanted to continue the chase in person, and Cam knew he had a healthy lead on the runners chasing him on foot. Plus, he could hop on a light-rail train out of the Financial District or grab a BART train to another city in the Bay Area altogether from inside the station. He didn't plan on doing either. The idea of being trapped on an underground train sounded too much like a potential trap. But the mere possibilities meant that his pursuers would have to consider them, also.

Cam walked through the tunnel toward the main station concourse, keeping his demeanor calm, his hood down, and his expression placid. There were security cameras everywhere, as well as transit police. He kept his senses sharp, avoiding any physical contact with people in the crowd. The frenetic energy from the streams of commuters pouring through the station helped shield him even further. Up ahead, he saw the exit that would point him toward Union Square. He could easily get a cab for the quick ride to Chinatown from there.

The otherworldly calm persisted, lending him a cold detachment that massaged away his burgeoning panic and gave his observations an incredible sense of detail, surrounding everything with a hard-edged clarity. It was an odd feeling, but every time he thought to question his state of mind, those thoughts were quietly tucked away for later when he wasn't on the run.

A pair of uniformed police officers, one Black, one white, stood guard up ahead, casually scanning the crowd through matching wrap-around sunglasses. He doubted that they were on the lookout for him but didn't want to risk showing his face if they were. He casually altered his course toward the side of the concourse, then knelt down and pretended to fix his shoelaces. A glance backward revealed a pack of office-casual tech workers heading his way. Most of them looked to be dark-skinned South Asians he could probably blend in with well enough. As they started to pass him, Cam stood and slotted himself in just behind the group, careful not to cause them any alarm. He pulled his handheld out as they all strolled past the police officers and kept his gaze pointed down, using his peripheral vision to stay in formation. But the cops never clocked him–if they'd even been looking for him in the first place–and he broke off from the group toward the station exit. He was almost home free.

Then an unknown voice called out from behind. "Hey, you!"

Cam ignored it. If it was meant for him, it couldn't be a good thing.

"Hey, you," came the shout again, "hold on a second!"

Cam kept ignoring it as he walked up the stairs toward the open-air plaza outside the station. Then his proximity-sense went wild, and he felt a hand on his shoulder. Without thinking, he reached up and grabbed the stranger's hand while twisting down and around, pulling their arm with him. The stranger cried out in pain as Cam quickly put their arm in a lock and forced them down onto their knees. They were white, possibly in their late thirties or early forties, with thinning brown hair, wearing a preppy style sweater and khakis. Probably not one of the Boss's bandits, then. "What the fuck do you want?" Cam growled.

"Nothing, I swear!" they cried out. "He just told me to try and slow you down if I saw you."

Damn, they were with the Boss, after all. Cam looked back toward the station entrance and saw one of the cops looking his way. Shit. He shoved the preppy stranger hard onto the ground, then turned and ran, bounding up the nearby stairs and emerging onto the street level near the Powell Street cable car turnaround. A noisy crowd had gathered nearby to wait for the cable car, cheering as its bell clanged wildly on approach. Cam ducked around them and took off up Powell, eyes peeled for any shadowy figures dressed all in black hiding among the shiny tourist faces all around him. He'd already lost whatever advantage he'd gained from cutting through the underground station. And the cops were a possible new complication that he didn't need at all.

He caught a sudden glimpse of unexpected movement in his peripheral vision, triggering his proximity sense again. There was no time to think, only to react. He broke right, between two parked cars, and dashed across the street before turning back up Powell. An offended shout behind him caused him to look back, and he spotted one of the familiar black uniforms shoving some unsuspecting bystanders out of his way.

They'd caught up with him already. He needed a new plan. Running all the way to Chinatown was not a great option. They could just follow him, and he'd be exposed the whole time. He could double back and jump on the light rail, but that could leave him just as trapped. If he wanted to seriously shake those bastards, he needed something better than a bit of misdirection. There was always the Haas. He'd never used a gun outside of video games, but he had a strong feeling that was about to change soon.

Cam dug a hand into his bag and pulled the Dominator out, casually shoving it into the back waistband of his pants like he'd seen countless TV crooks, spies, and hard-boiled policemen do. Newly armed, he sprinted across Geary, with the Union Square plaza to his right, toward the taxi stand that was just ahead. His danger instinct flared up again, so Cam sidestepped to the left just as an arm came around to grab at him. He swept his right foot out and tripped up the failed assailant, knocking them face down onto the sidewalk.

He glanced to his left and spotted another of the Boss's soldiers rushing across Powell toward him. The cab would have to wait. He took off to his right, up into the crowded plaza, winding around the turbulent maze of loosely packed tourists and office workers. Ahead of him, he glimpsed a second black uniform moving toward him from a dozen meters away. He darted to the right but then pumped his brakes when he saw a third emerge from the crowd in that direction, too. They'd boxed him in.

A charmingly smooth voice called out from behind him. "That's quite enough, Mr. Maddock!" Cam turned toward the sound and confirmed what he already suspected. It was the Boss. "You've led us on such an exciting little chase today, haven't you? But that's over now, so why don't we–"

Everything around him suddenly stopped. The raucous din of the crowded plaza dulled to a low murmur as the light around him dimmed. The whole world lost focus except for the bright, sharp figures of the Boss and his three mercs as they slowly but surely inched their way toward him. Somewhere inside his head, Cam heard the furious whisper of mental calculations measuring distances, angles, and velocities, processing faster than normal conscious thought. He shifted his weight slightly to balance his stance, pulling the Haas from his waistband and flipping the safety off in one swift, fluid motion. Cam pointed the gun at the closest uniform, angled slightly downward. The trajectory of the shot almost lit the air like neon. Then, in an unbroken string of movement, he gently squeezed the trigger, shifted his aim to the left, still low, and fired again. Shifted. Fired again. He shifted once more, this time aiming higher, and pointed the gun straight at the Boss's chest.

The world suddenly returned to normal as the echoes of three shots reverberated around the busy plaza like drunken bar-goers trying to find the door at closing time. Each of the three mercenaries collapsed from the brand new bullet wounds in their right legs, each shot perfectly placed just above their knees. It all went down so fast that the oblivious people jostling for position around him hadn't quite figured out what happened yet. But the Boss knew. His empty hands went up, offering surrender, the gentle amusement of his grin muddled with mild frustration.

"Just give me a reason, asshole," Cam growled.

"So, this is how it's to be, Mr. Maddock?"

"I don't even know what the fuck this is!"

"Oh, but I think you will soon enough."

Then someone to Cam's right let out a terrified shriek, and the carefully orchestrated chaos around him quickly dissolved into a mass panic, with everyone screaming, shouting, and running away. A smile flickered across the Boss's face, and, shaking his head ever so slightly, he stepped back and disappeared into the crowd.

Scowling, Cam quickly stuffed the Dominator back into his bag and ran, using the spiraling confusion around him to hide his escape. When he saw a taxi idling just ahead on Powell, he jumped into the back, startling the driver.

"Holy shit, you scared me," the driver said. "What's happening out there? I thought I heard gunshots."

"Yeah, I think I did, too," Cam agreed, breath heavy from exertion and an impending adrenaline crash. He pulled a handful of cash from his wallet and flashed it toward the driver. "Maybe we should get out of here?"

"You got it." The driver flipped the meter flag over. "Where to?"

"Chinatown."

TONY

Tony sat down on the only empty furniture in his cousin's room, an unmade double bed. Between rushing to get out the door, and the rush of riding his motorcycle up to Chinatown at breakneck speeds, he was a little out of breath. He brushed the hair back from his face and set his helmet down next to him. His cousin, Felix, lived in what was euphemistically termed an efficiency unit. At some point, people must've considered having everything you own within arm's reach to be efficient. Next to the bed was a small desk and stool, with a medium-sized flatscreen mounted on the wall above them. There was a tiny kitchenette with a microwave and mini-fridge in the corner, and a small en suite bathroom, a luxury for a unit like that. It was crowded and, due as much to his cousin's poor housekeeping as its small size, was pretty cluttered. The walls were painted a sickly yellow that cast a jaundiced pall on everything in the room. Tony looked over at Felix, who was sprawled lazily on the only other actual seating in the room, an old, ratty, paisley fabric upholstered easy chair. "Damn, Felix, is it the maid's day off again?"

His cousin rolled his eyes. "Whatever, dude. I'm sorry I let my membership in the secret hideout club lapse. "

Tony laughed. "Yeah, I really need to start hanging out

with a better class of villain."

Felix snorted. "Lemme know how that goes. Say, when's your friend gonna get here, anyway?"

That was the million-dollar question. Cam hadn't been very forthcoming with details. But Felix hadn't objected when Tony asked if they could lay low at his place for a while. He was used to hanging under the radar since he was basically a low-level crook himself, putting his halfway decent coding skills to work as a tech for the more criminal elements in the family.

Tony shrugged. "Soon, hopefully." Cam's call had caught him off guard. While the two of them liked to joke about how Tony was the one who had it together, Tony knew, deep down, that it was probably Cam who really had the goods. He was the smart one. He was good at strategy and planning. And he was the one who could provide for himself, so he didn't have to rely on the generosity of his parents like Tony did. If Cam called on Tony for help, he really must've been in some deep shit. "He didn't exactly want to get into details over the phone."

Felix nodded. "Yeah, I guess that makes sense."

When Tony got to the restaurant, he'd left strict instructions with his sister, Summer, to take Cam upstairs the minute he arrived. She wasn't thrilled about it, mainly because Tony was shirking on his offer to help out during the dinner rush. But she liked Cam as much as he did, so she agreed to the plan anyway. And Tony didn't mind taking a little grief from her over it. He'd already been reconsidering whether or not he was gonna show up to help anyway.

Once he'd squared things away with his sister, Tony went right upstairs to his cousin's place. While having such a large family could sometimes cause a lot of drama, he appreciated having so many folks he could turn to when he really needed to.

Felix shifted in his chair. "I heard you were at Emphasis last night."

Of course, he had. The DJ was his cousin, too. Tony smiled as he remembered dancing with–whatever her name was. Had he forgotten her name already? He really needed to stop smoking so much if it was gonna fuck with his memory like that. Hopefully, he wrote it down somewhere. "Yeah, it was really poppin'. Got a girl's number, even."

"Damn. You're such a fuckboy, Tony," Felix announced, sounding impressed. "I wish I had those kinda chops."

Tony scoffed. He knew his cousin was kidding around, but he considered his chops to be well earned. He'd been shamed mercilessly as a kid for being overweight and acne-prone and had taken to frequent gym workouts and elaborate skincare routines to maintain his body and face. On the other hand, Felix hardly ever showered, despite having the luxury of his own bathroom, and had never worked out a day in his life. But he still had perfect skin and zero percent body fat somehow. Why did he have to get the good genes? "Hey, you got the Zhang chops, too, right? You just gotta be a little more confident in yourself, dude."

Felix nodded as his cheeks darkened in embarrassment. "Yeah, you're probably right," he admitted, then shrugged. "But who's got the time for dating these days, anyway? In fact, you're lucky you called today since I usually have so much going on."

While he liked to talk up how much of a big-time player he was, Tony knew better. "Right. We both know that your only plan today was to jerk it to some Miranda Chambers porn and then play Chaos Seed."

Felix chuckled. "Well, half of that plan is done already." He yawned extravagantly, then got up off the chair and went over to the little kitchenette. "You want something to drink?" he asked as he opened the door on his mini-fridge.

"Nah, I'm good, bro. Thanks, though."

Felix nodded and bent down to dig through whatever was in there. They heard a knock on the door, then it opened, and Cam walked in. He looked flushed, like he'd just finished a workout. "Hey Cam, come on in." He waved toward his cousin. "This is Felix."

"Hey," Felix answered without looking up before finally grabbing a can of beer from the refrigerator. He opened it with a loud pop.

Cam nodded at him, then slipped off his bag and sat down hard on the bed next to Tony. "How's it going here?"

"Here?" Tony waved him off. "Who gives a shit about that? What about you? You're not looking so great. Are you gonna tell me what's going on?" Cam looked at him questioningly, then shot a side glance at Felix. Tony nodded, understanding Cam's subtle request for some privacy. He must've really had something juicy to share. "Hey Felix, could you run downstairs and grab us some pot stickers?"

"Hey, why do I–" Felix began, but Tony silenced him with a look. He sighed. "Yeah, ok. Sure, I'll head down." He set the beer down on the counter and walked out of the room.

Tony looked at Cam expectantly. "Good?"

Cam nodded, then took a deep breath. "Ok, here's the deal. Some kinda mercenary gang is after me, and I don't know why. First, they broke into my apartment. Then they tracked me to my workshop somehow."

Tony sat there, wide-eyed, as Cam gave him the rundown. No wonder he looked a little winded. He was describing the plot from a Hollywood spy-thriller. A fight? A foot chase through the city? Soldiers in black uniforms? A gun battle in Union Square? That's not even close to what he expected to hear. "No fucking way, dude! Are you sure you're alright?"

Cam shrugged. "I'm alive if that's what you mean. Otherwise, I guess that depends on your definition of alright."

Tony nodded in agreement, but he was having a rough time taking that all in. Was he really looking at the same mild-mannered Cam that had to be talked into going out? Just yesterday, they'd been smoking up after a successful video game raid. Suddenly he was talking like a video game character come to life. "I mean, shit. Like, you really shot all those guys?"

Cam nodded, then frowned. "I don't know how, but yeah. I've never even held a gun before today, but somehow I knew exactly what to do. Right then and there, at least. But it was like that with everything. One minute I'm running for my life, and the next thing I know, I'm all Jack Sterling, super spy."

That was precisely what he'd sounded like. He was only missing the tuxedo and suave, British accent. "Jesus, Cam. That's–"

"Fucked up," Cam interrupted. "I know."

Tony shook his head. Why was Cam so down on himself? Didn't he hear his own story? "Hell no, man. That's fucking badass, is what it is! And here I thought I was the fearless one." Suddenly full of nervous energy, he stood up and went to the mini-fridge. "But who the hell even were these guys?"

"That's just it, Tony. I don't fucking know." Cam took a deep breath. "I've been racking my brain trying to figure it out. The main guy was seriously some kind of cat stroking, spy movie villain. Plus, he had a whole army of gun-toting mercenaries. I got them on video, though. Three of them, at least."

Tony bent down in front of the fridge and poked around through the contents. There were a couple half-full, plastic soda bottles and way too many packets of soy sauce, even if Felix did live above a restaurant. "You think they may be cops? Or spooks?"

Cam shook his head. "Cops? No, not the way they acted. They had uniforms, but I never saw a badge once, and nobody actually shot at me." He shook his head again. "I don't think they were spooks, either. But I don't know. These guys were definitely bad news. I can tell you that much."

"Shit." Tony grabbed a beer and offered it to Cam, who shook his head no. He cracked it open himself and sat back down on the bed. He took a long swallow while he let the situation sink in. "I guess we can't exactly go to the cops with this, either."

Cam frowned. "No way. I mean, I never would've, but I just shot three guys in the middle of Union Square. I'm sure they're very interested in talking to me because of that."

Tony sighed. "Yeah, the boys in blue don't really go for that sort of shit, do they? You're probably lucky there weren't any around there at the time. You know, shooting first and asking questions later."

Cam chuckled ruefully. "Yeah, I felt like a quick getaway was my best move."

Tony nodded. He was glad he'd suggested his cousin's place

as a hideout. Hopefully, it was off the radar enough to get overlooked by whatever uniformed baddies were on the hunt for his pal. "For sure. And you'll be safe here for a little while, at least, until we can figure something else out."

Cam didn't seem all that confident in Tony's assessment, but he nodded anyway.

Suddenly, Felix burst into the room. "Dudes!" he barked as he rushed over to the TV. "You gotta see this!" He grabbed the remote and switched the TV on, flipping through the channels until he found the local news. A well-groomed TV anchor was sitting at his desk in the studio. Behind him was a video image of a reporter standing in Union Square.

"–and now for more information," the smooth-talking anchor said, "we're going live to the scene with field reporter Isabel Navarro. Isabel?"

"Thanks, Tom," the reporter replied as they switched to the new location. "As you can see behind me, the SFPD has closed off Union Square plaza to the public. According to an SFPD spokesperson, multiple shots were fired earlier this evening during a standoff between several unknown persons. Details about the incident are still sketchy, as are witness reports. Witnesses claim that as many as three individuals were shot by an unknown assailant. However, police have been unable to locate any shooting victims so far and have only confirmed that there are no known fatalities. I'll remain on the scene to report any new details as they unfold. In the meantime, back to you in the studio, Tom."

"Thanks, Isabel," the anchor said as they switched back to the studio. "If you're just joining us, gunfire rocked the Union Square plaza in downtown San Francisco earlier this evening. Police have not released any details, but we've obtained a cell phone video of the incident from a bystander. I must warn you that what you're about to see is very graphic and may disturb sensitive viewers." The screen switched to a shaky, portrait-style video. The camera panned right, across the crowd, until Cam came into view. Tony, Felix, and Cam all watched in rapt amazement as Cam, in the video, whipped a gun out of his waistband and fired three shots in rapid succession before the person holding the phone turned and ran. Then the screen switched to a freeze-frame from the video. It was an image of Cam, standing motionless, gun pointed at something offscreen, his face looking curiously calm, almost serene. The anchor reappeared on screen, next to another photo of Cam. "Police have not yet released the shooter's identity, but we've tentatively identified the suspect as twenty-six-year-old Cameron Maddock, seen here in this photo from his Spillr profile. Anyone with any information on the shooting is advised to contact the SFPD at the number you see on your screen."

Tony gave his cousin a look, and Felix hit the mute button. Then Tony looked over at his best friend, trying to reconcile what he'd just seen with the person sitting right there next to him.

Cam looked pained. "Yeah, I know."

"Yeah, so much for going to the cops," Tony confirmed. "But dude, I gotta say. You seriously kicked some ass there! I mean, it's not like I didn't believe your story, but seeing it onscreen like that–damn."

Felix eyed Cam warily. "Dude, who even are you?"

Tony shot him an evil look. "Shut the fuck up, man. Cam is my friend."

Felix waved a hand over at the screen. "Ok, sure, but–didn't you just see all that? It was like watching Jastin Kenzi in Bullet Cry or some shit. Except in real life."

Tony wanted to protest further, but he didn't necessarily disagree. He knew Cam better than probably anyone, but even he had his doubts. Before he'd heard Cam's story about his escape from the men in black, he'd never in a million years have expected his friend to be capable of pulling stunts like that. Yet, having seen it recorded for posterity, he couldn't deny that his friend could pull some freaky shit—pop, pop, pop, faster than he could even process it. He looked over at Cam warily. There was clearly a lot more to him than met the eye.

Cam seemed to be reading the reaction in the room. "Look," he said, warily, "it's ok if you want me to go—"

"Hey, no way, man," Felix assured him, "you can hang here as long as you need to. Nobody here is gonna turn you in to the fucking pigs or nothing."

"Yeah, forget that," Tony chimed in, smiling. "I mean, knowing how well you can handle yourself, I'd rather stay on your good side."

Cam laughed. "Thanks, guys. I just wish I knew who those guys were. Or at least who the Boss is. I mean, why didn't they splash his Spillr pic all over the news?"

Tony remembered what Cam said about the break-in. "Hey, didn't you say you got them on video?"

Cam nodded. He reached into his pocket to pull out his handheld. "Yeah, I do. Right here." He tapped the screen to wake it, then tapped through a few menus, pulling up the video footage. Then he found and connected to the screencast app on Felix's TV, put the video on the big screen, and hit play.

The three of them all watched as the two men in black uniforms spoke to each other, then a third guy, who Tony figured must've been the Boss, entered his living room. It was creepy hearing him talk to Cam once he'd figured out that Cam was onto them somehow. Finally, The Boss looked straight at the hidden camera and smiled. Then he walked over and reached down toward it. Just as his hand covered the field of view, it went black. Cam tapped the screen and backed the video up to the point just before it blacked out. The casual smile on the Boss's face was horror movie-level creepy.

Tony exhaled dramatically. "I don't know about you two, but none of those guys looked like cops to me."

Felix chuckled. "Yeah, it's gotta be some kinda black bag shit or something. You sure you're not a Chinese spy?"

"That's not funny, dude," Tony warned his cousin, even though he'd been wondering the same thing himself. "He's not even Chinese."

Felix stopped smiling. "Sorry."

Cam waved him off. "It's fine. Honestly, I wish I was a spy. Then I might have a chance at figuring this shit out. As it is, it's only a matter of time before they start looking for you, now, Tony."

Tony hadn't thought of that. "Me? Why are they looking for me?"

"Besides the fact that my name and picture are all over the news? Those guys had access to my phone, at least enough to track it. If the Boss can do that, he can get my call records. And, if he does, it won't be too difficult to figure out who I'd go to if I were in trouble."

"Oh, shit," Felix muttered. "He's right."

"So, I can't stay here," Cam confirmed, "and neither can you."

"Shit," Tony swore quietly. That was an unexpected wrinkle. He sighed. "Ok, maybe so. But where do we go?"

Felix looked at them thoughtfully. "You know, you may not be a Chinese spy, but you've kinda got the next best thing here."

"I do?" Cam wondered.

Tony immediately knew what his cousin was talking about, and it wasn't something he was willing to consider. He shook his head. "No way, man."

"Just think about it for a minute," Felix admonished his cousin. "If they can't find him, and they start looking for you, who else can really help you but Uncle Huang?"

Tony shook his head again. His family had deep roots in the city, especially in Chinatown. And some of them dabbled in less than savory affairs. "I don't think I want Uncle Huang's help, Felix. I can't see how that would actually make anything better."

"Who's Uncle Huang?" Cam asked.

"You didn't hear this from me," Felix replied, "but Uncle Huang is big in the local Tong, which is sort of like a cross between a gang and a club. If anyone can hide you in this city, it's him."

Tony frowned. He didn't want to admit that his cousin was probably right. It wasn't a position he'd ever been in before, but if someone were to tell him he needed to hide from a bunch of guys with guns, then Uncle Huang would've been his first thought, too. "Shit. Ok, so maybe that's not a terrible idea. It's just, I don't know what he'll ask for in return for his help."

"There's only one way to find out," Felix assured him. "But you're family, and you're in trouble. It's not like you're going to him for a loan to pay off your drug dealer or some shit."

That seemed reasonable enough. Tony knew that Felix was speaking from experience there. "Ok," he agreed, sounding more resigned than assured. "I'll call him. Gimme your phone, Felix."

"My phone?"

"Yeah, genius. If someone's gonna be looking for me, do you think I should let them see Uncle Huang's number on my call log?"

Felix rolled his eyes, then handed him a phone. Tony scrolled through it for a moment, finding Huang's number, then tapped the screen and held it to his ear. It only rang once before being picked up. "Hello," a brusque voice answered in Cantonese.

Tony's brain immediately switched gears. "This is Zhang Weitian," he replied in his best Cantonese. "I need to speak to my Uncle." Felix, realizing that Cam probably couldn't understand him, leaned in and whispered translations.

"Wait one moment, please," came the reply. Tony knew it wouldn't take long. He'd called his Uncle's personal number, and whoever answered would likely be near him. After a moment, his Uncle Huang spoke. "Hello, nephew. It's a surprise to hear from you."

Tony grimaced. He was shitty at keeping in contact with important family members, and it was never fun to be reminded of that. "I'm sorry to disturb you, Uncle. I hope this is a good time."

"Nonsense, you are not disturbing anything. I always have time for my favorite nephew. How is your family? Your sister? Is everything alright?"

Tony gave him a quick rundown on the family, assuring him that everything was fine. "But they're not why I called you. Do you remember my friend Cam? He's here with me now. We're at Felix's apartment."

"I assumed as much," his Uncle interrupted, "since you're calling me from his number."

Tony explained the situation as best he could, glossing over some of the more unusual details. "And now we think that it's best we get somewhere they won't be able to easily find us."

There was a brief silence on the other line before his Uncle spoke again. "I see. Give me a moment, nephew." Tony couldn't make out the muffled speaking he heard. But he could guess what his Uncle was asking about. After a few moments, his Uncle spoke again. "You are referring to the incident in Union Square?"

"Yes, Uncle."

"That was your friend Cam who shot those people?"

"Yes, Uncle."

"I see. I will help you, of course. But I would like to speak to Cam first. Please put me on speakerphone."

Tony pulled the phone away from his ear. "He wants me to put the call on speaker." He set the phone down on the bed between them and tapped the speaker button. "Ok, Uncle Huang," he said in English, "you're on speaker."

"Thank you, nephew. Cam, we've met before, yes? You were at my sister's house for our mother's birthday celebration last year?"

Tony recalled the party he was talking about. It was a huge affair, with at least a couple hundred people in attendance. If it was anyone else, he would've been surprised to hear them remember such a detail. But not his Uncle. He remembered everything.

"That's right, sir," Cam answered. "I think I did meet you there."

"I thought as much. My sister has told me before that she thinks of you as a son, Cam, which makes you family, as much as my favorite nephew Tony." Felix frowned when he heard that but stayed quiet. "I don't mean to be rude, Cam, but I have to ask. Other than what happened today, is there any reason that you may be wanted by the police?"

"No, sir, absolutely not," Cam assured him.

"Of course. And you have no idea who those men are?"

"No, sir. I haven't seen any of them before today."

"I understand," Tony's uncle confirmed, "and I'm frankly very disturbed to discover what seems to be an outside criminal gang operating in my city without seeking my permission first. I'll have to check with the Mexicans and Russians to be certain, but I would be shocked to find that they'd violated our understanding. In the meantime, Tony, I will send you to a safe house in Daly City. I won't have anyone harassing my family while this all gets sorted out. You'll both be safe enough there for the time being. Write down this address." Cam grabbed his handheld and opened a text file, where he typed the address that Tony's Uncle recited over the phone. "I'll send one of my people to the restaurant to pick you both up and take you there, but I want you to have the address just in case."

Tony smiled. "Thank you, Uncle."

"It's nothing. You're family, and for family, I would do no less. Contact me when you get there, and we'll figure out what to do next. In the meantime, I intend to find out all I can about what's happening in my city. This is all very unsettling." He fell silent for a moment. "Both of you, be very careful, please. I don't want my sister to become aggrieved over this."

"Yes, sir," Tony agreed. "Goodbye," he added, but his Uncle had already disconnected. "Okay, then. I guess now we wait. Hey, whatever happened to those pot stickers?"

Felix rolled his eyes. "Sorry, I got a little distracted."

Just then, there was a knock on the door. It opened before anyone could get up, and Tony's sister Summer came in. "Hey, guys. Uh, Tony? There was some guy downstairs just now asking about you. We told him you weren't here, but I'm not sure he bought it."

"Who was it?"

Summer's eyes went wide, and she pointed at the face on the screen. "Him."

CAM

The Boss already found him again, just like he'd done at Union Square. He made it look easy, and Cam wondered if they had some other way to track him. He knew it couldn't have been his phone since he'd trashed it. But there were always other options. They could've been tracking his handheld somehow, as unlikely as that seemed. Or, they could've been tracking his person, which was even more unlikely. But he'd been out in public enough times that someone could've spiked him with some kind of tracking device. There wasn't time to worry about that, though. He had to deal with the situation at hand first.

"Shit. How would the Boss know to look for me here?" Tony wondered aloud.

"Is he still downstairs?" Cam asked Summer.

"No," she said, "he left. Hold on." She pulled a phone from her pocket and rapidly tapped in a number. "It's me," she said after a few moments. "Have someone take a look out the window and see if there's anything suspicious out front." She listened to their reply. "No, I'll wait. Do it now." Summer's manager voice was much sterner than her typically casual tone and left no room for argument. After a few moments, she spoke again. "That's what I thought. Thanks." She hung up the call. "Bao said there's a couple of suspicious white guys parked in an unmarked car across the street, but no sign of our visitor."

"So, they're still watching the place," Tony said. "Shit."

That was no good. After Union Square, they were probably out for blood, too. Things were getting complicated. If it were all still just about him, he'd have a lot of options. But he'd involved Tony and, by proximity, Tony's cousin and sister as well. That meant he had to consider their safety, too. The fact that people had been left behind to watch the place might mean that they didn't know if Cam was there or not and that the Boss had gone to investigate other potential hideouts. Which might also mean that, by staying hidden, Cam was putting other people in danger, too. Hell, for all he knew, they'd hacked his Farstorm account and were tracking down the Goobers, who were all the way out in—The Goobers! Of course. Cam knew what they had to do. "Tony, we have to get out of here. Now. And we have to let them see us doing it."

"What?" Felix exclaimed. "Why the fuck would you do that? Just wait for Uncle Huang's people to handle it."

But Cam shot Tony a knowing look, and after a moment, saw the realization hit him. Tony nodded. "Shit. You're right. The Unholy Vault."

Cam nodded. "The Unholy Vault." He stood up and grabbed his bag.

Tony started looking for his jacket, but Felix wasn't on board yet. "What the fuck is an unholy vault? Will someone tell me what's happening?"

"Felix," Cam said calmly, "I have no idea how these people already found this place, but they have. And as long as I'm here, you're all at risk. Right now, they're probably hitting up all of my potential hiding places, letting me know that they're looking for me, and giving me a chance to show myself. I don't know how long that window will last, and I don't want them deciding to come in here to get me."

Summer and Felix both looked unsure, but Tony nodded again. "If we let them see us leaving," he added, "we can draw them away, and Uncle Huang's guy can look after you two until we get to the safe house. It's just like this campaign we did in Farstorm called The Unholy Vault." He grabbed his helmet then looked at Cam. "Let's go." Cam nodded, then followed Tony as he walked out. "There's an extra helmet down in the back room. My bike is around the corner."

Felix bounded out of the room behind them. "But what do I tell Uncle Huang's guy?"

Cam looked back as he followed Tony down the stairs. "Just tell them what happened and that we'll meet them at the safe house." He patted his pocket. "I've got the address."

Tony led Cam down into the kitchen, then turned and went through a door in the back into a combination back-office and storeroom, with an old, paper-strewn office desk and chair on one side, and a shelving rack filled with cleaning supplies on the other. He found the motorcycle helmet sitting on the floor by the desk. After picking it up, he handed it to Cam. "Are you ready for this?"

Cam shrugged. "Does it matter? We gotta do it anyway."

Tony flashed a wide grin. "You know it. But this is gonna be dangerous. You remember how to ride, right? How to lean into turns with me and stuff?"

Cam smiled and slapped his friend on the arm. "I sure do, man. Let's do this."

Tony nodded, then led Cam back behind the restaurant to a door opening onto the street, around the corner from the front entrance.

On the way, Cam popped his earbuds back in, then dug around in this bag and found his spare set. When they got to the door at the end of the hall, he handed them to Tony. "Put these in. I can patch us together via my handheld so we can talk to each other." Tony shrugged, pulled them out of the case, and slid them into his ears. Cam tapped on the screen of his handheld, then tapped through a couple of menus before he heard the connecting tone. "You reading me, Tiger?"

Tony nodded. "Loud and clear, Mad Dog." He slipped his helmet on. "Get your helmet on, and zip up your hoodie, cuz it's gonna be chilly. And make sure your bag is hanging in front of you so it'll sit between us. Otherwise, you might lose it."

Cam nodded, slipping his bag around to the front. He took another look at his handheld, pulling up the address for the safe house. "Ego, come online," he said.

"Online and ready, Cam," Ego announced.

"Verify, whiskey jar golden braid."

"Verify," Ego replied, "silent night solemn vow."

"System status?"

"Systems are nominal."

"Whoa," Tony exclaimed, "is that your AI program?"

"Voiceprint, Tony Zhang, confirmed," Ego said. "That's correct, Tony. I am Ego. How can I be of assistance?"

"I need directions to the address on my handheld from my current location," Cam instructed. "Fastest possible route. Reroute for traffic and obstacles on the fly."

"Affirmative, Cam. From your current location, head west-northwest for 20 meters."

"Contextual street directions for driving only, please. Oh, and monitor local police comms for any related incidents, or any incidents along the route."

"Confirmed, Cam."

Cam slipped his helmet on and shoved his handheld into a pocket before giving Tony the thumbs up. Tony pushed the door open and leaned out to see if anyone was waiting, but the coast was clear. He stepped out and walked the short distance to his waiting bike. Cam followed while Tony fished his keys out of his pocket, then waited while Tony straddled the machine. His pride and joy, a Matsui Hornet, was a sleek, red and silver, midsize, Japanese motorcycle with a 750cc engine. It probably wasn't going to win any street races with two people aboard, but it was hopefully fast enough for what they needed. Cam slipped on behind Tony, putting his feet on the rear pegs, and wrapped his arms around his friend's midsection.

"Okay, Mad Dog. You ready for this?"

"Let's do it, Tiger."

Tony flipped the key, hit the starter switch, and the engine roared to life. He revved it a few times, then slipped it into gear. He gave it a little gas as he slowly let out the clutch, just enough to turn them around and head back up to Grant. They took the corner after barely slowing to a stop, then pulled forward toward California. Halfway up the block, parked on the right, Cam spotted a dark gray, late model, Delis Crown sedan that may as well have had the word stakeout flashing above it in bright pink neon. "I see the car."

"Ok, let's stop next to it. I want 'em to see me."

"You got it."

Tony hit the brakes and stopped once Cam was next to the driver. They weren't paying him any attention, so Cam knocked on the window. The Crown driver, startled, turned to see who was there. Cam reached up and lifted his helmet's dark visor, making eye contact with the mercenary behind the wheel. Then he winked. The driver scowled, then started to open the door, but Cam quickly kicked it shut.

"Gun it, Tony!"

Tony didn't hesitate, twisting the accelerator, and they took off, stopping a short way ahead at the next intersection.

Cam looked back to see the driver trying to pull the Crown back into Chinatown traffic. "Ok, they're following."

"Then let's give 'em a good ass chase!" Tony twisted the accelerator again, and they surged forward. He slowed them as they reached California, looking ahead to gauge the turn, then, seeing his opening, quickly gunned it. They leaned right as they took the corner onto California, with a few startled pedestrians scampering out of their way. Then Tony opened it up, and they zoomed forward into the thick of rush hour traffic. As Tony expertly slalomed the Hornet around the vehicles on the road, Cam looked back to see their pursuers behind them.

"What do you think?" Tony wondered. "California to Gough to Geary?"

"Ok, yeah. Ego, reroute us to those directions."

"Confirmed."

"That thing is crazy, Cam," Tony said. "Does it tell jokes?"

"Of course I tell jokes, Tony. How else can I get you to lower your guard and ease my eventual takeover of humanity."

Tony laughed. "Holy shit, it tells jokes!"

"Now isn't the time, Ego," Cam declared. "Disable humor emulation."

"Affirmative."

"Spoilsport," Tony offered, followed by a sudden curse. "Shit, red light. Hang on!"

Tony downshifted and twisted the accelerator. They veered left around a slowing car, then continued all the way into the oncoming traffic lane before zipping through the intersection, narrowly missing the rear end of a truck as it crossed over California. A horn blared behind them as another driver swerved to avoid hitting them. When they got to Larkin, Tony took them left into the empty lane reserved for the cable car stop and twisted the accelerator again. The slowing cars on their right almost seemed to blur. The light ahead was green. There were more horns behind them, so Cam carefully turned to look over his shoulder to verify that their pursuers were still on their trail.

"Still there?" Tony asked.

"Yep," Cam replied. "Don't lose 'em too soon. Let's get farther away from the restaurant first."

"Yeah, yeah, ok."

"Just don't let 'em actually catch us, though."

"I know, I know." Tony inhaled sharply as he carefully maintained his speed. "Hold on, this one is gonna be tight." Traffic slowed to a stop behind the turning vehicles blocking the intersection ahead, one waiting to turn left, the other slowing to turn right. He swerved them left into the empty cable car lane, then veered into the space between the turning cars, shooting across Van Ness as the stoplight turned yellow. "Hell yeah!" Tony shouted, then released the accelerator, bleeding off some of their speed on the uphill stretch of road. A chorus of car horns trumpeted behind them as their pursuers veered into the oncoming lane just to make it through the intersection.

Tony chuckled. "We don't wanna make it too easy, right?" He maintained their speed for their final block before lightly squeezing the brakes and slowing them for their turn onto Gough. The wide, three-lane, one-way street was also packed with rush hour traffic, forcing Tony to slow them further.

Cam looked back to see the pursuing Crown take the corner behind them way too fast, sideswiping a parked car in the outside lane. He chuckled lightly. "Ooh, I bet that had to hurt."

"How much longer should we let them tail us?" Tony wondered.

"I think probably Geary. It'll still be easy enough for us to outrun them there, and we can always detour around a block or two if we need to."

"True enough. Yikes, hang on." They swerved to the right as a car in front of them slowed suddenly and turned left.

Cam inhaled sharply as they passed within inches of a cherry red sports car fender. "You realize that I'm never going to not be hanging on, right?"

Tony laughed as they turned right onto Geary. It was one of the main east-west thoroughfares in the city, a broad and mainly straight route to the ocean. Cam turned back and saw their car chase buddies make the same turn.

"Should we lose them now?" Tony asked.

"No time like the present." Cam held tightly as Tony twisted the accelerator, and they rapidly picked up speed. He glanced back again and saw the Crown struggling to weave around traffic as their pursuers tried to keep up with them.

"They're starting to fall behind."

"Alright. I'm gonna take this left on Arguello, then try cutting across on Balboa." Tony squeezed the brakes hard, then turned them left off of Geary, before making a right on the next block and pouring on the speed once more. The Hornet seemed to love it, purring like a kitten in need of attention as they zipped down the narrow, two-lane road. After a few blocks, he turned them left again, then right onto Balboa.

Cam looked back but couldn't see any sign of the Crown. "Looks like we lost our tail. Ego, what's the best route to our destination from here?"

"Turn left on Park Presidio Boulevard in approximately three point five kilometers. Continue south on Nineteenth Avenue for–"

"Got it, Ego," Tony interrupted. "Uh, thanks."

"You're welcome, Tony."

"You don't need to thank it, Tony," Cam admonished him. "It doesn't have any feelings."

"But Ego likes it. It said you're welcome."

"That's because I programmed it to do that."

"Oh, yeah."

While the traffic was still heavy, it was easier to manage since they were no longer being chased. When the pair pulled to a stop at a red light, Cam took the chance to stretch his legs a bit. He'd felt them tensing up while he worked to keep from slipping off the Hornet. They'd hopefully left their pursuers behind them for good. They only needed to stay ahead of whatever way the Boss and his crew were using to track him down.

They were soon cruising through Golden Gate Park. Cam

hadn't been there in at least a year. It was still early enough in the day that the fog hadn't rolled in across the western half of the city yet, but he could feel the temperature dropping already. He'd forgotten how bright and green the park was since he spent most of his time among the concrete and glass towers on the other side of the city. The waning daylight filtered through the leaves and needles of the eucalyptus, pine, and cypress trees as dappled shadows cavorted across the streetscape. Strangely, it reminded him of the times he'd escape from his overbearing parents to the woods behind his childhood home, where he'd lay on a tree-covered hilltop watching the clouds pass overhead beyond their leafy canopies.

"Shit. Looks like Nineteenth is a mess," Tony announced, interrupting Cam's daydreaming. "We should cut over to the Great Highway on Lincoln.

Cam lightly shook his head, dragging his attention back to the bike and the road. "Ok, sure. You prolly know the way better than I do anyhow. I don't think I've even been to Daly City."

Tony laughed. "I guess that means you haven't got any Filipino in you."

Cam snickered. "No, but I've had a Filipino in me."

Tony groaned. "Oh lord. I should've seen that one coming."

After heading all the way west down Lincoln, they turned south onto the Great Highway. The route ran parallel to Ocean Beach, with the grand old Pacific on their right, stretching majestically to the far horizon. Cam flipped his visor up, immediately relishing in the humid, salty air as it cooled his face. Traffic was loose that close to the water. It was too late in the day for any sunbathing and too late in the season for most tourists. The beach was another place in the city Cam didn't visit often. He mostly got his water fix living so close to the Bay. Like Puget Sound back in Seattle, the Bay was lovely and calming. But the endless expanse of the ocean was something he could easily get lost in. He longed to pull off his stuffy helmet but knew better, so he settled for leaving his visor flipped.

A tone sounded in his earbuds. "Alert. Police bulletin issued for a motorcycle belonging to Weitian Zhang in connection with the Union Square shootings. License plate number one-one-Zulu-five-four-niner-seven."

Shit.

"Are they fucking serious?" Tony asked, sounding exasperated. "They called the fucking cops on me? What kind of criminals would even do that? I guess our sightseeing time is over. We gotta move."

Cam flipped his visor back down just as the Hornet started to pick up speed. He kept his eyes peeled for any black and white SFPD or CHP cruisers. The sooner they got to the safe house and off the streets, the better.

They swerved left and right, using the road's entire width to dance around slower moving traffic. The Great Highway started to curve inland, where the beach turned into shoreline cliffs, but Tony kept up their speed. Not so fast as to call attention to them, but quicker than the pace of regular traffic. After all, on the Hornet, they'd draw just as much attention for going too slow. They were speeding past Fort Funston when Cam felt a piercing sharpness flood through him again. He fought it, briefly, concerned about what he'd end up doing on the back of Tony's bike. After all, he was no Jastin Kenzi, no matter what the video evidence had to say about it. But the feeling was relentless, crowding through his thoughts like early morning shoppers at a Black Friday sale. Once it settled into place in his subverted mind, he knew why it was back.

There was danger behind him.

Cam whipped his head around, looking back up the curving roadway, scanning for something, anything. Then he spotted the other motorcycle about a mile behind them. Its rider, dressed in all black gear and a deep red helmet with a dark tinted face shield, dipped their head as soon as Cam spotted them, realizing they'd been made. "Gotcha," he muttered with a smirk. The other rider hunkered down over their handlebars as their bike began to pick up speed, rapidly closing the distance behind them. "Tony, we've got another tail."

"What? How do you–"

"Behind us," Cam cut in, "on a black Apex Panther. Rider in all-black gear and a red helmet. Gaining fast."

Tony took a quick look in his mirror. "Shit. Hang on." The pair started to accelerate rapidly, and Cam gripped Tony tightly. "That bike's a lot faster than mine. He won't have much trouble keeping up."

Somehow he'd been found again, just like before. He was clearly being tracked. But how? And yet, something about this new tail felt different than the others, too. "Ok, but we can't let them catch us."

"No worries on that front. He may be faster, but I'm better." A short stretch of road magically cleared ahead of them, and Tony twisted the accelerator hard, quickly gaining speed and distance from their pursuer.

Cam could feel his senses building and updating a constant

mental picture of his surroundings. He found himself anticipating Tony's maneuvers, leaning left or right into their turns almost before they even happened. The bike suddenly surged forward as Tony sped them up again, slipping between a double-line of slowing cars to clear a stoplight that was about to turn red. Then he let off the speed just a little after they cleared the intersection. "Shit, that was close," he said, sounding breathless. "I haven't ridden like this in forever. Good thing I haven't lost my touch."

"Yeah, you got this, Tiger."

"But how do you think they found us again so fast?"

Cam let out an irritated snort. "I don't know. Police cameras? Anonymous tip? I don't think it really matters right now."

"Yeah, I guess you're right. As long as I don't see any disco lights in my mirror. The last thing we need is a televised police chase." Tony gunned it through another intersection, veering into the shoulder as a car crossed their path, then smoothly pointing them back onto the road like a pro. "Piece of cake! By the way, we're coming up on the ramp to Highway One. Should we stay on Skyline and try to make it to the safe house, or should we take the ramp?"

Cam quickly weighed the options. "Take the ramp. I don't think the safe house is a good option at the moment. These fuckers seem to be able to track me no matter what I do, and I don't want to lead them right to it."

"Yeah, you're prolly right. Let's lose this tail first." Then Tony gunned it, keeping to the right for the highway onramp.

They quickly sped up, cruising well past the posted speed limit as they merged with the highway. They must've been going over a hundred at that point. But Tony was totally in his element as they slalomed around and even between the speeding cars on the highway. They were soon in the far left lane, and then the shoulder, kicking up a rooster tail of dirt and sand as they picked up even more speed. Cam would've found it exhilarating if he wasn't so focused on their pursuer. He could feel the Panther on their tail like he was pulling them along on a leash. Glancing back, he spotted the other rider's red helmet as they fought to close the gap between them.

"Tony, they're catching up."

"I know, trust me. I'm gonna try something crazy." He pulled in front of a slower-moving station wagon, then suddenly hit the brakes, smoking the brake pads as they quickly slowed. The driver behind them slammed on their brakes in a panic, then swerved to the left to keep from hitting them, blowing out one of their front tires in the process. The car's front end hit the pavement in a shower of sparks, then slammed into the side of a delivery van as it strayed into the left-hand lane. Cam turned back and saw the Panther swing into the narrow shoulder, barely scraping past the car wreck in progress before another car smashed into the back of the growing pile up. "Who's Jastin Kenzi now, bitch!" Tony shouted.

"Holy shit," Cam muttered quietly. The other rider managed to stay on their tail somehow despite Tony's stuntman riding antics. Whoever they were, they were highly skilled. Cam knew then that Tony would be forced to act more and more recklessly with the way things were going. Their odds of somehow surviving this ride, much less escaping their tail, seemed to plummet before his eyes. There had to be another option. Maybe, if they stopped briefly to let Cam off the bike,

Tony could still get to his uncle's safe house without him. Cam appreciated what his friend was doing for him, but it no longer felt like he was doing anyone any good by trying to escape his pursuers.

"Hey Tony, I think, maybe–"

But, no. There was another option. Cam still had the Haas in his bag. He'd only fired it three times, so there could be as many as a dozen more shots remaining, assuming it was fully loaded when he took it from the soldier in the alley. Hanging onto Tony with his left arm, Cam pulled his right arm back and reached into the bag. He felt the gun grip, grabbed it, and pulled it out.

"Dude," asked Tony, "what are you doing?"

"Focus on the bike, Tony. I'm just changing the rules of engagement." Cam took a deep breath, then looked back and found the Panther. Swinging his arm out, he leveled the handgun and squeezed the trigger. Blam! But the other rider was already dodging somehow and swerved out of the shot's path impossibly fast. The bullet struck the cab of a pickup truck instead, harmlessly lodging in the vehicle's oversized frame.

"Fuckin' A!" Tony shouted. Cam had felt Tony tense up at the sudden noise. Since he never lost control of the bike, Cam paid him little attention.

But their pursuer had somehow anticipated his shot. Cam's initial instinct about them being different somehow was on the nose. He shifted his aim and fired again, then, faster than an eye blink, shifted again and fired once more. Time slowed to a crawl as Cam's perception sped up to inhuman levels. He watched as the other rider reacted to his second shot, then corrected again for his third. Still impossibly fast.

His second shot exploded into the pavement, while his third shot blew out a headlight on a distant minivan, causing it to swerve dangerously into the center median. Whoever that was had to be more than just a hired gun. They were reacting at the same speeds he was. That definitely changed things.

From his slow-time vantage point, Cam watched as the other rider, steering the Panther one-handed, reached their other hand out towards him, balled into a fist, and shot out a fiery blue energy bolt. It narrowly missed, shrieking right past him and striking a car just to their side. The vehicle tumbled from the force of the blast, then violently exploded. It was all Tony could do to swerve and miss it while keeping the bike upright. Cam held tight as a piece of the burning wreckage glanced off his helmet.

"God damn! What was that?" Tony shouted.

"I don't know." His face tight with concentration, Cam turned back to return fire, aiming not for the other rider but for the pavement ahead of them. The bullet struck the roadway, violently ripping small pieces of concrete and dust into the air. The Panther wobbled dangerously as the other rider plowed through it. Cam prepared to fire again when there was another flash from the Panther rider's outstretched hand. He instinctively leaned to his right, directing the bike out of harm's way as another searing bolt shot past them, hitting the road ahead and to their left with explosive force, sending chunks of pavement and earth into the air.

"Jesus Christ!" Tony called out.

They banked as the road ahead curved left into the coastal foothills. Traffic had thankfully grown sparse, but Cam knew they couldn't keep playing this high-stakes game of chicken for much longer. At least their pursuer wasn't actually trying to hit him with whatever sci-fi weapon they were firing. They wanted to stop him, yes. But they'd avoided hitting him directly so far. They seemed a little too ok with him being severely injured in a motorcycle crash, though.

Cam scanned the traffic behind them, then aimed and fired at a car between them and the Panther. Two could play at that game, after all. The shot missed, hitting the highway, so he fired again, and the driver's side tire exploded off the rim. The car immediately swerved right into the other rider's path. Their pursuer slammed on the brakes, smoking the Panther's tires, then swung their bike to the left around the crashing vehicle. They were just too good, he begrudgingly admitted. He had seven shots remaining at most, but before he could choose another target, the Panther rider fired their mysterious weapon again. Cam leaned to the left, ever so gently, steering them out of the potential path of another blast. The scorching energy bolt shot wide to the right, exploding into a tree on the side of the road in a fury of fire and earth. The tree fell into their path, but Tony managed to swerve at the last moment to avoid it.

"We're almost to the tunnel," Tony said frantically, interrupting Cam's focus. He meant the Devil's Slide tunnel, which opened just a few years back. It cut a straight shot through the rocky Devil's Slide promontory along the Pacific Coast and was an awful place for a motorcycle chase. They were about to be sitting ducks, with no room to maneuver, as they sped through the nearly mile-long, single-lane tunnel.

Still, they careened along, the highway curving through a small seaside town, with the vast ocean looming ominously to the west. The road narrowed to just two lanes, so Tony took them into a turn lane to sail by the traffic waiting at the stoplight ahead before snaking through the woods beyond it.

They were rapidly running out of time, and Cam needed to act fast. He waited until he could see the Panther come around the curve behind them, rapidly closing the distance between them. Then he pointed the Haas back a final time and emptied the gun's clip, adjusting his aim slightly between each shot–blam, blam, blam, blam, blam–before the slide clicked back, empty. This time, Cam had thrown more bullets at the Panther than the rider could dodge, and his third shot struck the bike's front tire. The motorcycle's front rim crumpled under direct contact with the road surface, dropping the fork down to kiss the concrete in an electric rainbow of sparks. The rest of the Panther tipped forward–obeying Newton's immutable first law of motion–lifting the back end and launching the rider into the air. Cam saw it all happen in tantalizing slow motion as the rider flung their hands forward like a helmeted superhero taking flight. But their battle wasn't quite over, as the flying rider let loose one more glowing blue energy bolt. It shot forward, almost slowly enough for him to follow its progress past his head, before striking a rocky outcropping just above the tunnel entrance. He watched in impotent disbelief as a wall of stone crashed down onto the highway ahead of them.

Tony's body slowly tensed under Cam's grip as he started to squeeze the brakes, but Cam already knew they couldn't stop in time. There had to be another choice. He closed his eyes, taking refuge in the quiet confidence of his mind, despite the situation's hopelessness. The other presence in his head, the one he realized had been there this whole time, wound its way through the fires of his racing thoughts like a cool breeze, undeterred by the looming prospect of imminent death. There was one final option, he recognized, without even fully understanding what it was. At least it was an escape. He knew that much. And it was his only remaining option at that point. Yes, he thought, feeling the rising tide of desperation threatening to break through the profound stillness that held it back. Do it.

Cam opened his eyes to see the world passing by at barely more than a crawl. The collapsed entrance to the tunnel, creeping ever closer toward them, lit up in an explosion of purple-white brilliance. Part of him began to recoil in horror. The part that was in control reassured him that all was going according to plan. Cam corrected his lean just so, pointing them straight at the brightly shimmering blue-violet oval that blossomed into existence just ahead of them. Cam could feel Tony's body tense further inside his grip. He focused his thoughts on Tony. Just keep going. We'll be safe if you just keep going. The bike's front tire finally contacted the fiery wall of radiance, and Cam smiled as the whole world became a dazzling light show around them. Then they were gone.

TONY

Tony's world suddenly descended into near darkness. He blinked madly as his eyes tried to adjust, then let out a strangled cry as he fought to maintain control of the speeding motorcycle. He squeezed the brakes, but the tires had no purchase on the rocky ground below them. The road was gone. Flashing purple afterimages flared in his vision as he struggled to keep the bike upright. They were careening along a bumpy dirt trail, and it was all he could do to keep from spilling the bike and crashing. Trees blurred as they rushed by on either side while he desperately bled off their remaining speed, but it was no use. The motorcycle hit something just as they flew out from the trees into a grass-filled clearing. A rock, probably. But he finally lost control.

The motorcycle flipped into the air, sending both of them flying. Tony tried to pull himself into a fetal crouch before hitting the ground, letting his momentum carry him forward into a graceless roll when he landed. When he finally stopped, he found himself awkwardly sprawled on the dirt, surrounded by waist-high wild grass. Tony lay still for a moment while his racing thoughts settled down. He had no idea what just happened or where they were.

"Tony!" he heard Cam cry out. "Tony, are you okay?"

He let out a low groan. "Ugh. Everything hurts. But I think I'm ok." Tony tentatively moved his limbs and found that everything worked well enough–until he got to his right leg, which blossomed with a sharp burst of pain. He definitely hadn't stuck that landing. He gingerly took off his helmet, then pulled Cam's earbuds out and slipped them into a pocket before settling in and laying there in the tall grass, trying to figure out what was going on. He couldn't hear anything other than the rustling grass. No traffic. No people. No signs of civilization. Then he heard Cam walking toward him. A moment later, Cam pushed his way through the grass into the small clearing Tony carved with his body when he landed.

Cam crouched down next to him. "Can you move?"

Tony gave him a weak thumbs up. "I'm good," he answered, his voice sounding strained. "Just taking a minute to enjoy laying here. What happened?"

"Honestly?" Cam sighed dramatically. "I don't think I could explain it. But there doesn't seem to be any signs of more trouble."

"Well, that's an improvement, at least." Tony hoped that was true. He didn't like his chances for surviving another mad getaway, considering how the last one went. "I was getting pretty tired of being chased and shot at by some alien fucking death ray. What the hell was up with that?"

"I don't know." Cam held out his hand, offering it to Tony. "Come on, lemme help you up."

Tony reached up to grab Cam's hand and pulled himself up off the ground, favoring his other leg as best he could. He tried to put some weight on his right leg but grimaced in pain. "Oh shit! Ok, I guess I'm not totally undamaged." Cam helped him keep his balance until he managed to stand on his own. "There. Now what?"

Cam pulled his handheld from his pocket, revealing a spider web of cracks across the screen. "Shit. Well, this thing isn't gonna be any help." He stuffed it back into his pocket while Tony patted down his own pants. Aside from Cam's earbuds, there was nothing to be found.

"Uh, looks like mine's just plain gone." Tony grimaced, then glanced around them. "Where the hell are we, anyway? Where's the highway?"

"No fucking clue. I can't even hear it from here." Cam looked back toward the trees. "We came from that way before we crashed, so I'd guess probably over there somewhere."

The memory of the blinding flash, then suddenly finding himself on a dark stretch of tree-lined dirt that barely counted as a trail, was still very fresh. "Hey, speaking of the crash, did you happen to see where my bike went?"

Cam looked behind him and pointed away from the woods. "No, but I assume it went somewhere in that direction."

Tony glanced toward where Cam pointed. The only signs of his baby were several spots where the tall grass was torn up. He feared the worst. While he may have been able to survive a tumble like that, he didn't have much hope for the Hornet doing the same. "We should find it and see what kind of shape it's in. I mean, it's probably wrecked, but a guy can hope, right? Cuz otherwise it's gonna be a long walk, and I don't know how far I can go on this leg."

Cam nodded. He took Tony's arm over his shoulder and helped him limp along, following the path of destruction through the tall grass. His bike must've bounced around like a rag doll in the dryer. They found a deep ravine at the end of the trail, with his bike's remains at the bottom.

Tony looked down at the wreckage of his pride and joy. The whole front fork had come entirely off the frame, and the rear wheel was nowhere to be seen. "Well, shit. I guess that's a lost cause. We'd need a crane to get that thing outta there. Maybe even a helicopter." That totally sucked. But there was no reason to focus on it at the moment. They had bigger fish to fry. He looked over at Cam. "Ok, now what?"

"I guess we should head back the way we came." The forced confidence in Cam's voice was evident. "Pacifica can't be more than a mile or two back. We might be able to find a phone there and call your uncle and maybe get a ride before whoever's been hunting me finds us again."

They turned back toward the woods and started walking, stopping briefly to retrieve Cam's messenger bag from where it landed. Tony spotted Cam's helmet sitting on the ground nearby. A big gouge was cut out of it, probably from flying wreckage. "Wow, dude, look at the cherry on top of that helmet. If you hadn't been wearing it, you'd be dead." Then he laughed. "What am I even saying? People have been after you all day! A little bump on the head is nothing compared to alien death rays."

"It's been a fucked up day, hasn't it?" Cam slung his bag over his shoulder. "Getting lost in the middle of nowhere is almost a nice change of pace."

Tony put his arm around Cam's shoulder for support again, and the pair started their slow trek back to civilization. The daylight was waning, so they didn't have any time to lose. Tony had questions for his friend, and it seemed like as good of a time as any to bring them up. "Can we talk about what happened back there, Cam?"

"What do you mean?" Cam asked innocently as if he didn't know what Tony meant.

Well, if Cam wanted it spelled out, Tony would be happy to oblige him. "I mean using the highway for target practice, for one. I've never seen you as the violent type, but that's the second time you've done your Fingers of Fury act today. Since when do you go in all guns-a-blazin' like that?"

"I didn't really have much choice," Cam said unapologetically. "I still had the gun, and I figured I should probably defend us." Tony saw him look down, searching the ground for something. Then he directed them toward the path they'd ridden in on. If you could even call that riding. "I don't know what you expected me to do. I've got no fucking idea why any of this is happening. I don't know why they keep showing up like that or how they keep finding me, and I couldn't think of any other way for us to shake them off our tail."

"Yeah, that dude was one hell of a fucking rider," Tony replied, then fell silent. He let the silence linger for a few moments. He'd been giving Cam the benefit of the doubt all day, but some pretty fucked up stuff had happened. Tony didn't regret anything that he'd done and would gladly have done it again to help his friend. But Tony had some doubts about just who his friend really was. "Cam, I know you like to play your cards close and all, but I gotta ask. Where did you learn to do all that shit? All joking about Jastin Kenzi and Calvin Gibbs aside, I've only ever seen someone handle a gun like that in the movies."

"Oh, and you've seen a lot of real-life gunfights, I suppose?"

Cam was deflecting, and Tony knew it. "You know what I mean."

Cam sighed. "I don't fucking know." Tony started to

117

protest, but Cam cut him off. "I'm serious. I've never held a gun before today. I've never even been in a fight unless you count all the times my folks smacked me around. I don't have any idea how I knew those things. They just came to me, like–" He stopped, shaking his head. "I don't know. It's all fucked up."

Tony frowned. "Hey, you can tell me. It can't be any more fucked up than the–"

"Alien death ray," Cam interrupted. "Yeah, I know. It's just–it's like there was something there with me in my head." He paused again, taking a deep breath. "It felt like I could sense that motorcycle behind me, you know? Like, when you can feel someone staring at you, even when you're not looking at them. And when I needed to fight those guys or use the gun, the knowledge was just there in my head all of sudden, like I'd known it my whole life."

With anyone else, Tony would've been sure he was being fed a line of bullshit. He couldn't fathom manifesting all those hidden skills like that. But he knew Cam, and if his friend claimed that's how it happened, then that's how it happened. "So, not just alien death rays," he said, chuckling to soften the dour mood, "but Psi Force MasterMinds, too?"

Cam laughed. He and Tony recently had a watch-party marathon of the cheesy retro sci-fi series. "Swift and savage, we fight as one!"

"Behold our power!" Tony called out, finishing the battle cry. "I gotta hand it to whoever that rider was, though, with his mad wicked riding skills. I could never pull off those moves one-handed like he did."

Cam nodded. "Yeah, that was something else, wasn't it? I hope we don't see them again for a while."

"More like ever." Or at least not until Tony got his bike fixed and ready for a rematch, he thought.

Cam shook his head. "Except we know that won't happen. Whatever it is they want from me, it seems like they'll keep trying until they finally get it. I think we can count on that."

Tony nodded. He hadn't forgotten. "I know, dude. It was just wishful thinking." He glanced over at his friend as they limped along through the woods. "You wanna know what I think is going on?"

"I don't know. Do I?"

"It's obvious, isn't it?" Tony held up his free hand and started to count with his fingers. "You're adopted. You don't know where you're from. You're mad smart, like hella mad smart. And now you can sense danger and fight like a fucking pro?" He smiled. "It's simple. You're an alien, dude. And some kind of intergalactic hit squad is tracking you down to bring you back home."

Cam flashed him a wry grin. "Yeah, in a body bag. But you forget, I've been to the doctor before, and I've had blood work done. I'm one-hundred percent, grade-A human."

"Since when have you been to the doctor?" Tony wondered aloud. "I've known you for what, three, maybe four years? You've never been sick once that whole time."

Cam flipped his hand dismissively. "Back when I was a teenager. My parents got some shrink to put me on meds trying to put a stop to my unruly behavior."

Tony laughed. He'd heard the stories about Cam's unfortunate upbringing. But the reminder made him grateful for the close ties he had with his family. "Once a troublemaker, always a troublemaker, eh?"

Cam smirked. "Yeah, well, I did my best, but my uber-

Christian parents had pretty high expectations for the little, brown, heathen, savage boy that they rescued from damnation."

"You're lucky," Tony replied in a deadpan tone. "I heard damnation can be pretty awful."

Cam chuckled. "Well, after today, I'm not so sure I got a good deal anymore."

Tony nodded as they continued to pick their way along. "Yeah, this really has been a rough one. But at least you're the hero in this story. I'm just the sidekick."

Cam's jaw dropped in mock outrage. "You're jealous of me? At least no one's trying to kill you."

"No, I'm just collateral damage."

Cam stopped them. "I'm sorry, dude, but you're way too cool to be the sidekick. If anything, you're the hero swooping in to save poor little old me with your superior motorcycle-riding skills and shady underworld connections."

Tony laughed. "Don't forget my rugged good looks and effortless charm!"

Cam laughed, too. "There's the Tiger I know and love. Now, we just gotta–" He started to move forward again, then stopped and looked down. "Tony?" Cam pointed at the ground.

Tony looked at where Cam was pointing. "What?"

"The tire tracks. They start right here, in the middle of the path."

Tony squinted his eyes to see what Cam was talking about. "Tire tracks?"

"The tracks from your motorcycle. I've been following them this whole time."

Tony awkwardly leaned forward to get a closer look at the

darkened path. With the waning light from the setting sun, it was hard to see any detail at all. "Wow, dude. You can really see those?"

Cam looked at him strangely. "Yeah, of course. They're right there at your feet."

"It's pretty dark, man. I can barely see them."

Cam sighed dramatically. "I must have good night vision, I guess."

"See?" Tony gently patted him on the shoulder. "Alien." He laughed, then urged them forward. "Come on, we're almost out of the woods. We should be able to see the road soon."

"I'm not an alien," Cam muttered as they emerged from the woods to stand out in the open again.

A gorgeous vista unfolded in front of them. Rolling, grass-covered hills sloped down to the shore, with the expansive ocean retreating off to the distant horizon. Tony looked beyond the familiar hills toward the– "Whoa."

"Yeah, it's really pretty up here," Cam offered.

Tony looked at his friend, confused. Could he really not see what was right in front of him? So much for good night vision. He pointed down toward the shore. "See that stretch of sand? I think that's Pacifica Beach."

"Ok, sure," Cam said once he had it in his sights.

"Dude?" Tony waited for a response, but Cam didn't offer any. "Dude, if that's Pacifica Beach, then where the fuck is Pacifica?"

Tony noticed it right away. There was no city there. There was nothing there but rolling hills. He looked further north up the peninsula at what should be San Francisco, but there was nothing there either. No skyline. No lights. Nothing.

Cam suddenly looked shocked. "Holy shit. Ok, that's pretty

fucked."

"Fucked is right." Tony felt like he was finally about to lose his cool. "There's no road! There's no city! There's nothing where there should definitely be something." He looked at Cam again and, for the first time, felt their uncomfortable closeness. "Ok, I didn't want to say anything before, but we're here because you did something to us, right? I mean, I could hear you mumbling to yourself in my earbuds, then all of a sudden, you squeezed me really tight, and there was this super bright flash, and then bam! We're in the middle of the woods."

Cam looked a little guilty. "What are you trying to say?"

"I'm trying to say–" What was he trying to say? His memories of it were jumbled. He'd been so focused on controlling the bike. "Shit. I don't know." He looked back at Cam, realizing that he wasn't feeling anger but fear. "Did you like, cast a spell or something? Teleport us to some faraway land?"

Cam rolled his eyes. "You're right, Tony. I'm secretly an alien wizard."

Tony just threw up his free hand. "For fuck sake, I don't know, ok? I've seen way too much shit today that shouldn't be possible, including a motorcycle stunt rider who can shoot alien death rays outta his hand. And now we're standing here on this hilltop, and there's no city where a city definitely should be." He felt a little queasy. "Shit, I gotta sit down."

Cam gingerly helped him to the ground. "Hey, Tony, things will be ok. We'll figure this out, I promise."

"Figure what out? Like, where all the fucking cities and people went?" Tony's anxiety started to feel like it had back when he was bullied in school. He felt powerless. And he was worried about his leg, too.

While Tony tried to calm his breathing, Cam left him alone for a few minutes to search around and gather some wood for a fire. He'd found a spot nearby that was pretty flat and clear, so he dumped the wood there and gathered some large rocks to make a fire ring. Then, using a portable torch from his bag, he got a fire going. After helping Tony over to a spot next to it, Cam dug through his bag and found a couple of energy bars he'd stuck in there at some point. He split one in half to share with Tony, who was pleased to discover that he had half a joint tucked into his pocket.

"I was saving it for my work break." Tony pulled it out and offered it to Cam.

Cam got that burning, too, and soon they were passing it back and forth between them, getting pleasantly stoned next to the fire. Between the fire, the joint, and their beautiful surroundings, it would've felt like an enjoyable evening campout if they weren't stuck in some strange place with no cities or people.

"I think we went back in time," Tony confessed as he passed the joint back to Cam. It was the only explanation he could come up with that made any sense to him. "Think about it. The landscape looks pretty much the same. There's just no civilization."

"Ok," Cam said, "but if it's time travel, what if we went forward in time, and the cities are just gone, like in that one documentary channel show?"

"Oh, shit, yeah! I forgot about that one." He looked around curiously. "Except there'd still be evidence that there was a city around, right? Like a vine-covered skyscraper skeleton or something."

Cam laughed at the thought. "That would be majorly cool."

"Yeah, totally. If we're still alive tomorrow, we should hike up the peninsula and see."

"I don't think you're gonna do much hiking on that leg, though."

Tony had forgotten about that already. "Shit, you're right. It's too bad that my bike was totaled."

"Not really. I mean, it's not like there are any roads anyway."

Tony grunted. "Oh, yeah. See, that's why I think we went back in time. Otherwise, there'd be a crumbled highway down there, too." He looked around warily. "Hopefully, there aren't any dinosaurs and shit."

Cam stifled a laugh. "Dinosaurs? No way!"

Tony played at being offended for a moment but ended up laughing along. "Hey, did you ever see that movie where the guy opened that time travel theme park that had a dinosaur collection?"

"You mean Exhibition Dino?" Tony nodded. "Oh yeah, totally. Both the original with the claymation and the big-budget CGI remake that came out a few years ago."

"Which totally sucked!"

Cam scoffed. "Totally sucked."

They both sat quietly, passing the joint back and forth until it was gone, then Tony flicked the roach into the fire. As he sat on the edge of that unknown hill, stoned enough that his leg wasn't bothering him much, a lot of the feelings he'd been ignoring finally started to resurface. When he'd rolled out of bed that morning, still suffering from his vicious hangover, he was at least looking forward to an easy day. Get stoned. Help out at the restaurant. Maybe text that girl from the night before. Shit, what was her name again? But then there was the call from Cam and the televised shootout in the middle of the city. Then came the motorcycle chase, which, if he was honest, was kinda fun. Then came the second motorcycle chase, which was way more exciting than the first and a lot less fun. Then came the second shootout, this time both with him and an alien death ray involved.

Tony loved his friend Cam, of that he had no doubt. He thought back to when they'd first met, after raiding together in Farstorm. He'd connected with Cam, in part, because he was so much different from a lot of Tony's other friends–in a good way. For the most part, he was totally unimpressed with Tony's family or their means, which was a breath of fresh air as far as Tony was concerned. Sure, Cam was always the quiet one. Not shy, so much. Just reserved. Like, he'd talk your ear off, but only if he thought you were worth it. Still, Tony was sure that his buddy Mad Dog was the best friend he'd ever had.

He didn't regret what he'd done that day. His friend had been in need, so he helped. That's what friends do. But Tony was sure that Cam did something to bring them to where they were. Whether it was an intentional thing or even a conscious thing, he didn't know. And then there was the question of what they were going to do about their situation.

"How are we gonna get out of here?" Tony asked, trying to keep the worry out of his voice.

Cam sighed. "I don't know, man. I've been thinking about it, trying to remember what exactly happened. But I just can't. It's almost like a dream, you know?"

"I don't know about that," Tony said, then chuckled. "My dreams are usually different. Less alien death rays, more Miranda Chambers."

Cam laughed. "Well, there's no accounting for taste."

"Do you think you could do it again, though?" he asked cautiously. "I mean, whatever you did to get us here?"

Cam sighed again. "I don't see how I could. I don't really remember doing anything the first time. It was like I was watching it all happen, but I wasn't in control."

Tony nodded. "Like the fighting stuff and the guns, right?"

Cam perked up. "Yeah, totally!" Then he sagged back down again. "It's not helpful, I know. But somehow, I'll figure it out. I have to."

Suddenly there was a rustling noise in the woods behind them. They both froze as they heard the sound of approaching footsteps.

"Shit," Tony whispered. "They found us."

Cam shook his head. "No, it couldn't be them. Whoever that is, they're not exactly trying to sneak up on us."

Tony thought it over and realized Cam was probably right. He wished he was as sure as Cam sounded, but he wasn't convinced they were out of danger yet. "I hope you're right, but help me back up, just in case."

"In case of what, gimpy? You're gonna run away on your one good leg?"

Tony laughed. "Don't be an asshole. Just do it, would you?"

Cam groaned but stood up, then reached down and helped Tony to his feet. The rustling and footsteps grew louder until a man emerged from the woods near where the path began. He was tall and dressed in practical, almost tactical style clothing, wearing a gray long-sleeve shirt and darker gray vest, black cargo style pants, and worn but functional black boots. He was built but not too bulky and, despite his size, moved with an almost dancer-like grace. His dark hair was shaved close to his scalp, and his sienna face featured friendly eyes and a radiant smile. He was really handsome, Tony had to admit, even if he didn't really swing that way.

"Hi there," the guy chirped pleasantly. Tony couldn't tell how old he was, but he guessed maybe thirty. Or perhaps a young-looking forty. "Sorry to bother you, but you didn't happen to see anyone crash a motorcycle around here recently?"

Tony groaned. "Why? Are you some kinda cop or something?"

The guy seemed to be amused by Tony's question. "Not exactly, no."

"Ok," Tony challenged, "then who the hell are you?"

The guy chuckled, then held his hands in apology. "Alright, I'll be honest. I know it was you two who crashed the motorcycle. I was just trying to be funny." He made a point of looking around. "In case you haven't noticed, there's no one else here. It wasn't that hard to work out." Then he flashed them a friendly smile.

Dang, he was charming, too. Tony looked to Cam for backup.

"Yeah," Cam chimed in, "there's just us. And you."

"And me," a heavily accented voice said from behind them. Russian, maybe. Tony and Cam both turned to see a thin, pale woman with short, spiky, black hair, dressed in tight-fitting jeans, a loose, white shirt under a dark jacket, and much newer looking, or at least, better cared for boots.

Tony looked from one to the other and laughed. "Oh, I get it. You're some kind of low-budget, b-movie, anti-heroes with hearts of gold."

The man shook his head but kept his smile. "I don't think

I've ever been described like that before."

Tony rolled his eyes in exasperation. "Listen, I don't care if you're school crossing guards, either tell us what the hell's going on here or go back to whatever military surplus store was having a two-for-one sale."

The man laughed, but the woman just frowned. "I do not get it."

"Of course you don't, Tasha," he said, still chuckling, and then he pointed at Tony. "And you aren't exactly winning over your savior's hearts and minds with your savage fashion critique."

Tony was about to reply, but Cam jumped in to bring them back on point. "You're Natasha?" he asked the woman.

"No. Natalia. Natalia Leondrova." Her accent was thick and definitely Russian. "Is only Tasha for short." She pointed at the man. "He is Jerusalem Finn."

"Just Finn is fine. And you both are?"

"I'm Leon," Tony answered, then pointed at Cam. "And he's Reginald."

Cam snickered before he could stop himself. "Yep, that's me. Reginald Butterberry."

Finn raised a suspicious eyebrow, then reached into a pocket in his pants and out a wallet. "That's interesting," he said casually as he opened the wallet and pulled out an ID card, "because, according to this driver's license, Leon, the State of California thinks your name is Weitian Zhang of San Francisco."

Tony's hand shot back to the pocket where his wallet was supposed to be, but it obviously wasn't there. It must've fallen out during his tumble in the tall grass. "Ok, fine," he admitted, "but I go by Tony. And it's not like Jerusalem is all

128

that believable of a name."

Finn looked mildly offended, but Tasha laughed. "Oh, so now you get the joke," he said pointedly.

She shrugged. "Is funny."

Finn sighed. "Whatever." Then he put the license back in Tony's wallet and tossed it over to him. "Listen, Tony and Reginald, or whatever your name actually is–"

"It's Cameron," Cam interrupted. "Or just Cam."

Finn nodded. "Ok, Cam then. I'm sure you've both realized that you're somewhere you're not supposed to be. Well, we're here to help you."

Tony visibly relaxed. "Oh my god, thank you. I'm really tired of getting chased and shot at, and we can't figure out if we've been sent to the past or the future."

"Is past, of course," Tasha offered. "You are lucky to be found before dinosaurs get you."

"Wait," Tony said, shocked. "What?"

Finn laughed. "She's just messing with you, Tony. You haven't traveled through time. But you still shouldn't be here, so I'd really love for you both to explain how you are here."

Tony looked over at Cam with an eyebrow raised. He wished he'd known they were going to be interrogated so that they could've prepared their stories. But considering how well the fake name went over, it probably wouldn't have mattered.

Cam shrugged. "I don't have a good answer for that, and I'd really like to know where here is, exactly." Then he looked over toward the coast and pointed. "There should be a city there. And a highway. But there's not."

Finn nodded. "Ok, then why don't you just tell us what

happened that led you here. And maybe we can help answer your questions after."

Tony looked at Cam and nodded. Finn and Tasha were their only source of help, and they hadn't pointed any guns at them yet. It didn't look like they were even carrying any. It couldn't hurt to see what the pair could offer them. So Cam told them an abbreviated version of the story, leaving out some of the details that he probably didn't think were relevant. But he told them about the Boss and his crew, being chased, and the mysterious motorcycle rider who shot some kind of beam weapon at them. "And when we got to the tunnel, there was this bright flash of purple light, and then we appeared here. Well," he pointed into the woods, "in there, actually." He pulled out his handheld. "And since this thing is busted, and his phone is missing, we decided to walk back to town to get help. Only there's no town there anymore."

"Hey, you didn't happen to find my phone, too?" Tony asked suddenly.

Finn shook his head. "No, I'm afraid not." Then he looked at Cam. "And that's a fascinating story. You've never seen any of those people, or that rider, before?"

Tony shook his head. "We didn't actually see the rider at all, cuz of the helmet."

Finn looked at his partner Tasha. "You think it's–?"
"Yes."

He nodded, either in agreement or resignation. "So, we should probably–?"

"Yes," said Tasha firmly. "We must." Finn didn't seem so sure. Tasha looked at him carefully. "You are thinking something different, though." It wasn't a question.

"This is clearly an unusual situation. You see that, right?"

130

She grimaced, then let out a resigned sigh. "I do. But is your call. You answer to them. I answer to you."

Tony groaned in exasperation. "Look, I appreciate that you have the kind of buddy-cop rapport where you can finish each other's sentences and shit." He looked at Cam. "But we could really use some answers. Or at least a ride."

Finn nodded, but his pleasant expression was otherwise unreadable. "You're right on both counts. First, we'll take you back because it's not safe for you both to be here. Then we'll answer your questions the best we can. Sound good?"

Tony nodded enthusiastically. "Hell yeah!"

Cam just smiled. "Ok, where do we go?"

Tasha walked up from behind and put her arms over their shoulders like they were old pals. "Is not far, my friends."

Finn gave them both a big smile. "There's just one thing we need to do first."

Tony suddenly felt a spot of cold pressure on the side of his neck. He turned, putting his hand over it, and saw Tasha holding some kind of injector in each hand. Cam had a hand on his neck as well, his expression a battle between confused and betrayed. Tony was definitely leaning more towards betrayed.

"Oh, man." Tony was starting to feel dizzy. He shot Tasha an accusing look. "Did you have to do that?"

Finn looked at him sympathetically. "Yeah, we have this routine, Tasha and I. Plus, it's just easier this way. But you'll both be fine. I promise."

Tony tried to stay alert, fighting the drug's effects, but he knew it was a losing battle when he stopped feeling his legs. His surroundings started to get blurry as he slumped to the ground. Then everything went black.

THE AGENT

«STATIC»«FLASH»

She begrudgingly surveyed the virtual scene, projected before her in exquisite detail. It was angled so that she looked down on her virtual self from above. Although she'd been moving at very high speed, the playback crawled forward in super slow motion. Every decision, every action, was laid bare before her. Just like before, she watched herself prepare to fire her particle blaster. Then she saw her target fire off his slug thrower incredibly fast and somehow strike her bike. She'd already watched this scene repeat many times, and it was always the same. The tunnel was there, and she knew that his capture was inevitable. She fired. Then the sudden flare of Cherenkov radiation burst forth, almost lovely in hues of blue and violet, and he was gone.

She'd failed.

After being thrown from her bike, the landing had been excruciating. Her combat armor valiantly absorbed much of the impact when her body slammed into the pavement at nearly twenty-seven meters per second. But she'd been badly injured nonetheless, enough so that it wasn't worth the extensive repair required to make her body functional again. Her emergency internals kept her alive long enough to transfer her mind to a new body, free of any injury or lingering effects from the impact. Still, watching it happen, she remembered how it felt well enough.

"Again," the disembodied voice of the Intelligence instructed, at once hollow and ghostly, yet still full of menace. She'd often tried very hard to emulate that tone. One day she would succeed.

The loop reset and began to replay at an agonizingly slow speed. She remembered her rage and disappointment at her target's victory. But she also remembered her surprise when he'd suddenly outmaneuvered her. She respected an adversary that could somehow manage to change the rules like that, to change the stakes.

The Intelligence remained silent for a moment after the replay finished. It may as well have been an eternity. Then it finally spoke. "Your failure was unexpected, but much about this situation has been unexpected." That same tone, lacking in any tangible emotion yet still somehow threatening. How much of that was she projecting onto it herself? "We now have clear verification that this individual is the one we have sought all this time. That is no small consideration. Given the circumstances, we will overlook this recent failure of yours. It is unlikely that future circumstances will allow any additional failures to go unpunished."

She was relieved. Not to avoid punishment, of course. She'd endured that often enough, and it was unlikely to be more painful than the injuries she'd watched herself experience in the replay. No, she was grateful to have another chance to succeed. Her success is what drove her. She would be disappointed to have this task given to another. "Of course," she acknowledged. "I will begin at once."

"You will wait." That was an unexpected response. She usually knew better than to have those kinds of expectations and silently chastised herself for her brief emotional response. "You will watch. We know they have been looking for him, too, even if they do not know what he is. We calculate a high probability that he is now in their care. If not, he soon will be. And then they will look for you next. You will wait and watch for them to make their move. You must be prepared."

"I will be prepared."

"You misunderstand. Your success in this matter is imperative. You are not suitable as you are for what's to come. You must undergo alterations."

She found herself suddenly frozen in place, unable to move any part of her body. She could feel the probing begin, along with the surging sense of dread. This was going to hurt.

She screamed.

«FLASH»«STATIC»

FINN

Jerusalem Finn was thinking of a maté. He fondly recalled the drink's delicious warmth as he helped Tasha load the two people they were rescuing into the flyer. Finn had never been a fan of the caffeine-infused beverage before. But he'd had one recently, sitting on the brick-paved veranda outside of a tea shop in old Valparaiso. It overlooked the sparkling, blue, south Pacific, and he'd been gently caressed by the cool ocean breeze as he cautiously sipped it through a metal straw. For some reason, the experience reminded him of a pleasant memory from his childhood, playing on a sun-dappled beach with his siblings and friends not far from his family home. Thinking back on it gave him a welcome feeling of nostalgic happiness.

"Stop goofing off and help with this one," Tasha snapped. The rolling lilt of her native Russian danced merrily around in her English. "He is heavy."

Finn smiled apologetically. "Sorry, Tash. Just thinking about the old days for some reason."

Tasha shivered dramatically. "Of course, is cold here. Why can mysterious Gate anomalies never happen where is warm? Or near bar?"

Finn chuckled at that. "Stop reading my mind, comrade.

135

Besides, there was that one time we got stuck in the desert for a couple days. That was pretty warm."

"Yes, delightful. Except for giant fucking scorpions."

He chuckled darkly. That had been a hell of a day. "Yeah, but we probably don't have to worry about those here." He helped her secure an unconscious Cam to the padded platforms they'd opened up in the back of their flyer.

"Is true." Tasha grinned and brushed a loose chunk of her raven hair back behind her ear. "With our luck, is probably just dinosaurs."

"Well," Finn deadpanned, "if anyone were going to stumble on a dinosaur nest, it would definitely be you."

Tasha shot him a narrow-eyed glare, then checked the remaining straps.

Finn checked them as well, then felt a wave of guilt over what they'd done. It was their SOP for rescue pick-ups—sedate them, transport them back to somewhere safe, and wipe their memories before release. But he'd had a bad feeling during the whole irregular mission, and not just because it came on the tail end of several other recent anomalies that turned to disasters. It could've been a coincidence that it all happened that way, but his instincts told him otherwise. And so did Otto.

The statistical likelihood is large enough to border on relative certainty, his autonomous onboard AI system, or Otto, explained. During the thirty years he'd lived with the voice in his head, Finn had never known it to be wrong. Irritating, yes. Intrusive, definitely. But never wrong. He hadn't known what it would be like when the system was implanted after he turned thirteen and joined the Protectorate. But it turned out to be one of his most significant advantages in unusual situations like the one he was in. And he'd come to mostly consider Otto to be a close friend. How could he not? Otto knew him better than he knew himself.

"You are daydreaming again, Finn. We are set here. Can we go now, please?"

Finn shook off the train of thought, irritated with himself. "Yeah, sorry. Otto, button us up and prep for dust off."

"Right away, Finn," Otto replied over the onboard speakers. The rear section lights dimmed noticeably, and the side hatch lowered until it was closed. "Grav-gen online, mag pulse on standby."

Tasha nodded. "Thank you, Otto." She looked at Finn. "You want to take stick?"

He shook his head. Technically, neither of them needed to pilot the craft, but he knew Tasha would want to do it. It helped her feel in control of a situation to have some direct input. And Finn could tell that she was just as put off as he was by their current circumstances, given how her normally taciturn demeanor had morphed into full-on petulance. "Nah, you take it. I'll ride Nav this time."

She smiled and walked up to the forward cabin. Finn joined her as she sat in the pilot's seat and arranged the displays to her liking. He sat down in the other seat and strapped himself in. Once he'd pulled up the Nav display and set their destination markers, he swiped it over to populate one of Tasha's display areas. It either was a stroke of luck or another unlikely coincidence that they'd been somewhere they could quickly respond to the Gate anomaly. Not that the two people lying unconscious in the back of the flyer had been in any real danger. They could've probably held out for at least another day or so before they would've been in any trouble. As it was, they'd only been stranded for a few hours. But their presence there at all was still a big question mark in his mind.

Finn felt a slight pull as the flyer lifted off, then was pushed back into his seat as they started moving. The grav-gen compensated almost immediately, easing the momentum to a barely noticeable pressure.

"I've completed my scans," Otto announced over the speakers, primarily for Tasha's benefit. She was unenhanced and used external equipment to hear or communicate with Finn's onboard systems. Tasha hadn't partnered with him until she was fully grown, and it would've been perilously intrusive to wetwire her to the extent that he was. She wouldn't have done it anyway. *You keep magic voice inside head*, she told him when she'd learned about it. *I don't need supercomputer reading my thoughts*. "The one identified as Tony Zhang has sustained serious but non-life-threatening damage to his right leg," Otto continued. "Onboard med systems can stabilize the area, but he will need a full medbay to repair the damage."

Finn nodded. "There's a portable medbay pod at the Seattle safe house."

"My scans of the one identified as Cameron Maddock are inconclusive."

Finn raised his eyebrows in surprise. "What does that mean?"

"He does not appear to have sustained any damage, and his bio readings are supra-optimal. In fact, he's in such good health that it's a little curious."

Tasha snorted. "He is too healthy?"

"Precisely, Tasha," Otto confirmed in his usual matter-of-fact tone. "I'd need a med system to run a more thorough scan, but I've detected no signs of injury or physical trauma, either current or past, anywhere on his body. For instance, Tony's scan shows areas of blunt force trauma and contusions resulting from his recent vehicle crash. Cam's scan showed no such injuries. There are no contusions, no surface injuries, no damage of any kind. He seems to be in perfect health."

That was odd. Even Finn, who'd been genetically enhanced to help prevent injury and speed his healing, still had some evidence of past injuries. Repairs showed, no matter how good they were. "How is that possible?"

"I cannot answer that without a more conclusive scan," replied Otto.

"But you could guess," Tasha suggested.

"Yes, I could, but not with any accuracy. However, if you are asking me to guess—"

"We are," Finn said.

"He can't have avoided ever taking any damage," Otto shared. "Recent incidents are proof of that. I'd therefore suggest that, somehow, his body is capable of healing itself to such a degree that it leaves no evidence of any damage behind."

Finn thought about that. It was another item to add to his rapidly growing list of unlikely coincidences and abnormal events. First, there was the orbital station incursion. That was followed by the incident in Seattle. And then this. While neither of the two in the back had been able to identify their final pursuer, their description of the events left him with little doubt that they were dealing with the same aggressor. He didn't like it, not one bit.

"This stinks, Finn," Tasha announced. She must've been

thinking about the same thing he was.

"There you go reading my mind again, comrade," he said with a grin. "If you're not careful, Otto's going to be jealous."

She scoffed. "You are too easy. Small child could read your mind."

He laughed. "Good thing you like children so much." Finn enjoyed their camaraderie. It was one of the primary reasons he'd pushed the Protectorate to violate their SOP and let her join his team. Otherwise, he would've just wiped her memory and dumped her back in old Saint Petersburg. She was the first, and so far, only Prime human in service as a Protector, although her rank was strictly unofficial. But he'd never worked with anyone as effective as her, enhancements or no. Plus, he cared about her a great deal, as much as if she was a sister.

Finn remembered the one time they'd attempted to explore the possibility that they may be more than that to one another. It was an interesting failure. She was undeniably attractive in Finn's view. Although for Finn, that view was pretty broad, enough so that he'd been a popular intimate companion among many of his classmates at the Academy. But their efforts only resulted in one awkward night of slightly drunken sex that Tasha swore they were never to speak of again. In truth, one of the reasons they got along so well together is that neither of them was really the "settle down with a romantic partner" type. They were both strong, self-reliant, and tended to have poor luck with relationships that had romantic, emotional attachments.

"So, what is plan for these two?" she asked. "You do not want to bring them in?"

He shook his head. "I don't. There are too many unknowns

here, Tash. I think that what we were just dealing with has something to do with these two. Or at least, with one of them."

"So we bring them to Seattle. Then what?"

They'd just been in Seattle, starting their investigation into what happened to their missing agent, when they'd gotten the notification from Protectorate monitors about the unusual Gate activity. The fact that they'd discovered two people who could possibly be involved in what they'd just been investigating was too suspicious. "We heal the one who's injured, and then we wake them up. We need more information." He turned to look at his partner. "I don't like how this is unfolding. Every instinct I have is telling me that we're missing something vital here. Cam's got to be mixed up in everything that's been happening, somehow. At the very least, whoever it is that's been responsible for all our recent trouble seems to be very interested in him. That makes me interested in him. And I'm not ready to turn him over to the Protectorate so they can just sequester him in a safe house for debriefing and study. Then we'll never get any answers."

Tasha nodded begrudgingly. "Is risky strategy. But I agree, at least. If this is how you want to play it, then so be it. But, I am telling you, there will be trouble for breaking protocol."

He scoffed. "Maybe so, but when has getting in trouble ever stopped me from breaking protocol? Besides, I think this is big, Tash."

She eyed him warily. "I am not worried about consequences for you. You are hero. I am only sidekick. I worry about consequences for me."

"Don't start with that again. Nobody is going to wipe your memory. I don't care what they say."

141

Tasha scoffed. "I would threaten to hold you to that, but if I have no memory, how would I even find you?"

He laughed. "See, it's because of charming statements like those that people are afraid of you."

"Good," she said flatly. "I like people afraid of me."

It was an odd part of their dynamic that she was the scary one. But it suited her personality much better than Finn's. His upbringing focused on caring, cooperation, and service to the community for the greater good. He was something of an outlier, of course, and spent enough time around Prime humans that he could relate somewhat to their more selfish notions of self-reliance and personal satisfaction at the expense of others. Tasha was an outlier, too, and had risked her own personal safety many times for the greater good. But she was Russian, and Russians were good at scary.

"You may be interested to know," Otto announced, "that one of our guests has regained consciousness."

"Well, well," Finn said. "Thanks for the update, Otto."

"Is smart one, yes?" Tasha wondered. "Drug probably doesn't work as well on him."

<It appears that he is pretending to be unconscious>

<Otto, bring up the rear cabin lights, please> Finn asked silently.

The lights behind him brightened to their original level.

"You may as well stop pretending," Finn called into the back of the flyer. "You heard Otto, so you know we know you're awake." Finn undid his safety straps and stood up. He heard a low moan as he went back to the main cabin. "Don't try to talk yet. The paralytic takes a while before it completely wears off. Besides, we're just going to put you under again anyway."

He stopped in the space where their two guests lay. Tony was still completely out, but Cam had his eyes partially open. <Anything I should be aware of?>.

<According to my bio scans, his system has almost entirely metabolized both the sleeping and paralytic agents. He will be free of their effects shortly. A second dose should be sufficient to sedate him for the remainder of our journey>

Finn looked down at Cam as he reached into the med-pack sitting nearby and took out the injector. Cam's grogginess was dissipating and being replaced with fear or possibly anger. Otto could probably tell him for sure, but it didn't really matter. "Don't worry," he said softly. "It's only temporary. We'll wake you again once we've gotten to where we're going."

He saw Cam struggle weakly with the straps holding him down. Then he placed the injector against Cam's neck and activated it. There was a soft hiss, and Cam's eyes fluttered as he lost consciousness again. Finn examined his face once more. Something about it struck him as strangely familiar. <Why does he look like I should know him?>

<I have no data of you seeing him before today>

<That's not really an answer>

<His features and coloration suggest that he is of a familial origin similar to yours and are common among your people. Plus, I imagine you find him to be attractive>

Finn snorted. <You know what I find attractive?>

<Of course. I've seen everyone you've been intimate with>

He scoffed, then looked up toward the front of the craft. "Hey, Tash? Does he look familiar to you?"

"He looks like one of you," she called back.

Finn replaced the injector in the med-pack and returned

to his seat in the forward cabin. "I hadn't noticed that before. Otto just pointed it out to me." It would explain some things if it were true. The extraordinary healing abilities, for one. And the super metabolism. But that would mean that he was either lying about who he was and was able to fool Otto when doing it or that he didn't know who he really was. "Otto doesn't have him in his database, though, so he couldn't be one of us. But there is something about him." Tasha raised an eyebrow but kept her gaze on the controls. Finn rolled his eyes. "No, not that. I mean, the other stuff. His perfect health. Overcoming the paralytic. And the Gate."

Tasha nodded solemnly. "Yes, is definitely something."

The Gate anomaly they'd been sent to investigate was a rarely occurring temporary, trans-dimensional portal. Most of those portals, or Gates, as they were generally known, were either fixed and static or operated in cycles. The ones they knew about, at least. But this one had existed only for mere seconds, flashing on and off like a one-time strobe. At least the trans-dimensional designated location it led to was habitable and benign, if a little out of the way. They'd been lucky to be near a Gate that led there and that the Gate anomaly existed long enough for them to get a geo-fix. That was a lot more fortunate than he was used to for one rescue. "What are the odds that a Gate would appear right in their path, at the exact moment they needed it to escape?"

"The odds are–" Otto began.

Finn cut him off. "I meant that rhetorically, buddy."

Tasha looked over, thoughtfully. "You think he knew it would be there?"

Finn shrugged. "I don't know. If he did, then he's definitely hiding something from us."

"And if he did not," Tasha added, "then he is either luckiest bastard alive, or—"

Finn didn't like where that thought was leading. But it would do no good to deny it, so he finished her statement for her. "Or he can open Gates." Whatever the case was, they'd need some answers. And soon.

CAM

The first thing Cam tried to do was move his arms. He couldn't, at least not very much, but the straps were definitely gone. He opened his eyes and, after they adjusted to the light, saw that he was lying in a small room. He gingerly turned his head and inspected his surroundings. To his right, he could see a plywood-paneled wall painted light gray. To his left, in a folding chair, sat Finn, watching him. Cam tried to move his arm again but only managed to wiggle his fingers a little.

"It'll take a few minutes to wear off completely," Finn explained, "but once it does, you shouldn't feel any side effects. Can you speak?"

Cam worked his jaw muscles a little and felt them loosening up. He licked his lips, then tried to say something. "Fuck you." That felt nice.

Finn laughed. "See? You're almost as good as new." He shifted in the chair, leaning forward with his hands on his knees. "Now, I know you're pissed, and I get why you are. Hell, I'd be upset, too. But we needed to get you out of there and bring you someplace safe."

"Someplace that I can't know about, either, right?"

"Well, no, not exactly. It's complicated. But that's close enough for now."

Cam lifted his arms, stretching his fingers. Whatever they'd given him a double dose of was definitely wearing off. "And I'm supposed to be glad you went with the date rape drug instead of just shoving a bag over my head?"

Finn at least had the decency to look uncomfortable when he shrugged. "Yeah, well, I'm sorry about that, but, as I said, it's complicated. And normally, folks don't actually remember that part."

"Because you wipe their memories somehow."

Finn looked at him curiously. "Just how long were you awake?"

Long enough to score a point there, at least. "Does it matter? I'm at your safe house now, right? And I have no idea where here is."

"That's true enough." Finn stood up and walked toward a door on the far wall of the room. "Take a few minutes to get your bearings." He pointed back toward another door next to his chair. "There's a bathroom through there if you want to freshen up. We've also got food if you're hungry. Come out and join us when you're ready. We've got a lot to discuss." He smiled, then left.

Cam let out a frustrated breath, then flexed and stretched his body. At least Finn hadn't lied about the lack of side effects. He felt pretty good. Considering the way he'd been sleeping lately, he actually felt better than he had in days. But he wasn't thrilled to be waking up somewhere strange. He was even more annoyed with how he'd gotten there. Still, he couldn't bring himself to get angry. He was grateful to be someplace that was supposedly safe, even if it was only temporary. Maybe that was good enough for the time being. There'd been a lot of people trying to hurt him lately, but

Finn and Tasha had technically made good on their offer of help. And he was in a bed in a room with an open door, not a jail cell or a shallow grave. It would have to do.

The smell of salty, greasy food made Cam's stomach rumble. The last time he'd actually eaten was at breakfast before all the craziness happened, when, a day ago? At any rate, he was starving. He sat up and swung his feet around the edge of the bed. He didn't feel dizzy at all, so he stood up and went into the small but serviceable bathroom to relieve himself and freshen up. It felt utilitarian, like the plywood bedroom, as if he was in some sort of thrown-together emergency shelter. But it was clean and smelled faintly of some kind of unfortunately floral disinfectant. There were only a toilet and a sink in the bathroom, so he couldn't do much more than wash his face and hands. He checked himself out in the mirror and was surprised to discover that he looked none the worse for wear. Considering that he'd just been in a severe motorcycle crash, that was definitely good news.

Once he was done, he walked back through the spartan bedroom and out into an ample warehouse space. Giant LED pendants hung among rafters holding up a ceiling that was probably two or three stories high. His door was one of several along the nearby wall, each presumably leading to other utilitarian spaces like the one he'd woken up in. Hopefully, Tony was behind one of those doors. Stacks of large boxes and old crates lined the opposite wall, interspersed with pieces of mystery equipment covered in dusty tarps. It must not have been a heavily used space. A workbench covered with tools and equipment Cam didn't recognize sat in the center of the room. Next to the workbench was a seating area with a few mismatched chairs, along with a table and four folding chairs. Finn and Tasha sat at the table with a pile of Chinese takeout boxes stacked between them. When Tasha noticed him, she beckoned for him to come and join them.

Cam walked over to the table and took a seat next to her in an empty chair opposite Finn. "This all smells really good. Is any of it vegetarian?"

Finn nodded. "It's all vegetarian, actually." He pointed his chopsticks at each of the takeout boxes. "There's vegetable dumplings with sweet and sour sauce, tofu fried rice, Sichuan-fried green beans, vegetable fried rice, and vegetable spring rolls. There's also some brown rice and chow mein noodles. Dig in. I'm sure you're hungry."

Cam grabbed a plate and some chopsticks. "I'm fucking starving." His mouth watered as he started spooning contents of the different boxes onto his plate. When he picked up a heaping bite with his chopsticks and put it in his mouth, his eyes almost rolled back into his head. It was heavenly.

Tasha smiled at that. "Is good?"

He swallowed the bite he was chewing. "It's amazing." He picked up another bite. "Almost worth getting kidnapped for."

Tasha sighed. "You were not safe. Now you are safe." She fixed him with a firm gaze. "There is much you do not know."

Cam shrugged. "It doesn't look like I'm going anywhere. Maybe now you could explain it to me?"

"Yeah, we definitely owe you an explanation, eh?" Finn agreed, cutting in. He turned to Tasha. "If you don't mind, comrade, could you maybe give Cam and me some space to chat?"

She frowned, then put down her own chopsticks. "Fine, I will check on other one. Is past time for him to wake." She got up from her chair, walked over to one of the nearby doors, opened it, and headed through.

Finn grabbed a chunk of fried tofu from his plate. "The food is Tasha's way of apologizing, by the way," he explained before putting the tofu in his mouth.

Cam shrugged. "I've had worse apologies."

Finn chewed his food thoughtfully while he considered his reply. "You're taking this awfully well."

Cam used his chopsticks to spear one of the spring rolls. "You drugged and brought me to who knows where. But it's supposedly somewhere safe, and now you're feeding me. I don't really know that I'm in the position to push back much."

Finn grimaced. Cam must've been making him uncomfortable. That was too bad since he was definitely going easy on him. If Cam was honest, the discomfort on Finn's face actually made him even more handsome. But he wasn't ready to be that honest yet.

"I suppose that's true," Finn replied. "So, do you want to start, or should I?" Cam offered a wave of his spring roll, giving Finn the floor to speak. "Ok, the short version is that you've somehow found yourself as a subject of extreme interest, for lack of a better term, for a somewhat determined group of radicals. The fact that we stumbled upon you and your friend when we did is fortunate. We know very little about the people who are after you because, until very recently, they never operated out in the open like this. Since yesterday was a complete shit show, we made a judgment call to bring you both into protective custody. And, after I reported in earlier, my handler agreed that it was the right move." Cam tilted his head at the last part, and Finn continued. "But, you have questions."

He nodded. "Who are you?"

Finn looked thoughtful. Clearly, he was mulling over how much he wanted to share with Cam at that point. "Tasha and I work for a government agency that's responsible for dealing with situations like this one."

That was basically a non-answer. "Ok, if you won't tell me who you are, can you at least tell me who this group of radicals is?"

"We don't know."

Cam scowled. "Jesus. Fine, then who do you think they are?"

"Some of that info I can't share, but, again, we really don't know." Cam was about to protest, but Finn held up his hand to stop him. "We think they may be operatives of a shadow group that we've been hearing about but haven't been able to pin down. Over the past few days, though, we've seen at least two other incidents that are almost certainly related to what happened to you yesterday."

Cam's eyes went wide. "Wow. That was really yesterday?"

Finn nodded. "Yeah. You were only out for around 12 hours."

"It feels like it was so long ago." Cam looked around, curious. Things were so calm and quiet there. It was a welcome change of pace from recent events. "And this place is some sort of safe house?"

Finn smiled. "Yeah. It's not very pretty, but it's safe enough. And the whole building is shielded, so they won't be able to track you here. Hopefully."

"That's handy because they've been remarkably good at

tracking me down so far. Plus, there's takeout." Cam ate another bite of food. "So what about all that weird shit I told you about, like the magical portal to Fantasy Land?"

Finn reacted ever so slightly when Cam said portal. That was interesting.

"I don't have any good answers for those questions, but that's part of the reason I wanted to talk to you." He hesitated. "How much do you know about quantum physics and multiverse theory?

Cam laughed. "Enough to hold my own in a dinner party conversation, I suppose." That made Finn chuckle. Cam was surprised he actually found Finn to be kinda charming. Maybe he was feeling a touch of Stockholm syndrome.

"Well, the quick and dirty version," Finn began, "is that, somehow, you and your friend transited through a temporary inter-dimensional portal into a different universe."

Ok. That was not at all what Cam expected to hear. But if he was honest with himself, which was still open to debate, Cam hadn't really known what to expect as an explanation for what happened. At least Finn's answer was direct. "You're kidding, right? That's not a real thing."

Finn shrugged. "Nope. It really is."

"So, then your government agency does, what? Handles situations where people encounter one of those temporary inter-dimensional portals?"

He nodded. "Yep. We monitor and regulate any and all traffic between different parts of the known multiverse."

The known multiverse? Much like it had the previous day, Cam's reality took another weird science-fiction turn. Hopefully, his day wouldn't end in alien death rays like before. "Ok, but really? Inter-dimensional portals? The known multiverse? I mean, come on. If all that's true, why doesn't everyone know about it?"

Finn grinned. "Because it's a secret, of course. But I know about it. And now, you do, too."

Cam set his chopsticks down. His understanding of coding and tech was reasonably high, but his theoretical physics knowledge wasn't worth shit. He understood the idea of the multiverse. Hell, he'd seen plenty of examples of it in comics, movies, and video games. But to sit there and be told that not only was it all real, but that he'd actually traveled to a different reality? It was hard for him to wrap his head around. "I mean, this is some science-fiction level shit, Finn. Like, if we can travel between different—what, dimensions? If I can accidentally stumble on some portal between two different universes, why doesn't it happen all the time?"

Finn shrugged. "It does happen, although maybe not all the time. But that's partly why our agency exists. We help those who stumble through those inter-dimensional portals, which we call Gates, and we keep it all secret. But what happened to you? Well, that was actually something new. You see, the Gates are all pretty much mapped out. We know where they are and where they lead, and we've done a pretty good job of discouraging people from finding them. But the Gate you traveled through didn't exist until right before you went through it. And then it stopped existing again—as in temporary. It was highly unusual. Gates generally don't work like that."

Cam tried to sort through his memories of what happened. But, as he'd said to Tony, they almost felt second-hand, as if he'd watched them happening to someone else. And, if what he'd just been told was true, then Cam was looking at something beyond having a few hidden talents for controlled mayhem. Having a sudden and previously unknown expertise with firearms was one thing. But this was different. He knew that he had something to do with the Gate. He could feel it deep in his bones. And he'd have to travel down that rocky mental road at some point. But he wasn't ready to admit what he knew just yet–not to himself, and, charming or not, certainly not to Finn. "You know, from my point of view, this whole situation is highly unusual."

Finn chuckled. "Yeah, I'd imagine that's what it seems like."

Cam still wasn't getting his questions answered, though. In fact, he had more questions than he'd started with. Tony had jokingly accused him of being an alien. If parallel universes existed, who's to say that aliens didn't, too? That couldn't be true. There'd been plenty of chances for him to discover that he wasn't actually human. Unless there was some grand conspiracy to hide his true nature from him–one that his parents, his doctors, and whatever company he'd sent his DNA to were in on? No, there had to be another explanation. Something about him was definitely different. He couldn't deny that. But he still didn't know what it was. "Ok, let's say I accept what you're saying is true. Then what?"

"Well, that's what we need to figure out. Do you have any idea why those people are interested in you?"

Cam shook his head. "Believe me, I wish I did. It's not like I haven't been thinking about it. I mean, I suppose it's possible I have an angry client. But it feels like a client would just sue me, not drop some fanatical motorcycle ninja on my ass."

Finn laughed. "No, that's generally not a standard business practice. Tell me–you do some sort of tech consulting, right?"

Cam nodded. "Yeah, I'm kind of a jack of all trades when it comes to programming and tech. I code things, build things, and fix things. Like, the day before yesterday, I'd just finished a consulting gig on a biotech company's data security. Their head of network security wasn't thrilled with me, but I don't think he'd go full-on violent retribution over it."

Finn looked at him skeptically. "What kind of things do you build, exactly?"

"If you let me have my bag back, I can show you."

Finn nodded, then got up from the table and went behind the workbench area. He emerged a moment later, carrying Cam's messenger bag. "We checked it for weapons and trackers, but otherwise, your stuff is all here. Except for the gun, of course. Here you go." He handed the bag to Cam. "Where did you manage to pick up a Chinese copy of a Haas Dominator, by the way?"

Cam cleared a spot on the table so he could set the bag down on it. "I took it off one of the mercenaries who was chasing me yesterday. I figured it would come in handy. Which it did." He reached inside and pulled out his damaged handheld. "Here. I built this."

Finn took it and looked it over curiously. "You built your own phone?"

Cam gave him a furtive smile. "It only looks like a phone, but it's so much more. I gave it some significant upgrades–faster processor, more memory, an ultra-wideband transmitter and receiver, signal detector, inertial navigation–stuff like that. It's pretty handy when it actually works."

That seemed to impress Finn. "Wow. I gotta say, that's pretty cool. I'm surprised that you managed to cram all that in there."

Cam grinned. He loved talking about that stuff. "I had to custom print most of the fittings, and a lot of the tech was special-order stuff." He thought about his workshop and what the goon squad probably did when they visited it. Between that and his apartment, he probably had another huge mess to deal with when this was all over.

Finn looked at him thoughtfully. "But this is what you mean when you say you build stuff? You're not selling EMPs or things like that."

Cam looked at him with amusement. "Nope. If you were hoping I was a black-market arms dealer, sorry to disappoint you."

Finn chuckled. "Yeah, I guess that would've been too easy. Then your security work doesn't require you to be armed?"

Cam rolled his eyes. "It's data security. Firewalls, anti-hacking, that sort of thing. Before yesterday, I'd never held a gun outside of a video game."

Finn looked surprised. "You could've fooled me. I saw the news footage. Seemed like you knew what you were doing."

"Yeah, well, that was one of yesterday's many surprises. And it wasn't even the biggest one. Like, what the hell was the–" he tried to think of a better term than the one Tony used but failed, "–alien death ray?"

Finn laughed. "Alien death ray? Oh, I'm so going to call it that from now on. Tash will absolutely hate it. But, officially, it's a type of particle accelerator. Have you heard of coil guns?" Cam nodded. He was a gamer, after all. "They're sort of related. A coil gun uses an electromagnetic field to accelerate solid projectiles to high velocity. A particle accelerator uses more advanced field manipulation to gather and accelerate a mass of highly charged particles. Depending on the available power, they can do anything from stunning someone to burning a hole through an armored plate."

"See, that's the science-fiction shit I was talking about. I mean, that motorcycle rider was shooting at us with their fist." Cam made his own fist to demonstrate. "The kind of energy you'd need for a weapon like that would have to be massive. Even a coil gun is too big for someone to just carry around, and they didn't have anything like that with them on their motorcycle. So, how does that kind of thing even exist in the real world?"

Finn looked pensive for a moment. "The technology exists, obviously, to build it into, say, an armored suit. You saw it yourself. But it's rare. For someone outside of our agency to possess it is, well, troubling, to say the least."

So, no denial, then. But it still wasn't much of an explanation, either–just some high-level concepts and sci-fi buzzwords. Once again, Cam found himself with more questions than answers. And, Finn clearly knew more than he was letting on. "You know, if you want me to trust you, then you're gonna need to show me a little trust, too. I get that your job is to keep these things secret, but that cat's pretty much out of the bag, right?"

Finn looked at him for a moment, but Cam couldn't read him well enough to know what he was thinking. Before he could say anything, though, Tony's voice interrupted the moment. "Oh my god, is that food? I'm so hungry I could eat my fucking shoe." He came rambling over to the table, grabbed a plate, and sat down next to Cam. Tony gave him a quick smile as he started to pile food on his plate. "Glad to see you're up and about already. What did I miss?"

Finn laughed. "The way to a man's heart, right, Tony?" He looked at Cam again, smiling. "I hear you, Cam. And you're right. This is stuff we're supposed to keep secret. But you do need to know more. Look, just let me talk to Tasha for a bit, first. Ok?"

Finn excused himself to quietly confer with Tasha as they stood nearby, which left Cam to give Tony a quick rundown of the situation. To his credit, Tony seemed to take it all in stride. He even held most of his questions until Cam was finished.

"So lemme get this straight," Tony said between mouthfuls. "When we crashed my bike, we were in some alternate universe?"

Cam nodded. "That's what it looks like, yeah."

"Ok, wow." Tony considered that for a moment. He clearly had a million more questions rattling around in his head. "I guess I was way off then with my time travel theory. At least there weren't any dinosaurs to worry about." He took another bite, thinking while he chewed, then stopped suddenly. "Wait! Do you think there might be evil alternate versions of us out there, with goatees, like they always do on TV?"

Cam laughed. Leave it to Tony to put things into perspective. "I don't know." He rubbed his chin. "I mean, it would have to be an alternate universe for me to even grow a decent goatee. But you haven't considered the possibility that we're actually the evil ones."

Tony chuckled. "Shit, no way, man. If we were the evil ones, there definitely wouldn't be any take-out Chinese." He looked around the warehouse space. "Where are we anyway?"

"I don't know. They haven't told me yet. Hey, how's your leg feeling?"

Tony looked surprised. "Shit, I totally forgot about that." He leaned back and flexed it, showing no outward signs of pain and discomfort. "It feels great. I guess it must not have been that bad."

Cam frowned. "I don't know. It looked like you couldn't even walk on it. I thought it was at least a fracture."

Tony shrugged. "I guess not. Unless our kidnappers also have super healing abilities." He was about to take another mouthful of food, then stopped. "Hell, they probably do, right? They've got inter-dimensional portals and shit."

Cam nodded. That was probably true. If powerful particle beam cannons could be built into flexible armor suits, perhaps there was also a way to heal a fractured leg overnight. He shrugged and reached for a fortune cookie, then cracked it open. He popped a piece into his mouth while he checked to see what the little strip of paper inside had to say about his future. *Sometimes the best choices are the least obvious ones.* That wasn't exactly helpful. Cam flipped it over to see what was written on the reverse side. *Golden Flower Chinese Restaurant, International District, Seattle, WA.* That was way more helpful. He tapped Tony on the shoulder and showed it to him. Tony's eyes went wide with surprise.

"No way," Tony gushed, getting the attention of Finn and Tasha. "We're in Seattle?"

Cam rolled his eyes at his friend's lack of subtlety. "Nice going, genius."

Finn looked over and smiled, shaking his head. "That wasn't meant to be a secret, actually. But, out of curiosity, how did you figure it out?" Cam showed him the fortune from his cookie. Finn shot a glance at Tasha, who just shrugged.

"You say to get food," she said unapologetically, "so I get food. There was no instruction to get secret food."

Finn chuckled. "We really need to talk about your information security, Tash. I'm glad this wasn't a covert assignment." Finn took a seat at the table opposite Cam and Tony. "Still, as I said, it's not supposed to be a secret from you guys. We'd rather that the people following you didn't figure it where you are. At least, not until we're ready for them."

Cam raised an eyebrow. A statement like that could only mean one thing. "You want to lure them out of hiding somehow?"

Finn nodded. "There's a reason we're here in Seattle. There was an incident here before yesterday's fun fest. An agent was sent here to track down some unusual Gate activity, but we lost contact with him. Unfortunately, once we got here, we found out that he'd been killed. Before he went offline, the last we heard from him was that he was tailing a pair of suspicious individuals through the Market. We'd intended to investigate that before, well, you know the rest."

"What's the market?" Tony asked.

"Pike Place Market," Cam replied. Something about what Finn said seemed strangely familiar to him. That was happening more and more, too, like some kind of menacing deja vu. He recalled the feeling from when he'd first encountered the Boss, even though it was unlikely that they'd ever previously met. Cam had been to the Market before, of course. You couldn't grow up in Seattle and not visit Pike Place at least once. But the feeling was different than just an old memory. It was like he'd been there recently.

He couldn't explain how that would be possible since he hadn't been there for at least a decade.

Then there was the fact that whatever Finn and Tasha were investigating happened in Seattle, where he'd grown up. You didn't have to watch very many spy thrillers to see that it probably wasn't a coincidence for an incident in Seattle to lead the Boss and his hit squad down to his doorstep in San Francisco. But that still didn't answer any of his questions. It was just one more implausible thing that happened. And, considering all that he'd been through the previous day, it hardly rated at all.

He noticed everyone was looking at him. "What?"

"You were doing that thing you do," Tony explained, "where you think so hard people can almost hear it."

"He would not be good poker player," Tasha agreed.

Finn looked curious. Or concerned. Maybe both. "What is it, Cam?"

"I don't know. It's just, I'm actually from Seattle, right? I mean, I grew up here before I moved to San Francisco, at any rate. It feels like an unlikely coincidence for something to happen here, is all." Finn raised an eyebrow at that. "But, why the Market, though?" There was that feeling again, like he was on the verge of remembering something that was just out of reach. He considered what he wanted to say next. "Because what you said about your agent and the Market seems strangely familiar to me–almost like deja vu, you know?"

Finn seemed to understand. "Well, something about it will definitely seem familiar." He reached into a pocket and pulled out a slim, dark-gray disc about a hand's width in diameter and two or three centimeters thick. He set it on the table in the middle of everyone, then tapped the top of it. A circle of tiny lights appeared in the rim near the top edge, then a holographic image of a crowded marketplace materialized, floating in the air above it. Finn used a few fluid hand gestures to rotate it, zoom in on two people, then zoom in again on one of those people. Cam's heart immediately sank when he saw the face projected there.

Of course, Tony was too shocked by the display tech to notice what it was actually showing them. "Holy shit, is that, like, a real holographic projector?"

"Tony," Cam said patiently. "Look at the face."

It was the Boss.

"Oh, shit." Tony got it.

Finn nodded. "So, you can imagine our surprise when he showed up on the news in San Francisco the very next day. It seems pretty clear that whatever happened here involves you somehow."

Something about the whole scene kept tickling at Cam's mind, just underneath the level of conscious awareness. But the more he tried to remember it, the more it slipped away. It was like when you forget a word, but thinking about it just made it harder to remember. He pushed the thought away. "But who is he, though? Because he definitely knows who I am. He called me by name."

Finn looked up at Tasha, who'd been standing quietly behind with her arms crossed. "He is Tomás Aguilar," she explained. "Originally from Chilé. Former intelligence operative before becoming freelance radical, as best we can tell. He used to work as contractor for different intelligence agencies and criminal gangs before disappearing five years ago. Until he showed up again day before yesterday."

Tony seemed impressed. "Wicked," he said breathlessly, then looked at Cam. "Dude, whatever you did, you're sure drawing some serious heat."

"Indeed," Tasha confirmed. "He is very dangerous individual."

It certainly helped explain how he could access the kind of resources he was flaunting the day before, especially the band of armed mercenaries tagging along with him. But it still didn't explain what he wanted from Cam badly enough to chase him around the city. He looked back at the holographic image of his face, that troublesome thought still scratching for his attention. Was there something else there? "He's talking to someone, right? Can I see who that is?"

Finn reached forward and rotated the image around, zooming in on a ghostly pale, hauntingly beautiful face with a short, blonde haircut in a practical but fashionable style.

Cam leaned in toward the projection, then sat back again. "Can you zoom out a little?" Finn obliged him, pulling the image back to show that they were wearing a nice raincoat and loose, flowing, white pants covered with a delicate blue floral pattern. Where had he seen those before? Cam searched his memories but came up with nothing. It reminded him of the dreams he'd been having recently and of trying to recall them the next day.

As soon as he thought of the dreams, something clicked into place. A sudden series of images assaulted him, flashing madly in his head. A crowded outdoor marketplace. An ancient fountain in front of an old hotel. A rooftop fight. A data crystal. His dream. Cam doubled over. The strength of his recall was almost painful—as if his memories were breaking through some kind of barrier.

Tony was off his seat in an instant, putting his arm around Cam. "Hey, dude. You ok?"

Cam nodded as he regained control of his faculties. His memory of the dream was suddenly as clear as if it had just happened. He took a deep breath, forcing himself to calm down. "Yeah, yeah, I'm good. I just remembered a dream from the other night. Only, I guess it wasn't actually a dream after all."

Finn had that curious but concerned look again. "What do you mean?"

Cam took another breath, recalling details from the dream, and waved his hand toward the holographic image. "Where this all happened–is there an old hotel nearby, next to a plaza with an old fountain in the middle of it?"

Finn and Tasha looked at each other and did that thing where they had a conversation with just their eyes. Finn nodded, then gestured at the projection again, pulling back on the zoom, then shifting the focus away from the two people. It was there. The plaza. The fountain. The hotel. Everything. "You saw all this?"

Cam nodded. It was strange viewing it from the image angle. He recalled seeing it through someone's perspective like he'd been watching from inside their head. He could even remember the noise and the smells. He reached out and tried to mimic Finn's gestures, rotating the view and zooming in until it was back on Aguilar's face. Then he slowly pulled the focus back until he saw what he was looking for. "Yeah, that's definitely what I saw in my dream."

Finn looked at him determinedly. "Really? Ok. Tell us everything you saw. You may be our only witness to what actually happened out there."

Cam related the events from his dream–or not dream, as it turned out–from the initial meet-up to the fight on the roof to the data crystal. Finn, Tasha, and Tony listened intently. When Cam was done, Finn excitedly turned to Tasha. "See, I knew it. I knew she had to be their Agent." He gestured to Cam. "Now, we have proof."

She shook her head. "What proof? He said himself, this is all dream. Is not enough. Not actionable."

Finn wasn't letting it go, though. "Ok, maybe it's not enough to take back to them, yet. But it's enough for us."

She shook her head again. "Every time you go off mission–"

"I'm telling you, it was her," Cam interrupted. "She's the one who took out your agent and got the data."

"You're sure?" Finn fixed him with a gaze. "I need you to be sure."

Cam nodded. "I'm positive. I never saw her face, but I recognize everything else, including Tomás. But it's more than what she saw. I remember how she felt, what she was thinking. It was definitely her." He looked back up from the projection. "So you think that whatever she picked up here somehow led her to me?"

"It sounds like you might know that better than we would. But it sure seems likely, doesn't it?" Finn wondered. "Of course, there's only one way to be sure."

Cam thought he knew the answer to his next question already, but he asked anyway. "And what's that?"

"We have to go back to the Market."

Cam didn't like the sound of that. It was a significant risk, considering recent events. "You said this all happened days ago. What's left for us to find?"

Finn thought about his answer for a few moments. "Well, our scanning tech is pretty sophisticated. You'd be surprised at the kind of evidence that can get left behind. But that's only part of the reason we'd go."

Of course, there was another reason, and Cam knew what it would be. There was only one thing they had that was likely to draw the attention of his murderous fan club.

Tony also worked it out. "You want to draw them out." He pointed at Cam. "And he's your bait."

Cam frowned. So much for safe and sound. "That's what she meant by going off-mission, isn't it? You want to dangle me out in front of Tomás and this Agent, the Mistress of Evil, after going to all this trouble hiding me from them?"

Tony chuckled. "Mistress of Evil. That's priceless."

Finn ignored that. "It's not ideal, I'll give you that. But time is not on our side here, Cam. The longer it takes us to find them, the more damage they'll be able to do." He fixed Cam with a gaze. "The more people that will get hurt."

That one hit home. While Cam and Tony managed to escape everything so far relatively unscathed, there was no telling how long things would stay that way. Cam thought about the other drivers on the highway during their motorcycle chase and the people he'd shot in Union Square. That wasn't taking into account Tony's family, who were probably still at risk, too. And that was all on Cam's shoulders, somehow. Tony's presence certainly was since he was the one Cam asked for help. And it was pure luck that had gotten them through it all alive and unscathed.

Whatever was holding his anger back finally dissolved, and Cam shot up from the table. "You know what? Fuck you. I didn't ask to get chased by a bunch of homicidal maniacs. I didn't ask to get rescued by the Mystery Adventure Team. I didn't ask for any of this. And now you want me to go back out there with a big fucking target on my back and the threat that, if I don't go, people are gonna get hurt? Hell. No."

Cam stormed off, looking for a door, a window, or any other way to get out of that place. When he finally found a door that led outside, he was unsurprised to discover that it was locked. Frustrated, Cam kicked it. Then he turned, leaned up against the wall, and slid down onto the floor, unable to escape and with nowhere to go even if he could. He sulked for a few minutes, but he really just wanted to be alone. It was a trauma response he'd learned at some point. When his parents fought with one another or violently punished him for something, he knew that the trouble was over, if only temporarily, once he was alone in his room. He thought about how he'd confidently marched through the streets of San Francisco like an action hero, down to the blink of an eye shootout in the middle of Union Square. Where had that confidence gone? How could he get it back?

Eventually, he heard the sound of approaching footsteps and then saw Tasha's backlit silhouette approaching him. He sighed. "Did Finn send you over here to play bad cop?

"I am not cop," Tasha answered dryly. "But if I was one, I would definitely be bad." Cam looked at her as she came to stand over him but said nothing. After a few moments, she broke the silence. "I don't blame you for being mad. I am mad, too. Situation is unfortunate."

Cam sighed. He didn't know her game, but she definitely wasn't playing the bad cop. "This is a lot of shit to process," he finally said.

"I know how it feels, believe me. Before Finn first found

me, I was walking alone in woods outside of St. Petersburg when I stumbled through Gate. I was in strange place I didn't recognize and didn't know how to get home. And then real trouble happened. Before Finn came to rescue me, I fought off huge Siberian fucking tiger. He was so impressed, instead of wiping my memory and sending me home, he asked if I wanted job."

"You fought off an extinct animal?"

She grunted. "It may have just been large cougar or mountain lion. But it was different universe, different Earth. Maybe Siberian tigers are not extinct there?"

Cam chuckled. "Ok, maybe."

She crouched down in front of him, her ordinarily taciturn expression softened with concern. "I know you think you have no reason to trust us. But we did rescue you, and we have not tried to kill you. Yet." She paused, holding his gaze with her own. He could see the good humor in her ice-blue eyes. "Finn is good guy. I trust him with my life. You should give him chance to help you, too."

Finn told him he wanted to help them find some answers. Maybe she was right. What more did he really have to lose? "Ok. But the minute you try to kill me, I'm out of here."

Tasha nodded, smirking. "Is deal. Now come back. We have plans to make." Then she stood and walked back toward the group. Cam took a moment to compose himself before he got up and followed her.

CAM

Even though he hadn't been there in more than a decade, the dream memories made it feel like he'd been to Pike Place Market a day ago. Just being in Seattle at all filled him with a strange nostalgia for his old hometown, too. Except for the occasional revenge fantasy of a trip back to confront his parents, he never really thought about returning. But standing there at the edge of the old marketplace, breathing wet, chilled air filled with the odors of fish, food, and the dark waters of Puget Sound, it all seemed comfortingly familiar. It was disconcerting, to say the least.

The group's plan was simple. Once he'd discussed it with Finn and the group, Cam felt his exposure level was manageable, if not ideal. The ideal would've been staying hidden in the ersatz safe house the whole time. But that would get him no further toward figuring out what was going on, and he really didn't want to spend the rest of his life in hiding. That wasn't his style. Plus, Finn promised to keep him as safe as he could. That wasn't totally reassuring, but it was a nice gesture. So Cam watched the crowds of buttoned-up tourists milling about like a flock of seagulls circling a pile of bread crumbs, mindful of any possible threats, while he looked for landmarks that he remembered from the dream.

Phase one of the plan had the group traveling downtown from the SODO warehouse, which served as their safe house and unofficial base. They drove from there in a newish, dark-green Yamoto Vagabond four-by-four that they'd stashed nearby. The truck had plenty of room for all of them, along with several duffel bags of undisclosed gear that Tasha and Finn loaded into the back.

As they drove along, Cam found himself surprised at how much the city changed since he'd moved away. At least a dozen new, gleaming glass towers had sprouted up to join the growing skyline. There were signs of new wealth everywhere–even in the seedier parts of Pioneer Square they drove through, heading north toward downtown and the central waterfront. There were also numerous signs of the growing income disparity that all the new wealth unleashed on the city's more impoverished denizens. Groups of street dwellers mingled among the tourists and residents of the neighborhood's newly gentrified, luxury condos. And the streets were fenced in by a wall of high-end Japanese and European luxury cars parked along the curb. In a lot of ways, it felt just like riding around the streets of San Francisco.

Tony loved it, though. He'd never been to Seattle before. In fact, Tony confessed that he'd never even been outside of California. Cam tried to imagine how the city would look to a first-timer, thinking back to his own, wide-eyed self as he first strolled the sidewalks of his adopted home. He ended up playing tour guide during the ride over, pointing out the places that he knew and sharing whatever trivia he could halfway remember. It was a strange period of normality on an otherwise bizarre day.

They eventually found a parking spot in a surface lot near

the Market. When Cam got out of the Vagabond, the first thing he noticed was the missing, double-decker, elevated highway that once cut the city off from the waterfront. The whole area seemed so much more open and inviting than how he remembered it. After a short walk, they found a long stairway that wound up the steep incline from the waterfront to the market, where it sat on the edge of downtown. At the top of the stairs, they took a walkway crowded with shoppers and tourists under a high, arched ceiling, past the famous Seattle gum wall, to the Market itself.

Phase two of the plan involved following the trail of events as Cam recounted them from his dream. Tony asked why they couldn't just go right to the plaza with the fountain, but Finn wanted them to scout the whole market to look for anything helpful they could detect. So they first stopped outside the covered area of the marketplace where Cam could get his bearings before leading them inside. Nothing was ringing any bells for him, though. At least half a dozen flower vendors were visible from his vantage point, mixed in amongst the stalls offering everything from trinkets to organic produce. And fresh fish, of course. While Cam scoped out their general surroundings, Tony spent a rapturous few minutes watching the famous market stall where the workers tossed giant fish around like they were playthings.

"I can't tell which flower stall it was yet," Cam finally announced to the group. "We should head in and start walking down toward the other end."

Finn nodded. "Okay. Everyone stay sharp and keep an eye out for trouble."

Cam led them across the brick-paved street and into the

covered section of the market. The boisterous crowd grew more difficult to navigate once they were in closer quarters under the roof. The first few flower vendors they passed weren't familiar. Cam wondered if the vendors had shifted positions in the intervening days or if the one he was looking for was even there. He recalled the vendor's face from his dream—a masculine face, wrinkled with age, possibly of Latino or Indigenous ethnicity. His memories from the dream were strange. The images sat in his mind like his own memories, fresh and clear, even though they were things he'd never experienced himself. He spotted another flower stall ahead. The vendor had their back turned, but they already felt familiar. Cam just needed to see their face.

Cam approached the stall. "Excuse me."

The flower vendor turned to Cam and smiled, the thick curtain of wrinkles on their russet face spreading wide. It was the vendor from the dream. "Hello there! Are you looking for anything in particular?"

Cam felt like screaming but smiled and nodded instead. "Uh, yeah, my friend was here a couple days ago. He picked up some lilies, and I wanted to get some for myself, but he couldn't remember who he'd gotten them from."

The vendor frowned. "Oh, I'm afraid lilies are out of season now, so they'll be hard to find. I don't have any, unfortunately, but perhaps one of the other flower vendors may still have some."

Cam feigned a look of disappointment. "Ah, that's too bad. I'll keep looking, I guess. Thanks." He turned back to the group. "This is the one," he said quietly, then pointed to his right. "From here, they walked that way."

"Yeah," Finn replied as he stared at the screen of a handheld scanner disguised as a phone. "I'm picking up some faint readings. Someone who's traveled through a Gate has been through here within the past couple of days." Finn had explained earlier that Gate travel often left behind residual traces of exotic matter that could be detected with the proper scanning tech. It wasn't anything harmful, he assured them. He even demonstrated that with the readings he got from scanning them. But there was often enough left behind to pick up on an otherwise cold trail.

"Ok," Cam agreed. "Do we keep moving?"

Finn looked at Tasha, who nodded yes. She'd been tasked with watching the crowd for signs of trouble. So far, she seemed to have found none. "Yes," she said. "Keep going."

Cam continued on through the Market, leading them through the rows of stalls as he pushed back on the weird sense of deja vu he was still feeling. He navigated through the crowd almost on autopilot as he struggled to keep himself present. Part of him kept thinking about what the Agent found in his dream. He remembered her certainty that whatever data she'd found on that crystal was important. But how did it relate to him? Had it contained any key that would help him unlock the mystery of his origins? But those thoughts were distracting him, so he put a lid on them and pushed his focus back to what he was doing.

He saw the end of the stalls ahead. The plaza would be just beyond that. Glancing around, he found the jewelry vendor from the dream where the woman identified her tail. He pointed to it. "That's where she spotted your agent. The hotel plaza is close."

Finn nodded. "I'm still picking up trace readings, so we're definitely on the trail."

"There is no sign of trouble yet," Tasha added.

Tony, who had been silent since they got to the Market, finally piped up. "Dude, this place is so cool. I wish we could check out that comic book shop we passed earlier."

"Sorry, man," Cam offered. "I wish we could."

"I know," Tony agreed sullenly. "To be honest, this is kind of what I imagined your job to be like. Doing all this sneaking around and stuff. You know, spy shit."

Cam laughed. He remembered his recent foray into the Bridgespan Biotech building's secure areas and Tony's surprise phone call while he was locking off all of Bridgespan's data. "Yeah, well, Jack Sterling, super spy's got nothing on Mad Dog and Tiger, right?"

Tony put his hands together to mock holding a gun, mimicking Sterling's signature pose from his movies' opening titles. "Dun, duh-dun-dun," he sang, improvising the familiar theme music. They both laughed, then quickly stopped when Tasha flashed them a dramatic scowl.

Duly chastened, Cam led the group out onto the plaza. Familiarity flooded through him as he stood where the Agent had. He felt himself looking through her eyes again. The hotel, which turned out to be The Pike Place Inn, was just ahead. He continued forward, leading them past the fountain. The plaza was reasonably crowded. Parents sat and watched their children playing while couples held hands and strolled next to the rising waters. Workers from nearby offices sat and ate their midday meals while buskers and street people called out to passersby to donate whatever they could spare. It was one of those engaging slice-of-life moments often found in large public spaces. And yet, everyone seemed blissfully unaware of the tragic murder that occurred nearby just two days earlier. They probably didn't even realize what the cones and police tape marking off a spot near the hotel were for.

As Cam watched everyone, a memory floated to the surface of his mind, unbidden. He was a young child, maybe five or six years old, and his mother held his hand as they walked through that same plaza. It had been set up as a festival or carnival, with temporary booths and games scattered around. Cam wanted a funnel cake, and his parents were not so quietly arguing amongst themselves about whether or not to buy one for him. In an uncharacteristic fit of generosity, his mother agreed to get one for each of them. His father, ever the pragmatist, had forbidden it, insisting that Cam didn't deserve one after having broken one or more of his parent's arbitrary and punitive rules that morning. But then his father left them alone to find a restroom, his sensitive stomach protesting against something he'd eaten earlier. Once they were alone, his mother took him right to the funnel cake booth and bought one for them to share. She gleefully made him promise not to say a word to his father. His father had known, of course. No amount of secret-keeping would overcome the powdered sugar sprinkled all over his face and clothes. But his father never said anything about it. It was a strangely pleasant memory. Cam hadn't thought about it in years.

He smiled wistfully, then turned his attention back toward the crowd. It was hard to pick up much detail. There were just too many people milling about. So Cam let his focus drift a bit, following the crowd's ebb and flow until the patterns started to emerge. Knots of people stood together in various spots around him, like shoals in a shallow river. Walkers flowed around them like eddies, sending ripples of movement through the crowd only to break on nearby clusters or objects. At that level, the localized chaos expanded into the smooth flow of constant motion. Then he caught a sudden disturbance at the edge of his vision. He looked toward it, but whatever movement he'd noticed was immediately lost in the chaos. It was enough to raise his hackles, though. "Something's wrong," Cam said bluntly.

Finn's casual demeanor disappeared. "What do you see?"

"Nothing, yet. But something's happening. I can feel it."

"He can feel it?" Tasha mused. But even she'd assumed a more defensive stance.

Finn glanced back down to his handheld device. "I'm not picking up anything new." Then he looked back up, carefully surveying the plaza and the unconcerned crowd. "But he's right. Something feels off."

"Shit," Tony muttered under his breath. "Here we go."

Cam shot a look back to his friend, partly to reassure him and partly to shut him up.

Finn just ignored him. "Tasha, maybe we—Shit!"

To an innocent bystander, everything would've seemed to happen at once. But to Cam, it all played out clearly, as the familiar sensation of intense focus suddenly slammed down on him, slowing the apparent flow of time around him to a virtual crawl.

A surprised cry broke out from the crowd as a young person pushing a stroller was suddenly shoved out of the way. Then an energy blast shot out from behind the stroller, aimed directly at where Cam had been standing, but Cam was already jumping backward out of its fiery path.

Finn raised his forearm at that same moment, and a hazy

176

curtain of blue light crackled into existence as a protective barrier between him and the shooter. The energy bolt slammed into that glowing curtain of light like it was a concrete wall, dissipating away from the point of impact in angry splashes of blue and white light. It was some kind of energy shield, Cam realized. He really had to get himself one of those.

Quickly dropping back into a combat stance, Finn braced himself as several more energy bolts smashed against his shield, which held steady. But the blasts pushed him back a few inches each time one struck. He dug his heels in, ready for the next barrage. "Tasha, get them out of here!" he called out. "It's too crowded. It'll be a slaughterhouse."

Tasha grunted in confirmation, grabbed Tony, then Cam, and pulled them both back toward her. "Come. Is not safe for you here. We go back to truck now." Cam noticed that she was already holding a handgun and wished that he had one of his own. While they'd discussed returning the Dominator taken from his bag, they'd ultimately decided against it. Although Cam already demonstrated his prowess with the Haas multiple times, having it made him too much of a liability, especially since he'd been on the evening news once already. Tasha pointed her two charges in the direction they'd come from. "Go back through Market!"

Cam nodded, his face serious. He grabbed Tony by the shoulder and pulled him toward the covered marketplace. It wouldn't be easy to run through there, as crowded as it was, but it presented many more places to hide or take cover than where they were. Tasha hurried along behind them, her gun held low and ready. The crowd in the plaza was already rushing around in multiple directions as people panicked and screamed.

Finn's assailant continued to fire blast after blast at his shield. Cam risked a quick look back, and he saw her. It was the Agent. Her shock of short blond hair stood at loose attention atop her head. Her elegant features were molded into a rictus of anger. It must've been her on the motorcycle, Cam realized, seeing her dressed in the same black combat armor that she'd worn on the Panther, minus the bright red helmet. He leaned close to Tony as they hustled away from the plaza. "It's her. She was the one that was chasing us on the bike."

Tony craned his neck to catch a glimpse as he was shuffled along. "Oh, wow, yeah. I recognize that alien death ray anywhere. Fuck!" He turned away and put his head down. "She just busted me looking at her."

"You two," Tasha spat, "less talking, more running for life."

The mob inside the covered Market was less chaotic but just as confused and crowded. Cam led them through it as he retraced his steps, eyes peeled, and senses stretched taut while he searched for danger. It was tough to stay focused around the uncontrolled madness, but Cam reasoned that worked more in his favor than against him. Near the spot where he'd spoken to the flower vendor, he caught a quick glimpse of the comic book shop Tony pointed out earlier. Instinct told him to double-check the storefront. Then he saw why. Standing just inside the shop, surveying the crowd as they passed by, was the Boss. Tomás Aguilar.

Cam quickly ducked his head down and turned away. "Tasha, at your three o'clock. Tomás in the storefront."

To her credit, Tasha didn't actually look. She just reacted. "Ok. Stay low, keep going, and find your way to truck. I will create distraction." She reached out and handed Cam a set of keys. He nodded, pocketing them, then grabbed Tony and moved out onto the street.

Tasha straightened up and made for the comic book shop. "Hello, little mudak," she called out derisively. "Why don't you come out to play with me?"

The street outside the Market was rowdy and hectic. No one seemed to know what the hell was going on, and several drivers trying to get through the teeming throngs of panicked shoppers and confused tourists gave up and abandoned their vehicles. Cam and Tony shared a knowing look, then began to push their way forward through the people around them.

"Next time we get ambushed," Tony muttered, "it should be somewhere easier to escape from."

Cam chuckled, glad to have his friend nearby, even if it meant putting Tony in danger. He was about to step around a curbside dumpster when he experienced a sudden sense of nearby danger. He grabbed Tony and pulled him down just as an energy bolt blasted overhead and slammed into another nearby dumpster. The sound was almost deafening as the explosive force sent the heavy metal box tumbling across the ground into a screaming crowd of tourists and vendors.

The blast came from the plaza to their left, which meant that it came from the Agent. Maybe she really had seen Tony looking at her. Or, Tomás had reported in before Tasha took him on. But the how and why could be left for later. Cam focused on their escape, grabbing Tony and pulling him up. "Come on, we've got to go."

"Yeah, no shit," Tony swore as Cam pulled him along. "This isn't my first shootout, remember?"

Cam grinned, then let newfound instincts and decade-old

memories guide him as he ducked back into the Market. He worked further into the building, aiming for a stairway that led to the Market's lower level. His proximity sense felt next to useless, with so many confused and frightened tourists scrambling around them. But he still managed to catch a flash of movement in his peripheral vision in time to see one of Aguilar's mercenaries barreling out of the crowd toward him. Cam quickly turned toward the runner, shoving Tony out of the way, and lifted his left forearm up as a defensive guard. The merc saw the move in time, though, bent low to avoid Cam's elbow, and plowed into his midsection, knocking him back onto the floor. The nearby crowd screamed and scattered, except for Tony, who ran up and kicked Cam's attacker hard in the side, knocking them off Cam and onto the floor. Cam quickly rolled over on top of them, grabbed their head by a handful of hair, and slammed it down onto the concrete floor. The mercenary kept struggling, so Cam did it again and felt the body beneath him go limp. He started to do it once more, but Tony grabbed him by the shoulder.

"Leave him! We gotta get outta here before any more show up."

Cam nodded and let go of the attacker's head, then stood up and took a moment to glance around at the crowd for signs of further pursuit. A second merc was trying to force their way upstream through the confused mass of people. "Too late," he told Tony, then looked down the nearby stairway. "Come on, this way." He hurried down the stairs with Tony right behind him.

"Where are we going?" Tony asked, breathless, as they reached the bottom.

"Still trying to get to the truck." Cam led Tony past a set

of more permanent storefronts–hawking the same touristy schlock that could be found upstairs–toward a lower-level exit from the building. "I'd like to lose our tail first if we can, though."

"Ok, just lemme know what you need me to do."

They pushed through large wooden doors at the end of the passageway out onto a concrete landing. There Cam found the long, rambling stairway that led back down to the waterfront. But he grabbed Tony and pulled him over toward the wall near the doorway before taking up his own position next to the door. After a moment, the door swung open. Cam lifted a foot and kicked it hard, knocking a black-uniformed soldier sideways and down onto the concrete. Cam watched them throw their hands out to stop their fall and saw a gun in one of those hands–another Haas, in fact.

Cam was moving before the merc even hit the ground. His mind raced at hyperspeed, plotting his course of actions faster than they could be carried out. In one fluid motion, he dove for the mercenary, grabbing their gun and disarming them, then rolled across them and came up on one knee. Cam flipped off the safety, then knelt down on the soldier's back, shoving the barrel of the Dominator into the back of their head.

"How many more of you are there?" Cam growled through gritted teeth. The mercenary tried reaching back to grab for the gun, but Cam just swatted their hand away and pushed the barrel even harder into their head. "Answer me now, asshole."

"There's one more at the bottom of the stairs," they spat anxiously.

"You'd better not be lying."

"I swear! I swear!"

"Then I guess we're done here." Cam lifted the weapon, and the soldier started to squirm again, so Cam smacked the back of their head with the butt of the gun, and the merc fell limp. Cam stood up, flipped the switch back to safety the weapon, then tucked it into the back of his waistband. He looked up to see Tony standing nearby, his mouth agape. "What?"

"Holy shit, dude. You've really got the moves, don't you?"

Cam rolled his eyes. He wasn't in the mood for Tony's fangirling, and they didn't have time for it anyway. "Never mind that. We've still got to get to the truck, and there's at least one more of these fuckers waiting for us down there." He pointed toward the stairs. "This way." Then he took off, already updating his plan of attack as the stairs wound downward. There were far fewer people around, so they're able to move much faster.

Tony bounded down the stairs on Cam's tail. "Hey, doesn't that mean we're just running toward another bad guy?"

"Yeah, but they don't know we know about them, so we'll have the element of surprise."

They were almost to the bottom where the stairs dumped out onto Western Avenue when Cam sensed danger once again. He reacted without thinking, shoving Tony forward as a sudden energy bolt burst down toward them, slamming into the pavement in an explosion of concrete and earth. Cam threw his hands over his head as debris rained down. She'd found them already.

Cam was quickly up and running again, dragging his slower-moving friend along behind him. He veered left, heading south toward the parked Vagabond, when a volley of blasts hit the pavement in front of them and knocked them both off balance. After he recovered himself, Cam grabbed Tony, and the pair scrambled back toward another set of stairs. At the bottom was a large parking lot, with the city's waterfront piers and Puget Sound beyond it. He wondered where the fuck Finn was.

As if in response, another blast boomed further behind them. Cam glanced back to see the Agent, perched on a landing halfway up the stairs, as a powerful shot struck her own energy shield. It didn't do any apparent damage but was still forceful enough to knock her down, sending her tumbling over the railing onto the next landing. Cam looked past her and saw Finn standing gloriously above her. His shield radiated a triumphant blue, and he had a strange-looking gun clutched in his right hand. In the distance, he mouthed a single word to Cam. "Run."

Needing no further encouragement, Cam resumed his race down the stairs, with Tony protesting loudly behind him. A faint wail of police sirens sounded in the distance, the telltale sign of cops undoubtedly on their way to the warzone in the plaza. Ahead, Cam could see the rough, dark waters of Puget Sound, with the shadowed peaks of the Olympic mountains looming large and foreboding in the distance. They reached the bottom of the long stairway just as another energy bolt shot in their direction. Cam twisted, faster than he thought possible, and grabbed Tony, pulling him to their right as the bolt slammed into a concrete barrier on the side of the stairs. Then they ran again, Cam leading Tony on a weaving trail through cars parked in the nearby surface lot. He hoped that would make them a more difficult target to hit.

Cam caught the sound of several more shots, each one

like the piercing screech of metal scraping against metal, and turned back to see Finn on the offensive, forcing the Agent to stop her advance and return fire. It was clearly an annoyance tactic since it wasn't really doing her any harm. But it gave Cam and Tony a chance to get her off their tail. They kept their heads down as they moved from car to car, working their way across the parking lot toward the waterfront beyond. Cam didn't have any idea yet where they'd go from there, only a vague sense that he was headed to safety.

There was still the possibility of an additional mercenary lurking nearby, and the sound of weapons fire behind them kept getting closer. Cam popped his head up, taking a quick look at his surroundings, before ducking back down.

Tony was panting from their efforts. He gave Cam a questioning look. "So, what's the plan from here?"

Cam shrugged. "I don't know. I'm kinda working this out on the fly. But there's some wharf buildings across the street. If we can make it over there, we may stand a chance of losing her long enough for Finn or Tasha to either take her out or pick us up."

Tony smiled. "I bet you wish you had that stealth cloak now, eh?"

Cam laughed. "Fuck yeah, I do." Then his face turned serious. "But no joke here. When I say go, you gotta haul ass, Tony."

Tony nodded. "I know. I'll be right behind you."

Cam nodded in return. He readied himself to run, then the shooting suddenly stopped. That was either very good or very bad. He wished he had a radio, or Ego, or any fucking way to communicate with the rest of his team. He needed to know what was happening back the way he'd come from. But he had no way to find out, so he chose to play it like they were still on the run, at least until he knew differently.

His back to the car, Cam slid toward the rear end and peeked his head out. The remaining soldier stood nearby with a gun drawn as they searched around the parked vehicles for Cam and Tony. Cam quickly ducked back into cover as he built a mental map of the threats he was facing. The mercenary was the closest to them and stood the best chance of taking them out, so they would get his attention first.

"Ok, stay low and follow me," Cam whispered. Tony nodded, and Cam crouched and walked toward the front of the car, then turned and slipped through the tight space at the head of the vehicle, working his way toward the remaining mercenary. He leaned out low into the open space next to the car and saw the soldier's profile as they walked toward where they'd been hiding before. Cam looked at Tony and pointed down to the ground, motioning for him to stay in place. Tony nodded again, then Cam snuck out from his hiding place, head still low, and quickly walked to the rear of the car. He poked his head out just far enough to see the merc stop and check the opposite side of the vehicle. Once the soldier started toward the next car, Cam rushed out from hiding and, in two steps, was right on his target's heels. He struck out with a low kick into the back of the merc's legs, knocking their knees forward. Then, grabbing their collar, Cam slammed their head into the trunk of a nearby car once, then twice. When he let go, the mercenary slid down to the pavement, out cold.

Cam crouched back down, picked up the merc's gun, and slid in underneath the parked car. Then he hurried back to where Tony was waiting. "We're clear," Cam whispered. "Are you ready?" He waited for Tony's nod, then turned and held himself in a runner's stance. "Now," he grunted, then launched himself from between the surrounding vehicles, hoping that Tony was on his tail. He was on his third step when a nearby car exploded into the air, knocking him off balance. Just as Cam started to recover, a second car launched upwards on a column of fire. The force of that blast sent him down hard onto the ground. His ears rang from the dual explosions, and his head spun, but he pushed himself up with a single-minded determination, stumbling forward across the road, heedless of any traffic that may have been there, his arms cartwheeling for balance. He'd reached the curb on the far side when he heard a shout.

"Cameron Maddock!" He turned, breath heavy, and saw the Agent standing on the sidewalk back across the street, surrounded by her shimmering blue shield. A pile of burning automotive wreckage was scattered loosely behind her like giant children's toys. Her right arm hung loosely by her side, her hand still balled into a tight fist. But her left arm was wrapped tightly around Tony, holding him firmly in place in front of her like a human shield. God damn it, Tony. "I do not wish to cause him any harm, Cameron. Nor do I wish to hurt you. But you must come with me. If you agree to do so, right now, I will release him to your other companions, unharmed. On that, you have my word."

Cam stood there dazed, chest raggedly rising and falling as he struggled to calm his breathing. This was it. She'd finally caught him. He had the gun but no shield to defend himself from her. And she had Tony, meaning the gun wasn't an option anyway. He gulped. "If I go with you, you won't hurt him?"

Her face was impassive, her expression placid and indecipherable. She gave nothing away. "I gave you my word. No harm will come to him by my hand. You need only to come with me."

"Why?" he cried out, exasperated. "What is all this for? What the hell do you want with me?"

Then, against all odds, the Agent gave him a friendly smile. "I want to take you home."

Home? Was this the answer he'd been looking for all along? It would've been nice to think so. But they'd been coming for him hard, so he doubted it. Not that it mattered. She hadn't given him much of a choice. He would do it just to save his friend. He was about to respond when he saw Finn run out to the sidewalk from the parking lot. Finn stopped in a fighting stance and pointed his alien-looking gun at the woman.

She casually turned toward him, her smile morphing into a sneer. "Hold your fire, Protector! I would hate for you to penetrate my shields and injure this poor individual." She tightened her grip on Tony, pulling him in closer. "Now, drop your weapon, lower your own shield, and stand down."

Finn scowled, then dropped his weapon onto the ground. His shield sparked and flickered, then dissipated into the air. "Just give this up, for fuck sake. There isn't a Gate within miles of here. You've got nowhere to run."

"I am not concerned with anything but Cameron's response to my request." She turned back to Cam. "What say you? Do we have an agreement?"

Cam looked at her, then back to Finn, who was clearly angry with the situation. Then finally, he looked at Tony, who was shaking his head, no. The poor fool was offering to sacrifice himself for Cam. That sealed it. There was no fucking way he'd let his friend get hurt anymore on his behalf. He made eye contact with the woman and nodded. "Yeah, we have a deal."

Her smile widened. Cam gulped, then started to take a step toward her, but some movement at the edge of his vision made him turn to see Tomás suddenly appear from behind another car. He stood up, gun in hand and pointed at Finn. Cam inhaled deeply, preparing to shout out a warning, when Tasha, running at full tilt, launched herself into the air and tackled Tomás just as he squeezed the trigger. For the briefest instant, Cam no longer had any doubt about her taking on and defeating an extinct Siberian tiger. The Agent turned as well, perhaps following Cam's gaze or sensing the motion behind her, but it was already too late for her to act. The gun fired, but Tasha had knocked his aim off when she tackled Tomás. The slug passed harmlessly by Finn, continuing its supersonic flight until it slammed through Cam's shoulder, shredding muscle, tendon, and bone before exiting behind him in a bloody mess. The force of the impact sent Cam flying backward, and he landed hard on the sidewalk behind him.

Cam lay there, stunned. Part of him knew he'd just been shot, but he was in too much shock to feel any pain yet.

The Agent shrieked in rage and dropped Tony to the ground. Then she pointed her fist at Tomás, who'd just thrown Tasha off of him. Tomás heard the Agent's scream and turned toward her with a look of shock when she fired an energy blast at him. That shocked look was the last one he ever made before the bolt of super excited particles tore through his head, disintegrating it in a cloud of steam and bloody mist.

Finn watched it happen, then looked back from that gruesome display to the Agent. The pair of them regarded each other for a long, drawn-out moment before both turned to Cam and took off in his direction. Cam was barely aware of what was happening by that point. He hardly noticed Finn. He didn't notice Tony at all, as his friend picked himself up off of the sidewalk and started to run after the Agent, shouting for her to stop. Cam was only aware of the Agent, of her terrible beauty, her face a mask of pure outrage, looking for all the world to him like an avenging angel flying to him on wings of shimmering blue light. She was death, and she'd come to take him to the netherworld. He started to feel cold as his lifeblood spilled out and pooled on the pavement beneath him.

Suddenly, he was no longer alone. The other presence in his mind was there. It flooded his body with calm, pushing down his feelings of pain and despair, replacing them with crystal clarity. He wasn't about to die, after all. He still had one option left. Yes, he thought with unhurried calm. Do it.

The blue-violet light flared instantly to life, growing into a blinding disc that hung shimmering in the air, just like when he was back on the motorcycle. Only, this time, it didn't appear in his path but in hers. The Agent barely had time to comprehend what she was seeing. Then she knew since she'd also been there when Cam was on the bike with Tony. But the understanding came too late, as her momentum carried her forward and through the portal, and she vanished with a fiery blue splash of Cherenkov radiation. That was when Cam saw Tony, who'd been right on her heels, reaching out to grab her as he was running, trying to protect his friend. Cam watched, his mounting horror smothered by the forced detachment, as his friend also disappeared in a violent blue flash of light. Then the light dissipated, and the disc was gone. Cam tried to move, tried to shout, tried to do anything, but his body was no longer his own as he lay there, bleeding out from the wound in his shoulder. Finally, the icy calm subsumed his racing mind, and everything went black.

THE AGENT

«STATIC»«FLASH»

She landed hard on her hands and knees, with only the soft, loamy soil to break her fall. Her shield had deactivated the moment she'd fallen through the unexpected portal. She'd been beaten by him again. For the first time that she could remember, she experienced a moment of doubt. She was the best of her kind. She was strong, powerful, and brilliant. She'd never failed in her assignments before, and yet she'd somehow managed to fail quite spectacularly. Twice.

She picked up a fist and slammed it down on the ground. Then she did it again, and again, and again until she let out a piercing shriek.

"If you're done having your little tantrum, lady, I could use some help here."

She looked up to locate the source of the voice. It was her target's companion. He lay sprawled on the ground before her, a body's length or so away. She remembered him running behind her in some foolish attempt to prevent her from reaching her target. He must have fallen through the surprise portal, as well. She didn't know whether to admire him for his naive bravado or pity him for his poor tactical skills in battle. "Help you? I should kill you."

191

The fool laughed softly. "Well, don't let me stop you. It's not like you ain't been trying and failing for the past two days." She watched as he gingerly pushed himself up to look at her. Based on how he moved, she thought it likely that he'd sustained a mild injury, perhaps a strained or pulled muscle. He looked her in the eyes. "In fact, I think this is the first time I've ever seen you when you're not shooting your alien death ray at me."

She regarded him closely. So, it would be naive bravado, then. She mentally reached for her sensors, trying to obtain his biometric readings, but she got no response. She searched for her other systems one by one–tactical, offensive, defensive–but got nothing at all. The portal had somehow knocked out her internal systems entirely. That would make things challenging. "I don't need a weapon to kill you, Zhang Weitian. Breaking your neck would make you just as dead."

He furrowed his brow. "Wow, lady, there you go using my government name, and I don't even know a damn thing about you. Real classy." He pushed himself up onto his knees, then slowly got himself on his feet. The way he favored his left side, along with his slightly labored breathing, meant she'd probably been right about the muscle strain. It could even have been a fractured rib. "Look, if you're not gonna kill me, then could you at least tell me where the fuck we are? Or maybe just what your name is?"

She took a deep breath to center herself. Her systems would come back online at some point, and when they did, she could call for a portal and get off whatever backwater rock she found herself on. In the meantime, she judged that it was time to try a different tactic. Zhang was not acting hostile and was certainly no threat to her. Like many from his world, he would undoubtedly respond to a softer approach. If not, when she did get out of whatever place they were stranded at, she could always take him to the Intelligence for a mind probe. Since he was identified as her target's primary companion, he must possess some helpful information about him. If not, she reasoned, he could at least serve as her hostage once more. That had nearly worked. And it would've worked, but for the bungling overreach of that idiot, Aguilar. Satisfied that she still had multiple opportunities to salvage her failure, she pushed herself up as well and stood before her unexpected companion. "I am called Omni. I do not have any information about where we are, though."

He smiled at her. "Hi, Omni. My friends call me Tony." He held his hand out, fingers straight, palm perpendicular to the ground. Without her tactical system, it took her a moment to realize that he was offering to shake hands, as was the custom of his kind. She stared at him a bit longer before reluctantly placing her hand in his and smiled. They shook. "Sweet. For a second there, I thought you were gonna leave me hanging." He released her hand, and she fought the urge to wipe it off on her tactical armor. "So, you really don't know where we are?"

"I do not." She took a moment to survey her immediate surroundings. They were standing in some kind of low, marshy area next to an expansive body of water. In the fading daylight, she could see a series of nearby hills, with a broad mountain range opposite them, in the distance. It was analogous to the landscape they'd transited from, although she could detect no signs of civilization. She looked to the skies, but there were no moons that she could see. It seemed that the portal had effected a dimensional transfer, then, but was tied to the same relative location. Until her systems came back online, that was all the information she had to go on. "We have clearly been transported to a dimensional alternate of our original location, although I do not know which one. It would seem that you were an unintended victim of your friend's attempt to remove me from the battlefield. It was a brilliant strategy if a little too effective, in this case."

He looked surprised to hear her say that. "Wait. You mean, Cam did this?"

Had he not known that? It was interesting that he would openly admit that to her. She smiled wider. "Well, I did not do it, and I certainly doubt that you did."

Tony chuckled in amazement. "Damn, he really is a fucking alien. I knew it."

She cocked her head to one side. This one's behavior was curious, especially compared to the others she'd dealt with from his world. She'd grown accustomed to receiving a more aggressive response from the people she chose to work with. "You have had doubts about him, then? About whether or not your friend is who he claims to be?"

He furrowed his brow again, shaking his head. He was very expressive. "No way, lady. Bros before hoes. I mean, no offense, but he's my ride or die. You're not getting anything from me."

While she didn't understand most of what he'd just said, she inferred the sentiment well enough and respected it, crude language and all. She smiled. "You misunderstand me, Tony. I am already aware of who your friend really is. I suspect, however, that you may not be." His expression changed. Confused this time. "In fact, I suspect now that even he may not be."

194

She gazed out across the rolling waters toward the distant mountains. The sky overhead was a rich indigo, melting into the horizon with a lustrous, dusky rose glow as that world's sun slowly set. Even someone as relentlessly practical and driven as she was could still appreciate its simple beauty at a primal, instinctive level. But the sunset meant that the local air temperature would soon drop to an uncomfortable level.

He looked at her plaintively. "I don't suppose you have anything to eat? I'm fucking starving."

She frowned. "No, I do not."

He frowned, then shrugged his shoulders. "Ah, well. It was worth a shot." He had a curious expression on his face. If she'd been able to sample his bio readings, though, she thought it likely that she would read fear. "So, uh, what now? I mean, are we just stuck here?"

"Only for the time being." Then she felt a faint pressure in her mind, which slowly expanded outward as her systems finally started to come back online. Clarity descended in a rush as she began to regain the full use of her sensors again. Her quantum entanglement communicator signaled that it was active, and she immediately sent a ping to the Intelligence with her location. Then she flashed a smile at Tony. "But it shouldn't be much longer, now."

«FLASH»«STATIC»

FINN

Finn was in shock. He couldn't believe what just happened, even as the chaotic events replayed in his mind. The powerful hit on his Gate sense meant that there was no doubt. But there was no time for analysis. They needed to grab Cam and get him out of there fast before anyone else showed up to spoil the party. He glanced over his shoulder to see Tasha standing over the headless corpse of Aguilar. "Tash," he shouted. "Forget about him. Get the truck!"

She shook her head. "Cam has keys!"

He huffed. Of course. Otherwise, things would've been too easy. "Fine. Then find us another way out of here." She nodded in acknowledgment, so he left her to it and took off across the street toward where Cam lay. There weren't any bystanders in the vicinity yet. They'd all been driven off by the weapons fire, and explosions. But that wouldn't last very long. Time. He needed more time.

<Otto, I need a diversion. I can't have any local police showing up here>

<Do you have anything specific in mind, or should I–>

He didn't have time for that, either. <Just take care of it>

<Alright, leave it to me>

Once he was across the street, he quickly knelt next to

Cam, carefully avoiding the growing pool of blood on the ground. It looked like he was still breathing. <Vitals?>

<Pulse is low but stable. Blood pressure is weak and dropping. You need to control that bleeding>

The emergency med-kit was all the way back in the truck, forcing Finn to fall back on his field medical training. He reached under his jacket and tore off a strip of his own shirt, carefully threading it under Cam's shoulder. He was grateful that Cam wasn't conscious and able to cause a fuss. Then Finn pulled the two ends of the strip tightly around Cam's shoulder and tied them into a quick knot above the entrance wound.

<Police have been directed to a false incident Northwest of this location. I took the liberty of jamming communications within my maximum radius as well, but I cannot guarantee the success of that>

<Thank you>

<A vehicle is approaching. I believe it's Tasha>

Finn glanced around and saw an older, gold-painted minivan rapidly approaching him in the opposite lane. Tasha was behind the wheel, grimacing. She turned wide to the right, then swung back and made a U-turn, pulling up next to Finn and slamming to a stop. Tasha jumped out, leaving the door open, then rushed around and slid the side door open. "Best I could do," she said breathlessly.

Finn couldn't help but roll his eyes. "It's fine. I was planning on stopping for groceries anyway." He looked down at Cam. "Come on. Help me get him inside."

She grunted, then hurried over and crouched down on the other side of Cam. Together, they lifted him as carefully as they could, Finn mindful of Cam's bandaged shoulder. Then they shuffled over to the minivan and set him down inside. Either it hadn't come with rear seats, or Tasha ripped them out. Based on the state of the carpeting, Finn figured it was probably the latter.

Tasha climbed in after him. "You drive," she instructed.

Finn nodded and rushed around to the driver's seat. There were tiny chunks of safety glass all over the floor, but the seat itself was clear of any. He pulled the door closed, then reached down under the seat to move it back and accommodate his height. Since Tasha hot-wired it, the engine was still running, so Finn shifted into drive and stepped on the accelerator. Their truck was parked nearby, so they could transfer Cam to it, where Tasha could access the medkit on the way back to the hideout.

<Otto, will Cam make it back to the safe house without treatment?>

<I'm unable to accurately determine that. With the amount of blood loss Cam is experiencing, I'd advise heading there directly, without delay>

"Tash!" Finn called back, "We're gonna skip the Vagabond and go right back to the warehouse."

"Is good idea. This vehicle cannot be easily tracked. Is too old." Cam let out a low moan. She looked down and frowned. "But you need to hurry."

Finn's face was rigid with determination as he pushed down on the gas pedal. He kept them to the right to avoid the tunnel, taking them down the old Alaskan Way toward the turn onto Atlantic to bring them into the city's industrial neighborhood. Traffic was mercifully light, but the old minivan protested every time he turned the wheel too hard. Tasha protested, also.

198

"Gah!" she cried out when she suddenly tumbled backward. "If I knew you would drive like this, I would have stolen better car."

Finn ignored her, focusing on his driving as best he could while his mind played back the incident. The Agent was definitely not a local, he reckoned. Whether her enhancements were wetwired in or only part of her combat armor, she was much more powerful and capable than he was. Her shielding was strong, and her particle weapon even stronger. His own shields could barely cope, and she'd nearly bested him. In fact, if he was completely candid in his assessment, she'd actually beaten him. It was Cam who'd managed to take her out. Quite literally, in fact. Cam, who she'd called by name. She clearly knew who he was, too. That left Finn with a lot of questions to be answered. Questions like where the hell the Agent was even from. Her enhancements were top of the line, and she was well-trained and capable. He'd almost burned out his own particle weapon, just knocking her down. But, despite her enhancements, she couldn't be Protectorate. He would've at least known of her if she was.

<Otto, tell me you got something off of her during the battle>

<Very little, unfortunately. Her shielding was as impervious to me as it was to you>

<Well, that's just wonderful>

<I did get excellent readings of her shield. And her weapon>

<Anything useful?>

<Her weapon operates on the same principles as yours, obviously. But it was definitely not a Protectorate weapon. It was far more powerful, for one. And the field technology she used was not Protectorate made, either>

<Yeah, way more advanced>

<Actually, no. It was a great deal less sophisticated in its field manipulation. But it made up for that lack of refinement with sheer power. The same could be said for her shielding>

<Where did she get the juice for that?>

<Unknown. She never lowered her shield, and I was unable to penetrate it with my scans>

<Any ideas?>

<Like yours, I'd assume her tech is somehow Nynari-based>

<So, what? She's part of some rogue Nynari splinter-group?>

<Or she's operating with stolen tech>

<Come on. Stolen wetware like that? It's not like stealing an actual gun. And never mind where she got it. Who would even install it?>

<Indeed>

<First, the orbital incursion. Then the first Seattle incident, the Bay Area incident, and now the second Seattle incident. She's running circles around us, Otto. What else can we pin on her or her group? They can't have just popped up out of nowhere and started swatting us down like that>

<I will conduct a records search, although I am limited to the data I currently have access to. But I've already assigned a high probability to these incidents being the work of Sable>

That thought had crossed his mind, too. The amount of verifiable data the Protectorate had on the shadowy organization they'd labeled with the code name Sable was laughably small. Its existence was more inferred than confirmed. But, unless there was another secret band of inter-dimensional radicals operating in the multiverse, that woman and her associates had to be part of it.

That still left the question of Cam and his mysterious ability to produce Gates, which was no minor issue on its own.

As if on cue, Cam let out a shout from the back of the minivan. "Jesus, fuck!" He unleashed another cry as the minivan took a large bump in the road. "What's happening!"

"Sorry, Cam," Finn called out from the driver's seat. "I promise we'll be there ASAP."

Still putting pressure on his shoulder, Tasha pushed him back down onto the floor with her other hand. "Stay still, vorobushek, or you will only bleed more." She turned to look at Finn. "I cannot stop bleeding with fucking piece of torn shirt."

Finn grunted in acknowledgment. "I know, I know, I'm going as fast as I can." He started to reach toward the glove box. "Maybe there's a first aid kit or something–"

Tasha reached forward and swatted Finn's hand away. "You drive. I will look." She looked down at Cam, took his free hand, and put it on the cloth over his shoulder. "Press down here. This will hurt but is necessary to stop bleeding. Ok?"

Cam nodded, his face twisted in pain, as he pressed the cloth down onto his ruined shoulder. "I got it."

Tasha reached around and grabbed the passenger seat, then pulled herself forward. She pulled the glove box open and started dumping its contents onto the seat. Then she found a white, plastic first aid kit buried at the bottom. She pulled it out and opened it. It was surprisingly complete.

Cam moaned again. "Finn, Tasha," he said quietly, "something's happening."

"What's that, Cam?" asked Finn.

Tasha let out a muffled grunt before scooting herself back

into position next to Cam. She set the first aid kit down next to him and pulled out a small roll of bandage cloth. Suddenly Cam reached out with his uninjured arm, releasing the pressure on his shoulder, and grabbed Tasha. She looked at him in surprise.

"What are you doing, vorobushek?" She put his hand back down onto his shoulder.

"There's–there's something in my head," Cam stammered.

Tasha shushed him gently. "Is ok. Everything will be fine soon."

Cam, suddenly frustrated, reached up and grabbed her arm again. "Listen to me, damn it. There's. Something. In. My. Head,"

Tasha stared at him, too shocked to reply. Finn turned back briefly. "What did you just say?"

"I said–"

Cam suddenly started to convulse. Tasha, shaken out of inaction, reached out and held him down, muttering angrily in Russian. Then the shuddering stopped. "What are you?" he called out.

"He must be going into shock," Finn announced, sounding disturbed.

"Tell me something I do not know," Tasha muttered, clearly at the end of her rope. She held Cam down as she tried to wrap the bandaging around his shoulder.

"What the fuck is a nano-colony?" Cam cried out. Then he fell unconscious again.

"Yop tvoyu mat'," Tasha grumbled as she worked the roll of stretch fabric around his shoulder.

"Did he just say something about a nano-colony?" Finn asked.

"He is delirious."

<Otto?>

<Yes, that is what he said>

Shit. Things kept getting stranger and stranger. First, the Gates. Then, something in his head, and then nano-colonies. Who in the hell was this guy? But Finn put those thoughts on hold. They were almost at the safe house.

<Otto, get the delivery door open. I'm driving us right inside>

<Opening it now>

<And prep the medbay>

<Already done>

He turned back to Tasha. "We're here. I'm going to pull inside and help you load him into the medbay pod." Finn drove around the corner and through the gate at speed, which earned him a squeal of protest from the old tires. The gate immediately started to close after passing through it before he slammed the brakes as he pulled the minivan inside the building. Finn threw his door open then rushed around to get the side door. "I'll get him. You go get the medbay pod ready."

Tasha nodded. She crawled out of the minivan and rushed over to the far side of the warehouse to the room with the medbay pod. The pod bore a strong resemblance to a giant-sized ceramic egg, smooth, shiny, and white. Tasha tapped on a softly glowing mark on the surface, and the egg split in two as the top half slid up and away. The pristine, padded interior lit up in a warm, soft glow. It had been reset since they'd used it to heal Tony's leg the night before and was already humming softly.

Finn reached in and grabbed Cam and then, carefully, using

all of his strength, lifted him up and out of the minivan. He was less gentle than when they'd loaded him in since time was no longer on their side. After quickly walking over to the room with medbay, past the waiting Tasha, Finn set Cam down in the pod's padded interior. Then the top half of the pod slid back into place and gently closed around him.

Tasha looked over at Finn. "I need nap. And drink. Probably not in that order."

Finn sighed. "You and me, both, Tash. You and me, both."

CAM

Cam woke up to darkness. He was in a warm space, lying on a reclined surface that felt like soft memory foam. As the roar of silence slowly dissipated, Cam could also hear the distant sound of two people arguing. For a moment, he flashed back to his early childhood, when he'd cower, alone in his room, listening to his adoptive parents having one of their knock-down, drag-out fights, fearful that it would end like it usually did, with someone getting hit. It used to be his mother, but as he'd gotten older, it more frequently turned out to be him.

The memories brought him no anxiety like they usually would've. Instead, he felt only a strange detachment, as if he was seeing them through a hazy veil of warmth and comfort. He tried to sit up but hit his head on the equally soft surface, a half-meter or so above him. A wave of dizziness came over him suddenly, and he let himself fall back onto the reclined surface.

His shoulder. He'd been shot. He carefully reached over to inspect the injury but felt only a bandage wrapped tightly around the area. There wasn't any pain. He must've been pumped full of meds. That would probably explain his lack of anxiety, too. He reached up with his uninjured arm and felt the surface above him. It was soft and curved, but there wasn't much more he could do to determine his location without any light. Was he in a coffin?

As he felt the overhead padding, something tickled at the edges of his mind, almost like a long-forgotten thought. He focused on it and suddenly felt his awareness expand. He was inside some sort of automated medical device. All around him were various mechanical manipulators and energy emitters, hidden from his touch by the soft, foam padding. A computer controlled it all. He could feel its presence nearby and mentally dove into the strange, alien programming language. After a few moments, it began to make sense to him. Programming was programming, after all. As he inspected and parsed the strange code, he found some files referencing him and his own injury. According to the files, the damage to his shoulder had been extensive. The blood loss alone had almost been enough to kill him. Had it not been for his own nano-colonies, it likely would've.

Nano-colonies?

In answer to his unspoken question, a wave of information flooded into his mind, and, suddenly, he understood what that meant. His body contained multiple colonies comprised of millions of nanites—molecule-sized constructs that could be programmed to manipulate matter on an atomic level. They'd done most of the work to repair the damage to his shoulder, reconstructing any damaged or missing bone and tissue.

That was some shit right there. It was probably the reason why he'd never been sick or seriously injured. But how was he able to sense the machinery around him? How was he able to read the machine code? Read wasn't even the right word for it since it hadn't been projected on a screen in front of him. Cam simply became aware of it and built an understanding of it in his own mind. How was that even possible?

Again, as before, his mind was flooded with information. It all seemed to open up and unpack of its own volition, and his awareness expanded even further. There was more alien machine code, different from that of the medical device, inside his head. Literally. He became aware of dozens of tiny crystal processors, each the size of a grain of sand, embedded within his body and connected to a forest of impossibly thin wires, mere nanometers thick, that flowed out through his head and body. It was a network of tiny, microscopic computers, and it was all inside of him.

Some of his recent experiences started to make sense–the sudden abilities, like knowing how to fight or use a gun. It could be why he had such an easy time with programming and code, too, since so much of it was present inside of him. That still left the question of how it got there. He had no memory of whatever radical surgery would've been required to implant all of that tech. He searched through his internal system, but even as his understanding of it grew, he still couldn't find the answer to that question. The thought chilled him. Who was he? What was he? Why had it taken so long to find out that, along with all the other shit that made him different, he was filled with technology that hadn't even been invented yet? Thinking back, he recalled the conversation where Tony jokingly called him an alien. How ironic that turned out to be when he could've been right all along.

His many questions all boiled down to where he actually came from. He could account for most of his life, except for when he was very young–especially the period between when he was born and when he was adopted. His parents had never been very forthcoming on the matter, although that hadn't been intentional. When they'd finally broke down and told him what they knew, it was very little. An infant turned up at a hospital emergency room one night. There were no witnesses and no footage on the security cameras. His parents didn't even know his actual birth date, so they celebrated the day they'd brought him home instead. He knew all of that to be accurate because he'd gone in and checked for himself, hacking into the police database and finding his case file. It was quicker to do that than to make an official request, and none of the records were redacted. But it only confirmed what he'd been told. Even his DNA test had come back inconclusive. The sample was compromised somehow, they told him when they refunded his fee. He'd thought about hacking into their database, too, just to be sure, but it would've been trickier than an old police server. And, in the end, he hadn't really cared.

Cam went back and further explored his internal system, hunting for some sort of interface beyond the random question and answer approach, which didn't seem very efficient, at least not when he was just figuring things out. There wasn't anything obvious, like a graphical or heads-up display. But he sensed that things were well organized. He'd already discovered the medical functions and what turned out to be sensors, enhancing his own built-in senses to a much greater degree. That was how he could sense the medical device he was lying in and even access and read the underlying code that operated it. Cam also found offensive and defensive functions located in other microscopic and nanoscopic-sized implants in his body. It turned out that he was full of tiny biomechanical devices and machinery.

Cam resumed inspecting his right shoulder and felt the bandage wrapped tightly around it. Gently probing the area, he was surprised to find that there was no feeling at all. He reached out with his awareness again, seeking his internal medical functions, and found overviews of the damage he'd taken and the repairs made. The dermal and vascular repairs were complete, but there was still a great deal of nerve, muscle, and skeletal tissue to rebuild. That was in process, so all pain and touch sensation to the affected area was blocked.

He had a million more questions, but time was wasting. The unanswered question that stood out the most in his mind was what happened to Tony. Cam continued searching his internal system. After a few more minutes, he stumbled on the emergency functions—including the ability to generate emergency trans-dimensional portals.

Shit. So it really had been him, after all. He'd created the Gates.

On some level, Cam knew that already, even if he hadn't understood how he was able to do it. It wasn't actually something he'd consciously done, per se. But it was a capability that Cam somehow possessed. He reached out with his awareness again, seeking the knowledge of how he'd done that—of how that system worked—and the information flowed through him. Suddenly, his knowledge of quantum physics expanded well past polite, dinner table conversation. But the knowledge didn't equate with understanding. Cam didn't actually know any of the underlying physics and thus has no frame of reference. So, while he knew that he'd done it, he didn't understand how he'd done it. Still, it was a start. He reached again but for something more specific. Where was Tony?

He discovered a log of the two Gates he'd created through the emergency functions that listed what were probably the dimensional coordinates for the Gate destinations. He wasn't sure what those coordinates meant precisely, but there was a clear pattern even with just the two sets of them. The Gates must've opened to the same dimensional coordinates but at different relative locations. So Tony had been sent to the same alternate universe that they'd gone to on the motorcycle, but to a separate area on that planet. He'd probably been sent to the same relative location that he'd left from. That left Cam with another, even more, essential question, though. Could he do it again? Could he open a Gate, except do it consciously, on purpose? He couldn't find a conclusive answer to that one, but the general sense that he got was: no.

Of course, it couldn't have been that easy. It meant that Finn and Tasha were still his only avenue for help in that regard. He paused to listen to the muffled sounds of their argument. They may not even be willing to offer their support since it sounded like they were still going at it. Could he actually listen in on what they were saying?

"It was total shit show, and you know it," he heard Tasha say suddenly. The quality was low and muffled, sort of like he was listening through a door or wall. But he could still easily make out what she was saying.

"Of course I know it," Finn replied, exasperated. "I almost got my ass handed to me. But we can't just turn him over to the Protectorate, Tash. Not yet, at least."

Tasha snorted. "You worry he will not be safe? Because he is not safe here. And neither are we."

Finn sighed. "I know. It's just–there's too much about this that doesn't feel right to me. Look, I know you're worried. Hell, I'm worried, too. But we promised to help him, right? I think we need a chance to do that before this turns into some kind of Protectorate circus."

Tasha laughed. "Is true. They can be bunch of clowns sometimes."

"And we still need answers," Finn added. "With the way things ended up at the waterfront, I only have more questions."

They hadn't realized that he was awake, apparently.

He needed to get out of the medical pod, so he sought a way to open it. He was met with a warning message letting him know that if he chose to exit the pod at that point, he'd need to keep his shoulder immobilized until the reconstruction work was completed. Then the pod offered him the option to wrap his arm in a sling, so he activated it. Dim, bluish lighting slowly came on around him. With it, he could see a section of the padding overhead slide open, and from it, a pair of narrow, silvery manipulator arms descend down toward him. While he tried to lay still, they fastened a tight sling around him, binding his arm in place across his chest. As the manipulator arms returned to their recessed hiding places, he took a moment to edit the data the machine stored about him while he'd been inside it. Given their indecision about what to do with him, he wasn't quite ready for Finn and Tasha to find out about all of the hidden surprises he'd just discovered about himself.

Once he was ready, he instructed the medical pod to open. There was a slight hiss, then a low hum as the padded dome above him lifted up and slid back behind his head. Things suddenly became very bright, but his eyes quickly adjusted. The muffled conversation stopped, then the door to the room opened. It was Tasha.

"You wake already?" she asked.

He nodded, then looked down at the bandage and his sling. "Yeah, looks like this thing is done with me."

She walked up next to him and inspected the bandage. "Is strange to be done so soon." She walked around behind him to access something on the open lid. "Hmm," he heard her say. "Was so much blood, but damage was not as bad as it looked. You are tough one to hurt. Readings show you will recover in time." She walked back around to his side and offered him her hand. "Let me help you up."

He grabbed her hand and, with her assistance, awkwardly swung himself around and into a sitting position. "Thanks." He slid off the edge of the medbay pod and stood up. There was a brief hint of dizziness, but it quickly passed.

She nodded. "How do you feel?"

He tried to shrug, but his immobilized shoulder made it difficult, so he gave her a grin. "Like I got into a fight with a mechanical bull army and lost. But there isn't any pain."

She smiled. "Medbay pod has good drugs. Come sit with us. We need to debrief. There is food, and coffee, if you like."

"Ok," he said, nodding. "Let's talk."

She smiled again, then turned and walked back out into the warehouse proper. Cam could smell the coffee as he followed her and saw a box of donuts and pastries sitting on the table in the middle of the room. Then his stomach grumbled, betraying his sudden, intense hunger. It was because of the nanites. They must've used a tremendous amount of energy to make the repairs, and that energy had to have come from him.

"I feel like I could eat a horse," he joked.

Tasha snorted lightly. "Horse would have more nutrition than box of donuts, but is all we have for now."

Cam stifled a sudden chuckle as he sat down at the table and poured himself a cup of coffee. After taking a careful sip, he grabbed a big pastry from the box in front of him and shoved a giant chunk in his mouth, relishing in the sugary sweetness as he quickly chewed and swallowed.

"I guess even getting shot doesn't dull your appetite," Finn said behind him. He walked around and stood across the table opposite him. "To be honest, I thought we might lose you at first."

Cam ripped off another chunk of pastry. "Can't talk," he said with his mouth full of food. "Eating."

Finn huffed and rolled his eyes. Then he sat down at the seat in front of him. "That's fine. You go ahead and eat. I'll start." He reached out and took a paper cup from a small stack nearby, then helped himself to some of the coffee. "I'm sure you won't be surprised to hear that what happened back there on the waterfront was a total clusterfuck." He took a sip of his own coffee while he waited for a response from Cam.

Cam narrowed his eyes as he swallowed another bite. Then he offered an awkward, one-shoulder shrug. "Don't blame me. I warned you she had alien death rays."

Finn smirked. "I'm not blaming you, Cam. Hell, I've got an alien death ray of my own. But, whoever the Agent is, hell, whatever she is, she very nearly took us apart at the seams." He shifted his expression, focusing intently on Cam. "But she knew you, didn't she? She called you by name."

The memory caused him to shudder involuntarily. "She sure did. But I still don't have any idea who she is, why she's after me, or how she's been showing up uninvited in my dreams." He took another sip of his coffee and avoided taking Finn's bait.

But Finn didn't let it go. "That's not exactly true, though, is it? She told you why she's after you. She said she wants to take you home. That seems like an awful lot of trouble to go through just to offer somebody a ride, don't you think?"

Cam frowned. "You heard her say that, too?" He looked away. Just because he was obviously at the center of an inter-dimensional scandal didn't mean he had to like it. "I don't know what she meant by that, but I doubt she was offering to give me a lift back to my place."

Finn looked unconvinced. "No, probably not. But there's obviously some kind of connection between you two. To start, there's the fact that you see her in your dreams."

Cam didn't enjoy being reminded of that, even if it was true. "I suppose you're right about that." Then he frowned again. "But it's not like I chose it, and it doesn't mean I'm part of anything she is."

"Hey, relax, friend. I'm not accusing you of anything here. If I'd thought you were one of them, I would've just turned you in before you even woke up the first time." He put his hands down. "But I get it if you're feeling a little rough around the edges right now, after everything that's happened."

Cam admitted to himself that he was being confrontational. Except for letting him get shot—which was only indirectly their fault—and being a little secretive, Finn and Tasha had been nothing but helpful. "You're right. I'm sorry. I am just a little shaken up by everything. And I'm worried about Tony."

Finn nodded knowingly. "That's understandable, too." He shifted in his seat to try and get more comfortable. "So, let's figure out what happened and what we can do next, ok?"

Cam looked at Finn. His expression was placid but otherwise unreadable. He needed Finn's help, and he knew that probably meant being honest. If Finn couldn't be trusted, he would've let him bleed out on the sidewalk instead of bringing him back to the safe house. "Ok, fine."

Finn smiled. "Good. So, here's what I know–or suspect. Somehow you're being tracked. That much is apparent–unless the Agent was waiting at the Market to make a move on the off-chance that we would show up, which is also a possibility, however unlikely it may be. Either way, I don't know how she did it. But she's gone, and Tomás is very dead, and there hasn't been any attention on this building since we got back here, so I think you're safe enough for the time being."

After Tomás kept popping up on his trail in San Francisco, it seemed likely that Finn was right. "Her soldiers kept following me, even after I left her engaged with you. And she still tracked me down, even after I should've thrown her off my trail." He thought about the battle–devastating blasts of energized particles slamming into the concrete near him, cars he'd just been hiding behind flipping and exploding. "Although, now that I think about it, I don't think she was actually trying to kill me."

Finn nodded. "Noticed that, did you? It looked more like she was trying to herd you. She definitely wasn't pulling her punches like that when she shot at me."

Of course, that was what happened. It wasn't like she was

a lousy shot. After all, Cam watched her place a blast in the precise spot to collapse the Devil's Slide tunnel opening after being thrown off her speeding motorcycle. Not to mention the shot that vaporized Tomás Aguilar's head. Cam shuddered again, thinking about that. "It makes sense if she really was sent to retrieve me." He thought back to Tomás and San Francisco. Even then, Cam was the only one to actually fire a weapon. And the guy he'd taken the gun from told him that his boss just wanted to talk. "She seemed pretty upset when Tomás shot me."

"He was aiming for Finn," Tasha shared, walking up from behind him while she rubbed a towel through her wet hair. "Was partly my fault he shot you instead." She'd changed her clothes as well. Tasha set her towel down, then poured herself a cup of coffee. She must've been showering while they were talking, Cam realized. She sat down next to Finn at the table. "Although he hardly had time to realize mistake."

"She would've hurt Tony, though," Cam replied grimly. "I'm sure of that." Then he remembered the Gate. "Not that letting him go did him any good in the end."

Finn sighed. "Yeah, then there's the Gate. One mysterious Gate appearance is unusual. But two, well, that's a pattern." He looked right at Cam as he said it, and Cam knew what Finn really meant by that. He knew that Cam created the Gates somehow and was waiting for him to admit it. There was probably no point in denying it.

Still, he couldn't resist being a little coy. "So yeah, I guess those temporary Gates aren't all that impossible, are they?"

Finn's expression didn't change. "I think I probably know the answer to this, but do you even know how you did it?"

There was no getting past that one. Not with Finn, at least.

"Not really. Until a few days ago, I couldn't even do it. It's never happened to me before."

"Of course. You have never been in actual danger before past few days." Tasha pointed out.

Cam looked at the back of his hands. "I mean, I'm a Brown guy in a white world, so I'm pretty much always in danger. But, no. So far, there's been nothing like getting chased and shot at–or actually shot–until very recently." Talking about it made him feel anxious. He took a breath, sending calm through the growing worry in his body, making himself ready to admit his deep, dark secret. At least that was something he had some experience with already. "Apparently, it was part of an emergency defense system. One of several things I didn't know I could do, at least until today."

Finn looked confused. "I don't follow."

Cam swallowed, then gave them a brief rundown of what he'd just learned about the strange tech that was inside him. Saying it out loud felt weird but strengthened his understanding of it and the fact that it was there. Once he'd finished, he looked at Finn and Tasha expectantly, but both of them seemed to be too stunned to talk.

Finally, Finn broke the silence. "Well, that's a lot of wetware to be unknowingly walking around with."

Cam frowned. "I'm telling the truth."

"Oh, I believe you. I mean, it's the only way you could've done what you've done. And it explains why you've walked away from a potentially lethal injury with nothing more than a sling and some bandages. It also explains what you said in the truck."

Cam didn't understand. "What I said?"

Finn nodded. "You seemed delirious–"

"He was delirious," Tasha interjected.

Finn scowled at her, then continued. "But you said something about nano-colonies and then told us that something was happening in your head. Now we know what that was."

Cam didn't really remember the ride over in the truck. It was mostly a blur. "Ok, so maybe I didn't know about it before because I didn't need to. And now, since I needed to use it, I became aware of it."

"You still think he is not one of you?" Tasha asked.

Cam pointed at Finn. "One of them?"

"Tash–" Finn started.

"Ask him what is in his head," Tasha instructed Cam.

Cam looked at her, then back to Finn, feeling more confused than ever. "Well?"

Finn sighed. "She means Otto."

That wasn't much of an answer. "What's an auto?"

Finn shook his head. "Not auto, although that's actually more accurate. Otto. It's a nickname for my autonomous, on-board AI system. Basically, I have a tiny quantum computer implanted in my skull."

Cam was shocked, which was surprising since he thought he'd pretty much reached his shock limit for the day. "Wait. You've got one, too? A computer in your head?" Finn nodded. Cam turned to Tasha. "What about you?"

Tasha shook her head and laughed. "No. Is nothing in my skull but brains."

Cam considered the implication that he wasn't all that unique after all. It was mind-boggling that he had that kind of hardware in his head without knowing it. At least he wasn't the only one who had it–not even the only one in the room. "Shit. For a second, I thought you were about to tell me that everyone had one, only nobody got around to letting me know."

Finn laughed. "Wouldn't that be something? Talk about conspiracies, right? No, it's still pretty unconventional, and the fact that you have one is even more so. It answers a few things, certainly, but it also brings up many more questions."

Cam sighed. "You don't have to tell me that. I've got a million of my own, mostly variations on how the hell that shit got into my head. But I've got no info about that, at least not that I could find."

"Your wetware sounds different than mine, too. For starters, mine's got its own personality. You've actually heard him already, way back when we were first transporting you in the flyer."

Cam thought back, recalling when he'd first woken up after being drugged by Tasha. There'd been a third voice, he realized. "That was your computer? It talks to you?"

Finn nodded. "Yeah. He provides me with tactical assistance and manages my internal functions and sensor suite."

Tasha snorted. "And he will be so smug, now. Otto was first one to notice you were different."

"So, is she right?" Cam asked. "Could I really be one of you?"

Finn shrugged. "I don't know. At this point, anything is possible, so I can't rule it out."

That wasn't exactly a confirmation, but at least it was a viable possibility. "When did you get yours? Your implant?"

Finn leaned in and put his hands on the table, looking thoughtful. "There's a lot we haven't told you, of course.

219

That's partly been for your protection. But it's also been, for lack of a better phrase, to keep from blowing your mind. I don't think there's much danger of that now, though." He looked over at Tasha, and she just shrugged. "I got my implants when I was thirteen when I joined the Protectorate. That's the organization Tasha and I work for. I'm what's known as Gate sensitive, meaning that, somehow, I have the innate ability to sense disturbances in space-time that are caused by the Gates."

That seemed awfully young to Cam. "You got your job when you were thirteen?"

Finn laughed and shook his head. "No, that's when I went to the Academy to learn how to do my job. I didn't get this job until I'd been fully trained. But the implants always go in better when you're working with a brain that's not fully mature. You can put one in an adult's brain, but giving the implant and its intelligence a chance to grow with its host generally works out better in the long run."

While that made sense on some level, it all still seemed pretty far-fetched. "Ok, I can buy all that, I guess. But there's a piece of your story missing, right? Obviously, all of this stuff exists unless I'm in some kind of coma-induced fantasy right now. But I know that none of this stuff should exist."

Finn looked at Tasha, who shrugged again. "You're not very helpful," he said to her.

"Is your story, is your decision," she replied.

Finn looked back at Cam. "Ok, well, you have a point. And, to be fair, I didn't actually say what government we worked for." Cam's eyes went wide, and he opened his mouth to protest, but Finn held out his hand to stop him. "Let me finish, please." Finn waited until Cam nodded. "You see, this

220

aspect of the multiverse isn't the only one that humans live in. I'm from an alternate Earth in a different universe parallel to this one. A world we call Turana."

And there it was, the other shoe dropping. Of course, it totally made sense how they knew of the Gates and possessed such advanced technology but kept it all secret from everyone. They weren't even from the universe Cam lived in. "So, what? You're aliens?"

Tasha barked out a boisterous laugh. "I am not alien. I am from Saint Petersburg."

Finn laughed along with her. "Technically, I'd be the alien since I am from a different planet. But I'm just as human as you, otherwise. And my ancestors came from this planet, of course, which we call Earth Prime."

Cam made a low whistle. "The Gates. Your ancestors went through the Gates."

Finn touched a finger to the tip of his nose. "You got it. Of course, that was a long time ago. Thousands of years, actually."

The implications from that were pretty fucking extraordinary. Another human civilization, developing independently from his own, for thousands of years. What were they like? "And you all have kept that secret this whole time?"

Finn nodded. "It wasn't a big deal until recently, especially the last several decades or so. And now, with Prime tech starting to really develop, it's even tougher. The internet is our biggest problem. But it's also been our biggest ally, in some ways."

That made sense. The net was the dream platform for conspiracy theorists everywhere. He could probably do a search and come up with thousands of hits on alternate dimensions and realities. But that was mostly the domain of nut jobs and the kind of thing that regular people just dismissed as fantasy. Even he'd have done so. That still left the original question unanswered, though. "So, could I be one of you?"

Finn let out a deep sigh. "As I said, I don't know. I don't think so, but it seems like that would be a possibility."

Cam looked surprised. "That's it?"

Finn grimaced. "There's no evidence that you are. There's no record of you or even someone who could be you. I mean, it's possible your birth was unrecorded, and maybe you ended up orphaned on Earth Prime somehow. Your wetware is definitely not of Prime origin."

That wasn't a very satisfying answer. The more Finn and Tasha learned about him, it seemed like the less they really knew. "That was a lot of possibles and maybes you just said, so I guess you really don't know. Maybe we should just table that for now and focus on what we're going to do for Tony. Like, maybe we should go and find him."

Tasha nodded. "Is a lot of sitting and talking so far. I like his idea better. But we don't know where Tony and angry woman went. Gate was only open for short time, and we did not stick around to run many tests afterward."

Cam smiled. "I know where he is. He's in the same dimension where you found us. Both Gates went there."

Finn and Tasha grimaced. "Ok," Tasha shared, "is maybe not so good plan."

Cam huffed in frustration. "Why not?"

Finn frowned. "If that's where he is, the only Gate we could use to get there is down in the Bay Area. And in a different dimension from this one. We're looking at a half-day of travel minimum. The only way to get directly there from here is through your Gate. The one that you don't know how to use, aside from when you're getting shot at."

That wasn't fair, but he couldn't really argue with that logic, either. "And he went there with her, too," Cam added glumly. "Who knows what she did to him? He could already be dead."

Finn nodded. "Yeah," he quietly agreed, "there's also that. Even if we'd set out right away, we wouldn't have arrived there yet at our best speed. Since you were painting the sidewalk pretty heavily with your blood at the time, we figured that you were in no shape to travel, anyway." He looked at Cam pensively for a moment, then he looked over to Tasha. Finn held her gaze for a moment, then looked back at Cam curiously. "You're sure that you can't open Gates on command?"

Cam shook his head. "Yes. The information is in there, somewhere. But I don't know the system well enough, and I haven't found it yet."

Finn looked up over Cam's head as if he was listening to something. "Ok. Otto says there may be another option. Of course, it's risky and may not work at all."

That was the first thing Cam heard that sounded like a possibility. "I'm listening."

"Well, it should be possible for Otto to, sort of, talk to your system. Maybe, if you're willing, Otto could scan your program matrix and help you figure out how everything works."

It was an astonishing proposition, having an AI from outside his head talk to the computer inside his head. The infosec expert in him was wary of hacking potential, especially since he didn't fully understand his internal system himself yet. But it would hardly be the most dangerous thing he'd done that day. And the possibilities probably outweighed the risks. "Ok, I'm in."

Finn nodded solemnly. "Alright." He stood up and gestured toward the wall of doors. "You should probably get back in the medbay pod, just in case something goes wrong." Then he turned to Tasha. "You ok going to retrieve the Vagabond by yourself?"

She scoffed and waved him off. "Da, of course. Will be piece of cake since I won't have to steal it." She got out of her chair and picked up the damp towel she'd set down next to her. "I will alert you if things go wrong," she added before walking away.

Cam pushed himself back from the table, then stood up and walked back to the room with the medbay pod in it. The curved lid was still open, and it was easier to get into it one-handed than to climb out of. Nestled in the reclined position of the medbay couch, he waited for Finn. He was nervous, so he breathed in and out slowly and evenly, trying to keep himself calm and keep his heart rate down.

Finn walked in, then, carrying a folding chair. He opened it and set it next to the medbay, then sat down. "Ok. You and I don't really have to do anything here. It'll be Otto doing the heavy lifting."

Cam nodded, his mouth tight. "Got it." Then he felt a strange sensation. It was a notification. He focused on it and received a connection request from Otto. Cam consented to it, then tensed up briefly before forcing himself again to relax. There were a few moments where he felt nothing, then a voice spoke in his head.

<Hello, Cam>

<Otto?>

<*Yes. I'm using your internal system to speak with you, much like I do with Finn. I am unfamiliar with your specific code structure, so I will run a quick analysis to determine its functions. You may briefly see and hear visual and auditory stimuli. Please do not be alarmed*>

<Ok>

Cam continued to lay there. After a moment, he jumped when he heard what sounded like wind rushing by his ears. Then he jumped again at the sound of a quick, sharp, piercing tone.

"You're doing great," Finn assured him.

Cam smiled at the reassurance, feeling a little like he was a child in a doctor's office, about to get a set of shots. Then he jumped again when a blob of bluish-green light popped into existence in the middle of his field of vision. "Whoa," he said quietly as the blob morphed and spread around in front of him. It started to change colors, adding in purple and reddish tones as it moved. "Ok, this is pretty cool."

<*I've completed the initial scan. Your system code is unlike anything I've encountered before, but there is a definite structure to it. I believe that the activation process may have been incomplete, likely because the pathways of the neural and physical interfaces have degraded significantly from years of disuse*>

<You believe?>

<*It's a figure of speech, meaning that I've assigned that possibility a high degree of probability. I also believe that this can be corrected. However, it will likely involve some physical and mental discomfort for you*>

<Discomfort sounds like it might a euphemism for pain, Otto.>

<I do not experience physical sensation the way you do, so I cannot adequately explain what you should expect. I can directly share with you what I intend to do, which may help you understand>

<Ok, do it.>

Cam's brain was filled with the knowledge of the procedure Otto proposed. The AI intended to simulate the missing years of use by artificially stimulating the pathways used to communicate and control various functions in his body. These pathways were biological in nature and were grown throughout his brain and body. Because they'd never been used, they'd atrophied, much like a muscle would from lack of exercise. When he tried to relate it to concepts he was already familiar with, the best Cam could come up with was essentially shock therapy.

Finn let out a low whistle. "Has Otto explained what is going to happen?" he asked.

Cam nodded. "Yeah. It sounds like it's going to suck."

Finn chuckled. "I remember when they installed Otto's hardware. I had to be conscious, of course, since it was brain surgery, although they blocked my pain receptors for most of that, and of course, the brain itself doesn't have any pain receptors." He took a deep breath before continuing. "But the worst part was when they grew the communication and control pathways. It felt like they'd set every nerve in my body on fire."

Cam gulped. That sounded a lot more extreme than discomfort. "So, you're saying this is probably going to hurt?"

"Well, it probably won't hurt as much as getting shot, but it will last a lot longer." He reached out, then and gently grabbed Cam's hand. Finn's hand was warm in his, and Cam

226

could feel the rough, calloused surface of his palm. "You don't have to go through with this. Eventually, as you and your system continue to interface, these pathways will strengthen by themselves."

"Yeah," Cam said, "the keyword there being 'eventually.' We don't have time to wait around for that to happen, though."

Finn nodded. "Then, you're ready?"

Cam's face was set with determination. "I am."

Finn squeezed his hand. "Ok. Otto is ready when you are."

<Let's do this, Otto>

<*Very well. I am sorry that this will be painful for you. Although I am not responsible for this situation, I still regret that this is necessary*>

That was definitely a sentiment he could identify with. He felt a sudden absence, presumably as his system went offline. Then there was a tickling sensation at the base of his skull. It was irritating, but no more than that, and something he could live with, at least temporarily. Suddenly a searing pain shot out from there, rapidly spreading down through his body and out through his limbs like someone was pouring molten metal through his veins. He gasped loudly and squeezed Finn's hand tightly, almost unconsciously, as the pain grew so bad he could hardly stand it. "Holy shit," he muttered through clenched teeth.

Finn held Cam's grip firmly. "Try to keep breathing," he said. "Breathing through the pain will help."

But Cam hardly heard him as the pain continued to spread in wave after wave of agony. Every muscle in his body tensed to the point of cramping. The light in the room grew brighter, and he squeezed his eyes shut as it flared to the point of being painful. Cam started to buck, unable to hold himself still as the pain rolled through his body, but Finn put a hand on his chest and pressed him down into the medbay couch. Finally, when Cam began to think he couldn't take it any longer, the pain stopped. He let out a slow, ragged breath. The relief at the sudden absence of pain felt almost cold. He kept his eyes closed, a tear slowly running down his cheek as he savored the return to calm darkness.

<I've completed the process. While doing that, I was also able to thoroughly examine your system and have created a neural map that should help you more easily access your system functions. I will share it with you now>

Otto's voice returned, or the idea of it, at least. Before, it was a dull presence, like hearing someone talk through a speakerphone. It had since gained the fidelity and depth of a high-end audio system. That clarity spread throughout his entire sensory range. The objects in his vision took on a richness and sharpness that almost seemed unreal. Even Finn's hand, held tightly in his own, felt firmer and more real. Then his mind filled with a new awareness of himself as Otto shared the neural map. All of his system functions became apparent, including, thankfully, his ability to create Gates.

"It worked," he said excitedly and closed off the connection to Otto.

Finn smiled. Then he let go of Cam's hand and placed it on his shoulder. "That's good. I don't think I could watch you go through that again." He grimaced tightly. "It brought up a lot of painful memories." Then he chuckled softly. "Not that it probably wasn't a lot more unpleasant to experience it."

Cam chuckled in return. The pain was all but a distant

memory already. Except for stiffness in his shoulder, which was still comfortably numb, he felt great, like he'd just woken up from the best night's sleep. He looked up at Finn and saw the same caring and concern in his handsome face that he'd heard in his voice. Finn's deep brown eyes were surprisingly gentle as they looked down on him. Then Cam was keenly aware, suddenly, of Finn's hand on his shoulder, of how he'd held Finn's hand tightly when the pain was happening. Finn's open displays of affection, casual body contact, and a sense of neediness brought on by much recent trauma all conspired against him, as he realized that he was very attracted to Finn. He felt a sudden tension in his groin. Oh shit. He willed himself to stop it from happening, much like he recalled doing during his puberty years, and, surprisingly, the tension eased. If the only benefit from having that new control over his body was to prevent unexpected erections, then the pain was totally worth it.

Finn, seeming to sense that something was amiss but not knowing what, calmly pulled his hand away and sat back into his chair. "So, I hate to rush the moment here, but there's still the million-dollar question. Can you do it?"

"Hell yeah, I can."

FINN

The nighttime landscape was peaceful and serene, softly illuminated by the light of a pale, glowing moon. The low, rolling, forested hills perched on the edge of the broad estuary were quiet but for the occasional owl hoot or wolf howl. Until the Gate appeared, that is.

Screeching birds scattered wildly as the otherworldly portal flashed into existence in the middle of a clearing. It stayed open just long enough for three figures to step through it, then snapped out of sight with a flash and lingering sparks of blue light.

It was the first time Finn had stepped through one of Cam's Gates himself, and the experience was a little thrilling, which was saying a lot for someone who'd seen as much of the multiverse as he had. Even the sensations from the Gate had been different from what he was used to.

Finn's eyes immediately adjusted to the low light, his pupils opening wide to take in the gorgeous nighttime scenery. The smells of saltwater and pine were almost strong enough to be overwhelming. The stars blazed like beacons above them, as bright as they would've been far away from any signs of civilization back home. And, where he was standing, civilization was as far away from them as it could get.

Once Cam had determined that he could consciously open and close his own Gates, it had taken all of Finn's considerable charm to make him wait for Tasha to return before they set off. Cam had only agreed once Finn had convinced him that having Tasha on hand could be valuable if there were any trouble, not to mention how angry she would've been with them both if they left without her. And Finn had allowed him to open a test Gate, as well. To be honest, even Finn had been excited about that, to witness the process when he actually knew it was coming.

"Now what?" Cam asked.

Finn looked around them. There was no way to know for sure, but it certainly looked like they hadn't changed position, only dimension. "Well, so far, your Gates only seem to allow dimensional transit, which I think means that we'll need to walk north a few miles." He looked back at the pair standing next to him. "I'll take point," he announced, then started to head north.

Tasha, who was wearing slender eyewear that enabled her to see in the dark, too, gestured for Cam to follow. "I will take rear," she announced, gesturing for Cam to head out.

Cam adjusted his pack and followed after Finn.

Finn had provided Cam with a new set of clothing at the warehouse, similar to what he was wearing. It was more rugged and practical than what Cam had been wearing before, plus the new shirt didn't have a giant, bloody hole in the shoulder like his old one. Finn also gave him a pair of sturdy but comfortable boots and a new backpack holding emergency supplies that he slung over his good shoulder. Plus, he returned the Dominator, now reloaded, that Cam wore in a belt holster. After the events at the

Market, Finn agreed that Cam would benefit from carrying it for some additional protection, at least until he became more familiar with his own offensive and defensive systems. Which, according to Otto, were more extensive than his own. Otto's interactions with Cam's system, while certainly helping to bring it to full functionality, had also provided a wealth of information, even if none of it was conclusive.

<His system was constructed on a program matrix like I've never seen> Otto had told him. *<I recognize it for what it is, and it makes sense on a quantum level, but it's definitely not based on the same root structures that I am>*

<Pretend I don't know what any of that means.>

Otto gave him the digital equivalent of a dramatic sigh. *<It means that it's not one of ours. But not just the system. Unless he was a radical, experimental one-off, nothing that Cam is wetwired for came from us. The firmware architecture may as well have been written in alien code>*

<Ok, but–>

<But from none of the alien code we already know and use>

Finn had heard that song before, of course. <Like hers?>

<I haven't seen any of her code, so I couldn't say>

<Then we just put this on our list of strange oddities and coincidences?>

<Our body of anecdotal evidence is massing, indeed, although we still lack anything categorical. That said, we've established a clear connection between Cameron and the Agent>

<But what do we know?>

<Cameron is wetwired with offensive and defensive capabilities that likely surpass your own>

Finn's logical mind told him that Cam had to be some kind of a sleeper agent, so deeply undercover that even he wasn't aware of who he was. But his instincts didn't agree with that logic. If he was a deep-cover sleeper, why was he fighting against the attempts to bring him back in? Had something gone wrong with his personality programming, leaving him unable to be activated?

Even if he was a sleeper agent, who was he an agent for? Did he represent the interests as Sable? Did he oppose them? One underground group popping up out of nowhere was alarming enough. But two? That was just plain madness. Still, Finn wasn't ready to hand the situation, and Cam, over to his superiors at the Protectorate just yet. Tash had made some good points about why it was past time to do so. But it still felt too much like he would've been handing them a report full of maybes and unknowns. And, despite Tasha's trepidation about how far outside their mission parameters they'd gone, Finn knew he was still well within his operational remit. He'd generally been given wide latitudes for dealing with trouble on Earth Prime. He knew that their current situation was no different.

Finn turned back to Cam and flashed him a smile. "So, how are you adjusting to having your new brain-buddy?"

"Is that what you call Otto?" Cam asked in reply.

Finn chuckled. "Not to his face."

Cam laughed. His mood had improved significantly after they'd done the painful procedure back in the safe house. "It's been weird, but a good weird, you know? And it's nice to have at least some explanation for my new superpowers."

"I can remember what it was like to suddenly have Otto with me all the time. At first, it felt like an invasion, but that was just the moody, teenage me, I think. Now, I couldn't imagine not having him there."

Cam looked at him curiously. "You call Otto 'him'?"

Finn nodded, smiling. "Yeah. He decided that he wanted to use masculine pronouns. Who am I to say no?"

Cam seemed to consider that, then nodded. "I guess so, yeah. I don't have a lot of experience dealing with self-aware artificial intelligences, especially one that's implanted in my head."

"Well, the stuff in your head is nothing to scoff at. The ability to create your own Gates? If you'd asked me if that was possible a few days ago, I would've said no. "

Cam lifted an eyebrow dramatically. "Yeah, well, I've seen quite a few things in the last few days that I thought were impossible."

Finn chuckled. "That's true, I suppose. You weren't exactly in a position to see any of this coming, were you?"

Cam shook his head. "No, not really. I've been swept up in the kind of adventure I've only ever read about or seen in the movies." He swept his arms out dramatically. "I mean, all of this? I'm on another fucking planet, another version of Earth. One of many, apparently, that I never would've even known about before all this."

While Finn had seen many people try to come to terms with how big the multiverse actually was, at least on a relatable scale, it wasn't something he'd ever experienced firsthand. He'd grown up knowing that humanity lived on more than one planet. "That's not your fault. Most Primes never even have the chance to learn that they're not alone in the universe. There's a lot you wouldn't know about.

Cam looked at Finn, his eyes narrowed. "You did say there were a lot of things you hadn't told me. Maybe now it's time that you did."

Finn sighed. He'd felt a lot more comfortable keeping his charges in the dark when they were still just innocent bystanders. But Cam was no bystander in all that was happening, and he definitely wasn't innocent. He deserved to be told. "Yeah, we usually don't do this sort of thing, having civilians along on missions like this. We tend to keep our operational activity within the Protectorate."

"Don't let him fool you," Tasha added from behind them. "Finn is always breaking rules. Today is just bigger rules."

Cam looked back at her and smiled, then turned toward Finn with his eyebrow raised again. "Well, we've got a ways to go before we get there. May as well lay it on me."

So Finn started telling Cam the story of Turana.

According to their ancestors, Finn explained, the Gates first appeared around twenty-five hundred years ago. There are many Gates, especially when you consider all of the different universes they appear in. But, for a planet the size of the Earth–

"How many alternate universes are there?" Cam interrupted.

"There's an infinite number of them," Finn replied. "But we've actually discovered and categorized several thousand through the Gate network. Now, stop interrupting."

For a planet the size of the Earth, there were relatively few Gates in total. There was one on California's central coast, discovered by a community of people living nearby. They were naturally wary of it. They first thought it was a tear in the boundary between the world of the living and the world of the dead, and they feared that the dead were going to come back through it. But, after communing with the spirits, one shaman announced that it was actually a portal to the spirit world. The shaman told the people they were being called to ascend and live with the spirits in their home plane of existence. It's understood that the shaman was one of the first people to experience Gate sense, which could've explained their understanding that it was something special, even if they didn't know why.

After a successful transit through the Gate and back, the shaman described a fantasy world with warmer, milder temperatures, lush vegetation, and strange animals that they'd never seen before. The stars in the sky were different, and there were two moons instead of one. It took some effort, but the shaman persuaded their tribal Chieftain to accompany them on another visit. When the pair returned, the Chief announced that his followers should prepare to migrate to the new world. Word of this spread, which led to several other Chieftains also visiting the new world. Eventually, this group of tribes all used the Gate to transit to the Earth-analogue planet it led to. Believing they were going to live among spirits, they called themselves the Chosen people.

After some time in the new world, and after several other tribes left Earth Prime to join the Chosen, the Gate mysteriously vanished.

According to historians, another Gate opened between the Chosen people's new world and their old one around a decade or so later. Unlike the original Gate, the new one led to a Prime island in the South Pacific. The Chosen sent a shaman through the Gate, who discovered the island and its people. The island people were naturally curious about the Gate and more than a little concerned with the strange people who lived beyond it. But the island Chief, who'd been preparing to send out a seagoing party to find new land, sent his oldest son back through the Gate with the shaman. When the Chief's son returned, he described the Chosen people's strange ways and the vast quantities of land and resources where they lived. It was fortunate timing. As a giant typhoon soon appeared on the horizon, and the Chief became convinced that the gods had sent the Gate to save his people from the storm. So he evacuated everyone, and whatever possessions they could carry, to the world of the Chosen people and, just as the hurricane was about to strike the island, the Gate closed behind them.

Despite the many challenges the two groups faced, their many differences, and even a few violent struggles, both groups managed to start living and working with one another in an uneasy alliance that eventually became a deep, trusting bond. Even though they had different languages and differing beliefs, they all shared the same, deeply held core values of honoring family, community, and all the bounty of the natural world. And, above all else, they had one crucial thing in common. They all believed that they'd somehow been transported to their new world by their gods.

Then, one day, they actually met some gods.

Those gods, it turned out, weren't gods at all. They were just people from another planet. They came from the planet Nynar, in yet another universe, and called themselves the Nynari. Nynar was the fifth planet in their system, between Mars and Jupiter, in place of the asteroid belt in both the Prime and Chosen people's universe. The Nynari discovered the new community of humans through their exploration of the Gate network. When they realized that those people were not native to that universe, they became curious about the Gate travelers and made themselves known.

The Nynari are a benevolent race, unlike some of the peoples that the Chosen's Prime cousins were eventually visited and then conquered by. After some time, they managed to convince the Chosen that, although they were indeed highly advanced, they were not actual gods. They were just neighbors, and they didn't want to be worshiped. They just wanted to help.

Even back then, the Nynari were already an ancient race and had advanced to technology levels far beyond even what Cam and his contemporaries from Earth Prime had developed. They were willing to share that knowledge and technology and only ever asked one thing of the Chosen people in return—to keep the Gates' existence secret from their ancestors on Earth Prime.

And thus, the people of Turana—which is what their world came to be called—flourished and thrived. Their original cultures blended and merged over time but, eventually, a movement emerged among the Turani who wanted something more. While most people appreciated the gifts of the Nynari and were content with how they'd built their society, some wished to have a closer relationship with their Nynari neighbors. They sought to live near them and create a community more in line with Nynari ideals. After talks with the Nynari leadership, those people were invited to settle on the Earth-analogue planet in the Nynari system, a world the Nynari called Andras. So they traveled there through the Gates and built another human society. Of the two newly settled human worlds, Turana was a more idyllic culture. Its people held to the idea of using Nynari technology only to coexist peacefully with the land and sea. But Andras grew to become much more cosmopolitan in nature, using their access to Nynar to become a technological paradise.

Finn revealed that he was Turani and worked as an agent of the Protectorate. The joint Turani, Andrani, and Nynari organization monitored travel through the Gate network, investigated any unknown dimensional disturbances, and maintained the network's secrecy.

"Wait," Cam interrupted again. "So your people–"

"The Turani," Finn corrected him.

Cam nodded. "Thank you. So, the Turani don't know about the Gates either, then?"

Tasha chuckled, but Finn responded. "Oh, no. We all know about the Gates. They're a huge part of our history, after all. We just keep them secret from you."

Cam frowned. "That doesn't exactly seem fair. I mean, your people are so advanced, and there are a lot of folks on my world that could really benefit from that."

"It's not about being fair," Finn pointed out. "At first, it wasn't even up to us. But, by the time we were first able to go back to Earth Prime again, it had been so long that we hardly recognized the world we'd left behind."

Turana and Andras had, between them, a total population of around one-hundred eighty million people. They'd both developed into peaceful societies full of abundance, each caring for their people's needs in their own way. Unlike their Prime cousins, they had no history of war or oppression. Adding Prime humans to the multiverse community, with their history of violence and warfare, was seen as a sure-fire way to bring everything they'd built to a swift end. But, beyond fearing for their own way of life, the Turani and Andrani peoples also had no wish to be conquerors over someone else.

"Besides, it's not like we've never helped you," Finn admitted. "There's been more than one plague that was cured and more than one disaster that was averted because we secretly intervened."

Cam scrutinized him with a penetrating gaze. Finn guessed that there was already a lot going on in Cam's head before all of this. He could only imagine how noisy it was in there now. He probably understood what Finn was explaining. Cam was pretty sharp. But Finn knew plenty of Prime humans who just couldn't wrap their heads around the idea that no one was going to come in and clean up their mess for them.

"Yeah, I guess I can see what you're saying," Cam finally acknowledged. "Honestly, the biggest reason I'm upset is that you're probably right. Even if you did start sharing your advancements with us, it wouldn't do most of us any good. They'd be hoarded by the rich and powerful and probably end up being used against the rest of us somehow."

Finn stopped and looked at Cam earnestly. The way the silver moonlight lit his cheekbones and the curve of his nose was quite arresting. Looking at him, Finn was again struck by how Turani he looked. "You know, I've spent a lot of time on Earth Prime, Cam, maybe even more than I have back home at this point. It makes me angry and sad to think about all of the shitty things Primes do to one another. But I know that there are plenty of good things on Earth Prime, too. And good people, like you."

Cam smiled and looked away. He was probably blushing, but Finn resisted the urge to check on the infrared spectrum to find out. "Thanks, Finn."

The group continued on in silence for a while. Cam obviously had plenty to think about, digesting everything that Finn just shared with him. But Finn had shared all that for another reason, too. He wanted to see how Cam would react. Not everyone on Turana or Andras agreed with the non-intervention policy, and, from time to time, some of the people who shared that dissent got together and started to make trouble. It was the most likely reason for what had been happening lately, and the enhanced Agent they'd been dealing with probably represented a new iteration of one of those groups. But Cam's understanding seemed genuine enough.

"So, how do you think the Agent figures into all of this?" Cam wondered aloud as if he had been reading Finn's mind.

"We honestly don't know yet," Finn replied, his voice heavy with frustration. "There have always been people, and even groups of people, that disagree with the way things are. Sometimes, even violently so. Until a few days ago, that's how we were approaching this. But this situation seems a lot different from those, especially given the Agent's interest in you."

Cam looked at him, frowning, his eyebrows raised plaintively. "So, you really don't know anything about who I am?"

Finn shrugged. "Well, there's what I knew about you before. But now I don't have a fucking clue, Cam."

Cam looked thoughtful for a moment, his features drained of color but glowing softly in the moonlit night. "So let's speculate, then."

"Ok. You can create Gates, right? You're not even opening one that already exists. You're actually forcing one into existence, temporarily, for as long as it takes you to cross it.

241

That's just–" He stopped. He was struggling with the idea himself still. "It's why Tasha wanted to take you in. There's only one group we know of that could possibly do something like this. Only, as far as we know, even they can't do it."

"The Nynari?"

Finn nodded. "Yeah. We know a lot about Gates, but most of that knowledge originally came from them. Still, I guess in an infinite multiverse, it's technically possible that you could've been born this way."

"Like how it's technically possible that I could win the lottery if I actually bought a ticket?"

Finn laughed. "Yeah, but with the way your luck is trending, I don't know that I'd rush out and buy one. It would probably try to kill you. But it's not just the Gates. All that wetwired hardware is definitely not naturally occurring, so someone had to put that there. I don't believe it was the Protectorate because we just wouldn't do something like that."

Cam didn't seem convinced. "But, you told me that you were recruited when you were only a kid."

Finn shook his head. "I was thirteen, which isn't as much of a kid for a Turani as it is for a Prime. And when I was tested for Gate sense, it turned out to be strong enough that I was encouraged to join the Protectorate."

"Encouraged?"

Finn nodded firmly. "Yeah, Cam. Just like it sounds. No one gets forced to do anything they don't want to do. Even after I graduated from the Academy, joining up was still a choice. I chose to do it, and I don't regret that choice. It's an amazing life, and it allows me to do exciting things, like stalk across an unknown planet in the middle of the night, telling the story of my people."

Cam chuckled. "I hear you. I actually was hoping to get a brochure when we're done in case I wanted to join up."

Finn smiled. "They don't print them in English, but you could probably translate it well enough, now."

Cam just smirked. "So, I'm not just a freak of nature then."

Finn nodded. "That seems pretty likely. Which brings me back to the only working theory I have, that you're some kind of Nynari experiment. Except you're walking around under the impression that you're not, so–"

"So that theory holds water like a leaky bucket, yeah." Cam stopped walking for a moment, deep in contemplation. "You know, I have a lifetime of memories, Finn. They're all from Earth Prime, and none of them involve a little radical implant surgery for my bar mitzvah."

"It's not just that, though," Finn added. "What you can do is extraordinary, in a literal way, and the fact that you can do it as easily as riding an elevator is astounding. Somebody had to come up with a way to do that. But who? Was it the Nynari? If so, then why haven't they told us?" He looked over at Cam. "And if they didn't, then who did? Because it sure as hell looks like someone did."

Cam sighed wistfully. "You know, aside from the fact that everything I believed about the universe turned out to be untrue, I've hardly had a chance to come to terms with all the hardware in my head, not to mention the whole inter-dimensional travel thing. But the idea that I was created in some illicit, alien gene lab and dropped into the not-so-loving arms of my asshole parents is not something I can easily wrap my head around."

Finn could see the hurt and confusion in Cam's eyes. He instinctively reached across and put a hand on Cam's shoulder. "It's kind of like finding out the Tooth Fairy was actually real all along, eh?"

Cam looked at him with feigned shock. "Wait, the Tooth Fairy isn't real?"

Finn laughed. "I'm sorry to be the one to break it to you."

Cam rolled his eyes. "It's alright. If there really was a Tooth Fairy, she'd probably try to kill me, too."

They walked on in companionable silence for a while. Tasha had been surprisingly quiet on their journey while he and Cam talked. But Finn knew she'd been through something very similar, herself. He remembered when he found her, tired, scared, and injured, standing over the corpse of an enormous, feline predator that she'd successfully defended herself against. She, too, had suddenly, and accidentally, discovered that there was a lot more to the universe than she'd been taught.

Soon they crested a small hill and saw the marshy shoreline spread out majestically below them. Since they first appeared on that world, the moon had risen in the sky and bathed the landscape with a cold, pearly glow.

"We are getting close," Tasha announced to no one in particular.

"Shit, Tasha," Cam said, with lightness in his tone. "You've been so quiet I forgot you were here."

She scoffed. "I am not enhanced super-warrior like you and Finn. It is harder for me to see in dark."

"I don't know," Cam replied. "I gotta say that I'm having a hard time believing a little darkness would be a big deal for you."

She shrugged. "Is not big deal for me. Just harder. Plus, you and Finn needed to have little talk, so you can find out

244

just how much there is you do not know." Then she looked at Cam. "Also, I do not trust you."

"Tash," Finn chided her.

She frowned. "I'm sorry. I'm not warm and fuzzy like Finn. I do not scare easily, and what you do scares me. But Finn trusts you, and I trust Finn. Is good enough for now."

Cam wouldn't be the first person to have folded under Tasha's brutal honesty, but he seemed to be taking it all in stride. "You may not be a super-warrior, Tasha, but you told me you fought off a Siberian tiger single-handedly. That's not exactly ordinary, either."

She laughed. "Maybe not in San Francisco. But you have clearly never been to St. Petersburg."

Finn just shook his head and started walking again. He'd been to St. Petersburg, so he knew she wasn't kidding. But Finn appreciated the effort that Cam was making with her, even though he didn't have to. He may need to pull Tasha aside at some point and ask her to go a little easier on him, though. He knew that Tasha had a little keener understanding of power dynamics when it came to race and identity than most Prime white women. But the two of them had never before been in a situation with such open and honest interaction with other Primes. Their usual process was rescue, transport, then memory wipe–one, two, three, and done.

<I am detecting traces of local space-time fragmentation consistent with the readings from the Gate that Cam produces.>

<Anything we need to worry about?>

<No. The levels are well within acceptable safety margins.>

Still, Finn couldn't help but feel a little alarmed. Otto had been able to make detailed scans of Cam's previous three

Gates–the one on the waterfront, the test in the warehouse, and the one they'd used to transit to their current location. He claimed that the instability the Gates created in space-time was sufficiently localized and brief enough to not cause lasting damage. While the physics behind the Gate network were well above his pay grade, Finn knew enough about them to understand that, however they'd initially occurred, they were potentially dangerous. Even stable Gates used for regular transit and commerce were violations of many accepted natural laws and were zones that were continuously monitored for signs of collapse. When a Gate did finally collapse, it mostly did so with little fanfare. But, on rare occasions, they did so quite spectacularly and caused an immense wave of damage that could be felt well beyond the universe they occurred in.

He thought back to the mission he and Tasha had on TDD-145, a pleasant and seemingly benign Earth-analogue, where a Gate had been exhibiting symptoms of impending collapse. It had started out as a routine milk run, with the pair acting as bodyguards for the data collectors from Protectorate Science. Since the Gate had been located in a forested region, the worst things they expected to deal with were a few local wildlife disturbances. But then everything had gone to shit, and they'd been lucky to walk away with their lives.

Cam stopped suddenly. "This is the spot," he announced. He pointed ahead. "The Gate would've appeared right there.

Tasha already had her handheld out and was waving it around and taking readings.

Finn stopped where he was and stood still for a moment, eyes closed. He could sense the telltales of Gate activity. It was the same feeling that he'd gotten on the other side at the Seattle waterfront, although much weaker, given how long it had been. "I can feel your Gate, still. It feels strange, somehow. It's not what I'm used to."

"What does it feel like to sense a Gate?" Cam asked.

Finn laughed. "That's like asking what sound tastes like. If you don't have the sense, there's just no frame of reference." He looked around carefully, trying to map the bucolic nighttime scene where he was standing to the Prime cityside waterfront. The shoreline was much farther out, so either the tide had gone way out, or the ocean levels were lower than they were on Earth Prime. If it weren't for all the footprints, there'd be no signs of anything like civilization where they were. He took a deep breath and noticed that even the air smelled different. That made sense, considering that there was no city to be found. It was also strange to be standing there, so close to where he'd grown up on Turana. Perhaps the area his ancestors had settled in looked like that once, too. "Ok, everybody, there's obviously no one else here, so let's everyone look for clues."

Cam narrowed his eyes in suspicion. "That's it? Just look around? Don't you have super-attenuated sensors or something?"

Finn nodded and pointed to his eyes. "Yep. Two of them are right here, same as you. And this is as good a chance as any to try out your own enhanced sensors."

Cam seemed to consider that. "Yeah, I guess I could. I want to be useful."

Finn didn't blame him. He would've felt a lot like the fifth wheel in Cam's shoes, too. Not to mention the guilt about Tony he was probably dealing with. Cam started to look around, and Finn left him to it, focusing instead on the two sets of footprints he could see on the ground.

<Otto, isolate and highlight the different sets of footprints, please>

One set of prints immediately began to faintly glow blue. They looked to be Tony's, based on the size and the markings left from the soles of Tony's shoes. As he followed them with his eyes, a trail began to appear. The second set of prints started to glow red, smaller in size, with markings consistent with combat boots. They must've been the Agent's. He found where the trail began, then bent down to examine the ground around that area. Interesting. Finn followed the highlighted path for a few meters until both sets of footprints just disappeared. That was strange. There weren't any apparent signs that they were picked up by a vehicle of any sort. Given who the pair were, that only left one option.

He closed his eyes and let his attention drift for a few moments. Gates were easy to sense when they were happening, but even when they were closed, they left lingering traces of the energy disturbances he could pick up on. The Nynari claimed that most living creatures could sense disturbances in the fabric of space-time, but that, for some, the ability was more pronounced. He had no additional sensory organ or anything like that. It was merely that his brain was able to process the myriad minute physical cues–vibrations, temperature differentials, even smells–into something resembling a feeling. As he lost focus, he started to pick up on something. Yes, that was it. There had definitely been a Gate there, although only for a short time and many hours in the past. Another day or so, and he wouldn't have been able to detect it at all.

<Otto, are you getting this?>

<Yes. The readings are evident>

<They Gated away from here, then?>

<So it would appear>

<Are you picking up anything like a destination?>

<Unfortunately, no. The readings are clearly the result of a Gate, but beyond that, they're fundamentally different from what I'm calibrated to decipher>

Damn. Finn looked over at Tasha, who approached him while she took readings of the area with her handheld. She noticed his attention and looked up. "You sense it?" she asked quietly.

He nodded, his face grim. "This is just getting stranger and stranger, isn't it?"

She jerked her head toward Cam. "Does he know yet?"

Finn shook his head. "No, not yet." He looked over at Cam, who seemed to have found the footprints as well, and was following them toward where he was standing. "You got something?" Finn asked him.

Cam looked up at him and smiled. "Yeah, I do." He pointed excitedly back toward where the footprints appeared. "It looks like they both came through back there. And came through pretty hard, I'd guess, based on the body prints they left behind on the ground. Then, they stood there, facing each other, before walking up this way. There aren't any signs of struggle, and she wasn't walking him at gunpoint, or the tracks would overlap. So he went with her willingly." He saw how Finn and Tasha were looking at him, then his face went sour. "But you probably figured that out already."

Tasha chuckled. "Welcome to team, new guy."

Finn rolled his eyes. "Relax, Cam. We're both way more experienced at this, is all. So what happened next?"

Cam looked back down, then followed the trail with his eyes until it stopped near where Finn and Tasha were standing. "Wait? The footprints just stop right there? That can't be–" Then they could see the lightbulb go off in his mind. "Shit. Another Gate."

Finn looked at Tasha with a grin, but she just snorted. "Beginner's luck."

But Cam's mind was already working, it seemed. "So they came here through my Gate, then walked over here, and left through another Gate? One that happened to be right here, right then? And is now gone?"

Finn nodded. "That's about the size of it, I'd say." Then he let Cam continue his train of thought.

Cam didn't seem happy with whatever he was working out. "But, according to what you've told me, that Gate should still be here, right?"

Finn nodded. "Yeah. It's certainly possible that it was a naturally occurring Gate that has since closed on its own or even has a regular open and close cycle. Those do exist."

Cam narrowed his eyes. He clearly didn't like the sound of that. "But what are the odds that there happens to be one of those right here, within spitting distance of where they landed?"

"With that kind of luck," said Tasha, "they should buy lottery tickets."

Finn had worked it out already, of course. It was the most likely scenario, and it neatly answered almost as many questions as it brought up, which was something of a first for them lately. But it wasn't a great answer, and he really wanted Cam to work it out for himself instead of being told. That way, he might more readily accept it.

250

Cam sighed. "So she can create Gates, too? Like me?"

"We don't actually know that, Cam," Finn replied gently, which was true. They only had evidence of a recent Gate manifestation and no additional signs of Tony or the Agent. The rest was all conjecture that conveniently happened to fit the facts.

The idea apparently didn't sit well with Cam. "But we already know that I'm connected to her somehow, right?" Cam asked. "I mean, I saw her in my dream. So tell me, what else could it be, then?"

Finn held back a sigh, reminding himself that Cam had every right to be a little upset about the situation. "Just because it's the only explanation we have that fits the facts doesn't mean it's the only possible explanation. Right now, the only thing we can say for sure is that we don't know."

"Remember," Tasha added, "is big multiverse. Many things can happen."

Cam shook his head. "But don't you see that it makes perfect sense? It's got to be why she's been looking for me." He got quiet for a moment. "She said she wanted to take me home, remember?" He threw his hands out dramatically. "That's why she's been chasing me. Because she and I are the same."

Finn put a comforting hand on Cam's shoulder. "Cam, we don't know that. And it doesn't make perfect sense. Think about it. If she could create her own Gates like you can, why hasn't she ever done so before? Why chase you down when she could just locate you and appear right in your path?" Finn waited while Cam processed what he'd said. "And even if she has the same abilities as you, that doesn't make you the same people." At least, Finn hoped that was true. The jury was still out, so to speak, given Cam's own violent behavior in the recent past. The primary difference that Finn could see, though, was that any violence Cam had perpetrated recently was purely out of self-preservation. The Agent was definitely more of a shoot first, then maybe shoot some more later, kinda person. Whether Cam believed that or not himself, though, still wasn't apparent.

Cam nodded slowly. "Ok, maybe you're right. But everything still points to some kind of relationship between us, right? And she's somehow the missing link in this chain. She knows who I am, Finn. Or at least she believes she does. And, since it looks like Tony was still alive when he left this place, that just makes it even more important for us to track her down. She's got the answers we need. We just need to find out where she and Tony actually went."

Finn nodded. "Yeah, that's an excellent question, too. Unfortunately, it's one that we don't have an answer for."

"I have readings," Tasha offered, "but device cannot determine where Gate led to."

Cam looked at her, his eyes narrowed suspiciously. "That device can't do it. Which means there's one that could, though, right?"

She nodded. "Yes. Protectorate computers can probably do it."

Cam looked at her in surprise as he realized what she was saying. "So, that means–"

Finn smiled. "We have to go to Turana."

CAM

Cam was surprised at how boring interdimensional travel turned out to be. It was exciting, at first, walking through lush greenery on the same land that had long ago been paved over and built up into a city back home. But that was hours ago and had since grown to feel like any other walk in the woods.

The three of them decided to walk back to their original transit point before opening another Gate. Suddenly appearing through a Gate in the middle of the Seattle waterfront wasn't exactly subtle. And it was likely that place would still be drawing a lot of heat from the big alien death ray shootout the previous day.

"So, how does all of this get explained to people?" Cam asked. "The particle beams and stuff? I mean, it's not exactly your standard terrorist attack, right?"

Tasha snorted. "Why not? Will be no footage. Emissions from your Gate would wipe any unshielded electronics within half a kilometer. Whatever does not get wiped, Protectorate takes care of. That leaves witness statements from shaky and scared bystanders, who really only heard booms and saw explosions."

Cam looked at her skeptically. "Come on. You're trying to

tell me that no one in the government knows about you?"

She laughed. "Some are suspicious, but most are too eager to look for enemy across border to think it could be anything else. Is no such thing as multiverse and inter-dimensional travel, remember?"

He sighed, knowing that she was probably right. Confusion and misdirection were both powerful ways to hide things, even in plain sight. Cam had used those tactics himself. But to think that a body as powerful as a national government could be that easily fooled? He already had a low opinion of them. They were just a bunch of rich, old, white men with money and power and were all fighting to keep it that way. That they could be so easily duped shouldn't come as much of a surprise. "Yeah, I guess I can see why that works well enough."

"To be fair," Finn added, "this kind of thing doesn't actually happen all that often. Or, really, ever. In the past, when we've had to track down bad actors, even they were reluctant to operate in the open on Earth Prime like that. I'm afraid this will probably get some people to start asking some difficult questions. Which makes it that much more important that we track down the Agent and the people that she's working with."

Which meant Cam would soon travel to yet another version of Earth–one that wasn't just a giant, unpopulated garden and actually had people living on it.

As they walked, the sky started to brighten and take on the rosy hue of dawn, even though it should've been far too early for sunrise. Finn explained that planetary analogues aren't always in sync across different dimensions and that sometimes the time difference was noticeable. In fact, he shared, they'd visited an Earth-analogue years ago that rotated so fast it only had an 18 hour day.

"Wow," Cam gushed. "That must've been freaky."

Tasha scoffed. "Was awful."

Finn laughed at her. "I keep telling you, there's no way you would've noticed the spin."

"You can keep telling me all you want," she replied with a huff. "It still made me sick."

Finn rolled his eyes but left it alone. Cam chuckled. Spending time with the two of them had given him an appreciation for their rapport. They were very buddy cop like Tony said. Hopefully, Cam would get the chance to let him know, too, once he'd worked out where Tony was and how he'd rescue him. Given everything he'd learned recently, it made sense for him to arm himself with as much knowledge as he could about his best new asset–himself. So he silently reviewed all the data in his internal system, the closest thing he had to an owner's manual for his body. It was strange, learning about all the things his body was capable of doing–things he hadn't known about for all the time that he'd lived in it. Enhanced vision and hearing. A comprehensive sensor suite that could passively and actively detect energy wavelengths far beyond what he could typically see and hear. Integrated shield generators. Complex field manipulators that would allow him to interface with machinery, electronics, and ordinary objects at a nearly telekinetic level. And, of course, the good old alien death ray. The list went on, but Cam was already overwhelmed.

At least he had Finn and Tasha's help, which reminded him that he could probably take advantage of the time to find out more about them, too. "Hey Finn, what was it like? Growing up on a different planet?"

Finn looked at him curiously. "So much for small talk, eh?"

Cam huffed. "Come on. I'm feeling like a fifth wheel here. And every time I wake up, I find out something else I believed about the universe is a lie. I just want to get to know you better."

Finn smiled and nodded. "Ok, point taken. So, what was it like?" He looked away for a moment, his expression unreadable. "In some ways, my childhood was like any other would be. There were parents and siblings. There was schooling and chores. I liked to play with my friends, and I was kind of a troublemaker."

"Was?" Tasha cut in with a chuckle.

Finn grinned. "What can I say? It's in my nature. I was definitely a handful growing up, though. One time, when my friends and I were supposed to be cleaning out a maintenance bay at the Guild, we ended up stealing a flyer and taking off in it. I don't know what we were thinking. We were in the air for maybe two minutes before Traffic Guidance forced us out of the controls and remotely piloted us right back. My mother was so furious with me. Although to this day, I don't know if it was because of what we'd done or how quickly we got caught."

Cam laughed. "Ok, I'm a little jealous now. My parents were fucking awful."

Finn looked at him sadly. "My mother was a rising star in the Engineering Guild, so I spent a lot of my time there. She's one of the smartest, strongest people I know. But family is a little different for us than it was for you. Family bonds are strong on Turana, but so are community bonds. We like to work together and look out for each other. That meant my parents could pursue their vocations, knowing that my siblings and I would be looked after. But it also meant that they were able to take the time to be parents without having to sacrifice their ambitions."

That was as much of an alien scenario to Cam as anything else he'd heard from Finn. He'd spent so much of his time growing up isolated from the community around him, his parents fearful of sinners who might prey on his young mind. "How did she feel about you joining the Protectorate?" Cam asked.

Finn took a moment before he answered. "Honestly? I think she was relieved. I was never going to join the Engineering Guild like her or my sister or the Science Guild like my sibling. I never had any direction as a kid, so the fact that I was meant for the Protectorate was a good thing."

At least Cam had never struggled with that. Once he'd discovered programming, he knew what his calling was. Even his parents had encouraged that to some degree, although if they'd known what he was actually getting himself into, they probably wouldn't have. "You said you joined up at thirteen? That still seems really young to me."

Finn nodded. "Yeah, I get that's how things were for you. But, once my Gate sense manifested, and I was tested for it, it was the perfect path for me to take, even then. I went to the Academy, where they trained us." He looked around as they walked on. "It's actually not too far from here, on Turana. We built a magnificent city around here, in about the same place as Seattle, called Kunoha. The Academy is the main Protectorate training facility, too."

"Really?" Cam asked excitedly. "So, it's almost like we grew up in the same place."

"Yeah, I suppose it is. Although I'd already graduated by the time you were born."

That shouldn't be surprising, considering what he'd initially guessed Finn's age to be. But the more he'd gotten to know him, the lower Cam revised his estimate. "I didn't think you were that much older than me."

"Ha," Tasha called out. "Is because he is so immature."

Finn rolled his eyes. "I like to think it's because I've kept my childlike sense of wonder all these years." He looked at Cam. "You're what, twenty-six?"

Cam nodded. "Yeah, although that's approximate since I don't know when my actual birthday is."

Finn frowned. "Oh, really?"

Cam nodded again. "I couldn't find any records of my birth. I was left alone in a hospital emergency room. No one ever saw who left me there. The doctors estimated that I couldn't have been more than a few weeks old at that point, but other than that, I'm a complete mystery. I used to hide that part of my story from the other kids at school. It was hard enough being the only Brown kid in the whole class. I didn't need to give them any more ammunition to use against me."

Finn put a hand on his shoulder. "Well, then you're probably gonna like Turana. Everyone looks like you and me."

That was surprising. In fact, Cam ignorantly assumed that in their version of Seattle, everyone was white, too. But, of course, they weren't. "You mean there aren't any white people?"

Finn laughed. "No, of course there are. They've come through the Gates, too, just like everyone else. There was even another Earth-analogue planet where a group of Prime

Vikings had unknowingly stumbled through a Gate and established a new settlement. But the early Protectorate ended up having to rescue them because it turned out that version of Earth was in the midst of an ice age, and they almost froze to death. We welcomed them, of course. But they're still the minority. We don't even call them white since that's a concept they made up on your world. And it wasn't until I started working on Earth Prime that I spent any time around many of them. It was also when I started to experience any real racism. But at least my training prepared me for that."

"Shit," Cam muttered. The way Finn described his home-world sounded a lot like paradise. Even just the parts about a loving family and no racism. "I bet I'd like it there." He turned to Tasha. "What do you think of it?"

She shrugged. "Is very nice place, but is not for me. I am too Russian. But I think you will like it."

Cam chuckled lightly. "What does that mean? Too Russian?"

She shrugged again. "I understand that place, Turana. I understand value of family and community because of where I am from. But I have fundamental difference. I am always preparing for worst to happen. Is our way because, for Russians, often things are bad. Russia has wealthy people, billionaires, but only very few. For most people, it is always struggle. But to struggle is Russian way, which we embrace. Turani way is about harmony, about expecting best. Is alien to me, if you will pardon pun."

He laughed. That struggle was something he was familiar with—like it was ingrained somehow in the human condition. Where Tasha grew up, it was just expected as a part of life.

Where he grew up, a pervasive "pull yourself up by your bootstraps" mentality meant that it was often lauded as a right of passage. Struggle builds character and all that. While that may have been true, he didn't believe in the need to rely on struggle to build character when that sort of thing could just be taught, instead. "Do you miss St. Petersburg?"

She shook her head. "No, not really. There I am not Russian enough. Is great paradox, I know." She smiled at him, then looked thoughtful again for a moment, her face softening a bit from her usual scowl. "I do not know racism, of course. Where I am from, everyone looks like me. But I do know about not belonging—too much this, not enough that. Life has always been that way for me. I have been to three different Earths. I do not belong on any of them."

Hearing Tasha admit something so vulnerable made Cam like her a little bit more. He'd suspected that her gruffness was some sort of defense mechanism, and it turned out he was probably right. "Yeah, I guess we both know a little about how that feels."

Circumstances made it hard for him not to veer into existential thinking. He had a whole life behind him questioning his own existence, after all. Usually, he had no problem shrugging it off. He existed, whether or not he knew about his own origins. In some ways, it was freeing to be devoid of an ancestral past. He knew too many people who were stuck in ruts created by their families, or their communities, leaving them forced to walk on paths that wouldn't take them to where they wanted to go. He'd had no such limitations, and once he'd managed to escape the temporary shackles of his own upbringing, the map to his future had been his own to plot. But, deep down, the question had always nagged at him because not knowing where he'd come from also meant not knowing the reason he even existed in the first place. He didn't care about it in terms of the grand scheme of all things. He lacked the more personal reason, the one that would tell him why the parents that created and birthed him had chosen to do so and, for better or worse, give him away.

Since his latest troubles had unfolded, Cam learned a lot more information to help answer those questions, pointing him in a direction he'd never even considered. Given the enhancements he'd been gifted with, it seemed much more likely that he'd been created with a purpose. That was something Cam could never have been sure about before. But the answers to why he'd been made, to what that purpose actually was, still remained frustratingly out of his reach, just like Tony was.

"What if we can't even save Tony? What if he's already dead?"

Tasha quietly sighed. "Is possible, yes."

"Tash–" Finn started.

"No," Cam interrupted. "She's right. I'm not giving up hope or anything, but I need to admit that's a possibility."

Tasha nodded. "He is like brother to you, yes?"

"I never had any siblings growing up," Cam confessed. "He's the closest thing I've had to a brother."

"When I was young girl," Tasha said, after a moment, "before I met Finn, I had brother who struggled to find work. He turned to crime, running with street gang. He would go out late at night, sometimes all night, sometimes for days. It was dangerous. Our mother always worried. But he always made sure there was food on table and bills were paid. When I needed new shoes, he bought them without complaint." She dropped silent for a few moments before continuing. "One day," she said, her voice low and quiet, "he left and did not come back. It made things harder, especially for my mother. She did not handle it well. We never knew what happened, but is most likely he was killed. If he was arrested, there would records. To this day, I miss him."

"Wow, Tash," Finn said softly. "I never knew that."

Tasha shrugged. "You have big happy family that I love. There was no reason to tell sad family stories." Then she pointed at Cam. "He has sad family, so I tell sad family stories."

"I'm sorry about your brother, Tasha," Cam offered. "That must've been hard."

"All life was hard for us. Was hard for him, so he became criminal. But he loved me, and I loved him. I'm sad for choices he made but glad he made them. He did what he had to do to protect us. You understand?"

She was explaining to him why Tony had done what he'd done. "I do. Tony was trying to protect me."

Tasha nodded solemnly. "Da. Tony was good friend, willing to make sacrifices to help save you. I hope we find him. But if not, he is still hero."

"She's right. It took some real courage to stand up to the Agent like that," Finn pointed out, "especially after what she did to Tomás."

Cam thought back to Tony complaining about being the sidekick. See, he thought to himself, you really are the hero of the story, my friend. "Yeah, I guess he is." Then he chuckled. "Although, I honestly didn't see what happened to Tomás. I was too busy dying and stuff."

"Be glad you didn't see," Tasha offered, shuddering. "I had

front-row seat. It was huge mess."

As they approached a clearing, their surroundings started to seem familiar to Cam. Because he'd been using his internal navigation to keep track of their progress, he knew they'd reached the transit point for the return Gate. "We're back at our return location."

"Thank god," Tasha moaned. "I need sleep."

"Yeah," Finn agreed, "as lovely as this little sojourn has been, it's time to get back home." He looked at Cam. "You're the doorman. Ready to rip a hole in space-time?"

Cam laughed. "Well, when you put it like that–" He reached for his internal system and instructed it to open a Gate back to Earth Prime. After a moment, a fiery blue-violet ring burst into view. Then he gestured for Finn and Tasha to go on through.

Tasha needed no further encouragement and was gone without a word. Finn smiled and shook his head, then stepped through afterward. Cam took a step forward, then felt a tingle of dizziness and stopped. He gently shook his head, recovering his focus, then stepped through the gate as well, and the population of the planet they left behind dropped from three back to zero.

Once he was back in the warehouse, Cam started to feel dizzy again. "Whoa," he murmured and began to lose his balance. He reached for the back of a nearby chair to stabilize himself but only managed to pull it back toward him. It crashed to the floor with a bang.

Finn quickly turned back to him. "Hey, Cam, is everything alright?"

"I, I d-don't know," Cam stammered. "I'm–"

Cam's legs seemed to fall out from under him, but Finn

was there, catching hold of him before he could fall to the floor. It was the last thing Cam saw before everything went black. Again.

TONY

Tony started to think nobody was gonna come let him out of his cell.

After Omni led him through the Gate, she'd taken him there and told him he would be fed, and then later, someone would come to retrieve him. It was for his own safety since their location was classified, and he was technically not allowed to be there. She'd smiled sweetly when she said it, but Tony was no longer sure she'd meant anything sweet at all.

The room was a plain, ten-foot square box, with walls and a floor made from a rough, gray, ultrahard material. The ceiling was some kind of giant light fixture that shone with a cold, white, even glow. Inside his box, there was only a cot with a pillow and blanket, a sink, and a weird-looking toilet that almost took Tony too long to figure out how to use.

Someone had eventually dropped off a tray of food, none of which he recognized. But he was hungry enough to try it, and it all tasted ok if maybe a little bland. After that, though, there had been no one.

It was eerie, being there all by himself. Aside from whoever slid the food tray through a slot in the cell door, there'd been no signs anyone else was in there with him. Tony occasionally heard weird noises, like the sounds of an old house slowly settling, but nothing else. He had no idea how much time had passed and had no way to entertain himself while he waited. He was incredibly bored.

Tony tried humming to himself while he let his mind wander, but his thoughts kept turning back to how he'd gotten stuck in some intergalactic jail.

The fight in Seattle had been unreal. Like, some serious action movie video game shit, with a lot more death rays and explosions than he preferred to happen in real life. And it was clear that his mild-mannered friend was packing some impressive, hidden, melee skills. What the hell had Cam gotten him into? Not that Tony was mad. It was just that he'd known Cam for years, and not once had he mentioned being a part of some secret alien death cult. But, innocent or not, the last he'd seen of his friend was when he'd just been shot and was lying, bleeding out on the sidewalk. Tony really hoped Cam was okay.

He shuddered, remembering Omni's steely grip, holding him fast inside her own humming, blue shield bubble. Then the gun went off, and Cam was shot, and Omni totally lost her shit. When she'd blasted that guy's head off, Tony didn't know whether he wanted to cheer or toss up his breakfast. And then everything else happened so fast. She let him go and started running toward his friend. He took off after her, hoping to maybe trip her up or at least delay her somehow. That led them both through the Gate and suddenly marooned in a barren, unpopulated version of Seattle. At least she'd started being nice to him then.

And she'd kept being nice to him, in her own way, until he'd been locked in his cell.

"So, what, you're some kinda spy, right?" Tony asked her while Omni led him through the stale, almost barren corridors of whatever facility they'd entered. "Like Tasha and Finn?"

She didn't answer him right away, and he started to think she wasn't going to at all, so he just focused on watching her ass as she walked in front of him instead. But Omni spoke up after a few moments. "I am, in the sense that I operate covertly, like those others you spoke of. I do not represent the same organization, though. They are in the business of keeping things secret. We are in the business of making things known."

"So, what? You're some kind of freedom fighter, then?"

She laughed lightly. "No, nothing like that. We just represent different interests than they do." She stopped, then, and turned back toward him. "Tell me, Tony. You knew nothing of inter-dimensional travel before this all happened, correct?" He nodded. "And you knew nothing about the existence of the technology you have seen recently?" He nodded again. "Well, those others you spoke of are the reason you know nothing about any of that. They have ensured that you stay ignorant of how things really are." She turned and started walking again before making her final statement. "We will soon change all of that."

Tony lay back on the cot, which was surprisingly comfortable, at least, and continued humming to himself. He'd gone through several songs on the last Fortune Scarlet album before there was a clunk outside his door, and it whooshed open, revealing his jailor, Omni. She looked in on him, resplendent in her deep black combat suit, her stance casual in the way that only someone of supreme confidence could achieve, with one eyebrow slightly cocked. She may have been evil, but she sure as hell was hot for a white girl.

"I was wondering if you'd forgotten about me," he said, trying to keep his tone casual.

She strode into his cell like she owned the place, then sat down on the edge of his bed near his feet. "My debrief took somewhat longer than I'd expected." She fixed him with a steely gaze. "That was partly because of your presence. I acted against protocol, bringing you back here." Then she reached over and placed a gloved hand on his thigh, and he suddenly found himself willing away a burgeoning erection. She stroked his leg lightly. "But I managed to convince them that your presence has some value to us, and now it's time for you to demonstrate it." Then she squeezed his thigh right above his knee, and he almost lost it. He hated that.

"Sure, sure, whatever," he said, trying to wriggle out from her iron grip. "Just tell me what you need me to do."

She tilted her head to the side, looking at him curiously, then released the pressure on her grip slightly. "I need you to tell me what you know about Cameron Maddock."

"About Cam?" Maybe, if he played his cards right, he could find out once and for all why she'd been chasing after him. "There's not much to know. He works in tech, he's a closet romantic, and I think he's an Aries. Or maybe a Taurus. Why? Are you interested? Cuz if you are, I can tell you right now that you're definitely not his type." She tightened her grip again, this time shooting right past uncomfortable and into pain. "Hey, ow! What the fuck, lady?"

But her grip did not relent. Instead, Omni leaned in closer and spoke so quietly that he almost couldn't hear her. "You misunderstand me, Tony. I am not here to play word games with you. I will ask you questions, and you will answer them truthfully and to the best of your ability. Otherwise, you have no value to me. Do you understand?"

"Yes," he spat through gritted teeth. "I understand."

"Very well." She sat back and released her grip on his knee. Then she stood up, folded her arms, and looked down on him, her face serious. "Now, let us start again. Tell me what you know of Cameron Maddock. Start with the Gates."

Tony nodded, his breathing heavy and anxious. "Ok, alright. I don't really know anything about that, of course, but I can tell you what I think. I think he can open them. Gates, I mean."

She frowned at him dramatically. "You think? But you do not know. Why do you think that?"

He gulped. "I've seen it happen twice, now. But then, you did, too, right? You were there both times."

That answer didn't seem to satisfy her, but it didn't make her angrier, either. "How is Cameron connected with the Protectorate agents?"

Tony shrugged. "You mean Finn and Tasha? I don't know, man. I mean, I just met them, right? They could all sing in the same show tunes choir for all I know."

Suddenly she lashed out, backhanding him viciously across the face. "Do you really think I will find your insolence charming? Now, answer my question!"

He sat back up, gently rubbing the cheek she'd hit. "Fine, shit." He took a deep breath. "He can't be connected with them, can he? He's never mentioned them before, and he seemed just as surprised as I was by them and everything that's been happening. And, honestly, they seemed to be just as surprised about him as he was about them."

She balled her hands into fists, and he flinched instinctively, but she just placed them on her hips. "So, before the incident on the motorcycle, you had never seen him act strangely or behave in such a way to make you think he was not an ordinary human being?"

Tony shook his head sullenly. "No, never. That day was the first time I saw him do anything unusual. Like the Gate. Or the thing in Union Square."

Omni's gaze went up and to the left like she was reading something hovering in the air behind him. He forced himself not to look. "Yes, during the attempt to make contact with him, when he decided to shoot those people in cold blood."

He furrowed his brow in surprise, unable to help himself. "Cold blood? Shit, lady, he had a bunch of gun-toting villains chasing after him. I think it's safe to say that he was provoked."

She eyed him carefully, and he wondered if she was deciding whether or not to hit him again. Then she nodded. "So, it appears that you do not know anything useful, at least consciously. That means we will have to dig a little deeper, then."

He was about to ask her what she meant but yelped loudly instead as she reached out, hooked a hand under his shoulder, and roughly hauled him up into a standing position. "What the fuck, lady!"

It must not have been the right angle for a backhand since Omni made a closed fist punch to his face instead. Stars burst in his vision, and his head snapped back painfully. It wasn't enough to knock him out, but it left him dazed, and he hung limp in her unyielding grip. She pulled him out of the cell, handing him off to someone he could barely see. Two someones actually, as another set of hands grabbed his free arm. She said something to them in a language Tony didn't recognize, then turned and walked away. He shook his head lightly, trying to bring his sight back into focus as he felt himself get carried down the corridor. As his vision cleared, he glanced to his sides to see who was carrying him–two tall, helmeted guards, each wearing matte-black body armor. Their grips were as strong as hers had been, so he didn't entertain any ideas about trying to escape. Hell, just her freaky strength and unpredictable violent streak were more than enough to dissuade him of any jailbreak fantasies.

Tony could feel his eye swelling already. It would be a hel-luva shiner soon. He should've known that her friendliness wasn't going to last. He'd played the game anyway, taking as much advantage of her kindness as he thought he could get away with. But it looked like the beatings had commenced. It was an inefficient way to get information from people. He had several relatives and acquaintances who were part of his uncle's operation, and he'd heard their stories about it. Pain-induced information was never reliable–even if it was the truth. Better to just outright ask for information, his uncle had told him. Even if you didn't get the truth, which you'd get only rarely, you could often learn as much from the lies you were told.

After being hauled along behind Omni for a short distance, they approached the corridor's end and a sizable, sealed doorway. When they reached it, the door slid open, leading to a circular chamber that served as a junction, opening onto a half-dozen other corridors. Omni led them into one of those, much longer than the previous one had been, that ended in another sealed doorway. She placed her hand on a glossy, black disc that was set into the wall next to the door, and it slid open to reveal the clear night sky.

As they stepped through, Tony first thought they were headed outside. Then he noticed that they were actually surrounded by a large, clear, half dome. It had to be at least a hundred feet in diameter. The chamber floor was made of the same rough, gray material as everything else he'd seen. A small, raised dais anchored the center of the room, dramatically lit from underneath. Outside the dome, Tony could see a barren, rocky landscape with no signs of life. Sharp-peaked, craggy mountains rose darkly in the distance, and the sky was full of more stars than he'd ever seen in his life. He wondered, briefly, if they were in a moon base. But that didn't seem right. Part of him understood that the gravity was too strong and that the horizon's curve would be more evident if they were on the moon.

Omni took him from the two guards, who then stepped to the sides of the doorway and stood motionless as they resumed their guarding. Holding him firmly, she pushed Tony forward toward the dais, stopping a few feet short of it.

"What is this place?" he asked quietly.

She ignored his question. "Intelligence," she loudly announced in English, "I have brought you the companion."

"Very good, Omni," said a deep booming voice, or Voice, that seemed to be broadcasting from everywhere and nowhere at the same time. "Place him onto the dais."

What the fuck was going on? "I'm fine right here, thank you," he shouted. "Maybe someone could fill me in on what's happening, first, before we get all friendly."

Omni shot him a quick glare, then hauled him up onto the raised platform. She transferred her grip, holding him by his upper arms, and positioned him so that he was standing more or less straight up. The light from below began to shine brighter, and she let him go, but he still couldn't move. His body seemed frozen in place. He felt a slight vibration under his feet, then the sensation of a cool breeze was blowing down on him from above, even though there was no actual air movement. That wasn't so bad. He tried to say something, but it only came out as a muffled groan since he couldn't move his jaw or his tongue. His heart started to pound, and his breathing became rapid as he began to panic. Omni watched him impassively, arms crossed as if she'd seen this sort of thing plenty of times, and it barely merited her interest.

"Preparation complete," the Voice announced. "You will now submit to us, Zhang Weitian, so that we may know all."

They used his government name again. How'd they even know it? Tony felt a pressure in his head, then, like his mind was somehow being squeezed, and his thoughts became sluggish. He tried fighting against it, forcing himself to think clearly. This was met with a sudden burst of pain in his head.

"Fighting it will only make it worse," Omni calmly explained. "Just let it happen, and it will be over soon enough.

He grimaced, still trying to push the invader out of his head, but was powerless to stop it, and the forced mental assault continued, unabated. Memories were dredged to the surface of his mind, some fresh and distinct, some with the dreamlike quality of things that happened long ago, each one feeling like sandpaper drawn across the surface of his mind. Eating his maa maa's dim sum as a child. The day he bought his motorcycle. Getting into a fight at school with a white kid who was picking on his sister. Kissing Lilly Xuan, the first time he'd kissed a girl. There was no rhyme or reason to it, just the sense that some powerful force was sorting through his life story at random. Then came the memory of the first time he'd played Farstorm with Cam. He gasped as the force in his head grew stronger, encouraged that they'd found something they were looking for. Other memories of Cam began to surface, appearing and disappearing again so swiftly he hardly had time to recognize one before he saw another. They appeared more or less in chronological order, replaying his entire relationship with Cam as it happened. Then they started to slow enough to be coherent. His phone call with Cam while he was on the run. Seeing Cam on the news about the incident in Union Square. The frantic motorcycle chase that led them to the uninhabited world on the other side of the Gate. The conversation with Tasha and Finn where Cam realized he'd dreamed of Omni. Then everything stopped. Tony let out a ragged breath as the pressure in his head ceased. He stood on the dais, still frozen in place, his body drenched in sweat, every nerve ending raw and tender.

"We have found something," the Voice stated.

The view in front of him slowly dissolved into the secret Seattle warehouse. He saw himself sitting at the table with Cam. Finn and Tasha were standing on the opposite side. They were all looking at the holographic projection of Tomás when Cam gasped and doubled over. Tony saw himself jump off his seat to grab and brace him. After a moment, Cam seemed to recover, and Tony asked Cam if he was ok.

"Yeah, yeah, I'm good," holographic Cam responded. "I just remembered something I dreamed about the other night. Only, I guess it wasn't actually a dream after all."

"What do you mean?" asked Finn.

Cam took another breath. "Where this all happened–is there an old hotel nearby, next to a plaza with an old fountain in the middle of it?"

Finn and Tasha looked at each other, then Finn nodded and manipulated the projection to zoom out and reveal the surrounding area. "You saw all this?"

Cam nodded. "Yeah, that's definitely what I saw."

Tony saw the realization creep across Omni's face as she watched his memory play out. "He–" she said, her tone uncharacteristically unsure. "He saw me in his dreams?"

"He possesses an immense potential for power," replied the Voice. "Despite his lack of training, it seems he may have somehow gained unconscious access to your quantum entanglement communicator."

She stood there for a moment, her face impassive, while Tony tried to make sense of what he was seeing. The fact that they'd pulled this memory from his head and turned it into some kind of immersive VR scene was mind-blowing enough. But he knew that wasn't the critical revelation. Cam and Omni were connected, and whoever it was that just rooted around in his head like they were looking for a twist tie in the junk drawer was the force behind them both.

Omni's face lit up into a twisted smile. "If he is connected to me like this, we can use that to draw him out again. On our terms." Then she looked at Tony, and his blood chilled. "And we can use him."

"Yes," agreed the Voice. "But we must act quickly." Suddenly, whatever force that was holding him immobile ceased, and Tony collapsed awkwardly onto the dais. "Take him to the Genetics Lab. We have much work to do."

Omni summoned the two guards from their post by the

door, who marched over to him and hauled him to his feet. They held him there for a moment while she grabbed his chin and pointed his face toward hers. "It seems you will be valuable to us after all, Tony. But you do not need to be awake for this part." Then, before he could even process what she'd just said, she hit him with a perfectly placed palm heel to the bridge of his nose. His head snapped back, and everything went black.

CAM

Cam came to while he was lying down inside a dimly lit, white space. Waking in strange places with no memory of how he'd gotten there was becoming a regular habit. Hopefully, he'd figure out how to kick it sooner rather than later.

There was a low thrum emanating from somewhere behind him. As Cam regained his focus, he realized that he'd heard it before. He was in the vehicle that Finn and Tasha had used to transport him and Tony on the night they'd first been rescued. Or, at least, the same kind of vehicle. His head ached a little, and his senses felt dull and gray. He mentally reached for his internal systems, but there was nothing there beyond an ominous blank spot. That must've been related to whatever caused him to pass out. Frustrated and a little afraid, he decided to let Finn and Tasha know he was awake.

"Hello?"

"Hello, Cam," answered a familiar voice. "Are you feeling better?"

"Otto?"

"That's correct."

"Where am I?"

The lighting around him gradually grew warmer and

brighter. "You are in the passenger cabin of a flyer, traveling between Gates while you're en route to Turana. Your vital signs were weak, so we thought it best to let you rest. How are you feeling?"

Cam groaned quietly. "Groggy and sluggish. And my internal system is gone now, too."

"We scanned you in the medbay pod before transferring you to this flyer. Although we could detect your wetware implants, I can get no signal from them. They are likely offline."

That figured. Cam finally discovered his real-life super-powers, and a day later, they'd already been taken away. "I thought you fixed that?"

"So had I. Unfortunately, I have no experience with a system like yours and had to make my best guess about how to fix it."

Cam couldn't really fault Otto for that. At least it worked for a little while. "So, what now?"

"Once we've transited to the city of Kaseka, we intend to meet up with Finn's sibling and request their assistance. Lhasa is a Master in the Science Guild, and their expertise could be beneficial."

Cam sighed, then pushed his frustration away. Things would work out one way or another, and it was better to focus on the fact that he was en route to an alien city. After all, that was cool as shit. "How long until we get there?"

"We're nearly there. We're currently descending on approach to the transit Gate."

Before Cam could even ask, the flyer's walls began to brighten, then became transparent, providing him a panoramic view outside the vehicle. Cam sat up and leaned back on the couch that spanned the chamber's left-hand side. Looking out through the now transparent wall, he saw rolling, grass-covered hills and valleys stretching off into a great flat plain in the distance. The other side displayed a commanding view of the vast expanse of a blue ocean. The Pacific, he guessed. Or, at least, its local equivalent. The flying craft was descending rapidly. It looked as if they'd be on the ground in just a few minutes.

"Ah, you're awake!"

Cam turned at the sound of Finn's voice to see him emerge through the forward bulkhead. "I'm starting to lose track of how many times this week I've passed out and woken up someplace new."

Finn laughed. "Yeah, you've become a regular damsel in distress, haven't you?"

Cam scowled mockingly. "Well, the old memes are the best ones, right? So, what's happening."

Finn gave him a brief rundown, echoing what Otto had already told him. After they'd landed, they planned to bullshit their way past the Protectorate monitors on the Turana side of the Gate since they were essentially sneaking Cam through.

That came as a surprise to Cam. "So, what? I'm illegal there or something?

"No, nothing like that," Finn assured him. "It's just that we don't want to make a big deal about the fact that you're a Prime, especially since we want to see Lhasa before we go anywhere else, like the Protectorate, for instance."

His assurances sounded sincere, so Cam went along with things for the time being. The Gate was located close to the city, Finn added, and there'd be a pair of

Protectorate monitors on duty to keep unauthorized people from traveling through it.

Once they'd landed, a section of the wall on the right side of the main cabin slid out and folded upwards, allowing everyone to exit the flyer. The sleek, curvy, wedge-shaped vehicle was glossy and white on the outside. Cam couldn't see any visible indication of jets or engines or even the windows. He had to remember to ask about how it worked at some point.

The flyer was parked on a large, flat surface covered with crushed rock near a wide, pillar-shaped, circular building made of white stone. The building had an open, arch-topped entrance facing the landing area. Once Tasha and Finn collected their shoulder bags from the rear of the flyer's main compartment, they led Cam into the building, where a glowing, blue-violet oval hung in the air on the far side of the sizable, circular room. Like the Gates he'd made, it was an apparently flat surface surrounded by glowing spasms of blue-violet light. Unlike Cam's Gates, it was more irregular than oval. Aside from cabinets and equipment hanging along the walls, the room was otherwise empty.

"This is it?" he asked.

Tasha chuckled. "Wait until you see other side. Is much more impressive." Then she stepped through the Gate.

Finn looked back and gestured toward the Gate. "Come on, buddy. Let's get through so we can get to Lhasa's." Then he stepped through as well.

With a shrug, Cam walked over and stepped through the Gate into another new world. The room mirrored the shape of one he'd just been in, with a high ceiling that cast warm, bright light evenly throughout the space. But the similarities ended there. The curved walls were paneled with different colored woods in an ornate, decorative pattern, with colorful wall hangings interspersed around the room. Two Protectorate Monitors in bright, patterned, black, red, and white uniforms stood watch behind a high counter, their faces lit from underneath by unseen displays set into the countertop. One of them, well-muscled, with ruddy, brown skin and dark hair cropped short, chatted amiably with Finn in a language that Cam didn't recognize. It had a musical quality that English lacked and blended long, soft vowels and sharp consonants. Ahead was an arched doorway leading outside, where Cam could see the bright blue sky of Turana.

Tasha talked with the other Monitor, who had long dark hair and the same ruddy, brown complexion as the first. The way they were smiling bashfully, especially when Tasha reached out and put a friendly hand on their arm, made Cam sure that they were flirting. While they'd finished talking, Finn and the other monitor grasped each other's forearms in what could've been a handshake. Then Finn walked over to Cam.

"Ok," Finn said quietly. "We're all set here, so let's go. I'll explain more once we're outside."

Cam nodded, then followed Finn as he turned and walked out of the room into a fantasy world. The Gate facility was located in the foothills above what he knew as Monterey Bay. The familiar ocean glimmered brightly in the distance, with diamond sparkles of fiery sunlight rolling along the surface of the water, threaded by long frothy whitecaps of the ocean waves. But the city built along the curve of the bay shore was truly wondrous. Tall, curving, colorful towers rose majestically among long, low, arched-roof buildings and stately dome-shaped structures. Surrounding the buildings were lush parks and woodlands. It looked as if the towers had grown up from the forest below. Cam saw many dozens of flyers zooming above and curving between the buildings. Farther off, on the northern side of the city, stood a slender, glass-sided tower that was taller than the rest. The tower's sides were faceted, giving it an almost crystalline appearance. The whole thing was breathtaking.

Finn, who'd been standing next to him in silence, put a hand on his shoulder. "Isn't it beautiful?"

Cam nodded. "I've never seen anything like this."

Finn chuckled lightly. "No, my friend, you definitely have not. But we can't stand around here for too long. I don't know how long the story I told the Monitors will hold up." He turned and walked over to a smaller, glossy, white flyer parked nearby.

After one final look at the view, Cam turned to follow him. "Story?"

He hadn't told the agents at the Gate who Cam really was, Finn explained. Instead, he'd passed Cam off as an Engineering Guild trainee from one of the smaller communities along the coast north of the city who'd accompanied Finn on a survey mission and was being taken back to the Guild to report in. It was a flimsy story at best, but at least it got them through the Gate.

"Do you do a lot of survey missions?" Cam asked as he climbed into the flyer after Finn and took a seat next to him. There was only a single cabin, with two rows of seating, one behind the other. The interior viewscreen wrapped all the way around, offering panoramic vistas, even sitting on the ground.

"It's all we do for the most part," Finn replied, "aside from rescuing the occasional strays. We investigate anomalies, too, of course. And when we find new Gates, we make sure that they're safe and, if they're not, we do what we can to make them safe."

Tasha climbed into the flyer behind them, a mysterious smile on her face.

Finn snickered as he touched a spot on the control panel in front of him to close the main hatch. "Did you finally say yes?"

"I did not," she replied as she slid into a seat in the second row. "But is still nice to be asked."

Finn smiled but shook his head. "You know she's never going to give up, right?"

Tasha smiled. "You shut up and fly. We keep your sibling waiting."

Finn shook his head, still smiling, and touched another set of controls. The flyer responded, climbing into the air, then sailed smoothly forward toward the city's towers. Finn explained that their plan was to visit his sibling before they did anything else. As a Master in the Science Guild, Lhasa had valuable knowledge and access to sophisticated scanning equipment, which might help them learn more about what made Cam tick, exactly, and hopefully help them all figure out what was wrong with Cam's wetware.

Their flight path took them low over the foothills outside the city, then soared up higher as they started to pass over buildings on the city's edge. The structures were well spaced from one another, with clusters of smaller buildings surrounding each of the towers like jeweled suppliants gathered to worship at their idols' base. Cam couldn't see anything resembling a road network. There were various pathways through the parkland that people walked on, along with teardrop-shaped vehicles that Cam assumed were probably some type of ground car.

Finn played tour guide as they flew, pointing out the different Guilds that each tower represented, including the Engineering Guild, the Arts Guild, the Medical Guild, and others. The crystalline building was the city's Protectorate Headquarters. It had an apparent Nynari influence on its design and stood out from the broader, curvier structures surrounding it. While the towers all represented Guilds, with some Guilds possessing more than one, not all of the clusters were anchored by them. The others belong to clans, Finn explained, which were large, extended family groups. The Turani who didn't join up with a Guild usually stayed with their clan since there were always plenty of opportunities available there. Sometimes, people even switched back and forth, moving from clan to Guild to clan, or even Guild to Guild. Although they were always encouraged to choose something that benefited their clan or the community, people were free to choose their own paths. That way, everyone had a chance to be helpful, and everyone was taken care of.

After the short flight, their flyer banked and looped around one of the towers. The brightly colored, intricately decorated building curved upward from its broad base, growing narrower as it went, before fluting out slightly at the top. There was a graceful, organic style to its design, at once seeming delicate but also incredibly sturdy. Cam couldn't see any windows, except for a tall, narrow strip that ran from the base almost all the way to the top. As they descended toward a vast, flat, circular pad on the ground, Cam realized the structure was much larger than he'd initially guessed it to be. Once they were on the ground and out of the flyer, he had to crane his neck pretty far back to see the top. It had to be at least a hundred stories tall.

"One-hundred-three, I believe," Finn said when Cam asked him. "I don't know for sure, but I know it's more than four hundred meters tall. Only the Protectorate tower is taller."

The entrance to the building lay under a sweeping, fluted overhang. There were no doors, but Cam felt himself pass through a pressure curtain as he walked under it. Inside, the primary feature of the space was clearly the impressive, full-height atrium. The vast, open-plan chamber on the main floor was laid out with different clusters of specialty and activity areas. Cam saw groups of seating, workstations, and even places where people gave talks or lectures, with large, holographic displays showcasing relevant images next to them. Off to one side, near the interior wall, was a buffet, with long stations of different food and beverage choices. When Cam looked up, he could see that the interior was lined with ring upon ring of balconied walkways, one after another, all the way up to the glass-roofed skylight at the top. Like the exterior, the interior was decorated with color blocks and patterns, including long, narrow, colored strips of cloth that hung from far above. Despite feeling strange and foreign to him, it was very welcoming and homey. The space was beautiful to behold, and one more item he added to the rapidly expanding list of things he'd never seen before. Cam was starting to feel a little bit like a tourist.

Finn led them off to the side of the atrium to a nearby bank of lift shafts. As they rode upward, Finn explained that the lifts used controlled gravity fields to move the platforms to the correct floors as they rose up along the side of the tower. They eliminated the need for the clumsy mechanical equipment that would've been required for such a tall building and allowed the shafts to curve. Cam could barely begin to imagine the exotic physics behind such a setup.

The group stopped and got off about midway up the tower. The wrap-around walkway had a polished wooden railing atop a clear balustrade on the interior side. A ring of arched doorways lined the exterior side, broken up periodically by darkened windows and vibrant wall art. After a short walk, they stopped at an entrance marked in a script Cam couldn't understand. The door slid open, and they went through it into a large room that somehow combined the look of a comfortable, brightly colored sitting room with a futuristic hospital radiology department to a strange but pleasant effect. The interior-side wall was lined with cabinets and shelving filled with various storage containers and equipment Cam didn't recognize. The exterior wall was a single, massive viewscreen, much like the ones Cam had seen in the flyers, offering an impressive view of the parklike city and the vast ocean beyond it. There was a remarkable amount of greenery in the room, and the far wall was decorated with wall-hangings woven in colorful, geometric patterns.

Someone wearing a brightly colored, floral-patterned lab smock was standing at a counter-height island on the other side of the room, near a larger version of the portable medbay pod back at the warehouse. They looked up when the group entered and smiled. Cam could see the family resemblance right away. Aside from their long, shiny black hair, and slightly narrower face, they were almost the spitting image of their brother, Finn. They waved hello, and said something Cam didn't understand.

"English, please, dear sibling," Finn replied. "This is my friend Cameron Maddock. He goes by Cam. Cam, this is my sibling Lhasa, child of the Wolf Clan and esteemed Master of the Engineering Guild. You can just call them Lhasa, though."

Ah, Cam thought. Sibling. They must be non-binary, or whatever the local equivalent of that was. Back at home, he knew a non-binary person of Indigenous ancestry who referred to themself as Two-spirit. But Cam could ask about that later.

Lhasa turned their smile to Cam, although it was slightly clouded by confusion. "English? Oh, are you a Prime?"

"Guilty," Cam admitted with a smile. "At least, I was until recently. Now, the jury's kind of out on that."

Lhasa laughed brightly. "How exciting! I rarely get to practice my English with a native speaker. The jury is out? Your idioms are fascinating."

Tasha snorted. "If only you would learn Russian. Then you would hear such idioms."

"I'm sure it's still on their to-do list, Tash," Finn said, then turned back to his sibling and pulled them into a warm embrace. "It's good to see you again, Lhasa."

"And you as well, Jerusalem," they replied, then extracted themself from the hug. "It's been too long."

"You know how it is with the Protectorate, dear sibling. In fact, that's why we're here. I'm sending you some of Cam's medbay scans. He's uh, he's got some unusual circumstances that we've been dealing with. Could you take a look and maybe give him a scan of your own."

Lhasa reached back to pick up a set of thin, wrap-around

goggles, then slipped them on. Text and graphics appeared on the transparent surface. They flicked a finger on their outstretched hand, and the information began scrolling down as they read through it. While Lhasa looked at whatever their brother had sent them, Tasha went over to a wet bar area and filled three cups from a silver pitcher of water. She gave one to Cam and Finn each, then took hold of the third for herself.

"This is absolutely fascinating, Jerusalem," Lhasa murmured. They made a swipe gesture and cleared the graphics from their goggle screen. "I've never seen a Prime human with these sorts of enhancements before. In fact, I've never even seen some of these enhancements before at all." They looked over at Cam. "How did you acquire them?"

Cam shot a questioning glance at Finn, who just tilted his head toward his sibling and nodded. "I don't know. Until a few days ago, I didn't even know I had them."

Lhasa's eyes went wide with surprise. "You didn't know you had them? How strange." They went to the medbay pod and touched a blue-lit spot on the side. It split in two, and the top half lifted open to reveal a reclined couch inside. "Well, those scans were a good start. But I can get much more sophisticated readings here, perhaps even dating the age of the implants." They gestured toward the pod. "Please lie here, Cam, and make yourself comfortable."

Cam nodded, then handed them his water cup before crawling up and laying back on the medbay couch. Lhasa put the cup down on the counter, then stood back as more graphics appeared on their goggles. They reached out and began to interact with the space in front of them, and the pod started to hum. Finn walked over to stand nearby while

Tasha sat down in one of the chairs, pulling out her handheld to look at it.

Lhasa gasped. "This is incredible. Jerusalem, look at this." They made a swiping motion in his direction, and he tilted his head up slightly, looking at whatever information they just shared with him.

"Ok, what am I looking at?" he asked.

"If I'm not mistaken, that's a multiphase, quantum-entanglement communicator. Although it seems to be inactive at the moment. And look here." They swiped toward him again. "This appears to be an exotic field manipulator. If I'm interpreting these readings correctly, this would be powerful enough to actually affect inter-dimensional energy transference."

"If by all that, you mean opening and closing Gates," Cam offered, "then you're not mistaken."

Lhasa looked down at him, then over to Finn, then back to Cam, clearly puzzled. "You can do that? This is one of those newly discovered abilities?"

He nodded. "It is. Although I don't understand how it works yet. I'm still kinda new to the whole quantum physics game."

They looked away, their focus returning to whatever data was projected in front of them. "I'm a Science Guild Master, Cam, specializing in both genetics and exotic particle physics, and I barely have the math to fully understand it. But that's not the truly amazing part." They focused on him again. "It's all constructed from organic material. Everything. The QEC, exotic field manipulator, shield generator, particle accelerator cannons, even the quantum processor crystals implanted throughout your body. It all appears to have been grown in place. To manipulate genetics to that degree is astounding. And I have no idea how you can power all of it. We should get a gene sample." They made several small gestures, then gasped in surprise, muttering something that Cam didn't understand but, from their tone, guessed was probably a curse.

Lhasa went back to the counter they'd been working at and tapped the surface, activating a built-in holo-projector. Reaching out in front of them, they grabbed an unseen virtual object and moved it over into the projector space. A virtual representation of a DNA strand materialized there, slowing spinning. "This is your DNA, Cam."

He looked over at it. It was pretty, but that was about all he could work out from it. "Sorry, Doc, but I don't know what I'm looking at."

They smiled. "Of course. My apologies." They tapped something out in the space in front of them. The floating DNA strand shrank slightly and was joined by a second one. It was different from the first, slimmer and less complex. Lhasa pointed to the new strand. "This is a typical human DNA strand. Mine, in fact. It contains around three billion bases, with tens of thousands of genes expressed in twenty-three pairs of chromosomes." Then they pointed to the other strand excitedly. "This is your DNA. It contains nearly half again as many bases, expressed in forty chromosome pairs."

He had different DNA than a typical human? Did that make him an atypical human or something else entirely? "Ok, wait a minute. Are you trying to tell me that I'm not actually human?"

Lhasa frowned. "That all depends on how you define human, I suppose. By some definitions, no, you're not. But it's important to note here that all the necessary parts of human DNA are present in you. Human DNA normally has a lot of extraneous code in it, most of which control gene expression and some of which is just legacy junk code leftover from our evolution. But your DNA also contains the genetic blueprints for how your enhancements were grown. It also seems to allow your genes to express in ways that the DNA of most people cannot. So I'd say that yes, you are human. Just enhanced." They smiled at him warmly. "And since I'm a Science Guild Master, I'm qualified to make that call." He must not have looked convinced if their look of sympathy was any indicator. "I'm sorry if this information is upsetting to you. It's really rather exciting, from a geneticist point of view."

Cam sighed. He wasn't sure he understood what he'd just been told. He got it on a conceptual level, but the idea that he wasn't really human, just some kind of human-shaped freak of nature, didn't fit well with his self-image. "I'm not sure how to take the news that I'm some kind of genetic oddity, Doc. Although I'm surprised that it wasn't discovered when I did that home DNA test."

Finn coughed politely. "You took a home DNA test? When did you do that?"

"Maybe three–" Cam stopped as the realization hit him. "About three weeks ago. Shit. It was discovered, wasn't it?"

Finn nodded. "I can't see why that wasn't what kicked this whole thing off."

"But that still doesn't make sense," Cam protested. "They would've had to be looking for me already, right? Otherwise, how would they know to monitor DNA databases? And if I never submitted for a test, they'd never find me."

"Cam," Lhasa said softly, "someone obviously went to a great deal of trouble to create you. Just the DNA development alone is astounding and is many decades, if not centuries, ahead of what we can do here at the Guild. Then there are all of the organically grown, highly miniaturized enhancements that you possess. I work with the Protectorate on their Gate manipulation studies. We've only recently succeeded in developing a device that can sufficiently manipulate exotic fields to close a Gate without creating a massive, quantum spatial implosion. And that device wouldn't even fit inside of this room. Of course, they were already looking for you."

"I think the real question," Finn added, "would be how they managed to lose you in the first place."

Cam shook his head. "Well, the real question for me is still who they even are."

Lhasa gave him a sweet, sympathetic smile. "Hopefully, once I have a chance to analyze the results from your scans, I may be able to—what's the idiom? Shed a little light on that, too?"

Cam chuckled. Just like their brother, Lhasa was relentlessly charming. It must run in their family. "Ok, Doc. Hey, while you're poking around inside of me, can you figure out what's wrong with my internal system implants?"

They nodded. "Of course. I should ask, though. Why do you keep calling me dock?"

He laughed. "It's short for Doctor. Another idiom, I guess."

"Oh, Doctor. As in, a title awarded to someone who has achieved the highest level of formal education in a particular field of study." They walked back to stand near the medbay pod, manipulating the space in front of them. "I'll take another look at your scans. This may take a few minutes."

"Take all the time you need, Doc."

Finn moved in closer to the medbay pod and put a comforting hand on Cam's shoulder. "Sorry, Cam. That probably wasn't the easiest thing to hear."

Cam sighed softly, then shrugged. "Honestly, Finn, in a weird way, I'm kinda used to this sort of thing. I mean, being different from everyone around me is nothing new to me."

Finn smiled. "Some of the things you can do are pretty unique," he said with a wink, "but I've known you for several days now, and you haven't seemed like anything other than human to me."

Cam smiled back. It was nice to hear Finn say that, even if they were just starting to get to know each other.

"Ah, I see what the issue is," Lhasa announced from behind him. "You ran out of power."

Cam raised an eyebrow. "What, like my batteries are drained?"

"Well, yes, actually," they replied. "You see, wetware like yours and Jerusalem's is powered by bioelectricity, generated naturally by your bodies. This works for people like Jerusalem because they're implanted with organic energy storage structures that constantly retain the excess energy built up by their own biorhythms. I see that you have similar structures, but the energy used by the quantum field engine to open Gates is significant enough to outpace your body's own energy production. After using it multiple times, your power reserves were totally drained."

"Huh. That feels like it might be a significant design flaw," Cam responded. "How long before I recharge?"

"According to these readings, it's happening as we speak.

But I believe I can help it along by using the medbay pod to boost your charged state."

"You're going to electrocute me?"

Lhasa laughed. "Yes, but I'm going to specifically target the mycelial power storage structures in your body with a low-powered burst. At the worst, it may straighten your hair."

Cam reflexively reached up and patted the top of his head. "I guess that's a sacrifice I'll have to live with."

Lhasa moved their hands around inside the control space. "Ok, it's starting now." A tingling sensation spread through Cam's arms and legs as if they'd gone to sleep. "It should just be a few moments before you're fully charged, but your system should have enough power to be active already."

Hearing that, Cam immediately concentrated his awareness on the blank spot in his mind and finally felt a confirmation in return. He focused on his system status, and the dullness of his senses lifted away. Everything around him felt richer and more precise again. There was an insistent pressure in part of his mind—another alert. He checked on that and found that his shoulder had been healed and was one-hundred percent usable already.

"Wow, everything is back online, now," he said happily. "Thank you, Lhasa. Now, could somebody help me get this sling off?"

Lhasa smiled. "I'd be happy to. Just sit up."

He did so, and they helped him get the sling unhooked and unwrapped. He moved his arm around experimentally. There was no sign of pain or stiffness. "Wow, it feels great. You'd never know I got shot yesterday."

Lhasa gasped and looked at their brother. "He was shot

yesterday?"

Finn nodded. "Slug shooter. He was lucky he didn't bleed out."

"The nano suite must be a great deal more sophisticated than I realized," they said. Then they held out their hands in a shrug. "Not that I'm surprised to discover that."

"Speaking of surprises," Tasha said from the other side of the room. "I have message from Natia. She knows we are back and says we have one hour to report in before she sends squad to come collect us."

Finn sighed. "Well, it's not like we thought we'd go unnoticed forever. But at least we got you all sorted first, Cam." He looked at Lhasa. "Do you have what you need for your analysis?"

"Yes, I believe so."

"Ok, then we really shouldn't put it off any longer."

Finn and Cam both thanked Lhasa, who gave them each a big hug. They also promised to continue studying Cam's readings and let him know if they discovered anything important.

After the three of them left the lab suite, Cam's system alerted him to the presence of an accessible local wireless network. Once he connected to it, virtual data markers appeared in his vision, labeling the essential things around him. He could also read the wall signage he saw. His system must've been translating that for him. Cam mentioned as much to Finn and Tasha.

"Really?" Finn asked. "Can you understand what I'm saying now?"

Cam nodded. "Of course."

Finn chuckled. "Ok, good, because I'm speaking Turani."

That was surprising. Cam assumed it was English since he'd understood it. But with a bit of concentration, he could tell it was another language. Even though he was still new to using his internal systems, he could spot the difference between the two languages if he paid attention. "Wow, I guess I can speak Turani now."

Finn smiled and shook his head. "At least that will make it easier for you to blend in."

They rode the grav assisted lift back down to the ground level. Cam's thoughts returned to the unsettling news he'd just received as the group silently descended on magical waves of gravity. He'd long dealt with feelings of otherness, but everything he'd been taught about angst told him that feeling different was natural and just a feeling. But it turned out he actually was different. Only, he'd just found out about that. So his lifelong sense of being different from everyone around him didn't really apply, did it? Had he always been aware, on a subconscious level, that he wasn't really human? It was hard to say. Hell, did he even have a subconscious, or was it some quantum computer program that acted like one? Was there even a difference?

Cam shook his head, pushing those thoughts away. He'd always been good at compartmentalizing his feelings–a gift from the years of trauma he suffered at the hands of his adoptive parents. He couldn't afford to spiral into an existential crisis, not when so many critical things, including the life of his best friend, still hung in the balance. He'd just have to make time for that later. If there even was a later.

After exiting the lift, the trio walked back through the tower's large, open atrium toward the main building entrance. Outside, they found the flyer they'd used earlier still parked and waiting. The three of them climbed inside, this time with Tasha at the controls, and were soon back in the air, pointed towards the giant crystal tower rising elegantly in the distance. They were headed to meet with Natialara Dalirassa, Tasha told him, their Protectorate supervisor and handler. She was from Andras, the other settled human world Cam had just learned about. That concept still felt improbably strange to him. While he could wrap his head around the idea of multiple human-settled worlds in an abstract sense, he definitely hadn't fully grasped it yet, even as they flew past the fantastical towers populating the alien city of Kaseka.

Instead of landing near the Protectorate tower base, Tasha flew them up higher, approaching a landing pad that extended from one side of the structure about three-quarters of the way to the spire on top. The local traffic guidance system took control of the flyer, and they were gently lowered onto a spot demarcated with flashing lights. Cam watched through the viewscreen and noticed a lone guard standing nearby, resplendent in their black and scarlet body armor. The face shield on their helmet was opaque, lending a subtly ominous tone to their look. Once the flyer settled down onto the landing pad, the guard removed their helmet, revealing a lovely, full-lipped face, with sepia skin, large, brown eyes, and shiny, straight, black hair pulled back tight and done up in a bun.

"Welcoming committee," Tasha muttered.

"Relax," Finn replied, "it's just Alina. She likes you."

"If Natia sent her, you know she is too angry to come meet us herself."

"She may be angry with us now, but she'll come around once she finds out what's been going on." He took a deep breath. "Ok. Smiles, everyone. Otto, open it up, please."

The side hatch lifted open, and Cam could feel the cold wind gusting in from outside. Finn stepped out first, followed by Tasha and then Cam. Finn approached the guard, his arms spread wide. "Alina? How've you been? It was so nice of you to meet us up here." He leaned in for an embrace, which she accepted.

"It's nice to see you, too, Jerusalem," she said. They hugged briefly, then she let him go. Then she noticed Cam. "You've brought company?"

Finn nodded. "Oh, yeah. Ali, this is Cameron Maddock. He goes by Cam. Cam, meet my fellow Protector, Alina, child of the Lightning Clan and an Agent of the Protectorate. She goes by Alina, but most of us just call her Ali."

"Hi, Ali." Cam reached out to shake her hand, but his system prompted him to do what he saw Finn do back at the gate, so he reached past her hand to her forearm. "It's good to meet you."

"Same," she replied as she grasped Cam's arm. "Come on, you three, Natia asked me to bring you up to her office. Rumor has it the two of you've been bad."

"I am always bad," Tasha remarked as the group fell in behind Alina. She led them from the landing pad toward the indoor hanger through a large archway on the side of the building.

Alina laughed. "That must be why so many of us idolize you. We'd never get away with half the shit you manage to pull off." Tasha smiled when she heard that. But, even in the sudden shadow, Cam thought he saw her blush, too.

The group walked past the parked flyers arranged around the hangar's edges to a lift shaft at the rear of the space, taking them from the sixty-fifth floor up to the eighty-ninth floor. Cam listened in as they made small talk about a new training regimen for a fresh crop of recruits. Alina also asked after Finn's mother, who, Finn claimed, was doing as well as always. Once they were out of the lift, Alina took them across a large, open-plan workspace dotted with clusters of minimalist workstations where people, some in uniform and some not, sat, stood, or grouped together around projected displays. They were headed toward a glassed-in office set into one of the building's angular corners. Even from outside of it, Cam could see that the office's view was incredible. Someone was working in the office–presumably Natia–and waved them inside when they saw the group approaching.

"Well, that's all for me, then," Alina remarked, stopping outside of the office. "Good to see you both again. And nice to meet you as well, Cam." She gave them a small wave, then turned to head back toward the lift shaft.

Finn stepped toward the door, which slid open as he approached, and the others followed him inside. The office was minimally decorated, with a simple but dramatically arched slab of white stone for a desk. Several chairs upholstered in rich jewel tones were set in a semicircle in front of it. The real showpiece was the view, which looked west and south over the city and out across the grand expanse of the great ocean. Cam was quickly entranced by it.

"That spit of land down there," said the person at the desk in English, "is where the city of Monterey would be. I went once, a long time ago, but I imagine it probably still looks much the same now as it did then. Of course, there are no buildings there that can match this one for the view."

Cam nodded. "It's pretty spectacular."

"Natia," said Finn, "this is Cameron Maddock. He goes by Cam. He is referenced in our reports, of course. Cam, this is Protector Supervisor Natialara of Clan Dalirassa. She goes by Natia."

Cam tore himself away from the view to greet his host. "Nice to meet you, Protector Supervisor."

She smiled. "Just Natia, please." Then she stood and held out a hand toward the chairs across from her. Seen up close, she was quite striking, with deep russet skin and long, well-styled black hair, dressed in a mint green pantsuit with a contrasting, peach-colored top and matching boots. "Please, grab a chair, everyone, so we can get down to business." While the three of them each took one of the chairs, Natia touched a spot on her desk that caused all of the surrounding glass to turn a milky white, eliminating the views both into and out of the office. Then she sat back down. "Excellent. Now that we have a little privacy, I'd like to start by asking what the fuck you think you're doing sneaking a Prime human into Turana unannounced."

Tasha snickered. "Told you."

"We were hardly sneaking," Finn complained. "You've seen our reports. We just didn't announce ourselves to the Gate monitors."

Natia looked at him shrewdly. "Yes, reports that are strangely lacking in detail, I might add. And you also somehow found time to stop in and say a quick hello to Lhasa, I noticed. Is there something wrong with our scanners?"

Finn shook his head. "Come on, Natia, you've worked with Lhasa plenty of times yourself. Don't go getting all high and mighty on me."

She looked at him silently for a moment, her mouth set in

a tight line, then nodded. "That may be true. And you know I hardly ever question your actions." Tasha let out a polite cough at that, which got her a glance from Natia. "Be that as it may, stretching protocol is one thing, but throwing out the rulebook is another matter entirely. I presume you have a good reason for doing so."

Finn nodded. "I think we've finally gotten our first glimpse at Sable in action."

Natia's well-shaped eyebrows lifted in mild surprise. "I see."

Cam wondered what Sable was. Instead of asking, he reached into the local net to see if he could find any information. Unlike the network back at the Guild tower, it was totally locked up. But whoever programmed his system had anticipated the need to break through network security because he found several routines meant just for that, so he set them to work on getting through the local net's encryption.

Meanwhile, Finn reached into a pocket inside his vest, pulled out a thin wafer of crystal, and placed it on Natia's desk. It looked like the data crystal Cam saw in his dream. Natia put a well-manicured finger on it and slid it toward her, positioning it inside the blue outline of a circle that lit up on her desktop. A holographic projection activated above the desk, displaying a set of rectangular images. She selected one of those, and it grew to fill the projection space. It was Finn's view from the plaza in Seattle. After a gesture from Natia, the image became a video, and Cam watched the battle unfold from Finn's perspective, with repeated particle blasts flashing from the scattering crowd. Then the aggressor emerged, and the video stopped. Natia gestured, and the projection zoomed in on the Agent's face. Cam shivered involuntarily at her snarling expression. Natia gestured again, and the background imagery fell away from the projection, leaving only the Agent's face. Lines of text started appearing next to it, which were too small for Cam to read. Natia could, though, and what she read made her scowl. "That's not a lot of hard data," she said, finally.

"No, but what we saw was evidence enough," Finn countered. "She was wetwired to the gills, Natia, and she's not one of ours. That doesn't leave a lot of options."

She seemed to think that over for a moment. "You're right, of course. Ok, I've seen your report, but I want to hear firsthand what you've clearly left out."

Finn looked at Tasha, who nodded, then began to recount the events of the previous two days, starting with Cam and Tony's rescue, in her clipped, businesslike style.

As Tasha made her report, Cam got an alert that his network intrusion was successful, so he started a careful search for any references to Sable. There wasn't much to find, he discovered. But a local node, probably Natia's, had a file that told him Sable was an internal code name used to denote a suspected group the Protectorate was quietly investigating. Their existence had been deduced from some common data between a series of incidents stretching back over the previous five decades.

Very little was officially known about Sable, including who they actually were and what their goals may have been. One theory Cam found particularly interesting was that they'd been producing enhanced humans through the combination of human and alien genetics. Alien, Cam realized, must've meant the Nynari. If they were creating hybrids of humans and aliens, could he be one of those? He laughed nervously as the thought struck him, interrupting Tasha's report. The other three looked at him strangely.

"I'm sorry," he said hastily. "I was just thinking of something funny."

It was his turn to get a shrewd look from Natia. "Yes, well, perhaps it's time we actually got to the matter at hand, anyhow. Namely, you, and how you fit into all this."

Cam looked at Finn, who nodded. "Go ahead. We can trust her."

Natia smiled. "Yes, well, you'd better, since I'm just as culpable for what's happening here as you three."

"Well," Cam said carefully, "I think the reason I'm involved in all of this is that I'm one of them."

"One of whom?"

"Sable."

Natia looked surprised to hear that, and Cam took some momentary pleasure in cracking her otherwise highly polished facade. "I think you'd better explain what that means."

Finn jumped in before he could answer. "He's not saying he's an agent for them. But he possesses some inhuman enhancements and abilities that could only have been engineered. And if he's not one of ours?" Natia nodded, catching the inference. "That's why we stopped to see Lhasa," Finn added. "If he'd gone through one of the scanners here, there's no telling who would've seen that data. I can show you what—"

She held a hand up to stop him. "No, it's better that you don't, at least at this point." She leaned back in her elegant office chair and nodded. "It would fit, though, wouldn't it? If he's a product of some genetic black lab and was lost somehow, I doubt they'd waste much time trying to recover him once he'd been located." Natia fell silent for a few moments, lost in thought. "You brought him to Kaseka for protection?"

Tasha nodded. "In part, yes. But also, we need your help. Off record." Natia looked at her shrewdly, but her expression softened as Tasha described the situation with Tony and the phantom Gate. "But data requires Protectorate analysis to process, so here we are."

Natia sat forward, placing her hands on her desk. "I see. Alright, give me the data. I'll get it looked at by Quantum Analysis, but I won't tell them where it's from. Since they're getting it from me, they shouldn't ask too many questions." Tasha nodded, then pulled a data crystal from her pocket and set it on the desk. Natia grabbed it and slipped it into her jacket. Then she sat back. "There's one more thing. Your instinct to keep his identity and scan data off the books was probably a good one. We now have reason to believe that the attack on Ipuka Station was meant to cover the theft of some confidential Protectorate data. As a result, we now have to assume that the Protectorate may be compromised."

Finn and Tasha both looked very uncomfortable when they heard that. "Shit," Finn swore. "For how long?"

Natia shrugged. "We don't know. There wasn't much left to see, and the Agent covered their tracks well beyond what we could find. A thorough forensic analysis turned up some traces of what they were looking at before the station was destroyed, but the most damning thing we found was a set of off-log transmissions to the station in the days leading up to the attack.

"Shit," Tasha spat, echoing Finn's earlier curse. "So whole

attack was just ruse to cover for dead drop?"

"That's how things would appear," Natia confirmed. "Which muddies the water even further." She looked at Cam, then back at Finn. "If you think he's trustworthy, then that's good enough for me. I'll get your data analyzed right away, but in the meantime, you should bring him somewhere to wait outside of the Protectorate. Your mother could probably offer him sanctuary."

Finn nodded. "That was our thought, too."

Natia stood and attempted to brush away some nonexistent wrinkles from her impossibly smooth jacket. "Alright. Cam, I'm glad to finally meet you, even if the circumstances are less than ideal. Finn, Tasha, I'm counting on you both to keep him safe until we have some answers, which I will head down to Quantum Analysis to get shortly." Then she touched the spot on her desk that deactivated the privacy screens, and the windows all turned clear.

They'd clearly been dismissed, so the trio returned to the bank of lift shafts and took one down.

"That went better than expected," Tasha mused once they were in the lift. "I thought she would yell more."

Finn nodded. "She did seem to take that all pretty well. With what things look like, she must be more worried now than angry."

"Indeed," Tasha agreed. "Now, we finally have fun part."

Finn laughed. "Oh, yeah."

"What's the fun part?" Cam asked.

Finn smiled. "Now, we get to introduce you to my mother."

FINN

The Engineering Guild's central tower was just south of the Protectorate headquarters, surrounded by enough Guild buildings to qualify it as its own small city. Since it was so close, Finn suggested that they walk there to give Cam a chance to experience Kaseka on a more personal level. Tasha decided to bow out of the walk and grabbed a flyer to visit her own, rarely-used living quarters to clean up and change.

Unlike the Science Guild's atrium, the one in the Protectorate tower didn't stretch upwards for its full height. But it was still many stories tall and was anchored by an impressive fountain that featured a large, abstract, crystalline sculpture at its center. Finn led Cam through one of the large, open archways to a broad plaza outside the building. From a distance, the plaza appeared to be paved with geometric shapes made of different colored, sparkling stone, but up close, you could see that each colored area was actually covered in crushed gemstones. Cam didn't seem to notice it, though. He had a faraway look in his eyes that Finn guessed meant he was stuck in his head.

Finn stopped where he was, startling Cam. Once he had Cam's attention, Finn pointed down.

"Wow," Cam said, looking downward. "Fancy."

Finn raised an eyebrow. It was obviously going to take more than a lovely plaza to drag Cam back to reality. He turned and resumed walking. "This is amethyst," he explained as they walked across the plaza, the gemstone gravel crunching brightly underfoot. "Over there is ruby, sapphire, and emerald. The light-colored stuff is diamond." He pointed back toward the tower. "That's diamond, too."

"For real?"

Finn nodded. "Yep. Manufactured, of course, not dug out of the ground. And polished to an optically clear finish. Our materials tech is pretty advanced, and we don't have any sort of enforced-scarcity economy here."

"Ouch. Touché."

Finn chuckled. "Was that a little too harsh?"

"It's fine. It's not like I invented capitalism."

"No, your inventions are more along the technical side, right?"

"I suppose so, although I like to think of myself as more of a tinkerer than an inventor. Where I get really creative is writing code."

Finn raised an eyebrow. "Oh, really?"

"Yeah, I totally nerd out for programming."

"I guess that's not all that surprising since it's your job."

Cam nodded. "Sure, but it's way more than that. It's like, as soon as I sit down with a coding idea, I almost can't stop until I've worked everything out. It's that way with any kind of puzzle for me, really. Code, systems, strategy. I've got a mind for it, I guess."

Finn couldn't keep from smirking. "In more ways than one, it turns out."

Cam rolled his eyes. "You don't think that hasn't been on

my mind? Am I a coding genius cuz I've always had so much of it in my head? I mean, I've actually been writing my own AI."

Finn's eyes betrayed his surprise. "You have?"

"Yep. I mean, it's nothing like yours. It doesn't have any self-awareness or any personality beyond what I've programmed it to have. But Ego is better than anything out there on the market today. On Earth Prime, at least."

<It's no wonder he's taken to his internal system so readily.> Otto shared. *<It almost sounds like he was trying to create his own>*

<I was thinking the same thing. It can't be a coincidence, can it?>

<It's impossible to say. Perhaps he was influenced by his system on an unconscious level?>

<Or it's just how he was made>

<Yes, that's a possibility, too>

A vast, wooded area lay beyond the plaza, with a broad path winding through the trees. The air was warm, with a pleasant pine and oak smell to it. After the week Cam was having, Finn expected that it would be a nice change of pace for him to have a walk somewhere that didn't involve being chased by people who wanted to hurt him. Looking back at Cam, though, Finn could see that he was already back in his head.

<Maybe he just needs time to process everything> Otto suggested, guessing at what Finn was thinking about.

<Probably so. Only, we don't really have a lot of time>
<That's true>

"You seem a little distracted," Finn commented.

Cam seemed to snap back to attention, then looked a little

downcast. "Yeah, I guess I am. Sorry."

"It's understandable, considering everything."

Cam nodded. "Yeah, everything." He stopped walking, forcing Finn to do the same. "I know I told you earlier that what Lhasa said about my DNA and all that didn't bother me, but I guess that's not really true."

Finn smiled. "As I said, it's understandable. Do you want to talk about it?"

Cam seemed to consider the idea for a few moments, then nodded again. "It's just–I don't know. I feel human, you know? Or, at least, I think I do. I was raised as one, and I've lived my whole life around them. I don't know anything different. So to hear that I'm not, you know, human–I don't know how to deal with that."

Finn sighed and shook his head. "Ok, stop that."

"Stop what?"

"Stop thinking of yourself as not being human. You're as human as I am." Cam didn't seem so sure but didn't offer any immediate pushback. So Finn continued. "You and I both have similar enhancements. We've got computers in our heads and wiring throughout our bodies. The only difference is that mine were surgically implanted, and yours were grown. You heard Lhasa. All the parts that make you human are there. You've just got some extra enhancements."

Cam narrowed his eyes, then nodded. "Ok, maybe so. Except you made that choice for yourself, but someone else made that choice for me and fucked with my DNA to make it happen.

Then Finn understood part of the problem was Cam's Prime way of thinking. He smiled. "And that's wrong, to you? We do that sort of thing all the time here." Cam opened his mouth to respond, but Finn cut him off. "No, not custom-grown exotic field manipulators. But correction for genetic anomalies that could one day lead to cancer and disease. Stuff like that."

Cam still looked unsure. "That doesn't feel like the same thing. You're talking about parents ensuring the health of their offspring, not some alien genetics committee choosing from a list of options for their special order superchild."

"You are kind of stuck on that alien thing, aren't you? I grew up on a different planet, remember? This planet, in fact. Do I seem all that alien to you? Or does anyone else you've met here, for that matter?"

Cam shook his head. "No, I guess not. But you're still human, though."

Finn nodded. "And you've never met any people who aren't human. Ok, well, we'll have to change that, I suppose. But, in the meantime, maybe you can take my word for it that all the aliens I know are pretty decent people."

"People?"

Finn nodded again. "Yeah, people. Just like you and me. They may have grown up on another planet, and they may look a lot different than we do, but they're still people with a society and culture. They've got goals, and dreams, and a moral code, and all of that."

Then Cam laughed. "Shit, you're right. All of my experience with aliens is in fiction. Books, movies, video games, and shit. They're always either wise, mysterious elders hoarding the secrets of the universe or vicious monsters bent on the destruction of our species and total galactic domination."

Finn laughed at that, too. "In my experience, they're

310

closer to the former than the latter. The Nynari have had millennia to destroy us or take us over. They don't seem to be interested." Cam started to look around and appeared to see the surrounding woods for the first time. Maybe Finn had gotten through to him? "Did that help?"

Cam took a deep breath and nodded. "Yeah, I think so. Sorry about my existential crisis, there."

"Don't sweat it, Cam. And remember–if you're having trouble with anything, you can always talk to me."

"Thanks, Finn. So, how far is it to the Engineering Guild from here?"

"Not too far. Come on."

As they continued walking, Cam mentioned how all of the trees looked familiar. They were primarily local, Finn shared, although Turana had many trees that closely resembled their cousins from Earth Prime, including the coastal redwoods. But the area was just one of many like it throughout the city. Walking through it, you'd hardly know that Kaseka was a city of several million people.

"No way," Cam interjected.

"It really is," Finn confirmed. "It helps that we're firm believers in communal living, of course."

"Wow, it's so quiet here. It feels like the city disappeared."

Finn nodded. "Sure, although this place is as much the city as the buildings and towers are. Initially, those were all constructed in places where they'd have a minimal impact on the natural life here."

"So, the parks were here first?"

"Yeah, except this isn't exactly a park. It's just an area that we've mostly left alone." Finn stopped and crouched down until he could put his hands on the ground, then dug a partially buried acorn out of the path. "Not to get all preachy," he continued as he stood back up, "but the land, and everything that lives in it and on it, is a part of us, just like we're part of the land." He handed the acorn to Cam, who took it, then looked back at Finn curiously. "It's important to us, as a community, to be good stewards of the land we live on, so we're thoughtful about how we use it."

Cam smirked. "Not to get too preachy."

Finn laughed. "I know that's a lot different from how things are where you're from." He took a deep breath, savoring the scent of the nearby trees and the hint of ocean salt in the air. "Plus, it's a nice place to walk. I like to come through here when I want to unwind after getting an earful from my boss."

Cam laughed. "She was really something. I like her."

Finn smiled. "I thought you probably would."

"And she's from Andras?"

"That's right. Although she lives here now, of course."

"I hope I get to go there, too," Cam said.

Finn laughed. "You've really got a taste for inter-dimensional travel now, eh? Good thing you've got the means for it built right in."

Cam stopped, and Finn wondered if he'd maybe taken things too far, too soon. "You're right, I do," Cam agreed. "I keep thinking I need to be taken to places, but I guess I could just open a Gate there right now." Finn inhaled sharply in surprise, but Cam just laughed. "I'm just fucking with you."

Finn laughed out the breath he'd been holding. "Yeah, well, I'll be happy to go with you once we get this little mess sorted out first."

The pair emerged from the winding, wooded path into a large, outdoor market bustling with people. It was a good one for a first-timer to see, with dozens of vendor stalls, offering everything from food to artwork to clothing. Cam laughed when he saw all of it. "Are you taking me shopping? Cuz I haven't got any money on me."

Finn chuckled. "That's ok, you don't need any. Just take what you like."

"For real? You actually just take stuff?"

Finn nodded and led him toward a stand that offered colorful, handmade trinkets of various sizes. "That's right. People make and offer things because they want to. They enjoy cooking or crafting, and they want to share their work. They don't need to sell it because they already have housing, food, clothing, and whatever else they need provided for them." He picked up a brightly painted wooden figurine of a bird, thinking his mother might like it. Then he put it back down, remembering that the last time he'd visited, he'd already given her the exact same thing. "See anything you like?"

Cam sighed. "I guess I don't even know what I'd be looking for. Like, I haven't been home for, what? Three or four days? And I don't even know how long it'll be before I get to go back."

Finn reached over and put a hand on his shoulder. "Yeah, I guess you're right. I wasn't thinking about that when I brought you here. Sorry."

That got a smile out of Cam. "It's ok. I'd love to at least look through here. It's my first real-life alien marketplace, right?"

Finn laughed, then turned Cam around toward the other stalls. "Not to mention the well-known benefits of retail therapy."

Cam rolled his eyes dramatically, then grinned and started walking into the market center. The pair stopped off at a few places that caught Cam's attention, including one that offered a unique recipe for spicy roasted acorns. Or, at least, the local equivalent. Explaining that to Cam led Finn to tell him how, in the early days, the Chosen people had sometimes gone hungry since they didn't recognize much of the local plant and animal life, and not everything they found was edible. But some of the Chosen had brought acorns over with them, which they planted and grew in the Turani soil.

"So, basically, terraforming?" Cam asked before he popped a couple acorn bits into his mouth.

"I suppose so," Finn agreed. He'd never thought about it like that. "Of course, the local plants and animals eventually worked just as well for a food source once the Turani figured out what was edible and what wasn't."

A little further onward, they stopped to listen to a band of musicians performing. Finn recognized the peppy, upbeat song from his childhood, and it got him reminiscing about listening to it during his first festival at the Academy.

Cam must have noticed the look on his face. "This is catchy."

Finn smiled at him. "I had my first kiss when this song was playing."

Cam raised an eyebrow. "Oh, really? Were they pretty?"

Finn chuckled. "He really was. I also had my second kiss that same night, and she was pretty, too."

Cam laughed. "Damn, player. Look at you go."

<Tasha asked me to let you know that she's on her way to the Guild tower now.>

<Ok, thanks, Mr. Moodkiller.>

314

"Speaking of going, that's what we should probably do. I don't want to keep my dear mother waiting."

"Will there be food? Those acorns were good, but they kinda made me more hungry."

Finn laughed. "Oh, there will definitely be food."

As they started to walk toward the central Guild tower, Finn took the time to explain more about the Guild. The Engineering Guild was sizable, managing everything from machine construction and repair to maintenance on the city's quantum mainframes. People who joined the Guild were provided with the education to learn their desired trade, food, housing, and other necessities. Once a Guild member chose to retire from actively working due to age, they were free to stay on at the Guild and often fell into teaching positions. People rose to the level of Guild Master by demonstrating their mastery over a particular field. There were no politics involved. Although family relationships could often influence one's choice of Guild, skill and talent were still the only way to advance. And, of course, people were free to leave the Guild at any time, whether it was to join another Guild, return to their clan, or even just strike out on their own. There was at least one Guild Master for each specialization and a rotating Guild Master position to oversee them all. That was the position his mother held.

As the two of them approached the broad, arched entranceway to the tower, Finn could already feel the familiar energy up ahead—energy that matched his own excitement at being home again. He led Cam through the entry into another large, open atrium that, like the Science Guild's, climbed all the way to the tower's glassed-in roof. Since it was the Engineering Guild, the atrium featured maker stations, stocked with all the tools and supplies needed for working on small projects, in addition to the discussion areas they'd seen in the Science Guild atrium.

When Finn looked at Cam, his jaw had dropped.

"You like it?" Finn asked with a chuckle. After Cam told him of his own workshop and his propensity for making things, Finn thought he'd feel a little more at home in the Engineering Guild tower. And, after everything they'd been through, he wanted to see something that made Cam happy.

"Are you kidding?" Cam asked in response. "I fucking love it. This place looks amazing!"

Then Finn noticed his sister Oslo approaching. She was a little shorter and older than Finn, but there was no mistaking the family resemblance, even with her darker complexion. Oslo was dressed in a brightly colored coverall with a geometric pattern running in a stripe across the chest and arms. She had more gray in the mass of thick curls on her head than the last time Finn had seen her, too. He smiled and offered her a friendly wave. "Dear sister," he called out. His sister waved back, and when they reached one another, they clasped each other's forearms and then touched their foreheads together. Then they both turned toward Cam, who looked like he felt totally out of place.

"Dear sister," said Finn, "this is my friend Cameron Maddock. He goes by Cam. I brought him here to show him the famous hospitality of the Engineering Guild. Cam, this is my sister, Oslo, child of the Wolf Clan and a member of the Engineering Guild. She goes by Oslo and works in the Guild with our mother."

Oslo held out a hand in greeting. "It's a pleasure to meet you." Cam reached out and grabbed her forearm. Oslo

316

spared him from the forehead touch, though, which Finn was silently grateful for. "Lhasa told us you'd be coming by, so our dear mother is upstairs getting a meal prepared. They spoke very highly of you."

Cam's cheeks reddened slightly at the compliment. "That's nice of you. I haven't eaten anything except Chinese takeout and junk food for days."

Oslo gave him a strange look, then turned back to her brother. "He really is a Prime, after all? This should make dinner interesting."

"Go easy on him, dear sister," Finn offered, chuckling. "It's his first day on a different planet."

"I guess you don't have any Chinese takeout here, do you," said Cam, realizing his blunder. Then he looked at the siblings strangely. "But wait. You're Oslo, you're Jerusalem, and your other sibling's Lhasa. You don't have any of those cities here, either."

Oslo laughed and nodded. "You can thank our dear father for that. Part of his duties was maintaining our archival data on your geographical and political divisions."

"Plus, he liked to collect maps," added Finn.

"Oh, I totally get that," offered Cam. "I'm kind of the same way about old wireframe schematics, too."

"Indeed," said Oslo, who then, after a moment, added, "If you'd pardon my rudeness, but you speak the language awfully well for your first visit to Turana."

Cam looked startled. Maybe he hadn't realized he was speaking Turani? It usually wasn't hard to tell how Cam was feeling. Unlike a lot of folks from Earth Prime, Cam tended to wear his heart on his sleeve. It was one of the things about Primes that annoyed Finn the most. And he recovered quickly enough. "What can I say? It's a gift."

Oslo didn't seem convinced, but Finn didn't want to drag that out in the middle of the atrium. "Let's get ourselves upstairs, Oslo, instead of interrogating our guest out in the open."

His sister took the hint and nodded. "Of course. Once again, I beg your pardon. Please, this way."

Oslo turned and led them over to the nearby lift shafts on the side of the atrium.

"Sorry about that," Finn said to Cam quietly as they walked. "I didn't think to warn you about my sister's lack of manners."

"It's alright," Cam whispered. "I don't mind. I just don't want to get you in trouble."

Finn scoffed. "With her? She's not going to cause any trouble. She's family. Plus, our mother would kill her."

The three of them took the lift shaft to the sixtieth floor, then walked along the curved mezzanine until they reached a door marked with Finn's clan sigil, which resembled a stylized wolf's head. Finn pointed it out to Cam and explained that they used them the way Primes used family names. They went through the marked entrance into a generous gathering area. It was an ample space, with central seating around a low table and an abundance of artwork spread around the perimeter. A lot of art hung on the walls and pottery and small statues on shelves and pedestals. His father had been an avid collector, and his mother, despite her general disinterest, had been faithfully keeping the tradition alive in his honor. Several doorways led off from the space, and a giant viewscreen took up most of the far wall. That evening it was set to reflect the view outside the tower, with the slowly setting sun casting a rose-tinted glow on the city's many buildings.

Tasha was already seated there, and Finn's mother joined them as soon as they walked in. She was dressed in a multicolored, sleeveless wrap dress that draped all the way to the floor. Her long, black hair was pulled back into a thick, tight braid, and large, golden circles dangled from her ears. She gave Finn a warm embrace before he presented Cam to her.

"Dear mother, this is my friend Cameron Maddock. He goes by Cam. Cam, this is my dear mother, Arana, an esteemed elder of the Wolf Clan and most esteemed Master of the Engineering Guild. Her informal title is Guild Master, but she usually just goes by Arana."

Arana smiled warmly. "Thank you, Jerusalem. Hello Cam, welcome to my home. May I give you a hug?"

Cam nodded. "I think I'd like that, ma'am."

She laughed and pulled him into a quick embrace. "I see your Prime manners are well ingrained, but that won't be necessary here. Arana will do nicely."

Cam winced. "Sorry, it's my first time on an alien planet. I'm still sort of getting the hang of things."

"From what I've been told," she said kindly, "you will likely acclimate quickly."

Finn frowned, realizing what that probably meant. "Lhasa may have spoken out of turn."

Arana waved off his complaint. "Nonsense. If I'm to offer him Guild protection, it's only reasonable that I know what I'm getting us into. Besides, he's hardly the first person I've met with an implanted internal system."

"He is implanted?" Oslo asked, sounding confused. "But he's a Prime."

Arana clucked her tongue, and Oslo immediately looked down. "Please forgive my eldest child, who has not learned her manners nearly as well as you have, Cam. I've had some food brought up. Once Lhasa arrives, we'll eat. Then, after that, we can learn more about our new guest if he's willing to share." She added a wink to the last part. "In the meantime, I'll get us some tea."

She put a hand on Oslo's shoulder and led her back out of the room. Finn offered to show Cam where the facilities were, so he could freshen up, which Cam was grateful for. When Finn walked back into the gathering room, Lhasa had already arrived and was standing with Tasha. Finn immediately went to greet them.

"You told our dear mother about Cam?" he asked Lhasa after giving them a quick hug.

They pouted lightly. "As if any of us could ever lie to her, Jerusalem. Besides, it wasn't me that gave him away. She already knew about him and that you'd brought him to me for scanning and analysis."

Natia, of course. No wonder she'd suggested that they take Cam to his mother so quickly. "I'd say we've probably both been set up by my boss."

Tasha smiled. "Natia is crafty one. It comes from growing up around much political intrigue."

Finn nodded. Although Natia tended to keep her personal life much more private than a Turani typically would, she was still a Dalirassa. The exploits of such a prominent Andrani clan were well known even among their neighbors on Turana. "Old habits die hard, right?"

His sibling gave him a smirk. "Well, Natia looks out for you almost as well as our dear mother, Jerusalem, so I'm willing to forgive her occasional backroom machinations."

Arana and Oslo appeared with some of the food, so Finn, Tasha, and Lhasa helped them set the trays out on the low table in the center of the room. Cam reappeared shortly after that, and everyone took a seat and started to help themselves. The food was served family-style, and the earthy, spicy smells made Finn's mouth water. He'd never really acclimated to Prime food, although he found that indigenous American and Mexican cuisine was a reasonable approximation of what he was used to.

While they ate, Finn started off their family mealtime tradition by sharing a story about a recent visit to Istanbul, which resulted in Tasha and him almost getting hopelessly lost in Turkish Anatolia. Arana pointed out that Istanbul was one of Lhasa's potential names, which got a laugh from the group. Lhasa and Oslo each shared some updates on projects they'd been working on. Oslo specialized in mechanical engineering as a member of the Engineering Guild, which Cam was interested in enough to interrupt and pepper her with questions. Finn hoped that might win him some points with his sister, who seemed to relax and be more comfortable with Cam as the evening progressed. Tasha shared a short but complicated joke she'd recently learned involving several oddball characters and a small animal, which was funny primarily because of the convoluted way she told it. It got a polite laugh from everyone besides Finn and Cam, who were the only ones to pick up on her cultural references and thought it was hilarious.

Once dinner was over, the others set about cleaning up the dishes while Cam took the time to take in some of the artwork in the room. It was an eclectic collection built mainly by Finn's father. The wall art ranged from woven tapestries to photography to paintings. There was one piece Cam seemed to recognize, though, once he stood in front of it.

"Ah, I see you've found the Gladysz," said Finn, who offered Cam a cup of herbal tea. It was fragrant and tasted faintly of ginger. "Wojsław Gladysz was my dear father's favorite Prime painter, and our dear mother couldn't bear to part with it, even though she thinks it's hideous."

Cam chuckled, then took the tea and carefully sipped it. "It would definitely take some getting used to. Your father was a fan of Prime art?"

Finn shrugged. "Somewhat. He didn't have any particular fascination beyond maps, but sometimes things just caught his eye."

"It was his way," said Arana, joining them with her own cup of tea. "It was how he and I met, in fact. His parents were very conservative and tried to arrange a union for him within his own clan. But we happened to meet when I was new to the Guild, offering basic home maintenance lessons at his clan's learning center. From the moment we met, he courted me until he finally worked up the courage to ask me to become his marriage partner instead." She smiled. "I was happy he did. He was so handsome and intelligent. And he somehow managed to put up with me."

"He was a good parent," Finn agreed.

Arana looked Cam in the eye, then. "I want you to know, Cam, that you're welcome here as long as you like, and that will always be so. My dear Jerusalem does not often bring people to meet me, so when he does, I know it must be someone he cares for a great deal."

Finn was a little embarrassed to hear his mother admit

that, especially since he hadn't even considered his feelings for Cam to be more than a professional interest. But she'd raised him and probably knew him better than anyone.

Cam looked a little overwhelmed at her admission. He swallowed but kept his composure. "Thank you, Arana. That's very generous of you."

Arana smiled. "Of course. I can't imagine what it must be like for you to be here in this strange place. Hopefully, having a place you're always welcome will make it easier."

"It's been strange but fascinating, too. I don't have a lot of warm feelings for the people who raised me, but I've enjoyed being halfway adopted by my friend Tony's family, and you all remind me of them a lot."

Finn saw a momentary shadow of sadness cloud Cam's face at the mention of his friend's name. His mother must've seen it as well since she reached out and put a gentle hand on his arm. "I know that, among your people, there's the concept of a chosen family. We've always lived that way here. Our clans can grow quite large, so if you don't happen to be loved or respected by the people who birthed you, there are always plenty of others who will." Then she looked back and saw that everyone else had gathered around the seating area again. "We should probably get to business, though. Shall we?"

Cam nodded, and they all sat down again. Cam took the seat next to Finn, who started to wonder what Cam made of everything Arana said. While she wasn't necessarily cold, she generally didn't open up to people as quickly and warmly as she had with Cam. Finn appreciated it since it seemed to help put Cam at ease. But Finn definitely hadn't expected it. Then, there was her remark about how he must've been someone

Finn cared about deeply to bring him to her home. Again, it hadn't been out of character for her to say something like that. But it was unusual for him to witness. She was getting older and may have been softening as she aged. Maybe he needed to start visiting her more often. He smiled at Cam, received a smile in return, then turned to Arana. "So, dear mother, are you willing to offer Cam Guild protection?"

Arana nodded. "I have some questions for Cam first, but yes. Provisionally."

"You cannot be serious," Oslo complained, losing all sense of decorum before the discussion even started. "He's not even Turani. There's no protocol for a Prime to gain Guild protection."

Lhasa cleared their throat. "Although it's been some time, if you check the archives, dear sister, I think you'll find that many Prime transiters have been welcomed into Turani Guilds."

"Besides," Arana added, "as Guild Master, I'm well within my remit to do so." Oslo opened her mouth to speak, but Arana silenced her with a look. "Now, Cam, could you tell me a little about your situation? I don't need specifics. Just paint me a picture with broad strokes, so to speak."

Cam nodded, and told her the story of what had been happening to him, beginning with the incident in San Francisco, then Seattle, then finally what happened to Tony and their search for him. Finn was glad to see everyone listening attentively, especially Lhasa and Arana. Oslo's face was unreadable, though, which made Finn a little concerned, given her recent outburst. "And now," Cam said as he wrapped things up, "we're waiting for Natia to let us know what information the Protectorate can give us about the last

Gate we found and where Tony might be."

Arana sipped her tea, which had undoubtedly grown cold by that point. She looked to be deep in thought. "I see," she said after a moment. "Thank you for being so candid. It sounds like you've been through a lot." She turned to Finn. "How much of this have you kept from the Protectorate?"

Finn sighed. Of course, she'd ask him that in front of everyone. "They're not aware of his enhancements, specifically. Especially his ability to open and close Gates at will."

She seemed to consider that. If it shocked her, she showed no sign. "And Natia also shares your concerns?" He nodded, remembering what Natia told them, along with his earlier conversation with Lhasa. His mother probably knew that Natia shared his concerns already and was just asking him for the group's benefit. "That doesn't surprise me," she added. "I'll be honest. I've heard rumors of late, of strange goings-on with the Protectorate. Well, stranger than usual, I should add."

Finn was surprised to hear that. "You have?"

"I'm the most esteemed Master of the Engineering Guild," she said solemnly. "It's my duty to hear those things." She turned to Oslo. "You're still concerned, dear child?"

Oslo was silent for a moment, likely considering what she wanted to say next, given the formal way their mother just addressed her, along with the reception to her last outburst. "With all respect to you, dear mother, and to you, dear brother, but I have to say this. The things he can do," she said, motioning toward Cam, "aren't natural. He shouldn't be able to do them. They're dangerous things, which makes him a dangerous person. Is keeping him here even safe for him, let alone us? There's no group better able to understand and, if necessary, deal with him than the Protectorate." Then she looked at Cam cooly, his face showing minor concern. "I mean no disrespect to you, of course."

"So you say," Tasha said acidly.

Oslo didn't rise to the bait, though. "Our dear mother asked for my opinion."

Finn opened his mouth to reply when Arana raised her hand to stop him. "She is correct. I did so. And her concerns are not without merit, I might add." Then she looked at Oslo. "But you're out of line for speaking of Cam like he's not sitting in this room with you. He may not be fortunate enough to have been born among us here, but that doesn't diminish his humanity. You'd do well to remember that."

Oslo looked reasonably chastened at her mother's rebuke. "Yes, of course, dear mother."

Arana fixed her pointed gaze back on Cam, and Finn felt a twinge of pity for him. While the evening may have seemed like a friendly, family gathering at first, he'd known that it would become a sort of trial before the end. His mother was capable of great warmth and caring. But the qualities Finn often admired most about her were her great resolve and determination. It took nothing less than total mastery of one's craft to rise to such a position of authority as hers, after all. "Do you have anything you'd like to add, Cam?"

Cam hesitated and swallowed before answering. "I recognize the danger in what I can do. I've even seen a few examples of it myself recently. My best friend is missing, and possibly dead, because of me, so I understand if this isn't a burden you're willing to take on. But I'd certainly appreciate any help you're willing to offer me to find the answers I'm looking for because I don't know who I am, and I'd really like to."

Arana held his gaze for a few moments longer, then nodded. "Of course, and thank you again for your candor. Cameron Maddock, I hereby offer you the full protection of the Engineering Guild, effective immediately, until you yourself choose to renounce it. You'll be as safe within Guild walls as we can make you, and no one may remove you from here without your specific consent. In addition, I grant you the rights of provisional Guild membership. Should you decide to take up a trade, you may convert that one day to full membership." She looked around the room, making sure that everyone understood what she'd stated. They were all smiling except for Oslo, whose face was stony. "So, I say, therefore, let it be done."

Cam smiled, and Finn let out the breath he hadn't realized he was holding. Finn was glad things had worked out in their favor. His promise to help Cam had meant that, if his mother decided against them, Finn would've had to make a few very uncomfortable choices. But he had faith in his mother and in his family, or he wouldn't have bothered trying to gain their support.

Still, there was the question of his sister. Oslo had always been something of a naysayer. A devil's advocate, to put it into Prime terms. But she'd never openly defied their dear mother like that before, at least not that Finn knew of. He made a note to check in with Lhasa about that later. Spending so much of his time away from Turana meant that he missed out on many things.

Everyone got up from their seats and started milling about. Arana, Lhasa, and Tasha broke off into their own little circle.

Finn approached his sister, intent on at least mending the shaky bridge between them. But Oslo saw him coming and just shook her head in Finn's direction before scowling and wandering away. That bridge would have to remain unmended for the time being. Finn looked back and found Cam, pacing with apparent nervous energy, and walked over to him. "Hey," he said quietly, "there's something I want to show you if you're game."

Cam nodded. "Yeah, sure. To be honest, I could use a little fresh air."

"Perfect," Finn responded, smiling. "Let's go."

He led Cam out of his mother's quarters and back around the mezzanine walkway to the lift shaft. They rode the lift up to the eightieth floor, where Finn took him to a wide, curving, outdoor platform—one of his favorite places in the whole tower. When they walked through the pressure curtain into the cool night air, Finn inhaled deeply. It was fresh and sweet, with no trace of pollution and just a hint of ocean salt. He saw Cam do the same.

"Wow," Cam said, "it's so nice up here."

Finn nodded, smiling, and walked over to the railing at the platform's edge. From there, you could see across the entire city, looking north and west. The crystal spire of the Protectorate tower rose sharply nearby, glowing in fairy light pastel colors. Flyers zipped and zoomed around the city towers like fireflies. It was peaceful and surprisingly quiet for a city that large. He turned to look out onto the ocean as it crawled darkly away from the far horizon, the slow-rolling whitecaps of massive waves looking tiny and thin at that distance. Its cascading surface sparkled brightly in the light of the moons overhead.

"Holy shit," Cam exclaimed. "There really are two moons."

Finn chuckled. "I was wondering when you'd notice that."

"Have they always been like that?"

Finn nodded. "Yes, as long as we've been here, certainly. Our scientists think that may have been the point of divergence between our two worlds. When the cataclysm that created your moon happened, here it created two instead of one. That's just an informed theory, of course. It's possible our realities could've diverged before then, but without a time machine, there's no way to know for sure."

Cam looked up and stared at the brightly glowing orbs overhead. Finn knew the feeling, recalling the first time he'd seen the massive white satellite orbiting Earth Prime. That was how he really knew he was standing on another planet. It hadn't mattered that, literally, everything else was strange and different, too. But seeing that massive, single moon, instead of the familiar sight of Oya and Hona circling above him, had driven the point home. He imagined the experience was similar to what Cam was feeling when he watched him turn away and look back into the Guild tower, leaning on the railing behind him.

"So," Finn asked him, "how's the head?"

Cam chuckled. "Haven't had any complaints."

"Oh, wow," said Finn, groaning. "You really took it there."

Cam laughed. "Sorry. Force of habit."

Finn couldn't help but laugh along. "It's alright. I just wanted to make sure things hadn't become a little too wondrous for you, you know?"

Cam smiled and shrugged. "It's just–It's a lot to take in, you know? Every time I learn something new about anything, I barely have time to digest it before the next thing comes along."

"Yeah. Every time I take you somewhere new, you kinda look like a kid on Christmas morning who's just seen all the presents under the tree."

That got a laugh out of Cam. "I keep forgetting that you're from here because of jokes like that. I assume there's no Christmas here, right?"

"There's no Christmas here," Finn agreed, "although some people know what it is, at least. But this is one place the Christianity never managed to get a foothold. No Spanish conquerors."

Cam looked over at him, curiosity in his eyes. "But you must still have some kind of religion, right? Even your ancestors must have brought something over with them."

Finn nodded. "Of course. My ancestors were very spiritual. They had all of their creation stories and sacred practices that survived the transit to Turana. Some of us still practice versions of those, and many more honor their ideas without necessarily following the practices. Believing in higher powers is human nature, I think."

Cam frowned. Finn must have touched a nerve, but he let Cam have his feelings. Eventually, Cam spoke again. "When I was younger, I believed in God. Really believed, you know? It's what my family grew up with, and their family, and it's what they tried to pass on to me." Then he sighed wistfully. "But, when I noticed I was different from everyone around me, with different color skin, having different abilities and different attractions, I started to question everything. I prayed and prayed, asking God to take away the things I was thinking, the things I dreamed about. To make me the same as everyone else. For a while, I really thought the devil was coming to take my soul." He paused, and Finn stayed silent, watching and waiting. After a moment, Cam turned, meeting Finn's gaze with his warm, topaz eyes. "After I told my folks about my crazy dreams, they just told me it was all in my head. The drugs they gave me stopped it for the most part, but I never really changed. I only became more of who I am. I also became strong enough to walk away and try coming to terms with who I am. Who I thought I was, at least. Then you came along, and all this happened, and now I'm standing here, on a parallel Earth in a different dimension, wondering if I'm even human. And we're just doing what? Admiring the view?"

Cam was clearly agitated, challenging Finn to look away. But Finn held his gaze until he saw Cam calm down again, then smiled warmly.

"Yeah, as I said, we believe in gods, too." he shared. "And then, we actually met some. We even worshiped them for a while because we didn't know any better. They were beautiful and powerful, and their technology may as well have been magic, as far as we were concerned. But they kept insisting that they weren't gods and that they were not there to be worshiped. However advanced they may have seemed, they were people, just like us. Eventually, we believed them." Finn turned away, then, and looked out toward the horizon. "But we've kept a lot of our traditions going throughout our history. They're what tie us all together as a family, as a people. Even those of us who don't believe in actual gods anymore still recognize that there are amazing, wondrous things out there in the multiverse. Even if we don't think that all-knowing spirits are the forces at work behind everything, we can still appreciate those amazing, wondrous things all the same." He turned back to Cam, putting a hand gently on his shoulder. "For my part, I don't think there really are any gods, but I don't know enough to say for sure, one way or another. If there are gods, though–or spirits, or fate, or whatever, driving the multiverse forward–I'm glad they brought you and me together. And, I'm glad to know you."

Cam was left speechless for a moment, and Finn wondered if maybe he'd pushed him a little too far. But Cam finally smiled. "Thanks, Finn. Although, to be honest, I kind of wish we'd met under different circumstances because then this wouldn't feel so weird."

Finn laughed kindly. "Yeah, I understand. Things are how they are. In fact, there's an old saying among my people: On the longest voyage, even the horizon must surrender to the stars." He smiled, then pulled his hand away and turned to look out over the horizon one last time. "Anyhow, let me show you where you'll be bedding down for the night. We should get some rest. Hopefully, we'll get an update from Natia tomorrow. If we do, we'll need to be ready to act on it fast."

"Ok. And Finn? Thank you."

"Anytime, my friend."

OMNI

«STATIC»«FLASH»

Omni stood in silence, her gaze fixed on Tony, who'd been brought from the genetics lab, and firmly strapped to the chair he was seated on. Omni focused on the straps tying him down, around his ankles, his upper thighs, his wrists, and his chest. Dark splotches of bruising crept up from underneath the gag securely fastened over his mouth and under his right eye. His right eyebrow was split where she'd hit him, but the bleeding had stopped. She smiled.

"Hello, Cameron Maddock," she said, her voice steady and commanding. "I am called Omni. I have recently learned that you and I are connected and that you have been using that connection to spy on me. I am impressed. I would do the same if I were able to, I assure you." She reached out and grabbed Tony by his chin. He struggled, trying in vain to pull his head from her grasp, but she was too strong. She forced him to look up at her. "As you can see, your companion is in our care. It was rather neglectful of you to allow him to fall into the trap you set for me. But no matter. He is in excellent hands. In fact, I will let him tell you so himself." She let go of his chin, then reached up and pulled the gag down from over his mouth. "You may speak."

Tony took a ragged breath. "Don't listen to this crazy bitch, Cam!" he shouted, his voice scratchy and raw. "I'll be fine, just don't give her anything! You have to–"

Omni pulled the gag back up and cut off whatever he was trying to say, reducing it to moans and mumbles. "He may be fine for now, Cameron. But whether he stays that way or not is entirely up to you. You see, we are willing to make a trade, and the terms of this trade are simple. You will turn yourself over to me, and we will release him from our custody. I will be waiting at ten pm tonight, by Earth Prime reckoning, at the Seattle Space Needle. If you do not appear, I will kill him. You may bring your Protectorate friends to our meeting, but I will kill him if they try to pull any tricks. So, you see, if his safety and well-being are important to you, then you have no choice but to comply." Tony started to struggle, his muffled yell clearly audible through his gag, so she hit him with a firm backhand across the face, leaving him dazed and moaning. "Do the right thing, Cameron. It is time to end this conflict between us. It is time for you to find out who you really are. It is time for you to come home."

«FLASH»«STATIC»

CAM

Cam's eyes shot open in panic. He'd just dreamed about Tony–and Omni. She'd spoken directly to him, knowing that Cam was watching and listening to her. Had that been real, like the last time? He ran the whole thing through his head, desperate to remember the details. She'd said to meet her, where? But it was already fading.

"Shit, what did she say?"

As soon as he asked the question, the dream started playing back for him in perfect detail. He focused on it, then understood it for what it really was. It hadn't been a dream at all, but a transmission picked up by his quantum entanglement communicator. Omni deliberately sent it to him.

He needed to let Finn know about it right away, so Cam jumped out of bed, slipped on his pants, and left the room to find him. Cam didn't know which room Finn was using, but he heard some voices down the hall and followed them through the main sitting room to a kitchen area that adjoined it. Tasha and Arana were both standing there, chatting while they sipped steaming tea from earthenware mugs.

"Good morning, Cam," said Arana when she saw him. "I hope you slept–"

"I just heard from the Agent," he interjected. "Her name is Omni, and she figured out that I'm connected to her somehow, so she used that to send me a message. She has Tony, and she said that I have to meet her tonight, or she'll kill him."

Arana stood there silently, and Cam immediately regretted his rudeness. But Tasha was all business. "You are sure this is real message?"

Cam nodded. "Yes. My system received it and recorded it."

Tasha grunted and set her mug down. "I will get Finn," she said as she left the kitchen. "Then you will playback message for us."

Arana pulled another mug from a nearby shelf, filled it with tea from a carafe, then handed it to Cam. "Here, drink this," she instructed him with a motherly tone. "It will help calm you so that you can better deal with what's happening."

Cam wasn't so sure about that, but he accepted it anyhow. "Thank you. Sorry for being a little over the top just now."

Arana smiled. "You have nothing to apologize for. I know what it's like to feel that way. I remember when Jerusalem was a young Protector. His early assignments on Earth Prime were an especially trying time for me."

As peaceful and collected as she seemed to him, Cam couldn't imagine Arana stressing out about anything. He took a few sips of the tea and started to feel a little less edgy, just like she'd promised. "You seem to be coping with it pretty well, now."

She laughed. "Seem is the key. As Guild Master, I don't always have the luxury of allowing my true feelings to show through. But then again, my true feelings don't always reflect the facts of a situation, either. It's important to remember that." She looked at Cam thoughtfully, then took a sip of her own tea. "While I may never truly be at peace with the idea of my child willingly putting themself into harm's way, I try to take comfort in the idea that Jerusalem is walking his path, as he should be. You see, we each have our own path to walk. For some of us, that path can lead to challenges and difficulty. In that case, all we can do is face those challenges and then take the next step forward. And then the next. Until we reach the end."

Cam looked down into his cup, watching as a few tea leaves floated around on top of the steaming liquid. "I've never really believed in fate."

Arana showed him a gentle smile. "Ah, but there is no fate. To say our actions and decisions are all predetermined by some unknowable outside force is just lazy philosophy. Having a path, or a destiny, if you will, only means that all of the parts that make up who you are–your mind, your body, your choices–may lead you in a particular direction. But it's up to you to choose that direction, or not. For my part, I'd find it difficult to feel fulfilled, to feel as if my life had a purpose if I did not follow my path."

He frowned. "I don't really feel like I have that much choice in things lately. It's mostly just been a lot of things pushing and pulling me."

She set her tea mug down and placed her hands on the countertop between them. "There will always be outside forces impacting your choices. None of us live in perfect isolation. But you still have a choice, Cam. Even now. You can choose to meet with this Omni or not. You can choose to go with her, or not. You can choose to ask for help or not. We may not always like our choices, but we will always have them."

Cam didn't know how to respond to that. She was right, of course. He could choose to not meet with Omni. That would most likely result in Tony's death. Or worse. Just because it was a shitty option didn't mean it wasn't an option. But Cam would never make that choice, not when his friend's life was at risk. Besides, despite everything he'd recently learned about himself, he was still left with more questions than answers. And the answer to his most important question still eluded him. Who was he?

Just then, Finn hustled into the kitchen, pulling a shirt down over his head. Tasha followed quickly behind him, not quite pushing him. Finn was holding a holo-projector disc in his hand and set it down on the island countertop.

"Ok," he said, "Tasha told me what's up. Let's see it."

"Alright," Cam replied. He reached out into the local network and found the projector. Then he sent the file over and instructed the projector to play the message. An image of Tony strapped to a chair appeared above the countertop where the projector sat, and the four of them watched in silence as the message played out. It was difficult for Cam to watch it, awake and consciously aware. His feelings were all raw and close to the surface. By the end, he didn't hesitate to turn it off.

"She was smart," Tasha suggested as the image of Tony flickered away. "Was nothing in message to give away information she did not want us to know."

"You think it was staged," Finn offered. It wasn't really a question.

"Of course. Was totally staged. Nothing in her view but Tony and chair. Nothing around her, no sounds. Nothing to give away location." Tasha looked at Cam. "Was other dream like this? From her perspective only?"

Cam nodded. "Yeah. The only things I could see of hers were when she looked down at herself, or her hands came into view. So, what do we do?"

"We don't have a lot of time to decide," said Finn, "but we do have some. Enough to consider our options, at least."

Cam scowled. "Options? I'm not leaving him in her–"

Finn stopped him with a hand on his shoulder. "Nobody's saying that, Cam. Of course, we'll try to get him back. But we need to check with Natia. If she's gotten anywhere with the Gate analysis, we could possibly find out where she went and maybe where she is right now. Then we could take the fight right to her. For instance." He looked at Cam with sincerity in his eyes. "But, ultimately, it's up to you, Cam, and what you want to do. None of us here are going to force you, one way or the other."

"It doesn't matter what I want," Cam replied firmly. "I can't let her hurt Tony any more than she already has. I need to get him back, and I could really use your help with doing that."

Tasha and Finn shared a look. "We will help, of course," Tasha said, "but you should not discount what you can do on your own."

Finn nodded. "She's right. You've got wetwired weapons and shields, not to mention the ability to rip a hole through space-time. There's no telling what Omni might try to pull when we meet with her, but you've got all the tools you'll need to be able to defend yourself. That way, we may just be able to get Tony back without losing you in the process."

"Yeah, I guess that's right," Cam confirmed, even if he

wasn't sure that was the choice he really wanted to make.
Yes, he wanted his friend returned safely, and Omni had
already proven herself to be a formidable opponent with no
scruples. But Cam had already come so close to learning
who he really was, and the promise that Omni dangled in
front of him–the opportunity to not only discover his true
identity but his real home–was tantalizingly within his reach.
Still, there was always the possibility that she'd lied to him.
It wouldn't have been the first time someone tried to lead
him astray for their own selfish ends. But Cam wasn't ready
to completely eliminate the possibility of going with her if it
meant getting the answers he wanted. He'd just have to play
things by ear.

After Finn, Tasha, and Cam took some time to eat, then
get cleaned up and dressed, Finn brought them back down
to the ground level to return to the Protectorate tower. They
walked through the same marketplace that Finn and Cam
had visited the day before. It was even more crowded and
livelier than it was the last time, forcing the three of them, at
times, to squeeze through the teeming throngs. Some of the
stalls were not yet open for the day, and the open ones were
mainly selling fresh produce and cooked food. It reminded
Cam of the Farmers Market he sometimes visited in the San
Francisco Ferry Terminal.

Cam noticed a pair of teenagers at one of the nearby
stalls–one shirtless and showing off a lithe, muscular form
under their deep, earth-tone skin, the other dressed in fawn-
colored leggings and a long, colorful top decorated with
an intricate geometric pattern. They talked and laughed as
they looked over what the vendor had on offer but didn't
choose anything. Then they grasped each other's hands as

they walked away. Of all the things he'd seen so far, Cam was most surprised by such a casual display of intimacy. They could've just been friends, of course, but, even then, to see two masc-presenting teens comfortably holding hands in public like that was such a foreign thing to him—and it made him more than a little jealous. He recalled Finn's story about his first kiss, as well as the moment he and Finn shared up on the rooftop balcony later that night. Looking over at Finn, who was chatting quietly with Tasha, Cam tried to make sense of his feelings. There was no doubt that Finn was attractive. And under different circumstances, Cam would've been open to something happening between them. But he couldn't just ignore everything going on, not even for a quick roll in the hay.

He sighed and put the thought out of his mind. He needed to stay focused on his primary goal—getting Tony back. There was no time for any distractions.

Cam had fallen a bit behind Finn and Tasha, so he pushed his way past a group of people who were looking over their market finds. As he did so, he felt an unexpected hand on his shoulder. Cam turned to see who'd grabbed him, only to catch a last-minute glimpse of a closed fist as it smashed into his eye. His face blossomed with pain, overshadowing his complete and utter surprise. How had someone managed to get past his defenses and sneak up on him like that? He felt his awareness speed up and expand as he fell backward and put a foot back to stabilize himself.

Cam's assailant was tall and muscular, with dark, walnut skin and straight, shoulder-length, black hair, wearing a coverall similar to the one he saw on Finn's sister Oslo. The attacker stood before Cam, staring at him, utterly stone-faced, before suddenly stabbing a wand-shaped device at him. Cam felt a surge of EM radiation as he twisted his body to the side, out of the way, then chopped a hand out and knocked the attacker's arm out of position. A nearby market-goer shrieked as the attacker drove the tip of the wand into their lower back, and Cam heard the sound of a muted lightning crack as the device discharged into their body before they collapsed to the ground.

It was a terrible place for a violent confrontation, surrounded by so many early morning market-goers. That could've been why they'd chosen that moment to act. Cam might hold back out of concern for the innocent people crowded around him. But there wasn't anything he could do about it. Crowded or not, the attack was happening.

Cam brought the edge of his hand down on his opponent's extended forearm, forcing them to drop the stunner. Then he drove his other fist upward and struck their chin with a loud smack, flipping their head sharply backward before they crumpled to the ground, unconscious.

The fight wrapped up so quickly that people around him had only just started to realize what was happening. One bystander knelt down next to the stunned market-goer to check on them. Others surrounding Cam started backing away in panic and confusion. Cam ignored them, searching the crowd for signs of Finn and Tasha. He tried to scan the area but only picked up the mental equivalent of white noise and static. That must've been how his attacker was able to surprise him. Somehow Cam's scans were being blocked.

He heard some other commotion break out a few meters ahead of him. Finn and Tasha were being attacked as well. That made it a coordinated action against the three of them.

But using a stunner probably meant that, like Omni, his attacker only intended to disable him.

Cam pushed his way through the unruly crowd to get to Finn and Tasha. But he didn't get very far before he felt a new hand grasp his arm. He tried to pull away when another hand grabbed his other arm. Cam struggled to break free, but both grips were like iron, and he was pulled sharply backward and thrown to the ground. He looked up to see his latest attackers—one was femme, with chestnut skin, long, flowing black hair, and full, painted lips, the other masc, with skin the color of reddish clay and a shaved head. They both stared down at him. Like his first attacker, they were equally expressionless and stone-faced.

The long-haired attacker turned toward the stunner lying on the ground and lunged for it. Cam huffed, realizing he should've grabbed it earlier, and rolled toward them. He kicked a leg out, sweeping it into their legs as they bent to retrieve the stunner. They tumbled backward into the surrounding crowd, and Cam continued his roll, twisting himself around to get up onto his knees. The other attacker stuck a hand into their jacket, so Cam reached out and snatched the stunner off the ground. He had no idea how it was supposed to work. Just holding it, Cam could feel the power surging through it, which probably meant it was recharged, so Cam thrust it forward and pressed the tip into his assailant's abdomen. Instead of shrieking, they only barked out a loud grunt as the stunner released its built-up power into their body. Then they collapsed onto the long-haired attacker, knocking them back onto the ground.

Stunner in hand, Cam quickly stood up, assessing the crowd around him. So far, three people had managed to attack him with no warning. Without the ability to detect any attacks in advance, Cam needed to be extra vigilant about potential trouble. Mindful of his desire to avoid hurting innocent people, he quickly but carefully pushed himself into the crowd, heading for a gap between two nearby vendor stalls. He still had no idea what was happening with Finn and Tasha, but he was anxious to get into some open space where he could more adequately protect himself.

He emerged from the crowd onto a pathway worn in the ground between the stalls and continued forward until he saw someone standing at the end of the narrow gap. They were tall, muscular, and dressed like Finn in practical, utilitarian clothing, down to the chunky, combat-style boots. Unlike Finn, they had chestnut skin and straight black hair pulled tight and tied behind their head. They stared right at Cam, but, unlike the people who'd attacked him, they were smiling. It wasn't a happy smile. They looked deranged.

While outwardly loose and casual, their stance was also perfectly balanced for any number of potential attacks. Cam wasn't about to wait for one of those, so he dropped the stunner and powered up the particle blasters built into his forearms. But before he could even lift an arm, his opponent launched themself forward, closing the gap between them in two, long strides. Cam barely had time to dodge their forward strike, and the attacker's fist narrowly missed hitting his jaw. Cam threw out a weak hit towards his foe's abdomen, but they easily blocked it, then followed up with a closed-fist clothesline strike that smashed into the side of Cam's already sore head.

Still seeing stars, Cam jumped back to the side of the pathway, then ducked under another forward strike so

344

powerful it cracked the wall behind him. Using that wall as leverage, Cam pushed himself shoulder-first into his attacker, shoving them all the way across the gap into the wall on the opposite side. There was an audible whoosh as he forced the air out of their lungs. But it didn't slow them at all. They brought both fists down hard onto Cam's shoulders, then shoved him to the side. Cam stumbled but didn't fall. He turned back toward his opponent but felt a sudden sharp, stinging pain near the top of his arm and saw a small blade in his foe's hand, red with blood.

Cam ignored the pain and didn't even look at his shoulder, readying himself for the attack he knew was coming next. Then, suddenly, a voice cut through everything.

"Kosumi!"

The attacker seemed momentarily confused and looked over their shoulder to see Finn standing just outside the market. Kosumi looked at Finn for a moment, then turned back to Cam, raised their knife, and rushed forward. Cam sidestepped them but, instead of continuing the attack, Kosumi simply kept going, running off into the wooded area behind the marketplace.

Finn rushed forward and shot right past Cam. "Stay here and wait for Tasha," he called back as he entered the woods in pursuit.

"Fuck that," Cam muttered and took off in pursuit as well. The trees were well spaced, and there was little ground cover, so he quickly caught up to Finn.

"I thought I said to stay behind," Finn said as he ran, a little breathless from the exertion.

"You sure did," Cam replied as he ran alongside. He could see Kosumi a few meters ahead of them. "But that asshole seriously tried to ruin my day." The two followed Kosumi as they veered left and right through the trees, varying their path to make the chase more difficult. Then Cam saw them stop, suddenly, and disappear into the ground. "Where the fuck did they just go?"

"There's a ground entrance to a subterranean tunnel system up ahead."

As they approached the area where Kosumi had disappeared, Cam saw a square gray slab with a large, circular sewer cover on it. It started to iris open as he neared it. He really hoped it wasn't actually a sewer.

"Just jump in," Finn shouted as he ran up to it. "It's barely a four-meter drop." Then he leaped down into it.

Cam grimaced as he got ready to jump, then leaped in after him. When Cam hit bottom, Finn had already started running. He was about to follow, but Finn shouted to go the other way.

"I don't know which way he went," Finn added, "so we need to split up!"

"Okay, got it," Cam shouted back, then turned and ran in the opposite direction. The lighting in the tunnel noticeably dimmed as Cam got farther from the tunnel opening. Then, as the open hatch irised closed, the light disappeared completely. His eyes adjusted immediately, somehow pulling in light from nowhere to make the tunnel appear almost as bright as when it was lit, although washed of all its color. Cam kept moving until he reached a T-junction, where he stopped, unsure of which way to take. He tried scanning again but got the same meaningless noise as he did in the market. His sensors were still being jammed somehow. But the jamming seemed stronger to his left than to his right. If

Kosumi was the source of the jamming, then that could mean he'd gone that way. Cam went with it since it was the only lead he had and took off to his left.

As the tunnel curved to the right, Cam spotted a light source up ahead. His vision readjusted with the growing ambient light, the color gradually returning as he got closer and closer. The light source turned out to be the entrance to a chamber that was lit from within. Cam stepped through the entranceway into a large, rectangular storage room around ten meters across on the short side and twice that distance on the long sides. There were stacks of different-sized boxes set into painted areas on the floor throughout, but it wasn't full.

The white noise sensation Cam got from his scans was getting much stronger. If Kosumi wasn't hiding in the storage room, then he was certainly close by. Being a gamer, even Cam could see that the room was full of places to take cover. It would be an ideal space for an ambush. Cam primed his particle blasters at their lowest power setting, hoping that meant it would only stun his target. Then he closed one hand into a fist and slowly walked further into the room.

He crept forward, arm poised to fire his blaster, and peered around the first set of storage boxes. Nope, not there. He shifted to his left, then checked behind the next stack. Nothing there, either. Had he actually been in a video game, Cam would've just started shooting at the boxes, eliminating any potential hiding places. But that would be reckless in real life. Although his system translated the symbols on the containers into their corresponding letters and numbers, the codes were still meaningless to him. Cam wouldn't know if what he was shooting at was flammable or explosive.

The next stack of containers was a no-go, too, which left Cam with around a dozen more to check before he reached the end of the room. Assuming Kosumi didn't double back at some point. Assuming he was even in there at all. Maybe it was time to change things up?

"Kosumi," he called out. "I don't know what the deal is, but if you're looking to get me alone again, I'm right here waiting for you."

Cam got no response and was about to move forward again when he thought he heard a faint wheezing sound. Of course. While he couldn't scan the area, Cam could still hear just fine. He listened for it again, slowly increasing the sensitivity of his hearing until his breathing was so loud that he couldn't hear anything else. He filtered that out and listened again. Sure enough, Cam picked up the sound of someone else breathing nearby. It had to be Kosumi. He was ahead of Cam's position, behind a pile of boxes to Cam's left.

Cam took a moment to plan his next move. He could just rush over there, but taking a stealthier approach seemed like a better option. Cam surveyed his surroundings again, observing that he could go around to the right side of the room and remain unseen, then double back along the other side and, hopefully, approach Kosumi from behind.

He crept around to the right side of the closest box stack as quietly as he could, keeping his head down as he went. Cam moved past the first set, then the next one, before turning and creeping across to the other side of the room. Cam stopped when he heard a sharp intake of breath, then the breathing sound stopped completely. Had Kosumi started holding his breath?

Suddenly there were footsteps behind him. Cam whirled

around, pointed his arm, and blind fired his blaster. Kosumi dodged Cam's shot, then lunged at Cam with the blade again. Cam pulled his shoulder down out of the blade's path, then twisted around and used his momentum to strike the back of Kosumi's head with his elbow. Kosumi cried out and stumbled but caught himself on the nearby stack of boxes. Then he snapped back with a mule kick, hitting Cam in his chest and knocking him back on his ass. Kosumi whirled around and lifted his knife for another strike, but Cam raised his fist and fired, hitting Kosumi square in the chest. Even at its lowest power setting, it knocked Kosumi back into the far wall before he fell to the floor, face down, and stopped moving.

Cam quickly got up and went to where Kosumi lay, his fist pointed at him the whole time, ready to fire. He could see the gentle rise and fall of Kosumi's breathing, so he knew he hadn't killed him. Cam nudged his body with a foot but got no response. He did it again, a little harder, but still got no response. Then he noticed a small, black, oval disc with a single, tiny, red light shining out from the center of it fixed to the back of Kosumi's belt. Cam carefully reached down and unclipped it, then pressed on the red light with his thumb. The light faded, and Cam suddenly had his sensors back. He quickly reached out to contact Finn.

<Cam? Are you alright? Where are you?>

<I'm fine, but I don't know where I am. Some kind of storeroom, maybe. I'll send you my location. Also, Kosumi is here with me. I stunned him, and he's down>

<Okay, I'm headed right for you. I'll alert the Protectorate while I'm on the way> Then there was a pause before Finn added, <Nice work>

Once Finn arrived, he first inspected Cam's handiwork with Kosumi, then checked to make sure Cam was ok. "Let me see your shoulder."

"It's fine," Cam said. His internal system reported that his medical nanites were in the process of repairing the minor knife wound he'd gotten from Kosumi earlier. But he reached up and pulled the sleeve of his shirt up past where he'd been cut. The cut was still red and angry looking, but the skin had already closed up, and he felt no pain.

Finn seemed satisfied after he inspected the wound. "Looks like you don't even need a bandage. Not that I'm surprised." Then he turned to look at the unconscious body of Kosumi again and sighed.

"Who is he?" Cam asked.

"He's a Protector, like me," Finn replied, frustration evident in his voice. "Only, he shouldn't be here."

Cam waited for the story to continue, but Finn didn't seem to feel very forthcoming. "Except that he is here."

Finn grunted. "Yeah. There was an accident on a survey. Kosumi was severely injured. The last I heard, he'd been sent to a special Protectorate facility on Andras for care and recovery."

"Which is where he still is," added Natia as she walked up to meet them, with Tasha and a Protectorate support team in tow, "at least according to the facility records." Then she looked down toward Kosumi on the floor, as the support team, with Tasha's guidance, started to deal with his body. "However, I can see that is clearly not the case." Then she turned to Finn. "I am very much looking forward to hearing your report, Protector."

Finn smiled, then held a hand out toward Cam. "He's the

one you need to debrief, actually."

Natia raised an eyebrow, then turned to Cam. "Ok, then let's hear it. Tell me what happened."

Cam started to recount everything, beginning with Omni's message, and was surprised to discover that he could remember it all perfectly. But Natia was thorough and stopped him several times to clarify specific details. When she was finished questioning him, she stood there, arms folded tightly across her chest in a way that made her already pronounced shoulders seem even broader, with an almost severe expression on her face. Finn came over to stand next to Cam and saw the look, too.

"You don't seem thrilled, boss," Finn said lightly. Even he appeared to tread a little more carefully around her.

"Oh, you think so?" she snapped. Then she sighed and lowered her arms. "I'm sorry, that was uncalled for. But yes, I'm not happy. We've already retrieved five combatants from the marketplace, plus three bystanders with minor injuries. And then there's him," she added, pointing at Kosumi, who was being strapped onto some kind of floating stretcher. Seeing it, Cam had to stop himself from asking how it worked. "And the only connection we have between all of them is you, Cam, which raises so many uncomfortable questions. How did they know who you are? How did they know you're here? Who are they working for?"

"Honestly, I can't begin to understand what part Kosumi is playing in all this," Finn mentioned, "but the others could be working with Sable."

"But why?" asked Cam. "I mean, we've supposedly got that meetup with Omni tonight, right? Why would they send another snatch squad?"

"Precisely," agreed Natia. "Does this mean they have factions? Or are we unknowingly looking at more than one group of operatives?" She paused, shaking her head. Then she reached into a jacket pocket and pulled out a slim data crystal, handing it to Finn. "Speaking of your meeting, this is the analysis of the data from your Gate readings. The destination is inconclusive, I'm afraid."

"Shit," Finn muttered, taking the crystal from her. "That leaves us with one less option, I guess, even if it was a longshot."

"Indeed," Natia agreed. "I don't suppose there's a possibility that you'll consider Protectorate support for that?"

Finn shook his head. "No. The message clearly indicated that Tasha and I could come along, but that was it. Besides, it's in Seattle, so it's neutral turf anyway. It's not like she can have an army waiting for us there."

Natia pursed her elegant lips. "Before this incident, I might've agreed with you. Still, to be honest, I'll be glad to have you out of my hair for the evening while I get this mess cleaned up." She looked up as Tasha joined them. "And you two should be plenty of support, I suppose. It's not like Cam hasn't already demonstrated his proficiency for this sort of thing, taking out one of my Protectors single-handedly. Speaking of which–" She turned toward Tasha. "What's the word on Kosumi?"

"Attempts to connect to his implant were unsuccessful," Tasha replied in her usual blunt manner, "so he is being taken to AI support team at Protectorate Science."

Natia nodded. "Alright." Then she looked at Cam. "I don't suppose I need to tell you to be careful since you know better than any of us how dangerous this woman can be. But, if at all possible, I'd appreciate it if you didn't add yourself to her already impressive kill count tonight."

That was new information. "How impressive?"

"Two-hundred twenty-three," Natia admitted. "That we know of."

Cam gulped, but Finn put a friendly arm around his shoulder. "We'll be fine. He'll be fine. You'll see."

"Excellent," Natia said. "Then I'll look forward to getting your report tomorrow. In the meantime, I'm going to find out what got into the head of one of my Protectors." Then she turned with a flourish and walked away.

After she left, Finn took his arm off Cam and moved to stand in front of him. "Don't let her scare you. I know she can seem a little intense."

Cam nodded. "On my planet, she'd probably be a CEO."

Finn laughed. "On her planet, she'd be one of the ruling elite. She's part of one of the most powerful families on Andras. But she chose to go into service instead."

"Really?"

"Not to mention she can kick serious ass when she wants to," Tasha added admiringly.

Cam laughed, then made a mental check on the time. "Shouldn't we get going? How long will it take us to get back up to Seattle."

"We'll get going soon enough," Finn said, "and we're still ok on time. But first, we need to go see Lhasa. They left me a message while all this was going down. They've got some important news for you."

CAM

Finn led them back through the tunnel network to an underground parking area filled with small, four-wheeled vehicles. They reminded Cam of golf carts, except there were no steering wheels. Some of them had two banks of bench seating. Some only had one, with a cargo-carrying area in place of the other bench. After boarding one with a pair of bench seats, Finn explained that the carts and tunnels were used to transport equipment and people between the various Engineering Guild facilities without having to go outside. The vehicles were self-driving. Riders only needed to select their destination. Since Lhasa was planning on meeting with them at the primary Guild tower, using a cart was the quickest way to get back there. Plus, they were able to avoid another stroll through the marketplace, which Cam was more than okay with. Given his recent experiences with markets, he wasn't sure he ever wanted to go shopping again.

They continued on in silence for the rest of the ride. Cam was okay with that, too, since it gave him some time to think. He had a lot to think about, considering that, on four of the previous five days, someone had violently attacked him—usually more than one someone, at that. And one of those attacks had come dangerously close to killing him.

Had it really only been that long? It felt like he'd left his old life behind a lot more than five days ago. In many ways, it felt like he'd left it behind entirely. Cam had done and discovered so many things he never would've dreamed of before that he had trouble imagining things just going back to the way they were.

Then there was Tony. Cam felt a growing sense of guilt about what he'd done. Because of Cam, Tony was in the hands of someone with more than two hundred kills to her name, with only her word that no additional harm would come to him. It kept getting harder for Cam to hold on to the hope that things would be ok. On top of that was the fact that he really missed his friend. Although Tony had gladly and willingly helped him through a lot of what he'd been going through–which Cam appreciated immensely–he absolutely regretted getting him involved. Plus, it had been days since anyone had talked to Tony's family, and they were likely getting sick with worry about him. Cam couldn't even think of what he'd say if he was able to contact them. At least the guilt was helpful since it motivated him to save Tony and bring him back from wherever Omni was keeping him.

"You are doing thing again," he heard Tasha say. He looked up to see her turned around and staring at him. "Where face shows what you are thinking." She smiled, which made Cam smile.

"Sorry, I guess I've just got a lot on my mind."

She reached back and put a hand on his knee. "Even though I am not warm and fuzzy, for you, I make one exception. Everything will be ok, Cam. Have faith, and things will work out fine." It sounded so strained when she said it that Cam couldn't help but chuckle. Finn just plain laughed out loud, which made Tasha scowl. "Fine, but never say I did not try." Then she pulled her hand back and turned to face the front of the vehicle.

"We're here, anyhow," Finn announced, as the cart turned out from the tunnel into another parking area, pulling into an open spot between two parked carts. "The main tower is just up that ramp," Finn added, pointing to a nearby incline. They climbed out of the cart, and Finn led them up to the vast open space in the tower's atrium. It was crowded and frenetic with activity, but nothing was triggering Cam's defensive alert, so he allowed himself to relax. Then he spotted Oslo walking toward them, much like she had when he and Finn first arrived at the tower the previous day.

"Jerusalem," Oslo called out, getting Finn's attention. "I need to talk with you."

Finn raised an arm in greeting as his sister approached. " There's no time for that, Oslo. We're meeting Lhasa, and then we're off on more Protectorate business."

"This is important, dear brother," said Oslo, her tone almost pleading. "Please."

Finn sighed. "Fine. Tash, Lhasa should be here any moment now. Can you let them know what's up?"

"Of course," Tasha answered, nodding.

Finn smiled, then let his sister lead him off to a less crowded space nearby where they could speak privately. Cam watched as the two siblings talked. Whatever Oslo was saying was making Finn agitated. Cam knew he could just listen in if he really wanted to, but he figured he probably shouldn't, out of respect for their privacy. Thankfully, Lhasa walked up just then, sparing him from having to make a choice.

"What's going on with them?" Lhasa asked, nodding their

head toward their siblings.

"Don't know," Tasha replied. "Oslo wanted to talk."

"What were you thinking, Oslo?" Finn suddenly shouted, with Oslo frantically trying to calm him down.

Lhasa grimaced. "That doesn't sound good."

Finn stopped shouting, but the way he repeatedly and angrily pointed at Oslo as he spoke only made Cam more inclined to agree with Lhasa. Cam hadn't seen Finn really lose his cool yet, even in a wide variety of stressful situations, so it was a new experience. Then Finn pointed toward the nearby lifts. Oslo started to object, but Finn held his stance and kept pointing. Oslo finally nodded, looking chastened, then started walking away. Finn turned to see the group was all watching him. He scowled, then shook his head and made a shooing motion with hands before walking off in the direction his sister went.

Lhasa grimaced again, then turned to Cam. "I don't know what that was about, but I do know that you have to leave soon, and I have something I need to share with you first." Cam started to reply, but Lhasa shook their head. "No, not here. There is somewhere else that will be more appropriate." They looked Cam in the eye. "I know you're probably anxious to depart, but trust me. This will be worth it."

Cam and Tasha shared a glance, conspiring silently the way he'd seen her do with Finn. She nodded once, and he turned back to Lhasa. "Alright." Cam glanced over at Finn. "What about him?"

"He will catch up," Tasha assured him. "Let's go."

Lhasa nodded, then beckoned for them to follow as they turned and made their way toward the main building exit. Once outside, Lhasa directed them to a smaller version of the flyer parked nearby, about a foot off the ground. Curious, Cam reached out and looked it up on the local Net, finding that the vehicle, called a floater, used an anti-gravity system similar to the flyers, only less powerful since it was meant for ground use. He could sense the underlying knowledge of anti-gravity science hovering just outside of his awareness. But Cam left it alone, not wanting the delicious distraction that kind of engineering would bring him.

A gesture from Lhasa caused a slice of one side to pop out and slide open, allowing the three of them to climb inside and take a seat on the wrap-around couch that lined the interior. As with the larger flyers, the top half of the floater seemed transparent from the inside, giving them an uninterrupted view of the surrounding greenery and park-lined boulevards on the warm, sunny afternoon. Lhasa tapped a few commands on a black touchpad set into the seat next to them, then the door closed, and the vehicle started moving. On the way to their unknown destination, Cam and Tasha let Lhasa know what happened on the way to the Protectorate tower. Lhasa seemed shocked to hear about it, mentioning that they'd met Kosumi several times, and they thought he'd been a charming individual.

Cam enjoyed getting a new perspective on the city. They passed by a cluster of buildings that his system labeled as part of the Arts Guild. Outside one of the buildings, he saw a group of young people being led in a group dance, with the performers adorned in bright, colorful costumes. He wondered briefly if the dance had originated with the original occupants of the area or the islanders who later joined them. Of course, it could've been neither, or both, considering that several millennia had passed since they first came to Turana. After a few more turns along their programmed route, the vehicle glided up to a small, dome-shaped building. An arched doorway slid open, and they slowly pulled into a dark garage space. When the outer entrance closed, the ceiling overheads came to life, filling the room with bright, warm light.

Lhasa opened the vehicle hatch with a gesture and climbed out. Cam and Tasha followed, then waited behind Lhasa while they placed their palm onto a black wallpad. This caused the floor to start descending, taking them and the vehicle underground.

"Is this some kind of secret lair?" Cam mused aloud.

Lhasa laughed. "It's no secret, but access is highly restricted. This is my workshop, and some of the things I do here could be quite dangerous without proper safety protocols."

It wasn't clear how far they'd descended, but the floor eventually stopped moving. Then the wall in front of the group slid open, revealing a large, tall, circular chamber that even to Cam's alien eyes was clearly a high-tech laboratory. Tables, workstations, and a few medbay pods were set up around the room's perimeter. The room's center was occupied by a large, raised dais, at least ten meters in diameter. Cam walked in behind Lhasa and Tasha, then the wall slid closed behind him.

Cam immediately noticed a feeling of being cut off, as if his awareness had suddenly been shrunk from the world at large down to just the chamber he was in. "This room is shielded? I can't sense anything outside of it."

Lhasa nodded, then stopped at one of the workstations and put on a set of wrap-around goggles similar to those they'd worn in their office. They made a few gestures in the air in front of them, then turned to Cam. "I've opened the local network to you. Please access it."

He mentally reached out and found the network, then connected to it. His awareness was still confined to the room, but he could definitely sense the immense computing power available there. Lhasa must have some fancy toys. "Ok, done."

They took a breath, gathering their thoughts, then nodded again. "Well, I've spent some time reviewing your scan data, Cam. There is so much about it that needs further study. I can hardly imagine how much time it would take to digest everything. So, instead, I've focused on the area that interests me the most: your quantum field engine. Or, to put it in a layperson's terms, your ability to open and close Gates."

Cam smiled when he heard that. "Ok, you were right. This was definitely worth the detour."

Lhasa smiled and nodded. "Thank you." They turned toward the central dais and made a sweeping gesture. A holo-projector activated, displaying a giant, three-dimensional wireframe schematic, along with several columns of descriptions and annotated data. "This is your quantum field engine implant," they said. "I've obviously increased the scale. In reality, it's approximately ninety micrometers in diameter, or around the width of a human hair, for comparison. That in itself is a nearly miraculous piece of engineering that will take some time to properly analyze. So far, I've only been experimenting with possible functionality."

"Possible functionality? As in, I could do more with it than just open and close gates?

Lhasa nodded. "Yes, and I believe this will help you do just that. You see, I found the control programming in the static copy of your code that I kept."

"Wait," said Cam, suddenly stiff. "You copied my code?"

They made a soft frown. "Yes, but only a static copy of your operating code. Quantum programming works differently than standard binary code, of course, but having a copy of it is similar. And looking at your operating code is no different than reading a copy of a book you've written. I'm not actually reading you, just information."

He relaxed, realizing that they were right. It wasn't a copy of him. And he'd already encountered many differences between the quantum code in his internal systems and the binary code he'd written himself. Plus, any understanding Cam had of the quantum code running inside his implants came from the code itself, which was sort of a paradox. He knew full well that he'd otherwise be unable to write similar code from scratch, not without years of further study. Since he was definitely out of his depth, he reminded himself to trust Lhasa and nodded to continue.

"With that in hand, I was able to compose some additional operating protocols, based on my knowledge of our own quantum field engine technology. Although the physical differences between our equipment and your implant are, frankly, astounding, the nature of how they operate is still much the same." They made a gesture, and the schematic and data disappeared from the holo display, replaced by a three-dimensional graphic of a wormhole. "This is how a Gate normally works. There is an opening on either end, allowing energy, or matter expressed as energy, to transit between points in two different locations within the multiverse. These occur naturally throughout the known multiverse, but the quantum field engine allows you to create them for yourself by using some highly esoteric energy field manipulation to bridge two different points in multidimensional space-time, temporarily connecting them together."

A series of dashed arrows appeared in front of them, traveling from one side of the wormhole to another. Cam smiled. Suddenly he was back in school watching one of his teacher's slideshows again. Lhasa gestured again, causing the wormhole to wrap around into a U-shape, and the traveling arrows assumed the shape of the new path. "I am suggesting that your quantum engine is actually capable of much more than that. For instance, I believe it is capable of creating a Gate between two physical locations within the same universe." They gestured again, and one side of the wormhole increased in size while the other shrank. "I also believe that you could vary the size of the Gate apertures, the openings, allowing you to transit large physical objects or even just the energy required for information transfer." They looked back at Cam and gestured in his direction. "I'm sending you the control protocols for that now."

Cam, a little astounded, was still struggling to catch up. "So what you're saying is that I could essentially teleport? Like," he pointed across the room, "from here to there?"

Lhasa smiled and nodded. "Teleport? That's an English word, right?" They looked up and to the side, reading something in their own display. "Yes, I suppose that's an apt comparison."

"That could be very useful," offered Tasha.

Lhasa looked startled as if they'd forgotten Tasha was even there. "Yes, there are many potential uses. Once we're able to replicate this technology, it will revolutionize so many things. But the most astounding thing I discovered as a result of this research was how you're able to power the quantum engine—as well as your shields and your particle accelerators and any other internal system. Since the energy needs for a quantum field engine are far too great for your body's own energy production, it appears that you could use the quantum engine to power itself."

"Wait. What?" Cam asked, confused.

"What I mean is that the quantum field engine is capable of constantly maintaining a micro-width Gate to draw in all of the energy it needs. A small percentage of that energy maintains the Gate, while the rest is either stored or used as needed."

As clinical as that all sounded to him, Cam couldn't help but feel a little frightened. "You mean I could have a Gate inside me that's open all the time? Where would it lead to?"

Lhasa gestured toward the holo display, and it changed to a long string of letters and numbers that Cam assumed were coordinates. "According to your control code, it would lead here."

"Ok, but where is that?"

They smiled. "It's a dying star."

"What? Are you serious?"

They flashed a quick smirk. "I'd say that it's not as big of a deal as it sounds like, but it really is. Of course, the power Gate itself would be stable and should remain so for as long as you can siphon energy from the star. And, for your purposes, an energy source of that magnitude is essentially unlimited."

"So, shields will never fail?" asked Tasha. "Blasters will never run out of power?"

"Apparently not," Lhasa confirmed. "I located the relevant

systems in Cam's scans. They are quite elegant, sluicing the power flow according to immediate needs. The only limitations are those of the systems themselves."

Cam looked down at his hands, imagining them as weapons of unlimited power. "Yikes."

"So, now that I've blown your mind," said Lhasa, hesitantly, "would you like to try it?"

"In here?" Cam asked.

"Yes. This room has some robust shielding. If you somehow manage to explode or implode, the shielding should contain the brunt of the damage."

Their delivery was so dry, he wasn't sure if they were trying to be funny or not. He went with not. "Ok. What do I do?"

"Well, first, you need to locate the control code I sent you. It seems that your interface is primarily intent-based if I've read your code correctly. Meaning, you interact with your system on an almost unconscious level, yes?"

Cam shrugged. "If you mean that I think about stuff and it happens, then yes."

"Amazing," Lhasa replied. "Alright, think about the control code I sent you and about integrating it into your system. Then think about opening your power Gate. That should be enough to initiate that system, which should then do the rest."

Cam tried to do what she asked, thinking about the control code she'd sent him. He found it, just on the edge of his perception. After he mentally reached for it, it unpacked into his mind, giving him a sudden understanding of the power Gate and how to use it. He focused on that and mentally instructed it to activate. Then there was a slight buzzing in his head, which could've been imagined. Or, it could've actually been the micro-width Gate siphoning energy from a dying star to power a nanoscopic quantum field engine in his head that was capable of tearing through the very fabric of space-time. Just thinking about that was almost enough to give him a headache. "I think it worked," he said warily.

Lhasa nodded excitedly and pointed to a series of graphs in motion on their holo display. "It did. The readings I'm getting are astonishing, but otherwise, everything seems to be stable enough."

That wasn't exactly reassuring. "Ok, so now what?"

"Now, you should try to open a Gate from where you are to somewhere else across the room."

They made it sound so simple and, when he thought about it, it really wasn't that much different than opening a Gate to a different dimension. Cam reached into his system for the Gate process. He could already tell that it wasn't the same as before when it was more of an on/off function. Mentally selected the option to open a Gate, Cam focused on having one open right in front of him, extending to a point he chose across the room. Underneath those surface thoughts, his internal system processed impossibly complex calculations, adding to the buzz he felt after opening the power Gate. He assumed that meant things were proceeding how they were supposed to be, so he initiated the process.

A blue spark appeared in the air in front of him, then quickly expanded into an oval that was slightly larger than his height and width. A second spark simultaneously appeared on the opposite side of the dais and grew to the same proportions. Cam gulped, then stepped through, and found himself stepping out on the other side of the room. He looked around briefly, then turned to make sure that Lhasa and

Tasha were still back where they'd been. It worked! He stepped back through the Gate, ending up where he started from. Reaching for the Gate system again, he deactivated the process, and the Gates winked out of existence.

Lhasa clapped lightly, their face lit up by a ridiculous smile. Tasha stood with her arms folded across her chest, her face impassive. Then she smiled, too. "Of all impossible things I have seen," she said, "that was most impressive."

Suddenly, the door to the garage-sized lift started to slide open, and Finn stepped into the room. He looked around, seeing the three of them standing there with childlike grins on their faces. "Ok," he said curiously. "What did I miss?"

FINN

Finn thought he'd taken the news reasonably well. It had been a trying day for all of them, but once he'd heard what his sister had to say, things really went downhill.

"I'm sorry to interrupt you, Jerusalem, but I've got something I need to get off my chest," Oslo had said. It sounded suspiciously like his sister was about to admit to making a mistake. That was a rare enough occurrence, so he'd simply nodded for Oslo to continue. "Look, before I start, I should give you some context first." Finn nodded again, so Oslo shared a story of a Guild member who'd recently come to the Kaseka Guild from a community far to the north. Like Oslo, he had some disdain for the way things worked within their communities and a desire to see them changed. Like Oslo, he'd often felt shortchanged by the Guilds' structures and even society at large, as if he was meant for better things than what he'd been given.

Finn tried to object, but his sister held up a hand to stop him, admitting that they were attitudes she still hoped to change. But, hearing her new Guild mate express those same things had, at the time, helped her justify her own feelings. It never occurred to her, Oslo admitted, that she was being told those things for a specific reason. Finn suddenly understood where his sister's story was headed. He worked to keep his face impassive, remembering the hair-thin trigger his sister's own temper could have. After their family discussion the night before, Oslo went to one of the local community gathering spaces to unwind and found that her Guild mate was there, too. Once they'd had several drinks together, Oslo, still deep into her resentment, let slip what their family talked about, including details about Cam. It made her feel better to talk about it with someone who had a sympathetic ear, she allowed.

"Let me guess," Finn said, interrupting. "This Guild mate didn't show up for his shift this morning. And when you tried to contact him, you found out that he didn't actually exist."

Oslo seemed surprised, then irritated, that her brother guessed her story's outcome so easily. But she recovered herself quickly, to her credit, and confirmed that it was true.

If Finn hadn't already gone through such a trying ordeal that morning, he might've had the patience to keep himself from losing his temper. "What were you thinking, Oslo?" he shouted. "Do you have any idea what's been happening today?" Then he stopped himself and took a deep, calming breath. "I mean, you must, if you're telling me this now. And you must have some idea that you may be responsible. But you very nearly cost me, Tasha, and Cam our lives, not to mention the hundreds of innocent bystanders that all got caught in the crossfire."

"That's easy for you to say, Jerusalem. How was I supposed to know this person was some sort of plant trying to get confidential information from me?"

"It doesn't matter because that information wasn't yours to

share in the first place," Finn growled. "But you can be sure that this story will get shared." He pointed toward the nearby lifts. "First, with our mother, and then with the Protectorate."

"The Protectorate?" Oslo asked, suddenly sounding fearful. "You can't be serious."

But Finn was serious, and he made it clear that his sister could do so voluntarily or under duress. That would be her only choice in that matter. Realizing what that meant, Oslo reluctantly agreed.

Once Jerusalem and a browbeaten Oslo shared everything with their mother, she was nearly unrepentant in her fury. But soon, the disappointment set in, and by the end of their conversation, she looked as if she'd aged five years. It hurt Finn just to watch it happen. But Arana was also a most esteemed Guild Master, and she knew what her duty was. So she agreed to take Oslo to the Protectorate over Oslo's weakened objections, promising her that she'd be treated fairly but that things would be challenging for her at the Guild if she did not follow through.

After replaying the conversations in his head, it was still something Finn had trouble coming to terms with. Compared with that, Cam's newfound abilities to play fast and loose with quantum physics didn't really phase him at all. So to speak. He was also secretly glad that his mother took on the responsibility of dealing with Oslo's unintentional treachery. He knew that meant the Protectorate would probably go easy on his sister since, in the end, her mistake had been primarily one of ignorance and was forgivable. Finn just wasn't ready to do that yet and was glad to get back to dealing with something a little more straightforward, like Cam and the impending, multidimensional, hostage exchange.

The upside of Lhasa's lesson in theoretical quantum physics was that they no longer had to take a flyer to get up to Seattle. With the new control software Lhasa had created, Cam would be able to Gate them there, directly, if need be. It was a mind-blowing prospect, but Finn didn't have time for his mind to be blown. It was merely what they needed at the moment, and it opened up some fascinating new options.

Finn proposed that they take a little of their newfound spare time and practice some of Cam's new abilities. So Lhasa took them through to an additional section of their workshop, another underground, circular room, but one that was free of all the obstructions in the primary chamber. The foursome used the open space well, constructing battle strategies where Cam could quickly Gate himself from one part of the fake battlefield to another and remove himself from harm's way or flank an attacker. Cam came up with a few ideas of his own, including one where Finn would start running in a random direction, and then Cam would Gate him to another position, dropping him into place at full speed, pulse blasters at the ready.

The one hiccup that even Lhasa couldn't help them overcome was that they couldn't travel through the Gates shielded. No matter how many times they'd tried, tuning both the Gates and shields differently each time, active shields were always somehow always disabled by Gate transit. This was a common factor of Gate travel, so it wasn't much of a surprise. But Finn was never able to incorporate Gate use into actual combat before, so he was keen to see if it was possible.

Still, after just a few hours, Cam was operating like a well-oiled machine, using his blasters, shields, and Gates as if he'd been doing it his whole life. Earlier, Finn had sensed some reticence on Cam's part about their upcoming confrontation with Omni. He'd eventually begun to see only confidence and assuredness.

"He is ready," Tasha said quietly to Finn as they watched Cam's battle simulations.

"You're right," Finn agreed. "I gotta admit, I'm a little surprised to see how quickly he's developed. But then, he was pretty much built for this."

Tasha nodded. "You are not concerned? You have fought this Omni. If they come from same source, he could end up like her."

"Ah, the old nature versus nurture argument, comrade? My vote is on nurture. He grew up in a totally different environment. Hell, the whole reason we're doing this is that he's willing to sacrifice himself for his friend. Based on that alone, they're nothing alike."

"You make good point," she admitted, then added quietly, "but that leaves other question: Do we let him sacrifice himself?"

Finn frowned. "You mean if things go to shit, do we make sure that he comes back with us, with or without his friend?"

She nodded, her face grim. "Cam is basically superweapon, yes? Do we want him to fall into hands of Sable?

Finn wasn't sure how to answer that. He knew Tasha was right. Even watching Cam take on imaginary targets, Finn started to get the sense that he may not actually win if he ever had to go up against Cam. But would forcing Cam to sacrifice his own friend for the greater good even keep him on their side? He shook his head. "No, we don't. But I can't support the idea of forcing him to choose us over his friend. Even if it means losing him to Omni."

Tasha smiled and nodded. "Good. Was just checking." Then she sighed. "I think that will not be popular decision with some, though."

"Yeah, well, it's not like it would be the first time we made some waves at the office, right? I think if things came down to it, though, Natia would back us up to the Council."

She shrugged. "Maybe so. I do not know yet what will get us on her bad side, although there is no hurry to find out."

"Truer words have never been spoken, comrade. So, should we make a plan?"

She laughed. "We probably should. Would be nice change of pace instead of just storming in guns blazing."

Cam noticed the two of them talking and stopped his drill. "Are you talking about me behind my back again?"

Finn beckoned him to come over. "Yes. We think you're ready. It's time to make a plan."

Cam smiled and walked over to them, then the three of them returned to Lhasa's primary work area. Lhasa was still there, face buried in their goggles, standing at a workstation. They didn't even notice the three come back.

"First," Finn said, "let's get Otto onto the local network."

"I am here," Otto confirmed.

"Good. Now, we're going to the Space Needle, right? Otto, could you give us a layout grid on the holo?"

The central holo-projector came to life, and a three-dimensional Space Needle, along with the surrounding areas, was neatly rendered across the whole dais at approximately waist height. Finn stepped up onto the platform, wading through the projected graphics until he was standing next to the Space Needle, which was almost as tall as he was. "Cam, you used to live here. How well do you remember the area?"

Cam shrugged. "I went there as a kid a few times, but that's about it."

Finn frowned. "Ok. Then let's just start breaking all of this down."

Tasha and Cam joined Finn, and the three started labeling and defining everything from areas that were the most defensible to the best possible escape routes. There were several large buildings near the Space Needle, including a movie theater, a museum, and a large structure called the Armory that had been converted to serve as a food court and performance space. The group didn't know exactly where the exchange would occur, so they labeled the likely spots for that to happen and put together a few scenarios for each one. They all tried to combine the strategies as best they could to keep the number of options to a minimum.

The basic plan relied on the fact that, since Tony didn't know about all of Cam's abilities, Omni wouldn't either. Or, at least, Omni wouldn't be aware that Cam knew about all of his abilities and, more importantly, that he knew how to use them. Given that, there'd have to be a point where Tony and Cam were near enough to one another for Cam to throw up a shield around them both and then Gate them away. That would leave Finn and Tasha behind on mop-up duty, but they were anxious to have another go at Omni after the fiasco on the waterfront. The biggest unknown was whether or not Omni would come with support. She hadn't done so the first time she confronted Cam on the motorcycle. But she'd brought local support, in the form of the late Tomás Aguilar and his soldiers, when she faced them at the Market. So that remained to be seen. Since she'd explicitly allowed Cam to bring his Protectorate friends along, the group assumed she'd bring some of her own backup as well. In that case, they identified a fallback point that Finn and Tasha should try to get to if things turned nasty. Once Cam had left Tony in a safe location, he'd Gate back to the fallback point and offer support if needed, or escape, if possible.

Lhasa eventually joined them and volunteered to be Tony's caretaker once he'd been recovered, which everyone agreed was a great idea. Then Lhasa pointed out that, with Cam's ability to create what they called micro-Gates, he could actually use one to maintain comms with Finn and Tasha after he'd Gated away from the Prime universe.

"For real?" Cam asked, incredulous.

"Of course," they said. "It would be nothing compared to a Gate large enough to transit a person or an object. The power requirements drop off exponentially, although that's hardly a concern."

"Again," Tasha said dryly, "would have been helpful to know earlier."

"As soon as I discover the secrets to time travel, Tasha, you will be the first to know."

"Wait," Cam said urgently. "I hate to sound like a broken record, but is that actually possible?"

"Well, Cam, although the possibility of a time-dilated Gate is highly theoretical–"

"Nope," Finn interrupted. "I love you, dear sibling, but now is not the time."

Lhasa smiled. "Oh. Of course."

"Well, we have our plan," Finn announced. "Let's go collect your gear, Tash, and then we can be off."

"If we just Gate to Seattle safe house," she countered, "I could arm myself there."

Finn looked thoughtful for a moment. "Actually, that's as good a place as any. They'll probably be monitoring the local Gate, but the warehouse is strictly off the books. Aside from detecting your Gate emissions, we should be in the clear."

"I could drop the quantum shielding on the second dome," Lhasa offered. "Then, you could use it as a return point, too."

"That's perfect." Finn looked at Cam expectantly. "Are you ready for this?"

Cam nodded, clearly enthusiastic. It was nice to see him in such good spirits, especially before what could turn out to be a dangerous expedition. Finn hoped that what was to come wouldn't spoil things for him too badly. "Ready as I'll ever be."

Finn took a moment to hug his sibling and say goodbye. He left the Oslo incident unspoken since they'd undoubtedly hear about it from their mother. Then he smiled at Lhasa sweetly and kissed them on the cheek.

Tasha and Cam were already headed back to the second dome, so Finn hurried to catch up with them. Once they were near the center of the space, Finn watched Cam close his eyes as he interacted with his internal system. Then, a blue spark appeared in front of the group, smoothly expanding into the clean, bright, blue-violet oval of a Gate. Finn stepped through first, appearing in the darkened Seattle warehouse, lit only by Gate's indigo glow. Cam came through next, followed by Tasha, then the Gate winked out.

Finn adjusted his eyes to see in the low light, then found the light switch panel and turned on the interior lighting. The space looked exactly like they'd left it.

<Otto, check the security logs and make sure that no one else has been here>

<*Already done. The safe house is still secure*>

<Excellent. Time check?>

<*Two hours until the meetup*>

That left them plenty of time to pack up and get there. And maybe eat first. "Anybody hungry?"

Cam flashed him a smile. "I could definitely eat something."

Tasha shrugged and volunteered to go get take out from the Golden Flower again. It wasn't Finn's favorite Chinese place, but it was good enough, and Tasha seemed to like it a lot. Finn suspected that she was using the errand as an excuse to remind herself what it was like to be a regular Prime for a little while. She'd never said anything to him indicating that she regretted her choice to become a Protector. Well, never anything serious, at least. But, as he'd gotten to know her better, he began to recognize her occasional bouts of homesickness. It was to be expected. Even Finn felt them from time to time. But he was also able to go home again once in a while. She always refused to. The few times he'd offered to take her back to Saint Petersburg for a visit, Tasha claimed that she was no longer welcome there. But he thought he knew what she really meant. She no longer fit in there. That was a feeling he was more than familiar with. Every time he went back to Kaseka, he could see that things were pretty much the same as he'd left them. But he'd already moved on long ago.

While Tasha was away picking up the food, Finn took the opportunity to inventory their gear when he noticed Cam sort of hovering quietly nearby.

"Something on your mind, Cam?"

He squirmed a little bit before answering. "I'm sorry to bring it up, but I was wondering about what happened with your sister earlier."

Finn just managed to hold off the wince that threatened to appear on his face. That wound was still fresh. But Cam had a right to know. So without getting into too much detail, Finn explained how Oslo had been partly responsible for what happened that morning. Cam took the news about as well as could be expected.

"You're saying that your sister almost got me killed?" he exclaimed. "I knew she didn't really like me, but, damn."

Finn sighed. "You don't have any siblings, right?"

"No. It was just my parents and me. And I haven't even spoken to them in years."

Finn knew he was lucky to not only be close with his family but to have grown up somewhere healthy relationships were encouraged, and that family meant more than just the people he shared a genetic bond with. To him, Tasha was family, too. Working on Earth Prime had taught him that things could've been very different and that he could've been saddled with the expectation to maintain a false respect for the people who'd birthed him just because they were his family. The Turani people knew better than that. Being a good member of the community didn't mean being forced into unhealthy relationships with blood relatives. If you didn't get along with your family, plenty of others would be happy to have you join them. "Oslo and I have never really been that close. And she's always carried around a lot of bitterness. She's convinced that she's always been given the short end of the stick, so to speak. That she was pushed to join the Engineering Guild when it couldn't be farther from the truth.

And when she peaked early and realized she never had what it would take to be a Guild Master, I think it kind of broke her a little."

Cam seemed to mull that over for a minute. "I hate to say this, but I guess I'm kind of glad to hear that. I was worried that my presence caused a rift between you two."

Finn chuckled and shook his head, then put down the blaster he'd been assembling and leaned back on the nearby counter. "No. Your presence might've been enough to finally spur her into rebellion, but that was a long time coming, I think. If you hadn't come along, there would've been something else. So don't sweat it."

Cam smiled weakly. "I guess my only experiences with healthy family dynamics before now have been with Tony's family. It probably sounds dumb, considering everything, but adjusting to being a genetically engineered, interdimensional super-soldier has been way easier than figuring out how families are supposed to work."

"That's not dumb at all," Finn said assuredly. "Learning to relate to people is a lifelong process, and family relationships are just one aspect of that. You're single, right?" Cam nodded. "Has there ever been anyone special?"

"No," Cam replied, shaking his head. "I mean, I've dated here and there, but I haven't met anyone that I've really clicked with, you know? What about you?"

"There've been a few people that I thought maybe would be the one, but I haven't been in a committed relationship for a long time. That last one, well, let's say it ended badly."

Cam looked concerned. "I'm sorry to hear that. What happened?"

Finn frowned as he recalled the details. Even after all that time, there were still some painful feelings of loss when he thought about it. "He was a Protector, too. We were both working undercover duty on Prime, but we connected between assignments whenever we could. He was following up on a lead he'd gotten about a rogue Turani working with a South American drug cartel and ended up getting killed when the Turani tipped off the cartel that he was on their tail. They planted a bomb on his vehicle."

Cam frowned. "Wow, that sounds shitty. I'm sorry." He inhaled to speak again, then hesitated before finally speaking. "I guess I assumed that at some point, you and Tasha–you know?"

Finn laughed, thinking about that one time they'd both been curious enough to try it. "No, things aren't like that for Tasha and me. I mean, I swing in pretty much every direction, and she's definitely attractive. But we're too much like siblings, I think, for anything like that to happen." Whether or not Cam understood that wasn't clear, at least from his expression. Then he looked like he had something else to say but got cut off by Tasha's return with bags of takeout boxes. Finn stood up from the counter. "We can continue this later, I think," he said lightly. "Food's here."

The group converged on the table near the kitchenette and were soon dug into the different boxes Tasha picked up. Finn drilled them on the various defensive and escape options at their mission target as they ate, just to keep things fresh. Once they'd all finished eating, it was finally time for the main event.

"How are we gonna get there?" Cam wondered aloud. "I suppose I could open a Gate."

"That's probably not a good idea," Finn commented. "If

they detect the Gate, then they'll know something's up. We can drive, although the Vagabond could be on their watch list by now. Thankfully, we've got another vehicle."

Tasha smiled. "And this one, I drive."

Of course, the vehicle in question was an almost brand new Ganz-Auto-Werks Aurora, the sporty, German, top-of-the-line, four-door sedan that was a nearly ubiquitous presence in the garages of the city's tech elite. It was fast, reliable, and, because they were everywhere, practically invisible, which made it perfect for their purposes. It was sitting under a tarp in a dark corner of the warehouse. When Tasha pulled the tarp off with a flourish, Cam smiled. "Ok, this will do."

Finn and Cam helped Tasha prep and load up the gear. The three of them first snapped on body armor plates that fit neatly over their clothing. They were made of a lightweight composite material that Finn assured Cam would stop most bullets and blades. It typically would've felt like overkill to Finn, but after their absolute thrashing at the hands of Omni their last time out, and the unfortunate gunshot that wounded Cam, he wasn't about to take any chances. Since Tasha didn't have the benefit of a wetwired shield, she wore a shield generator. She also carried several particle beam weapons, including two small, pistol-sized blasters, as well as an extended range, rifle-sized version that was collapsed and concealed in a shoulder-slung bag. Finn armed himself with a blaster similar to what he'd used at Pike Place, tucked into a holster under his arm. He swapped his vest out for a dark, tactical-style jacket to hide the weapon.

Once they'd dressed and loaded the extra gear into the car's trunk, Tasha got in and drove it over to the large, sliding door at the other end. Finn slid the door open long enough for

Cam to walk out and Tasha to drive through it, then slid it closed again after she pulled out. He had Otto activate the security system while Cam got into the car's back seat, then he jumped into the front passenger seat, and they took off.

Nighttime gave the city a whole dazzling makeover. The soaring downtown towers glowed brightly from their interior lighting and fancy accents. Although Finn was used to the local architecture, the square, boxy buildings always had an alien appearance. Having attended the Academy in Kunoha, which occupied the same general area on Turana as Seattle, it also gave him a subtle thrill to be inside the Prime version of the city.

Tasha drove like a maniac, of course. She'd picked up her driving skills back in Russia, where the road rules were mainly gentle suggestions to be honored only when it was convenient. Her driving settled down some over the years, especially after Finn impressed upon her the need to blend in with the locals, but Tasha still pushed things to the edge of local standards.

It was a short trip through the downtown tunnel to the giant park where the Space Needle stood. They circled the area once, identifying the crucial landmarks, then Tasha found them a parking spot near their primary evade and escape point. Once they were parked, Tasha grabbed the weapons bag from the trunk, and they headed onto the park grounds.

<Comms check> Finn sent the group.

<*Receiving*> Tasha replied, followed by Cam.

<Ok. Everyone stay sharp and keep a lookout for our target> Finn let his focus drift for a moment, zeroing in on that nebulous sensation he always felt around an active

Gate. There was nothing. <I'm not sensing any Gate activity, so they either haven't arrived yet, or they're coming in on the ground like we are>

Finn looked over to Cam, who caught his glance and nodded. A few pedestrians wandered through the park grounds, but not many, considering the time of night. The weather was just on the uncomfortable side of chilly, and there was some humidity in the air from rain showers that must've happened earlier in the day.

<We've picked up a tail> Otto told him. <A single individual, thirty meters behind us>

<Are you sure?>

<Yes. I haven't done any active scanning in case they'd be alerted. But they're sending AI-level encrypted transmissions at regular intervals.>

<Can you give me a look?>

<Patching into the local security cams now>

A virtual display unfolded in front of him, showing a high-angle view of an individual, presumably male, following along the same path as them. They were pale-skinned, with a buzz cut, wearing a bulky, utilitarian-looking jacket that was probably too warm for the weather and was meant to hide weapons. Local merc, undoubtedly. Or, at least, attempting to look like one.

"We have a watcher tailing us," Finn announced. "Could be local help."

"At least that answers that question," Cam replied.

"I will split off," Tasha suggested. "Draw out any other watchers, then double back and meet you at Point Alpha."

"Understood," Finn confirmed.

Tasha immediately veered to her left, toward the Armory

building. There was no need to keep up the pretense of being out for a stroll. Their watchers would already know why they were there.

Finn and Cam kept walking toward the Space Needle. Other than their tail, who was still behind them, no one else had made themselves known yet. Finn was starting to feel a little antsy. They were approaching the meetup time and still didn't know exactly where they were meeting Omni. He didn't like it. He looked up and saw the towering structure rising into the sky behind the nearby buildings. When Finn looked back down, someone was standing in their path, facing them. It was another pale-skinned individual with a buzz cut who was dressed like the other watcher. For all Finn knew, the two of them could've been siblings. The mercenary stood with their arms casually at their side, but they made eye contact as soon as they knew they had his attention.

"Ok, I guess they have uniforms," he said quietly.

"Yeah," Cam answered. "Just like Aguilar's little gang did back in San Francisco, too."

They approached the waiting merc but stopped a comfortable distance in front of them. The soldier nodded in acknowledgment. "Cameron Maddock. Jerusalem Finn," they said, with a gravelly sounding, lightly accented voice. "Omni is waiting for you at the top of the tower. I will accompany you there. It should take no more than ten minutes for us to get there. She will wait for twenty, then depart."

Finn sighed. Of course, they hadn't planned for any action on top of the Space Needle itself.

"That's not what we agreed on," said Cam, an edge of

hostility in his voice. "Why can't she come down here?"

"I can't answer that," the merc replied. "I was only instructed to say what I already have. The rest is up to you. Now, we should depart, or it may take too much time to get there."

"Fine, then let's go," Finn agreed, forestalling any further arguments from Cam.

The merc held a hand out to their side. "After you," they said, without a trace of humor. "I insist."

Finn grunted, then turned to Cam and tilted his head toward the tower. "Come on. Let's get this done."

Cam nodded, the pair resumed walking once more.

<Tash, change of venue> Finn sent on the group comms. <We're meeting on top of the Space Needle. The observation deck, I assume>

<Lovely. I hear is nice view. I am following tail as they search for me. They are local help, clearly>

<We've got an escort now, too. Deal with your merc, then pick up our tail. Our exit is now a choke point, so identify any soldiers on guard and take out as many as you can, discreetly>

<Understood>

Finn glanced over at Cam, who gave him the faintest of nods, then looked up at the tower as they approached it. "You know," Cam said, casually, "I don't think I've actually ever been up there."

Finn smiled. "Me neither. It'll be a treat for both of us."

Cam chuckled, but there was no reaction from the merc. As they neared the base entrance, Finn spotted a sign stating that the observation deck would be closing at ten pm. He glanced back at the merc questioningly. "It's handled," the merc replied.

<They must've infiltrated the building staff> Cam sent. *<How long has this been in the works? She's only had Tony for a day>*

<Unless they set it up for another reason, and they're just taking advantage of it now> But Finn didn't like it either. He didn't like any of it.

<Merc one, neutralized> Tasha sent. There was no reaction from their escort, so it must've been a clean takedown *<Am now behind you. You have second tail besides escort. Will deal with them next>*

<Understood>

"Hold it," said their escort, suddenly. Finn stiffened immediately, then forced his body to relax. He turned around, and the merc opened their jacket and reached inside, pulling out a pair of laminated tags hanging on lanyards. Finn caught a glimpse of a slug shooter in an under-the-shoulder holster.

<Did you catch that, Otto?>

<Just ran the serial number. It's a Chinese copy of a Haas Dominator>

<Did they get a bulk purchase discount on those? That can't be a coincidence>

<I concur>

Their escort held out the laminated tags. "Put these on."

Finn and Cam each grabbed one and slipped them over their heads. The tags were printed with the Space Needle logo, along with the words Special Guest. That was how they handled the after-hours entry, it seemed.

The merc looked at them and nodded. "I'll need you to hand over your weapons."

Finn rolled his eyes, then pulled the blaster out from under his jacket and handed it over. Then the merc looked at Cam questioningly.

Cam held out his arms. "I'm not carrying anything."

The merc reached out and patted him down, then nodded, apparently satisfied.

When they got close to the elevator, an unarmed, full-figured guard in a branded security service uniform held out a hand to stop them. The red polish on their nails shone brightly against their ebony skin tone. "I'm sorry, hun. The observation deck is closed."

Finn held out his hanging badge, and the guard nodded. "Oh, of course, sir, my apologies. Go right up. Your party is waiting." They unclipped one end of a guard rope strung in front of the elevator then stood to the side. The elevator doors slid open, so Finn and Cam each stepped inside, followed by their escort, who nodded at the security guard. Finn couldn't tell from their exchange of glances, but he had to assume the guard was also a plant. When the elevator doors slid closed, their escort pressed the button marked Observation Deck, and the glass-walled box started to rise.

<When you see me make my move, stand back> Finn sent to Cam.

<Got it>

Reading Finn's intentions, Otto threw a graphic into his vision marking the weak points of the merc's stance. Once the guard started to shift to their right, Finn lunged forward without warning, scooping his right hand under the merc's right arm and pulling it out to the side. At the same time, he cupped his left hand and shot it forward to the base of the merc's skull, not stopping until their escort's face crunched against the glass elevator doors. Finn pulled his hand back, then shoved again, hearing another crack and feeling the merc's body go limp. He guided the body to the floor of the elevator as it fell, then reached into the merc's jacket and grabbed the Haas, as well as his own blaster.

"Talk about fast," Cam commented breathlessly. "I barely had time to react. Nice work."

Finn grinned at him while he shoved the Haas into the back of his waistband, then replaced his own blaster in its holster. "Help me move him to the back if you don't mind."

Cam reached down and grabbed one arm, while Finn grabbed the other, and the two moved the unconscious mercenary to the floor behind him. Finn was glad he was able to knock him out without killing him. The stink in a space that small would've been overwhelming.

Finn stood up straight, then reflexively fixed the jacket he was wearing over his body armor. Once the elevator reached the top, he was entirely composed. He glanced at Cam, who nodded at him, and the elevator doors opened to reveal the interior of the glass-walled observation deck. There was no one waiting for them, so Omni had presumably assumed her merc would be able to direct them to her location. Her mistake. They stepped out into the unoccupied space.

<Tasha, status?>

There was a brief pause before she replied. *<Merc two is neutralized. Approaching tower base>*

Then Finn had a sudden thought. He turned and stuck a hand in the path of the closing elevator doors, stopping them. Then he leaned in and flipped the Emergency Stop switch.

<Our escort is down in the elevator at the top. The second elevator has an unarmed guard, but I don't know if they're a plant or a bystander>

<Understood. Will take care of it. See you soon>

Finn nodded to himself, then turned to Cam. "Ok, let's go find her."

CAM

The view from the top of the Space Needle was almost as impressive as watching Finn in action had been. He'd hardly telegraphed his movements at all. Cam only caught it because he'd been looking for it.

Cam walked up to the large windows that canted out from the floor and looked out over the city. The moon had risen, large and bright, giving the clouds in the sky a faint, ghostly glow. Only one moon, though. After seeing two of them in the sky over Turana, it was almost a letdown.

He reached for his sensors, looking for any signs of life, such as body heat or movement. A wireframe graphic sketched out in front of him with a green icon indicating his position and a blue icon that must've been Finn's. There were five red icons on the opposite side of the deck. Two of them were outside, and the remaining three were each stationed near a doorway.

"Ok," Finn said, gesturing toward where all the people were standing. "I guess we go that way." He must've used his own sensors.

Cam nodded. "Looks like it."

<I'll follow your lead, Cam, unless things start to go south. Keep your focus on Tony. I'll handle the rest>

<Will do>

Cam could feel his heart start to pound as his glands dumped adrenal chemicals into his bloodstream. He took several long, deep breaths as he walked, oxygenating his blood.

A pair of tall, pale, muscular soldiers stood on either side of the doorway they were headed for, their stances wide, their arms held loosely at their sides. They wore dark body armor similar to what Cam had seen Omni wearing and had impressive blasters holstered at the waists. Their belts had blue-lit studs spaced evenly around their circumference. According to his system analysis, they were shield emitters. The weapons were ion pulse guns–essentially high-tech tasers on steroids or low-tech versions of his particle accelerator. His own shields would probably withstand any hits he took from them.

As Cam got closer, he realized that their skin wasn't just pale. It was gray and slightly mottled in a way that almost seemed like camouflage. It could've been the lighting that made it look that way, but Cam didn't think so. The guard on the right nodded at their approach, then reached out and pulled the door open. Cam stepped through without hesitating, walking out into the chilly night air. The panoramic view of the city was even better outside.

Omni stood off to his right, barely ten meters away. She held Tony firmly with one arm wrapped around his chest, echoing her pose from down on the waterfront. Her other hand was covering his mouth. Tony started to squirm right away, but Omni's grip remained unshakable.

"You are right on time, Cameron," Omni said, her voice projecting loudly despite the howling winds whipping around the outdoor platform. "Did my escort not make the trip up with you?"

"You mean your hired gun? Yeah, they did, but we left them back at the elevator."

She smiled. "You could have killed them for all that I care. This world has so many more just like them waiting for an opportunity like this. You, on the other hand, are unique."

He scoffed. "Is that why you're so interested in me?"

"I will be happy to explain everything to you, Cameron–who you are, where you are from, why you even exist. I have all the answers you seek. You just need to come back with me."

He shrugged. "I'm here, aren't I? Let me talk to Tony."

"Very well."

She pulled her hand off his mouth, and he immediately started shouting. "Get out of here, Cam! This bitch is totally fucked. Don't you dare fucking go with her. I don't care what she does to me. Just fucking save yourself!"

"Trust me, Tony," Cam shouted back. "Everything's gonna be fine."

Tony took another breath but saw the look in Cam's eyes and exhaled instead of shouting. It was clear he didn't like what was happening. But at least he seemed to understand that Cam had something up his sleeve.

Cam took a breath of his own, willing himself to be ready. "Ok, let's do this, Omni."

"As you wish, Cameron. Come to me, and then I will send this one to your Protector."

"No way," he said firmly, to her apparent surprise. "I don't know that you'll even let him go. No, we do it at the same time." Cam gestured back toward Finn. "You send Tony to Finn while I walk over to you." Omni hesitated for a few moments. It wasn't the group's only plan, but it was by far the least risky of them. He needed her to play ball. "What's the problem, Omni? Everyone will get what they want. You've got the advantage here anyway."

She fixed him with her piercing gaze for a moment, then relaxed. "Fine. I agree to your terms. Once I see you start walking, I will let this one go."

Cam made eye contact with Tony and nodded. Then he took a step forward. When he did so, Omni released Tony, who almost fell to the ground, before catching himself on a nearby railing. Cam hadn't realized that she wasn't just holding him back but also holding him up. What had she done to him? After Tony recovered himself, he stumbled forward, caught himself again, then slowly started walking toward Cam. "I hope you know what you're doing, Cam," he said.

Cam smiled as he walked closer. "I do. It's just like the trip we took last fall, remember?"

Tony looked confused for a moment. "What are you talking about?"

It could've been the trauma. Tony would usually pick up on cheesy wordplay hints like that quickly enough. But he was almost in place. Only a few more steps. "Just keep walking."

Then Tony really seemed to trip on something and stumbled forward. Cam reached out to grab him, but before they even made contact, he activated his shield, encasing the pair of them in an almost complete sphere of charged energy.

"No!" Omni shouted. "What are you doing?"

Cam ignored her. He knew that Finn would also activate his shield and probably eliminate the nearest guard before they activated theirs. But Cam let that all play out without him. His only concern right then was his friend. He'd already lost Tony once. He wouldn't let it happen again. "Are you ok?"

"I'll survive," Tony replied, his voice a little hoarse. He held Cam tightly, unable to stand up on his own.

Cam nodded. "Ok. Hang on tight." Not wasting any more time, Cam opened a Gate right below where they were standing. The pair immediately fell through it, landing roughly on the floor in the middle of Lhasa's workshop dome just before the Gate disappeared with a flash.

Tony looked shocked. "Holy shit! What the hell did you just do?"

Before Cam could answer, Lhasa came rushing into the room. "Cam! Is that Tony? Are you both ok?"

Tony scrambled back in fear. "Who is that? What's she saying?"

"This is Finn's sibling, Lhasa," Cam answered, trying to sound reassuring. "They're here to help."

"Oh, I forgot to speak in English," Lhasa quickly added. "I'm sorry. You must be Tony."

Tony looked at Lhasa, then back at Cam, and gulped. "I don't know what's happening, but–"

"There's no time to explain," Cam interrupted. "Lhasa will fill you in. I have to get back." He reached for his system, instructing it to open another Gate back to the Space Needle, close to the elevator entrance. "They need my help."

Tony didn't seem to understand. "They need your help?"

Cam looked at Lhasa, who nodded. "Go. I'll take care of him."

So Cam stepped through the Gate and re-emerged inside the Observation Deck of the Space Needle. He activated his shield as the Gate closed behind him, then raised his fists, setting his particle blasters to their maximum power. There was an icy breeze, no doubt from a broken window or two, and the shriek of blasters and their impacts reverberated throughout the space. He brought his perception and reaction speeds up to combat readiness with a thought and headed for the closest skirmish.

<I'm back> he sent on the group comm channel. <What did I miss?>

<One soldier down. Am pinned down in exchange with other two> Tasha replied. <My shield is down. Finn is exchanging pleasantries with Omni outside>

He glanced around and found Tasha right away. <I see you, Tasha>

She'd taken cover behind the remnants of a display counter, leaning out and firing at a soldier who had his back to him, then ducking back into cover when another soldier fired at her from behind. Cam calmly raised both fists and started bashing the nearest soldier's shield with his particle blasters. That soldier had the same armor, handheld blaster, and waist-mounted shield array as the previous ones. But Cam had unlimited power in his blasters, and his opponent's shield unit couldn't last forever. The soldier turned and started returning fire, pelting Cam's shield with blast after blast. Cam's shield sparked and flashed but held firm, although he still had to brace himself to balance out the force of the kinetic bleed-through. Once she'd spotted Cam, Tasha started trading fire with the other soldier using her rifle-sized blaster, leaving Cam to deal with his opponent on his own.

Cam soon found himself in a battle of attrition, waiting out the soldier's shields. He was in little danger, but he worried about Tasha, who was not so lucky. Thinking back to his practice that afternoon, Cam reached for his internal system and opened a small Gate right behind his opponent. With all the light and noise from the blaster fire, they didn't even seem to notice. Cam kept firing, pushing the soldier back a little farther with each blast until their shield made contact with the Gate and flared out. His opponent reacted with shock and stopped firing. But Cam didn't, peppering them with particle blasts until they toppled to the floor.

Cam looked over toward Tasha in time to see her opponent destroy the display counter she was hiding behind, leaving her unprotected. She dove and rolled to her right, avoiding the soldier's next blast, but had nowhere else to go.

There was no time to draw the soldier's fire, so Cam reached for his system again and opened a Gate inside the soldier's shield sphere, which flashed out in a burst of sparks. Then Tasha immediately aimed a high blast directly at the soldier's head, vaporizing it in a bloody mist. His body slumped to the floor, blood pooling from the steaming top of his exposed neck.

Tasha looked back to Cam and pointed around to her right. "Get to Finn!"

Cam nodded and followed the direction she was pointing with his gaze. He witnessed a series of flashes and then heard a shattering explosion as another of the interior windows blasted apart. He ran toward the commotion and found Omni locked in shielded combat with Finn. Cam saw her shift her fire from Finn's shield to the glass barricade on the outside of the mezzanine, battering it with blast after blast until the energy was too great for the glass to maintain its structure. It spiderwebbed, then blasted apart. Finn stumbled, then took a few steps back. It was clear that she didn't intend to wait until his shield failed. She wanted to force him off the mezzanine instead.

Cam used a broken window as an opening to fire at Omni from behind. At that short distance, the noise of the battle was enough to nearly deafen him, so he used his system to filter it out. His particle blasts struck her shield hard enough to cause her to stumble and stop firing. Omni turned to see who was attacking and spotted him. Her expression, already angered, went murderous. She mouthed a single word. "You."

He grinned, then kept on firing. Finn redoubled his efforts as well, and the two of them pinned her in place, advancing on her slowly.

<I'm glad you're back> Finn sent on their comms. *<My shields have taken a beating. I don't know how much longer they're gonna last>*

<Ok, then we need to end this>

Copying Omni's move, Cam aimed his right arm at the safety glass next to her, quickly shattering several sections after just a few hits each. Then he pointed both arms back at her and kept firing, slowly advancing to close the gap between them. Omni braced herself with her stance, aiming one hand at each of them as she fired, but Cam could see that he was still pushing her back.

Suddenly Finn's shield started to flare, and Cam knew Finn was out of time. Acting purely on instinct, he opened a Gate and quickly stepped through it to place himself directly between Omni and Finn. She howled in rage and pointed both fists at him, firing blast after blast. Their impressive exchange lit up the skies around them in a neon fantasy as they expended untold amounts of energy into the air around the Space Needle. It was only a matter of time before the authorities showed up—if they weren't already on their way—which would only result in more death. So Cam used his Gate maneuver again, opening a small Gate right behind Omni. Once her shield came into contact with it, it sputtered out of existence. Before she could react, he bombarded her with a series of blasts. Her armor absorbed most of the energy, but the force of the impacts sent her flying backward right through the opening in the safety glass he'd already made.

Omni shrieked as she fell over the edge of the platform. Wasting no time, Cam rushed to the opening and peered over the side to find her hanging from the halo truss that surrounded the edge of the mezzanine. She was in a precarious position, and he clearly had the upper hand.

Doubt, fear, and anger all mingled uneasily in his mind, his emotions finally overwhelming whatever enforced calm his system tried to maintain. While Omni didn't seem to want him dead, he had no doubts that she would've killed Finn if she had the chance. And after all the shit she'd put him through, and especially what she'd done to Tony, part of him wanted to just let her fall. She deserved it. But she also claimed to have answers to his burning questions. And, when it came down to it, it seemed like she was his best—and maybe only—path to finding out who he really was. So he pushed back on his rage, deactivated his shield, knelt down, and reached out a hand out to her.

"Give me your hand," he called out, shouting to be heard over the sound of the high winds. "I'll pull you up!"

Omni glared at him fiercely, then pursed her lips in resignation and tried to get a hand free to grab his. But her weight and the force of her movement were enough to pull the weakened truss loose, and Omni plummeted down to the ground below with a piercing, angry screech. Cam let out a ragged sigh as Finn and Tasha ran up behind him and looked over the edge.

"Wow," Finn said, clapping him on the back. "That was impressive."

"Was brutal death," Tasha added. "I approve."

Cam swallowed hard, hoping to bury the confusing swirl of adrenaline and horror he was feeling. "I wish it didn't have to come to that, though."

Finn nodded. "Yeah, well, she didn't exactly leave us with much choice, did she?" He looked over the edge and then back over his shoulder. "Say, could you do us another favor and use your Gate to get rid of the bodies in there?"

Cam nodded to Finn with a grunt. He reached for his system scanners to locate the nearby bodies, then sent each of them through a Gate into the corona of a dying star in a series of bright, blue flashes. "That should make it harder to figure out what happened up here. What about Omni?"

"We should get down there and recover her body," Finn answered. "It would help answer a lot of questions about who she really is and where she came from."

"Plus, I would like to kick it," Tasha added. "Multiple times."

Cam laughed nervously. That he could relate to. He was still full of anger. The thoughts of what she'd done to Tony and what she was trying to do to Finn kept playing back in his mind. But he was also sad. Despite being undeniably evil, Omni claimed to possess all the answers he'd been seeking. Maybe her body would at least provide some of those. He reached for his system again, opened another Gate that would take them to the base of the tower, and then stepped through. Finn and Tasha followed, and the Gate disappeared with a flash. He looked around, spotting the wreckage from where the truss had hit the ground but didn't see a body. "Shit." He hurried over but stopped when he saw the blood splatter from where she must've hit the ground. "I don't believe it," he spat. "She's fucking gone."

FINN

The three held an informal debrief session on the car ride back to the safe house. Actually, Finn and Tasha had a debrief session while Cam sat in the back and silently brooded. But Finn was inclined to cut Cam some slack, given his performance in the mission–leading ultimately to its overall success–and the fact that he'd essentially murdered someone for the first time. It was probably playing fast and loose with his senses of morality and self-preservation. Still, even with Finn and Tasha riding high on their win, it was a tense and, thankfully, short ride back to the safe house.

The mission was a success in almost every planned respect. Finn's team had suffered zero casualties, rescued Cam's friend Tony, and managed to eliminate a thoroughly annoying thorn in their side with Omni's death. Except that her death was only implied. Since they hadn't managed to recover her body, they didn't have any conclusive evidence to actually back up that assertion. But they were able to make some quick scans of the area and collect samples of her blood before the local authorities arrived on the scene. The amount she'd left on the pavement only further supported the supposition of her death. They'd left several unconscious mercenaries behind, but that didn't really concern him. Finn doubted that Omni's team was given accurate information about what they'd been hired for, and they provided a practical focus and diversion for the local authorities.

Once they arrived back at the safe house, Cam started to perk up again. When Finn asked whether he wanted to take a few minutes to clean up or head right back to Turana, he didn't even hesitate to open a Gate to Turana right after his enthusiastic yes and step through it.

Tasha shrugged, hoisting her gear bag over one shoulder, and followed suit. Finn wondered if he had time to grab anything before going back but decided not to risk having to take the long way home and followed right after her. It would take Finn a good while to get tired of having access to the convenience of instant Gate travel.

Finn emerged in Lhasa's empty workshop just as Tasha was leaving for the primary chamber. Based on what he could hear, that's where the party was happening, anyway. The Gate flickered away after he'd taken a few steps, leaving him with just a Gate sense afterimage, like the mental equivalent of looking into a bright light for too long. Cam's Gates were starting to feel more and more familiar to Finn and more like naturally occurring Gates, as well. But there were still differences. In fact, as Finn spent a moment mulling the feeling over in his mind, he noticed that it was refined in a way that even ordinary Gates weren't. It wasn't a sensation that he couldn't really put into words, but he could still tell the difference between them.

Inside Lhasa's main workshop area, he found his sibling gathered with Cam and Tasha around the medbay pods where Tony was lying.

"You need to remain still while I'm running the scan Tony,"

Lhasa admonished.

"I'm telling you, Lhasa, I'm fine," Tony implored. "I'm just a little banged up, is all."

"Just do what they're asking, Tony," said Cam with a smirk. "Otherwise, they might sick their mother on you, and you don't want that. Trust me."

Tony rolled his eyes, but Finn figured he was just playing out the protest to save face. "Alright, alright. No need to play the mom card. I'll behave."

Finn walked over to the others while Lhasa fussed about in the air in front of their goggles, directing Tony's scan. "It's good to have you back, Tony. Congrats on surviving the night with Omni. That can't have been any fun."

Tony nodded, then stopped when he heard a sharp breath from Lhasa. "Worst slumber party ever," he muttered as he tried to hold himself still.

"Ok," said Lhasa as they flipped up their goggles. "You're all done. You can sit up." Then they turned to Cam. "Now it's your turn."

Cam looked surprised. "Mine? What for?"

"You vigorously stressed the systems that you've only just started using," they explained patiently, "and that none of us entirely understand yet. I want to make sure that there's been no damage."

Tony sat up and hopped off the medbay couch, only showing minor stiffness in his movements. "You heard the Doc, amigo. If I gotta do it, so do you."

Cam smiled graciously. "You're absolutely right." He hopped onto the couch and lay back. "Happy?"

"Ecstatic," Tony replied with a smirk. While Lhasa started Cam's scan, Tony looked around the room in wonder. He took a few steps away from the medbay pod, still showing some stiffness and maybe a slight limp.

Finn had Otto pull the readings from his scan. Lhasa hadn't found any severe injuries, although they'd notated areas where he suffered multiple contusions from blunt force trauma, and his right hip was marked with a possible strain. Lhasa also screened him for foreign bodies and did a full genetic workup. They didn't have any records of his genome to compare against, but he registered as an unenhanced human, and he hadn't been injected with any toxins or tracers that they could find.

"If you think this place is impressive," Finn said as he approached Tony, "wait until we take you outside."

"I'm really on another planet again?" Tony gestured around the room. "I mean, this is clearly a sci-fi science lab, and all, but–"

"Yeah, you're on my planet now. I think you'll be pleasantly surprised."

Then Tony's stomach growled. He put a hand over it, looking embarrassed. "As long as there's food."

Finn laughed. "Oh, there's definitely food."

"Ok, Cam," announced Lhasa from behind them, "you're all done, too. Everything looks good, which, honestly, I'm not sure if I'm surprised about or not."

"Hey, Finn," Tony said quietly. "You're sis–I mean sibling. Are they single? Cuz they're totally fine!"

Finn chuckled warmly. "They're single, alright. Think you're up for someone like them? They're pretty much a genius, you know?"

Tony tried to look offended, then laughed. "Hell, I could tell that right away. I may not be the sharpest knife in the drawer, but I'm still smart enough to recognize when someone else is." He gestured toward Cam. "How do you think I manage to keep up with him?"

Finn laughed in response. "Point taken."

He saw Tony's eyes go wide, then heard Lhasa walking up behind him. "You got pretty beat up," they said to Tony. "You're fortunate that there doesn't seem to be anything serious enough to worry about. But even though there wasn't much physical damage, there could still be serious psychological or emotional impacts. If you need someone to talk to about what happened, my door is always open, as they say."

If Tony hadn't just confessed his attraction to Lhasa, the puppy dog eyes he gave them would've definitely given it away. "Thanks, Lhasa. I really appreciate that. Maybe after I get something to eat, we can go somewhere and talk?"

Finn carefully kept his reactions to himself, but Lhasa seemed to take his request in stride. "Are you sure? Of course, we could do that."

Tony practically jumped for joy, which would've been sad to watch, given how much it would've hurt him. "Sweet! Lemme go check on my boy, and then can we grab some food? I hate to keep harping on it, but they didn't really feed me, so I haven't eaten in a while." He smiled, then ducked away to go talk to Cam.

"Are you sure you want to be alone with him?" Finn asked. "I think he likes you."

Lhasa scoffed. "I can take care of myself well enough, thank you. Besides, he's cute. And I've always wondered what a Prime would be like in bed."

Finn laughed. "Lhasa–"

They held up their hands to stop him. "I know, I know. Honestly, I can't really pass up the chance to learn about the people who took him. He may have seen or heard something useful that the Protectorate might not get out of him."

"And there's my dear sibling."

They punched him lightly in the arm. "Your dear sibling, the esteemed Guild Master, thank you very much."

After yet another protest from Tony about how hungry he was, the group used the ground vehicle parked outside of Lhasa's workshop to return to the Engineering Guild tower. Tony was suitably impressed by Kaseka's nighttime glow, and Cam did a reasonable job of playing tour guide. Finn sent a message to his mother to expect company, then another to Natia with a brief rundown of what happened in Seattle, along with the promise of a full report the next day. He was surprised to get a reply from Natia right away, letting him know that they recorded a statement from his sister Oslo. She also shared that there'd been no new developments with Kosumi yet, which gave him a moment of pause, and told him to expect a visit from Alina shortly, which left him wondering.

His mother, ever the gracious hostess, somehow managed to put together a spread that even put their last group dinner to shame. Tony was entirely respectful of her, which Finn was grateful for. Not that his mother couldn't handle the casual obstinance and irreverent sarcasm that Tony was so good at. She'd raised Finn, after all.

During their meal, Cam shared what Lhasa discovered about him while Tony was being held by Omni, and Tony couldn't get enough of it. He made Cam demonstrate his shield, but Finn forbade any weapons or Gate demonstrations in his mother's rooms. There would be plenty of time to show that off somewhere more appropriate in the future.

After the group cleared the dishes and then helped themselves to sweetcakes and tea, Tony told the story of his ordeal, beginning with his fall through Cam's emergency Gate until his eventual rescue. According to Tony, he hadn't seen much besides a long hallway and the inside of his cell, which had been okay as far as jails go. As for the bruising, Tony admitted that Omni was pretty rough when she was questioning him. But once they'd realized that Cam was dreaming about her, and she made that deal for the exchange, she'd left him pretty much alone. Tony also tried to apologize for spilling Cam's secrets, but Cam wouldn't hear of it, insisting that he was just glad his friend was okay.

"Besides," Cam added, "she got what she deserved anyway."

"Fuck yeah, she did," Tony agreed. "She took the express elevator to hell." Then he looked embarrassed to have said that in front of Lhasa and Arana, but they both just smiled and shook their heads. Finn was instantly reminded of just how much Lhasa reminded him of their mother. They would probably make a great parent one day if they ever chose to become one.

Tony, feeling emboldened, asked Lhasa if they still wanted to talk, so they offered to take him on a walk around the tower grounds. The two of them thanked Arana for the meal and departed. Finn's mother bid everyone else a good night, reminding them that she needed her rest after a stressful day, and Tasha did the same shortly after, leaving Finn alone with Cam.

"What about you?" Finn asked him. "You had quite the day."

406

"Honestly? I'm still way too worked up to even think about sleep yet. I was actually hoping you could take me up to that rooftop overlook again."

Finn stood up and stretched. "I'd be happy to. Want to grab a couple of beers to bring along?"

Cam looked surprised. "Seriously?"

Finn mocked a little surprise. "What? You don't think we have beer?" Then he laughed, which made Cam laugh. After seeing how sullen and withdrawn he'd looked in the car ride back to the safe house, Finn was glad to see Cam enjoying himself again.

He went into Arana's kitchen and pulled a couple of beer bottles from the cold box. Then, after handing one to Cam, he led him back to the lift and up to the balcony they'd visited the night before. It was deserted, being so late, so they had the whole place to themselves.

Cam immediately walked over to the railing and looked down at the city below. "It's so peaceful up here. And the view! I mean, I have a decent view of the city from my apartment. Well, had, I suppose. If it even is still my apartment. But I didn't have anything like this."

"Yeah, there are a lot of nice things to see up here," Finn replied as he joined him. He undid the clasp that held the bottle top down, demonstrating for Cam so he could do it for his own, too. Then he took a generous drink from it.

Cam took a drink from his own. "Is this a wheat beer? It's nice."

"I don't know." He took another drink. "I'm ashamed to admit that I'm not much of a connoisseur."

That got another laugh from Cam. "Finally, something you're not an expert at."

Finn chuckled and rolled his eyes. "It's moments like this that keep me humble. Look, I know I keep asking you this, but circumstances seem to keep calling for it. So, how are you holding up?"

Cam frowned a little. "I think I'm ok. I mean, for these past few days, every one of them has brought me newer and bigger surprises. And that fight with Omni tonight? I don't know. I was just so full of rage towards her—for what she'd been doing to me and what she'd done to Tony." He looked Finn in the eyes, his expression earnest. "I hate to say it, but I really don't feel bad about what happened to her. She deserved it."

Finn nodded, then put a hand on Cam's shoulder. "It's normal to feel bad about something like that. But, in this case, I'd say it's ok not to feel too bad about it. If you hadn't done what you did, she certainly would've killed at least one of us. Probably me."

He expected Cam to shrug his hand off, but he didn't. Instead, he kept looking right at Finn. "I saw that your shield was going to fail, and I knew that if I didn't do something fast, she was going to hurt you. She'd already hurt enough people, and I couldn't stand the idea that one of those people was going to be you, Finn." Then he moved in closer until their bodies were almost touching. His eyes were soft and pleading.

That left him with some unexpected options, Finn realized. And, despite his better judgment, he knew which one he wanted to take. "I'd like to kiss you now, Cam."

"If you're asking my permission," Cam replied with a coy smile, "the answer is yes."

Finn smiled back, then Cam closed his eyes and leaned

in. Finn bent his head down until their lips were touching, and Cam pushed himself forward until there was no space between them at all. Finn could taste the beer on Cam's tongue as he pressed it into his mouth, but his lips were soft and tasted a little sweet. Finn moved his arm from Cam's shoulder down to his back, pulling him in even tighter. Then he felt Cam's hands as they explored his own back, his shoulders, and his arms. Finn felt himself harden and felt Cam's own hard groin pushing back against his. He didn't know how long the kiss lasted, but eventually, he stopped and pulled back, taking a deep breath. He looked into Cam's eyes, seeing the longing he felt reflected right back at him.

Suddenly a voice called out from inside the tower. "Hey, Jerusalem, are you–Oh, shit. Sorry." Finn looked over and saw Alina standing at the entrance to the balcony. He laughed softly and felt Cam pull himself away.

"Did anyone ever tell you what a mood killer you could be, Alina?" Finn asked, although there was no malice in his voice. Maybe just a bit of disappointment, though.

She at least had the decency to look embarrassed. "Yeah, you're honestly not the first. Hello, Cam."

Cam waved. "Hello, Ali."

"I assume you're looking for me for a reason?" Finn prompted her.

"Oh, yeah. Natia sent me." She walked over to where the two were standing and held out a data crystal to Finn. "She wanted me to give you this and to let you know that you've been ordered to report to the Temple, along with Tasha, Cam, and Cam's friend."

"The Temple?" Finn asked. "Is she serious?"

"What's the Temple?" Cam asked.

"It's the Protectorate headquarters, on Andras," Finn answered.

"She is definitely serious," Alina confirmed. "I was there when she got the call. After the Council got wind of what happened in the market this morning, they made Natia pass on the data about Cam to Andras, and, well, they are very interested in meeting him now."

Finn grimaced, but he'd known it was always a matter of time before the powers that be got involved with things. "At least they're asking, I suppose."

"I thought they ordered you," Cam pointed out.

Finn smirked. "Yeah, but if they weren't asking, we wouldn't even have the chance to talk about it." Then he smiled at Cam sweetly. "At least we don't have to go until tomorrow."

"That's good," Cam replied, with a wink, "because after the day I've had, I could use a good night in bed."

Alina coughed politely. "As much as I hate to keep killing the mood, they want you to report in right now." Then she looked up the sky toward the moons that had just come into view from behind the top of the tower. "Although, I suppose it's possible it took me quite some time to actually find you and deliver your orders. I was looking for at least an hour."

Finn grinned, then looked at Cam, who nodded. "Can we make it two?"

Alina shook her head. "I wouldn't recommend it unless you want to repeat this scene with Natia instead."

Finn was about to object, but Cam cut him off. "An hour is plenty, thank you. We'll meet you downstairs?"

"Works for me," Alina agreed. Then she turned and walked back inside without another word.

Once she was gone, Cam reached out and pulled Finn back over to him. "Now," he purred with a coy smile, "where were we?"

EPILOGUE

Omni woke up screaming. The memories of her rage and her fall from the tower were still fresh in her mind. She was glad the Intelligence let her keep those. A memory of her death was always a powerful motivator.

She flexed her limbs experimentally and found that she had no pain, so she pushed herself up off the cold surface she'd been lying on and swung her legs over to the side. One of the med techs standing nearby her started to protest, but she silenced them with a look. She'd died before, of course. She knew what she was doing.

Standing up from the med table, Omni brushed the wrinkles out of the smock she was wearing. Another tech, bolder than the first one, stepped forward, heedless of her glare, and ran a scanning wand in front of her. She permitted it, knowing that they were just doing their duty. Satisfied with whatever the readings were, they put the scanning wand back into a pocket on their tunic, then gestured to her left. Omni looked over and saw a folded uniform and pair of boots sitting on a nearby pedestal. She nodded at the tech in thanks then, despite her audience, removed her smock, and began to get dressed.

A door behind her slid open, and Omni detected footsteps

approaching her from behind. She recognized the pattern and gait right away, so she continued to dress without looking. It was Enioh, undoubtedly coming to retrieve her and present her to the Intelligence. Once she'd slipped on her boots, she turned to see the tall, gray-skinned, black-eyed soldier standing before her.

"It was a success?" they asked, their voice gravelly with the harmonics from dual sets of vocal cords.

That much was plain. Had her mission been a failure, Omni doubted that she would have been rebirthed. But the Ninaki valued their conversational gambits, so she swallowed her angry retort and nodded. "It was. The asset is now in place."

"Excellent," Enioh replied with a hint of a smile. Their tall, pointed ears twitched as well, giving away their evident satisfaction at her answer. "And they did not suspect a thing?"

"Not that I could ascertain," Omni stated, swallowing her irritation at the continued questioning. Nominally, Enioh was her superior, as all Ninaki were, but Omni officially reported to the Intelligence, who would be waiting to debrief her. "There were complications, though."

Enioh raised a furry eyebrow. Not for the first time, she was curious how a race that had developed so far removed from humankind had such remarkably human expressions. "Explain."

That was too much for her. "The Intelligence—"

"The Intelligence will learn of this in due time," they said, cutting her off. "I am asking you to explain it to me now. Do not make me ask you twice."

She forced herself to be calm and accepted the rebuke. "The subject seemed to have full command of his abilities, whereas, on our prior encounter, he did not even seem to be aware of them."

Enioh nodded, understanding. "I read as much in your report, yes. Our records of him are frustratingly lacking, as you know, due to the incident. However, from what we understand of his makeup, that does not surprise me. In fact, his power will likely grow exponentially now. Come, I have delayed you for too long. Let me not do so any further." They turned and beckoned for her to follow.

She nodded and fell in behind them, outwardly placid, inwardly cursing them for their arrogant insolence. The pair left the lab behind and exited into the corridor. As they walked through the facility, she ran a complete system diagnostic, ensuring that her new body was ready for her next task. She was surprised to see that she'd been upgraded again, although she didn't fully understand the nature of her new enhancements. The Intelligence would inform her of what she needed to know.

As they both proceeded toward the audience chamber, she realized they would pass by the cell where the prisoner was still being kept. She smiled, pleased with herself that she'd so masterfully played the role the Intelligence had given her. She was an expert at subterfuge, after all. But her anger during the exchange had not been entirely faked once she'd seen what the subject could do. And it hadn't been faked at all when he'd so thoroughly bested her. But his attempt to save her from her impending fall brought her up short. It was usually an act she would assign to weakness, and, perhaps, in his case, it was. It was also possible that his desire to gain the knowledge she'd promised him overrode his urge to kill her. Should that be the case, she thought of several possible options that could present. She knew she should share her thoughts on the matter with the Intelligence. For some reason, she desired to keep them to herself. Although should the Intelligence wish it, her mind was open to it regardless of her desires. But, one way or another, she would still have the last laugh.

She stopped as they passed the cell, peering through the tiny opening set in the thick door. The prisoner saw her looking at him and immediately jumped from his bed and ran to the door.

"Let me out of here, you fucking bitch! I told you everything I know. Why the fuck are you still keeping me locked up!"

She regarded him for a moment longer, enjoying the energy of this rage and fear. "Be calm, Tony. The Intelligence has a plan for all of us. Even you."

Yes, she thought. She would have the last laugh, indeed.

Coming Soon

Read more about Cam's adventures in Book Two of The Gates Saga, The Renegade Child, coming in 2022!

Excerpt from Steal The Demon, a Science-Fiction Novella

Kimiko was parked at a tiny table tucked under the massive viewport, trying not to fidget while she ignored the breathtaking panoramic view of *511 Davida*, the giant rock that *Davida Station* was orbiting. Of course, she'd seen it when she walked in. It was impossible to miss. A sea of twinkling lights shimmered on the dark surface of Davida like the nighttime windows of far off highrises, a distant city just over the curve of an impossible horizon. But the only civilization to be found here was in orbit, and the lights on the surface were the glowing marks of heavy industry. Like so many others in the Belt, the rock was a rich source of Ceresium, along with numerous other valuable elements and metals, and the pinpricks of light Kimiko had seen in the viewport were mining facilities.

It wasn't city lights that she saw, though, or mining facilities, when she'd gazed upon the station's craggy neighbor. To her, they were racing beacons, much like the ones she'd seen during her years in the Belt racing circuit. Back then, she'd flung her young body and bafflingly insubstantial ship into improbably high-g turns around rock after rock in what would seem like careless abandon to an observer, but was actually the result of precise calculations and intense training.

She sometimes pined for those days from her carefree youth, but not as much as she missed being in the pilot's seat at all.

But a news report about her father playing on the viewscreens above the bar had made short work of any reminiscing about racing out in the cold and black. Kimiko was surprised to see it, since it was already old news. At least she wasn't in that report, too. Something like that could've easily blown her cover, if any of the joes sitting at the bar spotted her after seeing her face shining down on them. She'd otherwise learned to live with the annoyance of being the daughter of someone notoriously newsworthy.

Kimiko considered it to be part of her *giri*, an ancient concept, culturally unique to the Downwell Earth islands her ancestors had once called home. She had a vague understanding of it–enough to have an idea of what it meant, but not enough to accurately describe it out loud. In one sense, *giri* alluded to responsibility or duty. Her father, Ichiko Hitomi, the (former) head of *Hitomi Shipping*, (formerly) one of the largest independent shipping and supply companies in the Belt, had once been duty-bound to ensure the well-being of the employees under his care. That was his *giri*. While it could be argued that he still had that duty, that *giri* could also have fallen on her, as his daughter, once he'd been picked up by the *Confederation Security Group*. But her father's absence had left him unable to fulfill his duties to his former staff and had left her affairs in a perilously unstable orbit. After the CSG had arrested her father on smuggling charges, *Confederation Compliance* had convicted him and sent him off to the Callisto mines in the Jovian system. They'd also seized all of his and his company's assets, leaving Kimiko with no resources and barely enough possessions to fill the tiny compartment in Motherlode that she could hardly even afford.

Giri also suggested owing favors or being in someone's debt. For instance, Kimiko had earned her reputation as one of the System's best pilots, thanks to her father's resources and the tutelage of her Uncle Shinzo. The *giri* she owed from that had pushed her to put those skills to use for *Hitomi Shipping*, where she'd also made a reasonably good living as a pilot and smuggler. But, following her father's downfall, the Hitomi name suddenly and irreparably transformed from an asset into a liability. Kimiko had submitted employment inquiries under that name for all of the pilot listings she'd seen on the Motherlode job boards. That was how she discovered that the weight of her father's disgrace overshadowed her own reputation to such a degree that she received a polite no from the few companies that even bothered to respond. Mostly, her inquiries were met only with silence.

What she was left with was her personal *giri*, or her duty to herself. With her father's absence and everything that meant, Kimiko needed to make a name for herself. Not literally, of course. She'd already done that when she jettisoned her identity as Kimiko Hitomi and transformed herself into Kimiko Yanaka, taking the name of her mother's family and giving up the well-deserved reputation that she had always traded on before. Kimiko knew she could earn it back. She was still a kick-ass pilot. But to do that, she just needed the one thing she no longer had access to–a ship.

That was why she planned to steal one.

That was also why she sat under the massive viewport in the bland, corporate, Confederation-run lounge on the edge of Davida Station. It was nothing like the dirty, friendly, hole-in-the-wall, dive bars that she frequented back on Ceres, but it was the only option that an uptight, straitlaced place like Davida Station had to offer. The lounge was crowded, at least, which helped her to blend in. And it was noisy enough to confuse most listening devices, which enabled her to maintain her operational security. Unfortunately, it was also prohibitively costly, which was why she'd been carefully nursing the *Pavonis Mons Genuine Martian Whiskey* in front of her while she waited to meet with a notorious hacker called Paradox.

She knew very little about Paradox, besides what she'd heard about and read on the Net. She felt a strange kinship with them, though, since they also had a reputation for being one of the best, or rather one of the most notorious, due to their prodigious and high-profile hacking activities. Everyone had heard about the *Confederation Data Bureau's* firewall breach, after all, not to mention the infamous *Erebus Station* hack. But the rest of Paradox's identity, including their appearance and their real name, was mostly a collection of wild guesses and complete unknowns.

To say that she'd been mildly surprised when Paradox agreed to meet with her would've been an understatement. Being on the CSG's *Most Wanted List* had understandably led them to become something of a recluse. But, when Kimiko had left Paradox a message at the secret Net address her cousin Kenji had dug up for her, she'd actually gotten a reply the very next day, and eventually, an invitation to meet with them in person. She was even more surprised when they'd agreed to meet with her at Davida Station.

It all could have been a set up by the CSG or a former rival of her father's, meant to entrap her so she could be sent off to join him on Callisto. But it was worth the risk for her. She had very little left to lose, at that point, and was honor-bound to act, anyway. So, when Paradox sent her a private, encrypted message link, she accessed it. That first message from them had really set the tone for their relationship, too.

Which ship would you like my help to steal?

So much for operational security. Had she been setting up a smuggling run, Kimiko would've spaced the whole thing then and there. But her smuggling runs had been done with parties that were carefully vetted by her father's organization, and they were little different than regular cargo shipments—mostly just quieter and more out of the way. And she'd never before directly engaged the services of an elite hacker—the closest she'd come was one of Kenji's ex-boyfriends, and he hardly counted. So she sent Paradox a cagey denial since she still didn't trust them, but wasn't ready to jettison the whole exchange after the first message.

But it's obvious, Paradox had responded. Then they sent a detailed log of all the Net searches Kimiko had done on the *Al-Zamani Shipyards* that shared Davida Station's orbit, digging for whatever scraps of information she could find to build her plan, a little bit at a time. *And I'm a hacker, not a shipbroker*, they'd added. *If you're looking to buy a ship, you've got the wrong individual.*

She shouldn't have been surprised by that. Any hacker who could waltz through the AI-security of a firewalled CDB server would obviously have no trouble looking at her Net data. But it still stung seeing her Net habits spelled out so clearly like that, especially after the effort she'd made to hide her tracks. Kimiko tried imagining how her father would've dealt with that, with all of his complex rules about honor and propriety. He probably would've felt just as spun out as she had at having her motivations laid bare so early in the negotiating process. She was nothing if not her father's daughter, after all. Deep down, she knew that she was just embarrassed. Perhaps he would have been, too. But she had no reason to be, and she certainly didn't need to be concerned with saving face. Why would someone like the infamous Paradox trade messages with her only to insult her?

So Kimiko told him which ship she had in mind. Then Paradox asked her what her plan was, and she told him that, too. It terrified her a little, committing her plan to some kind of record, no matter how private and secure it was. But it also felt good having a co-conspirator. She hadn't realized how much she'd missed having a team of some kind to work with, especially her old crew from before her father's arrest. And for whatever reason, Paradox seemed interested in being on her team. She asked them if they would help and, if so, how much they wanted to be paid.

I definitely want to help you, Paradox replied, then suggested an oddly specific figure that, after looking it up, she found to be exactly a third of the creds stashed away in her account on Ceres. Apparently, her bank's security was no match for the hacker, either. While it would be a big chunk of money to part with, it was obviously something she could afford, and she couldn't help feeling like they were letting her off easy–maybe even giving her the bait and switch. She didn't want to be on the hook for any favors to be named later, Kimiko told Paradox flat out, even if that meant spinning the upfront price a little higher. But they only responded with an anonymous account number and instructions for transferring the creds. A few minutes after she'd done as instructed, she received a confirmation at her public message address for a one-way, transfer-class, shuttle trip from Ceres to Davida Station, leaving in two days.

A polite cough interrupted her introspection. She looked over to see a male-presenting individual dressed in nondescript, gray coveralls, taking the seat opposite her. Everything about them was unremarkable, from their short, clippered, dark hair with hints of silver, to their olive-brown skin with the slightly gray undertones of someone who'd never been exposed to direct sunlight. Their coveralls had the Davida Station logo–a red, stylized, beam cutter with the plasma beam curling into a D and S–printed on the right-side breast pocket. If that was Paradox, they were either the most cliché, undercover CSG agent she'd ever seen, or a brilliantly disguised hacker.

"Hitomi Kimiko?" they asked.

That was an unexpected opening line. Not only had they called Kimiko by her former last name, but they'd also used the archaic method of putting her family name first. Kimiko raised an eyebrow in suspicion. "Sorry, Joe, there ain't nobody here by that name."

Her tablemate gave her a slightly creepy smile, once that didn't quite reach their eyes. "My apologies. Of course, you're Yanaka Kimiko, now. But you used to be Hitomi Kimiko. Born 2307 in Motherlode on Ceres, the only child of Hitomi Ichiko and Yanaka Misaki. Then you sent me a message from a rented, anonymous terminal in Motherlode using a Net address that you'd gotten from your cousin, Hiruma Kenji. I just needed to be sure it was really you."

She scoffed lightly. "And you're Paradox?"

They nodded.

"Well, it sounds like you've done your homework, Joe—except for the part that I'm not from Downwell Earth, and I don't put my last name first."

"My apologies," they replied, with a small nod of their head. Then they took a sleek-looking handheld terminal out of a pocket in their coveralls and tapped a command into it. Her own handheld buzzed in response. "While I'm good with data, I'm not very good with people."

Kimiko reached into a jacket pocket to pull out her own hand terminal and opened the waiting message to reveal an ID file that simply said *Paradox. He/him. Hacker.* Clever. She smiled, then put her terminal away. "It's fine. No need to get spun up about it."

"Thank you," he replied, then looked at her curiously.

"It's nice to finally meet you," she said. "I honestly had no idea what to expect."

He looked away, taking a moment to stare at the viewport. "That's to be expected, and it's not undesired," he said, then looked back over at Kimiko. "Between those who would like to employ me, and those who would see me caged, I'm a highly sought after individual. So, I prefer for most people to know nothing about me."

She imagined that was why he went to such great lengths to appear so ordinary. A lot of joes in his position—assuming that there were even a lot of joes who could be in his position as a hacker notorious enough to draw the attention of Confederation enforcers systemwide—might have tried much more elaborate disguises. But that sort of thing often backfired, in her experience. It was better to just hide in plain sight, Kimiko knew, by making yourself unremarkable enough to blend into everything around you. It was how she'd always managed to avoid getting caught on her smuggling runs. If she were to have seen him anywhere else besides sitting at the table across from her, she would have simply ignored him like every other joe in the background. The guy really was good. She had to give him that.

Kimiko looked down at her own attempt at a disguise. She, too, had gone for the low-profile look, ditching her standard flight jacket and jumpsuit in favor of a simple pair of tight, gray leggings, a black t-shirt, and a used, work jacket that she'd thrifted in Motherlode with the *High Orbit Mechanical* logo printed on the back. She kept the boots from her flight suit since they were so well worn-in and anonymous enough to go with anything she wore. She'd also kept her straight, black hair in the short, choppy, razor-cut style she favored since it was practical and easy to manage. There was nothing to be done with the ornate sleeve tattoo on her right arm–the one with the old-style chemical rocket weaving through a set of stylized rocks and planets–but the jacket hid it well enough. She'd added a little makeup, too, which she usually didn't wear–but just what she needed to de-emphasize her sharp cheekbones and make her eyes seem a little larger. There really wasn't much else she could've done, aside from springing for a quick facial sculpt, which was out of the question, and completely unaffordable for the time being, anyway.

"Your disguise is effective enough," Paradox offered as if he'd read her thoughts. "And your false ID is still secure, even if your legend is terribly thin. There is no indication that the local authorities are aware of your former identity. I checked very thoroughly before coming to meet with you."

"That's good to know."

He reached into another pocket in his coveralls and pulled out a data chip. Then he set it onto the table and slid it across toward her.

"What's this?" she asked as she picked it up.

"There are two sets of information stored on that chip. One is an early copy of the plans and schematics for the Al-Zamani Shipyard. The final plans can't be found anywhere outside of Al-Zamani's internal Net, but I located these on a server owned by one of the few contractors they'd hired during the initial planning phase. Unfortunately for us, nearly everything else was done in house, from planning to construction."

"Still, this is a pretty good find." While she didn't have a copy of the facility plans, she had pieced together the likeliest route for her infiltration based on a few conversations she'd had with another ex-boyfriend of Kenji's. His ex had actually worked for Al-Zamani for a short time on the General Maintenance crew–which was a polite term for a janitor. But if anyone knew where everything was, it was always the janitor. "What's the other set?"

He smiled. "Something I dug up on a *Confederation Defense Forces* server, actually. It's the full schematics for the *Shaitan.*"

Kimiko had initially chosen the Al-Zamani shipyard be-cause the ship she intended to steal was their new *Shaitan* class fast-courier spaceframe. Specifically, the very first *Shaitan*, a proof-of-concept ship they were using as a demon-strator craft. It was packed to the baffles with all the available options that Al-Zamani offered for that class, including integral shield generators and grav gen, various defensive weapons systems, and a well-appointed captain's cabin. Most of all, in addition to the standard drive, it had an experimental grav drive. It was a ship most joes could never in a lifetime afford, even if Al-Zamani ever chose to offer it for sale. "Wow, that's amazing. I can't wait to look them over."

"That is definitely a craft worthy of someone with your piloting skills," Paradox added.

"Thanks."

"But this is a dangerous path you're taking."

Kimiko frowned and then took a swig of the Genuine Martian Whiskey that had cost more than a month's rent, never once taking her eyes off the hacker. The amber fluid tasted smokey and vaguely of astringent, and coated her throat in a layer of liquid warmth. She'd ordered it neat, undiluted by water that had already been consumed and evacuated by countless Station residents. Not that she was averse to filtered water. It was all she knew. But if she had to spend that much on one drink, she'd be damned if she watered the fucking thing down. "I don't need you to tell me about danger, Joe."

"No, I don't suppose that you do. Nonetheless–"

"What is this?" she interrupted. "Why the sudden concern for my safety? I've already paid you."

Paradox nodded his agreement. "Indeed, you have. But this concern is not sudden. I've looked at your data, Kimiko, and the data says that you're reckless and prone to rash decisions. Your decision to steal a ship from a notoriously heavy-handed shipbuilder would support that analysis."

Kimiko laughed at the absurdity of his statement. "So, you're an analyst now?"

"I've always been an analyst. Hacking is merely the tool I use to access data. And now that we're meeting with one another, I can add more data to my analysis."

She frowned again. "Are you looking for reassurance, because–"

"I want to know why."

His face was still sincere, almost serene. Except for a few brief, tortured smiles, his expression hadn't changed once during their conversation. It would've come off as creepy on someone else, but, on such an ordinary-looking face, it suited him well enough. And Kimiko had to admit that it was fair for him to wonder about her motives. Paradox's legend was well known, and he had both the reputation and the evidence to back it up. But Kimiko was venturing well outside of her general area of expertise. "The Confederation did this to me," she said, finally, her voice tight and controlled. "They took everything from me. And I still tried to do it their way. I took my licks, and put my name in the pot for a new gig, any gig that would get me behind the stick again. But that didn't work." She took another swig of her whiskey. "But the real reason, I suppose, is that I want to hurt them for what they did to my father and me. And the only way I know how to hurt them is to hit them on the bottom line."

"And Al-Zamani was somehow responsible for your father's–"

She scoffed. "Don't be dim, Joe. They're part of the Confederation, too. Hurt one of them hard enough, and you hurt all of them."

Paradox examined her intensely while he held back his response. "I was once a tool of the Confederation," he admitted once he finally resumed speaking, "something that my corporate masters felt comfortable using and discarding, seemingly on a whim. While I would caution you that they are not a force to be trifled with, I understand the desire to cause them difficulty."

Kimiko hadn't known that about him. She doubted that many others did, either. She wanted very much to learn more about what that had meant, too, but she knew well enough to leave it alone. If he wanted her to know, he'd tell her. "That sounds terrible."

He frowned slightly. "It was." Then his expression returned to its usual serenity. "I appreciate your indulgence of my curiosity, and your candor. Although I had no intention of judging your motives, I am grateful to learn that they coincide with my own."

She nodded. "So, now what?"

"Now, perhaps we should review your plan."

Acknowledgement

The concepts for this book have been floating around in my head for some time, but it took a global pandemic to spur me into action and get them written down. I'm eternally grateful to my partner, José, for giving me the support and encouragement to give these ideas a voice. His insight and suggestions were instrumental in bringing this story to life. Thanks to my friend Eric, who has yet to say no when I ask him to read a work in progress, for his friendship and feedback. A special thanks to my dearest Abie, for sharing her brilliant mind and point of view, and to Aaron for helping determine the best place to stick the knife.

About the Author

Robert Roth (he/him) is a working-class queer nerd and author helping to overthrow the capitalist patriarchy one wry comment at a time. Besides writing stories and novels, he's written hundreds of magazine and news articles, dozens of published film and video scripts, and a four-act play. He lives in Seattle with his partner, where he enjoys writing and reading science-fiction.

You can connect with Robert at:
- 🌐 https://robertmroth.com/author
- 🐦 https://twitter.com/robbertrough
- 🇫 https://www.facebook.com/robertrothwrites

Subscribe to Robert's newsletter:
- ✉ https://robertmroth.com/mailinglist

Also by Robert Roth

Steal the Demon
A Science-Fiction Novella
For a score this stellar, who wouldn't break a few rules?

Life was good for ace pilot (and occasional smuggler) Kimiko Yanaka until the ruthless Corporate Confederation arrested her father and took everything away. Forced to make a new name for herself, she finds an unexpected ally in the infamous hacker Paradox. The pair set out to infiltrate the high-security Al-Zamani Shipyard orbiting 511 Davida and launch a truly cosmic heist!

Downstation Blues
A Science-Fiction Novella

Keep your friends close and your enemies closer.

Life can be rough for a young snatcher working the Downstation markets and corridors of EOS-1. Since Nix is Unregistered and forced to live off Upstation society's dregs, a rough life is the only one he knows. But when his orbit gets all spun out, and he catches heat from the hard-driven agents of Earth Orbit Station Security, Nix has to face some harsh realities about what he believes and who he cares about before he gets sent on the short walk and long drop on the Downwell Express.